Dark Hunger

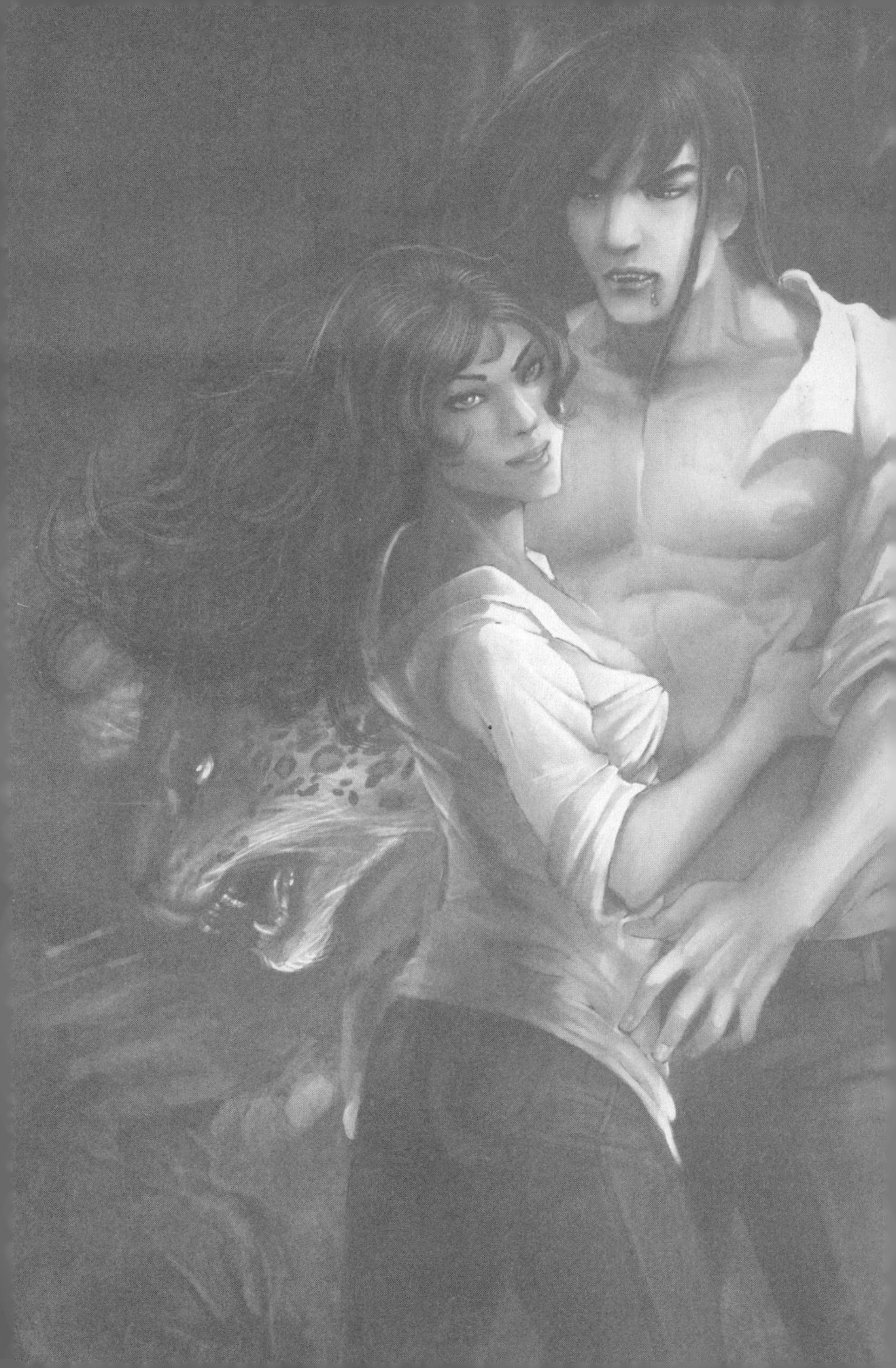

Dark Hunger

BY CHRISTINE FEEHAN

PENCILS BY ZID OF IMAGINARY FRIENDS STUDIOS
TONES BY IMAGINARY FRIENDS STUDIOS

BERKLEY BOOKS, NEW YORK

THE BERKLEY PUBLISHING GROUP
Published by the Penguin Group
Penguin Group (USA) Inc.
375 Hudson Street, New York, New York 10014, USA
Penguin Group (Canada), 90 Eglinton Avenue East, Suite 700, Toronto, Ontario M4P 2Y3, Canada
(a division of Pearson Penguin Canada Inc.)
Penguin Books Ltd., 80 Strand, London WC2R 0RL, England
Penguin Group Ireland, 25 St. Stephen's Green, Dublin 2, Ireland (a division of Penguin Books Ltd.)
Penguin Group (Australia), 250 Camberwell Road, Camberwell, Victoria 3124, Australia
(a division of Pearson Australia Group Pty. Ltd.)
Penguin Books India Pvt. Ltd., 11 Community Centre, Panchsheel Park, New Delhi—110 017, India
Penguin Group (NZ), 67 Apollo Drive, Rosedale, North Shore 0745, Auckland, New Zealand
(a division of Pearson New Zealand Ltd.)
Penguin Books (South Africa) (Pty.) Ltd., 24 Sturdee Avenue, Rosebank, Johannesburg 2196, South Africa

Penguin Books Ltd., Registered Offices: 80 Strand, London WC2R 0RL, England

DARK HUNGER

Previously published in the anthology Hot Blooded, published by Jove Publications, Inc.

This is a work of fiction. Names, characters, places, and incidents either are the product of the author's imagination or are used fictitiously, and any resemblance to actual persons, living or dead, business establishments, events, or locales is entirely coincidental. The publisher does not have any control over and does not assume any responsibility for author or third-party websites or their content.

PRINTING HISTORY
Berkley manga edition / October 2007

ISBN: 978-0-425-21783-2

PRINTED IN THE UNITED STATES OF AMERICA

10 9 8 7 6 5 4 3 2 1

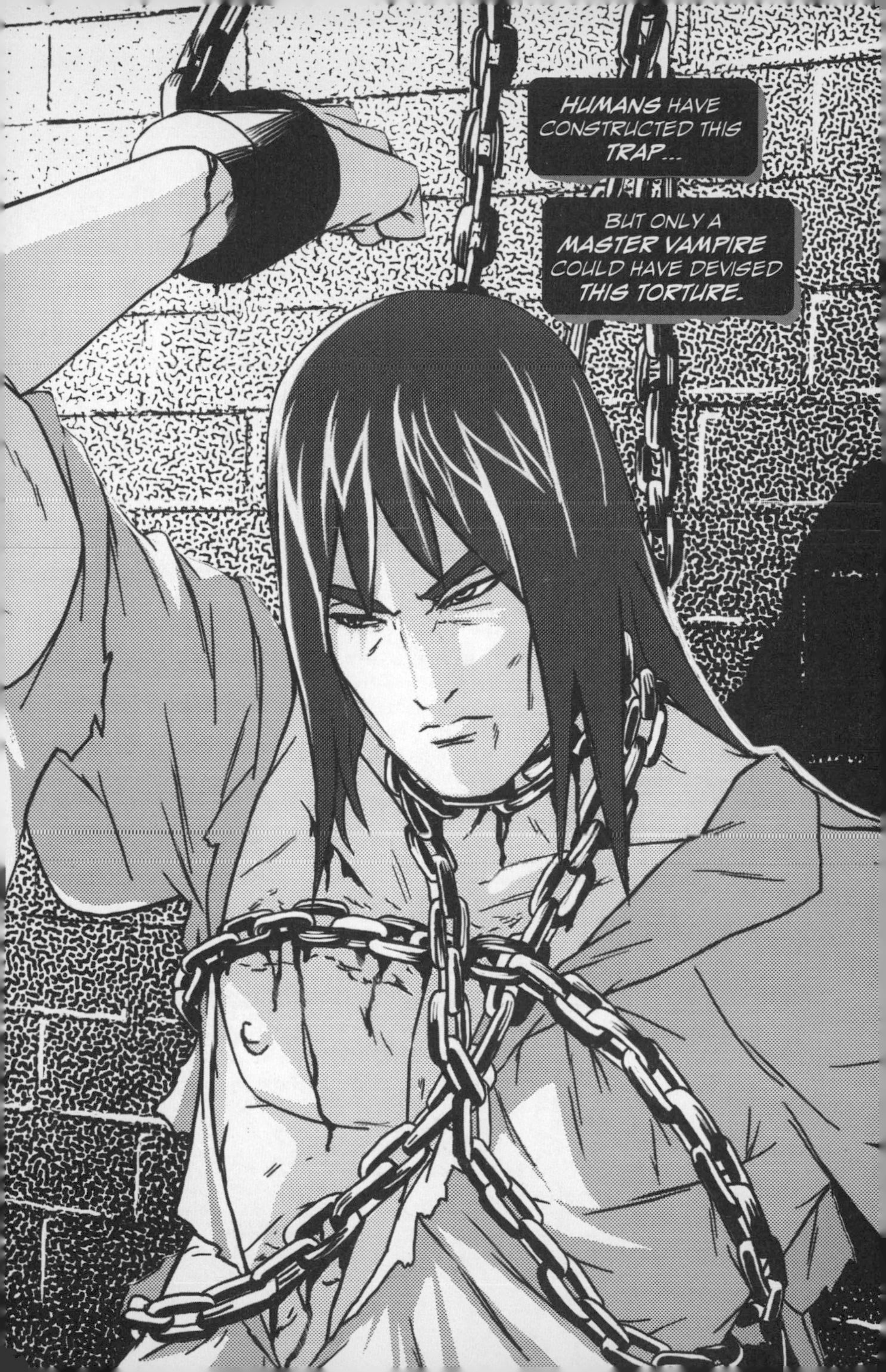
HUMANS HAVE CONSTRUCTED THIS TRAP...
BUT ONLY A MASTER VAMPIRE COULD HAVE DEVISED THIS TORTURE.

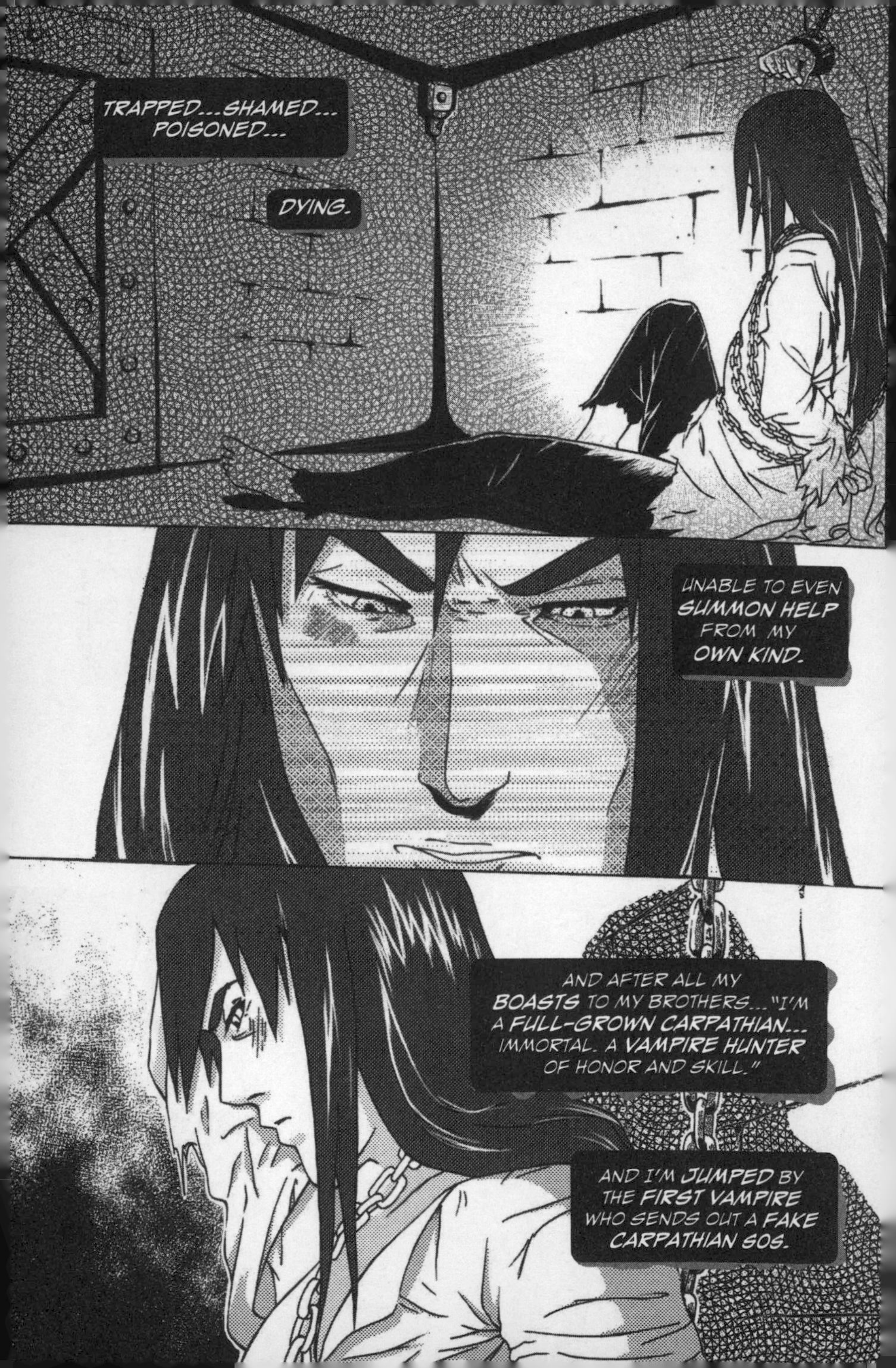
TRAPPED...SHAMED... POISONED...
DYING.
UNABLE TO EVEN SUMMON HELP FROM MY OWN KIND.
AND AFTER ALL MY BOASTS TO MY BROTHERS... "I'M A FULL-GROWN CARPATHIAN... IMMORTAL. A VAMPIRE HUNTER OF HONOR AND SKILL."
AND I'M JUMPED BY THE FIRST VAMPIRE WHO SENDS OUT A FAKE CARPATHIAN SOS.

IF MY BROTHERS SAW ME NOW, FIRST THEY'D *LAUGH.*

AND THEN THEY'D *WEEP.*

OUR ENEMIES HAVE FOUND A WAY TO *POISON OUR BLOOD*...AND EVEN *MY* SKILLS ARE NOT ENOUGH TO *BURN* IT FROM MY BODY.

THE *VAMPIRES* AND THEIR *HUMAN ALLIES* ARE CLEVER.

THEY'LL SEARCH FOR ME THE MOMENT THEY REALIZE THEY *NO LONGER* HEAR MY *THOUGHTS.*

BUT I WILL *NOT BE* BAIT FOR THIS *TRAP!*

OUR ENEMIES GROW MORE NUMEROUS AND MORE *DEADLY.*

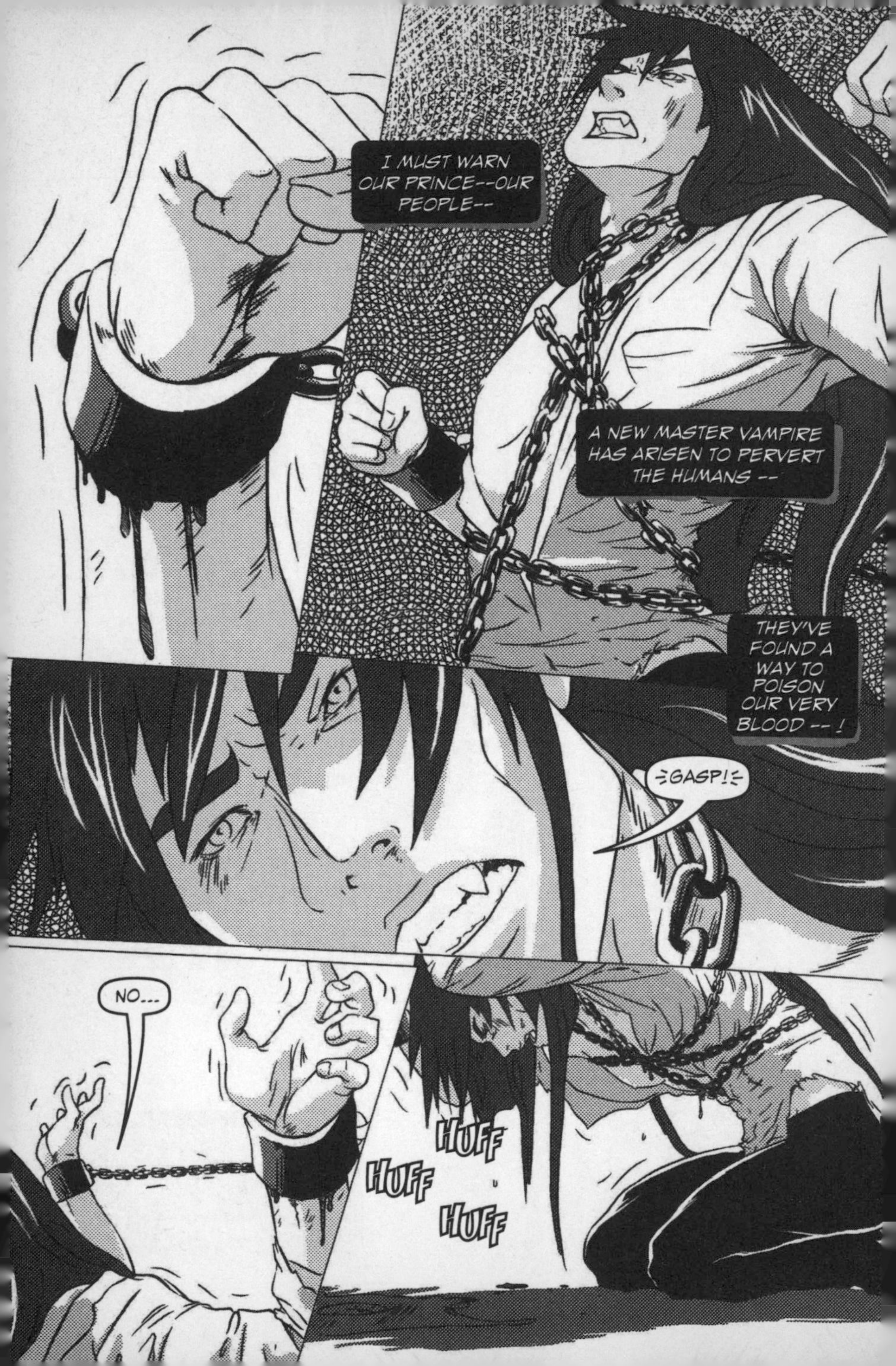
I MUST WARN OUR PRINCE--OUR PEOPLE--
A NEW MASTER VAMPIRE HAS ARISEN TO PERVERT THE HUMANS --
THEY'VE FOUND A WAY TO POISON OUR VERY BLOOD -- !
GASP!
NO...
HUFF
HUFF
HUFF

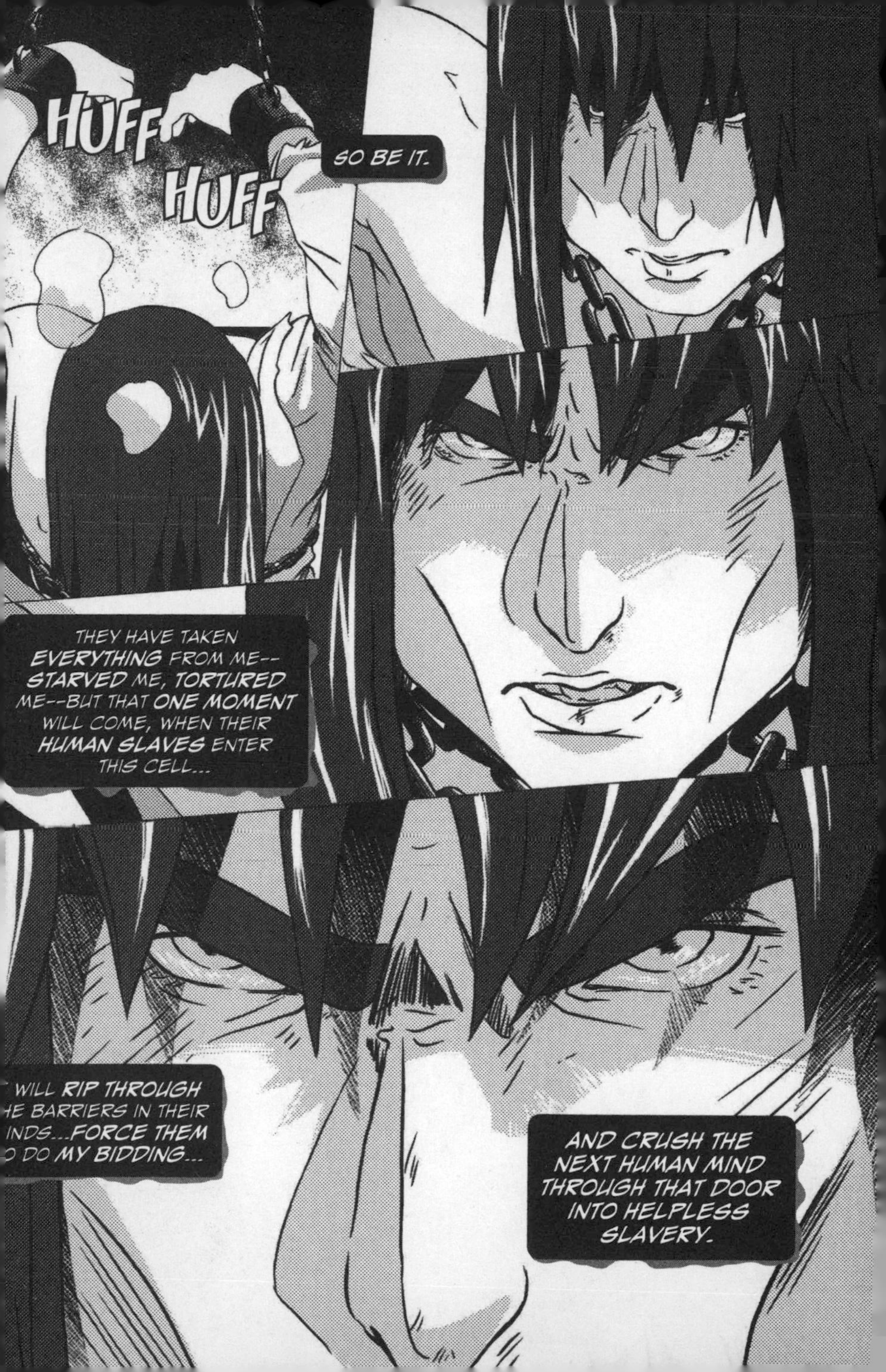
HUFF
HUFF
SO BE IT.
THEY HAVE TAKEN EVERYTHING FROM ME--STARVED ME, TORTURED ME--BUT THAT ONE MOMENT WILL COME, WHEN THEIR HUMAN SLAVES ENTER THIS CELL...
WILL RIP THROUGH HE BARRIERS IN THEIR INDS...FORCE THEM O DO MY BIDDING...
AND CRUSH THE NEXT HUMAN MIND THROUGH THAT DOOR INTO HELPLESS SLAVERY.

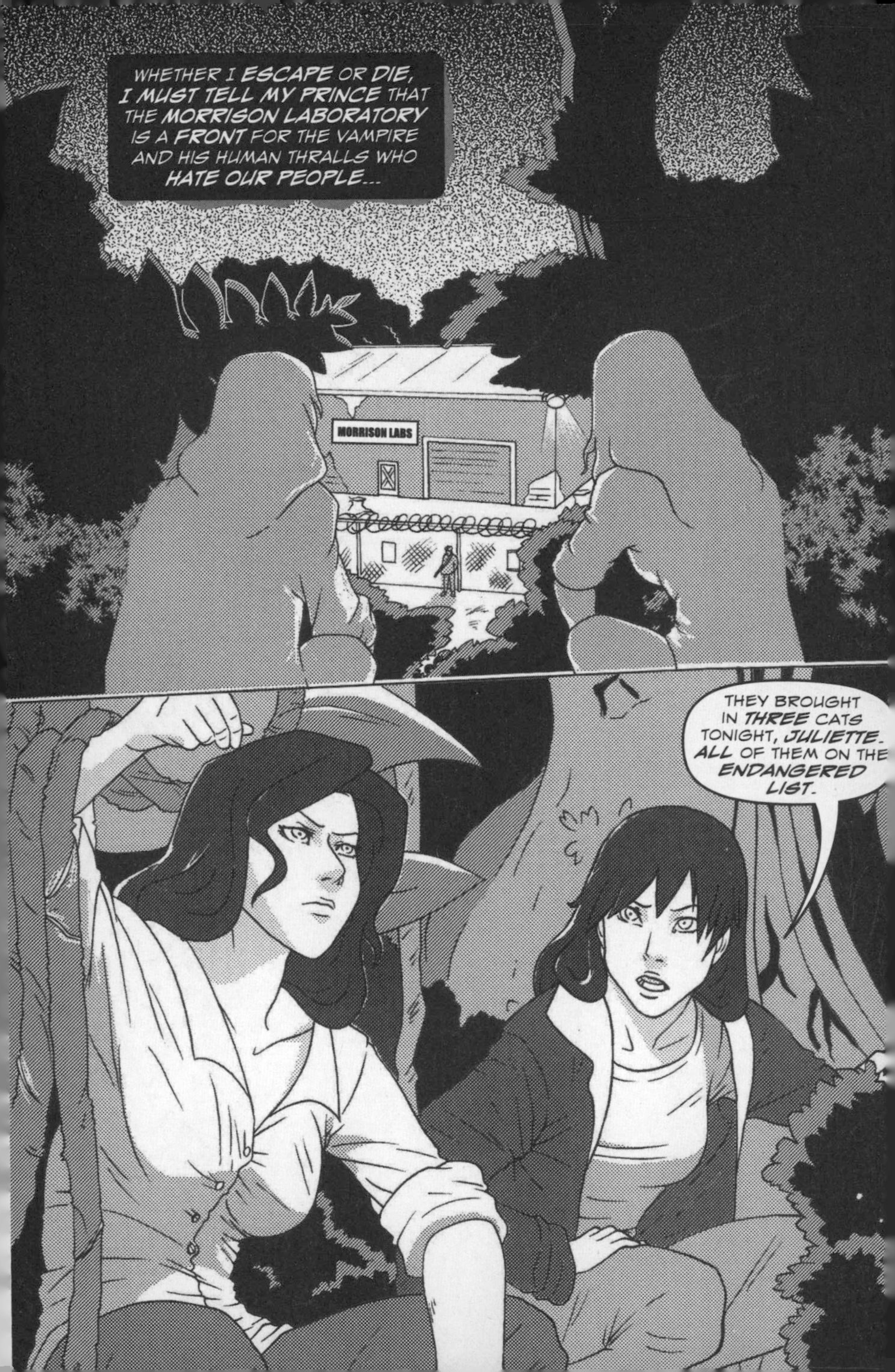
WHETHER I ESCAPE OR DIE, I MUST TELL MY PRINCE THAT THE MORRISON LABORATORY IS A FRONT FOR THE VAMPIRE AND HIS HUMAN THRALLS WHO HATE OUR PEOPLE...
MORRISON LABS
THEY BROUGHT IN THREE CATS TONIGHT, JULIETTE. ALL OF THEM ON THE ENDANGERED LIST.

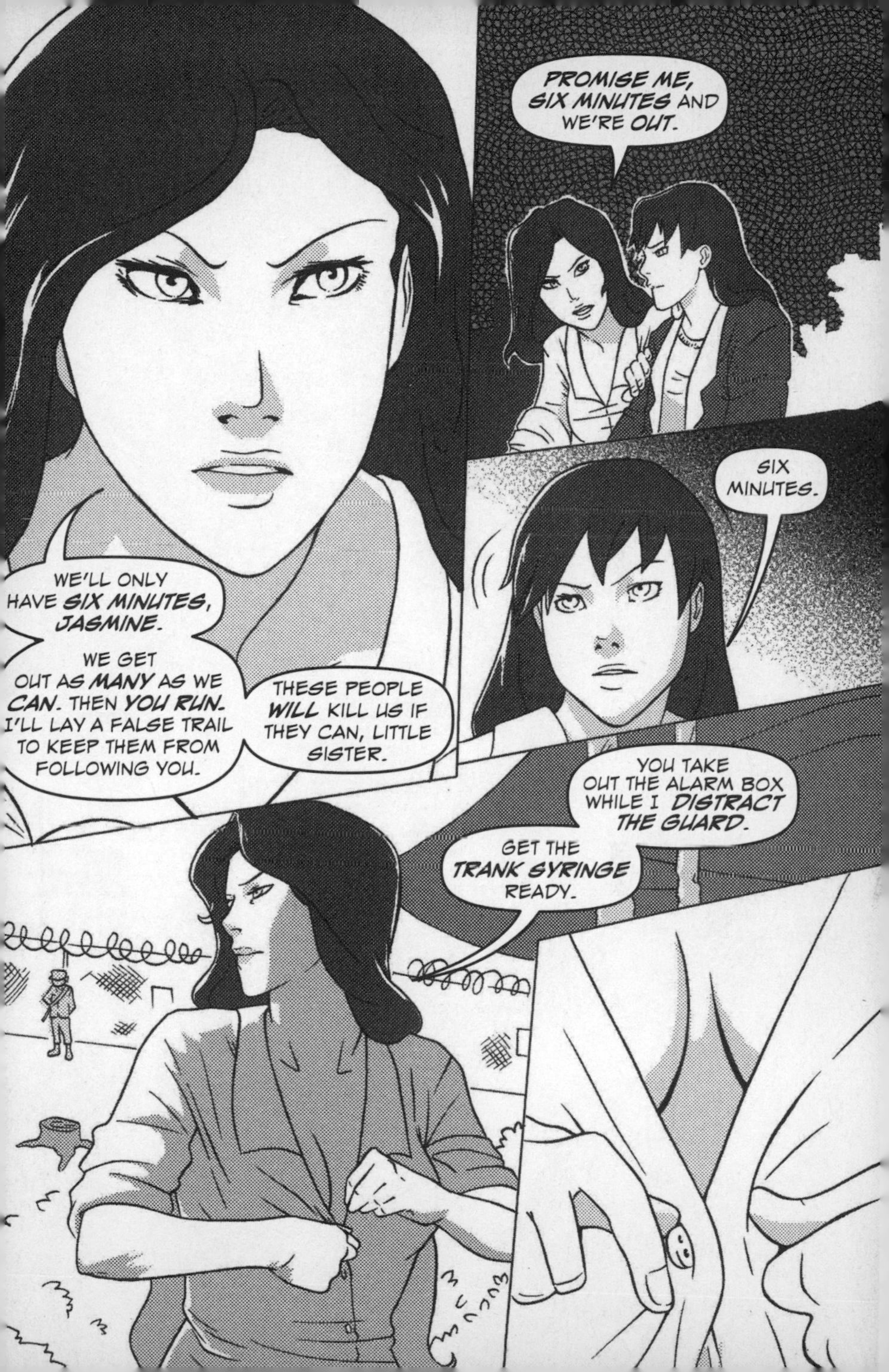
WE'LL ONLY HAVE SIX MINUTES, JASMINE.
WE GET OUT AS MANY AS WE CAN. THEN YOU RUN. I'LL LAY A FALSE TRAIL TO KEEP THEM FROM FOLLOWING YOU.
THESE PEOPLE WILL KILL US IF THEY CAN, LITTLE SISTER.
PROMISE ME, SIX MINUTES AND WE'RE OUT.
SIX MINUTES.
YOU TAKE OUT THE ALARM BOX WHILE I DISTRACT THE GUARD.
GET THE TRANK SYRINGE READY.

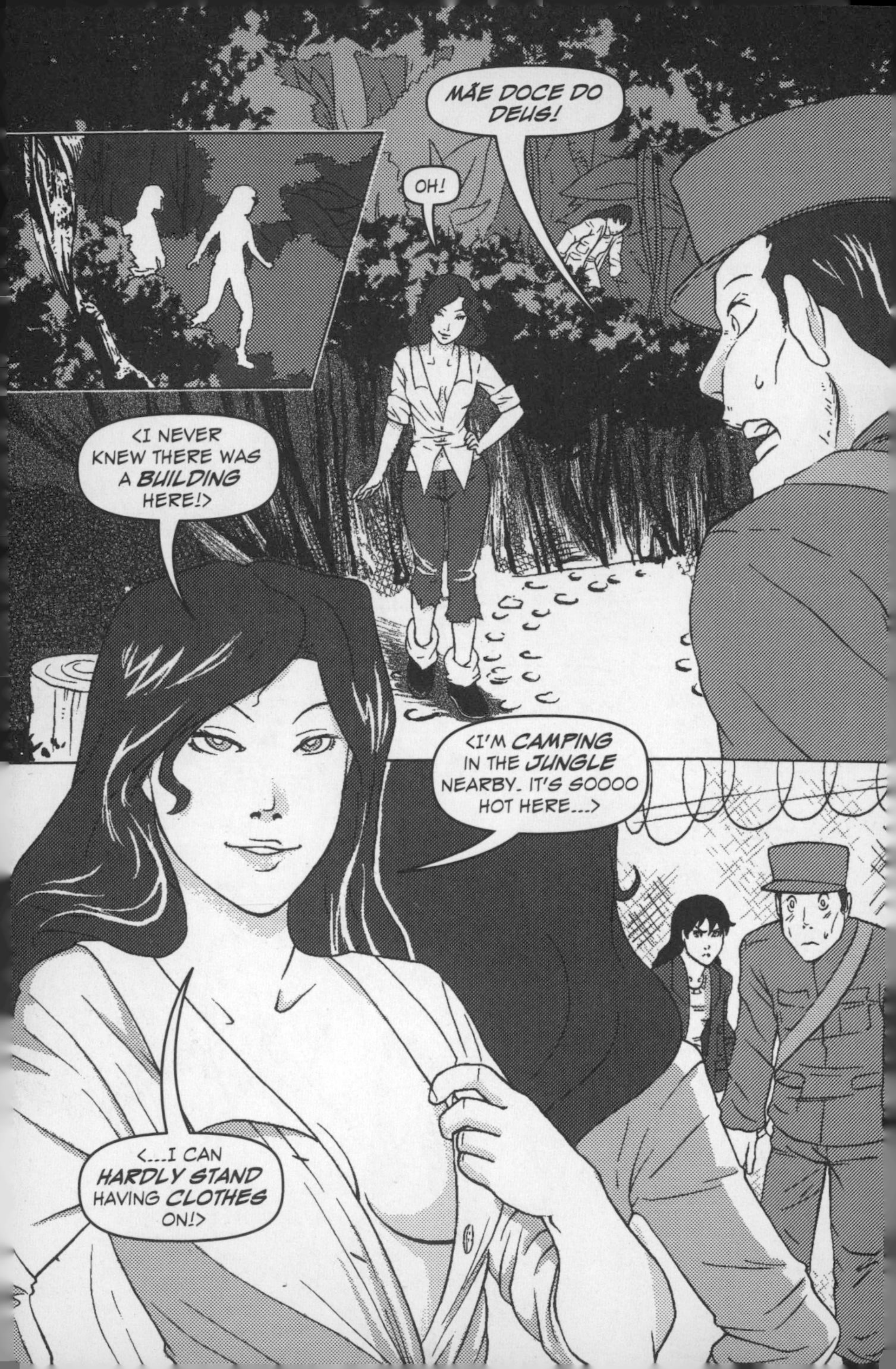
OH!
MÃE DOCE DO DEUS!
<I NEVER KNEW THERE WAS A BUILDING HERE!>
<I'M CAMPING IN THE JUNGLE NEARBY. IT'S SOOOO HOT HERE...>
<...I CAN HARDLY STAND HAVING CLOTHES ON!>

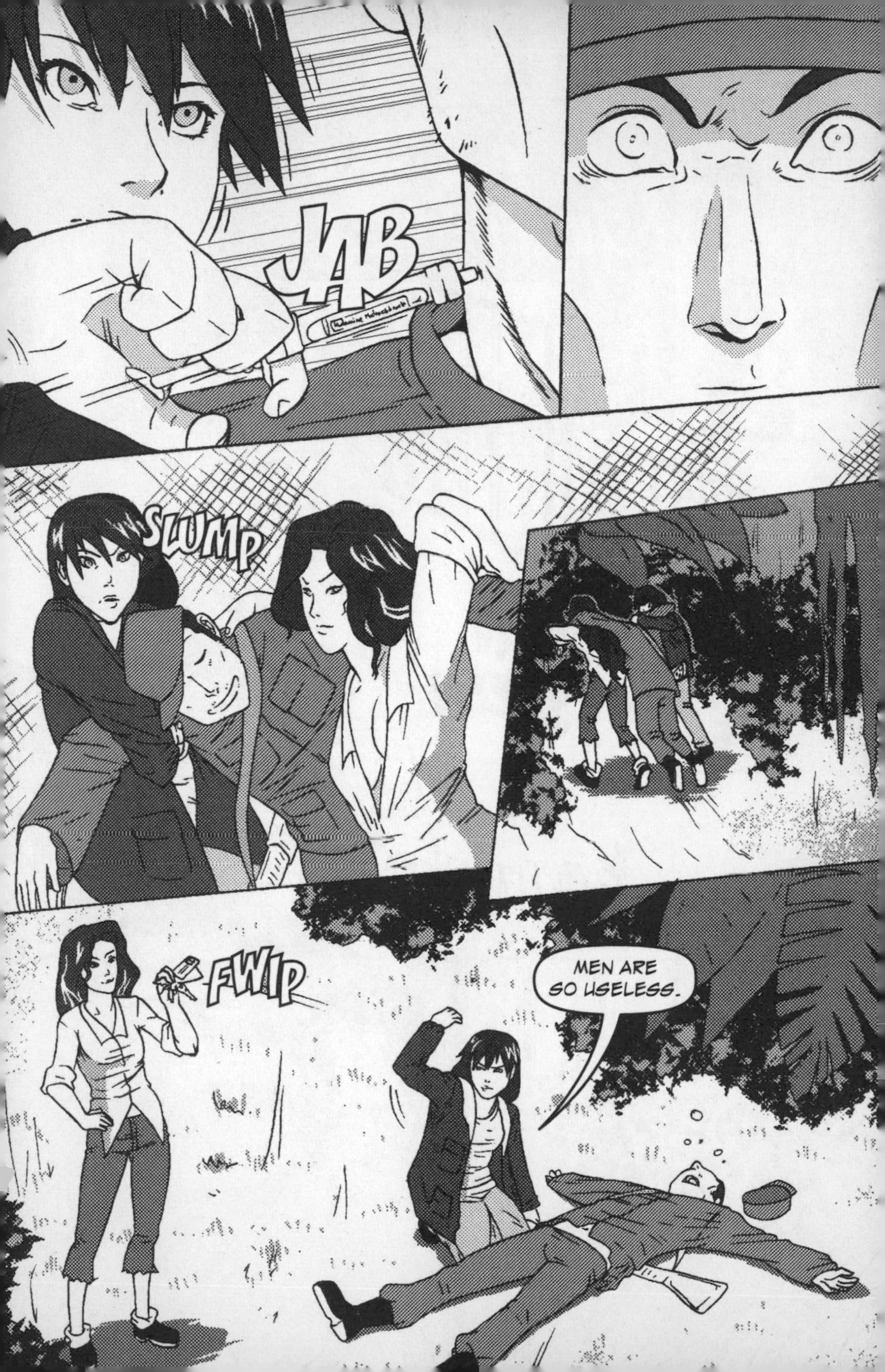
JAB
SLUMP
FWIP
MEN ARE SO USELESS.

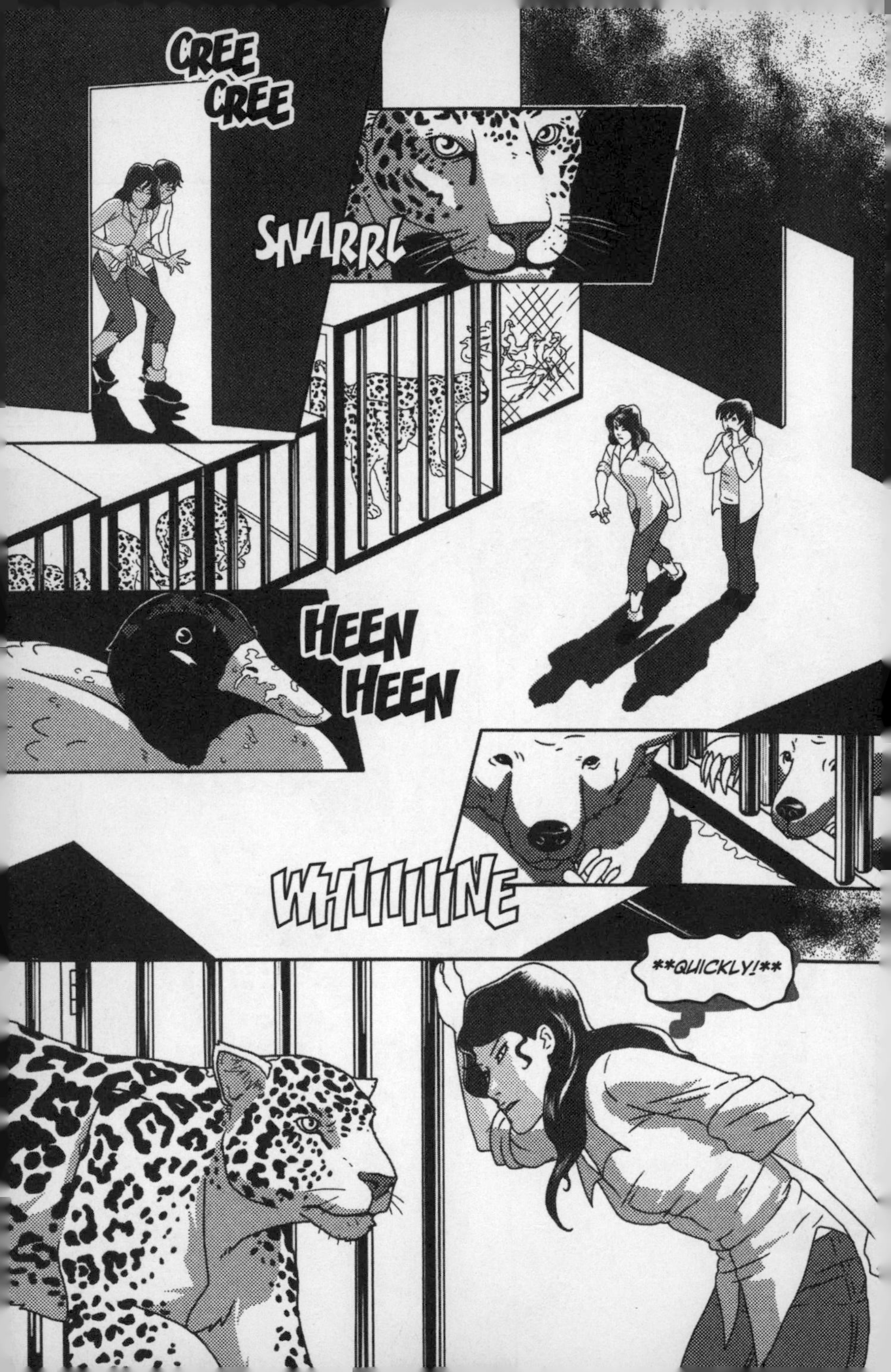
CREE CREE
SNARRL
HEEN HEEN
WHIIIIIINE
QUICKLY!

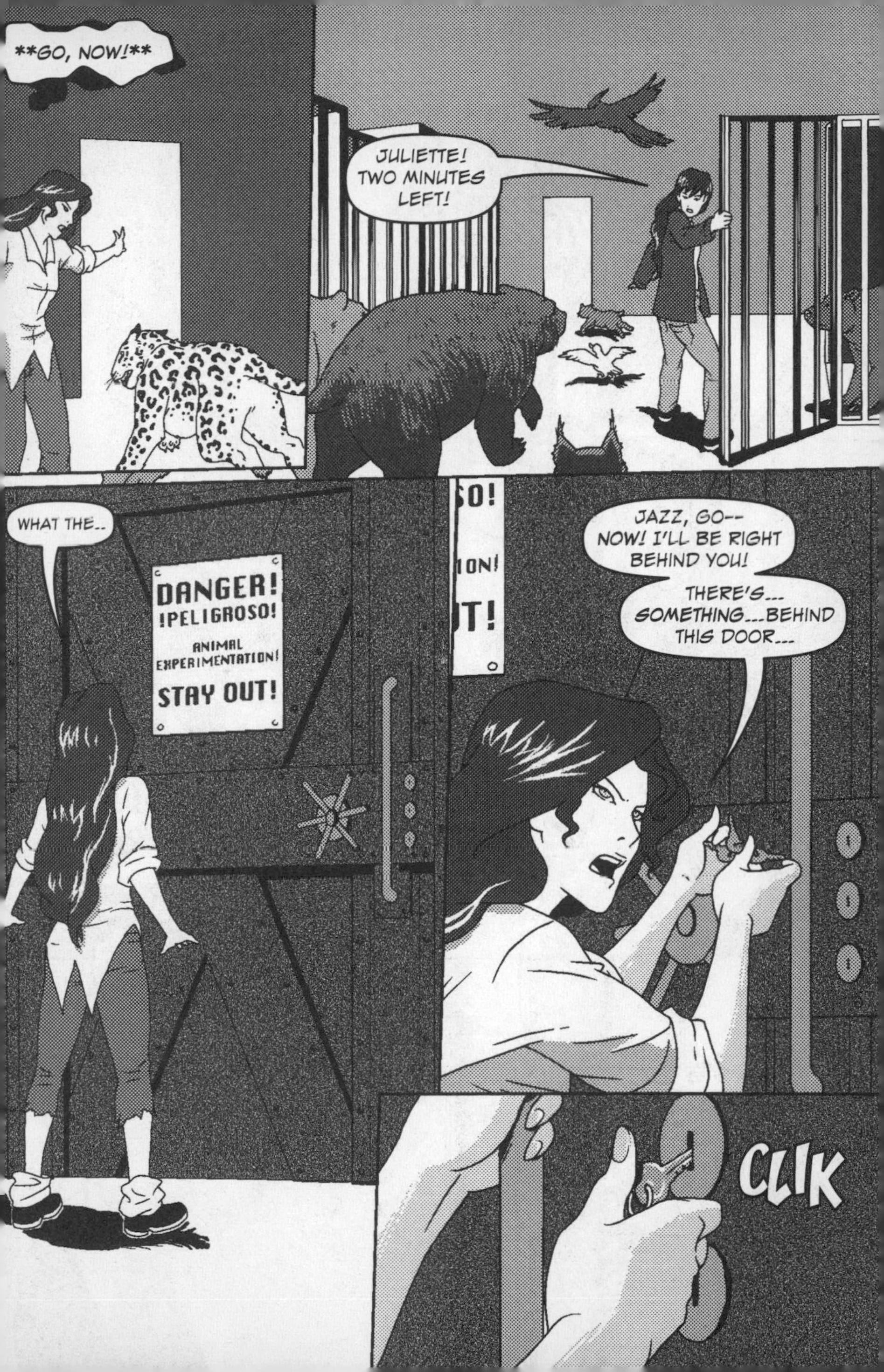
GO, NOW!
JULIETTE! TWO MINUTES LEFT!
WHAT THE..
DANGER! !PELIGROSO! ANIMAL EXPERIMENTATION! STAY OUT!
JAZZ, GO-- NOW! I'LL BE RIGHT BEHIND YOU!
THERE'S... SOMETHING...BEHIND THIS DOOR...
CLIK

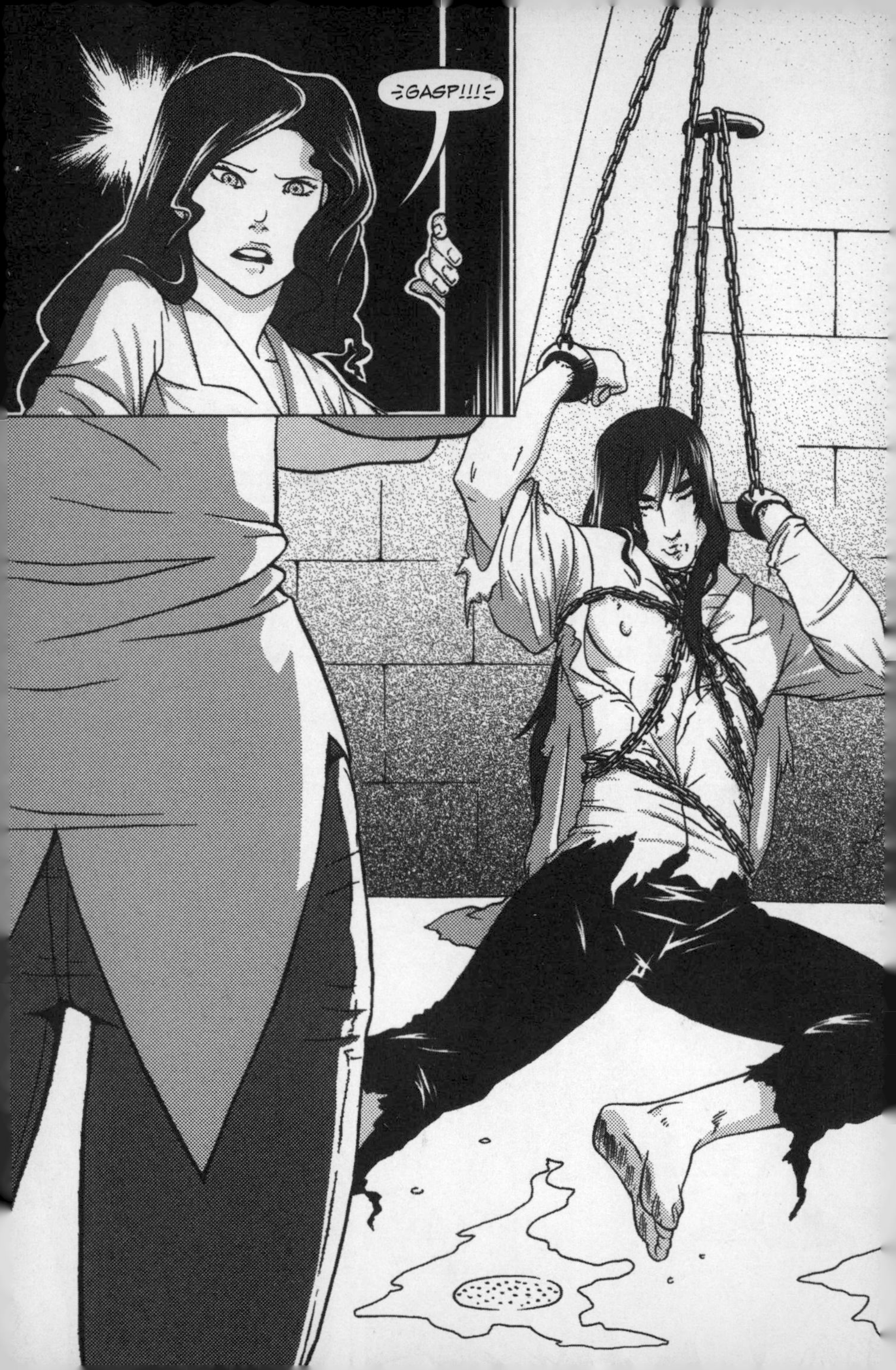
GASP!!!

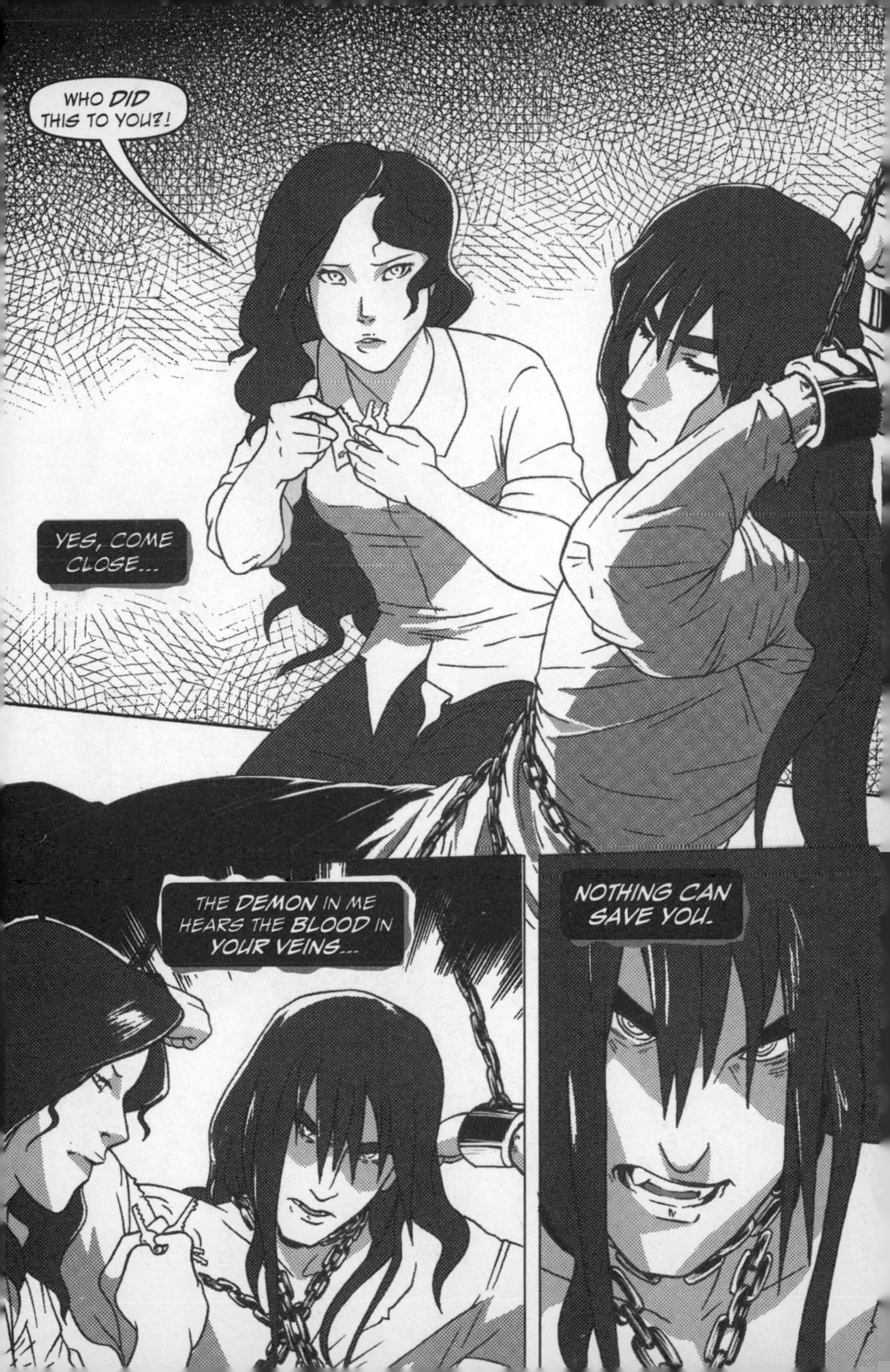
WHO *DID* THIS TO YOU?!
YES, COME CLOSE...
THE *DEMON* IN ME HEARS THE *BLOOD* IN *YOUR VEINS*...
NOTHING CAN SAVE YOU.

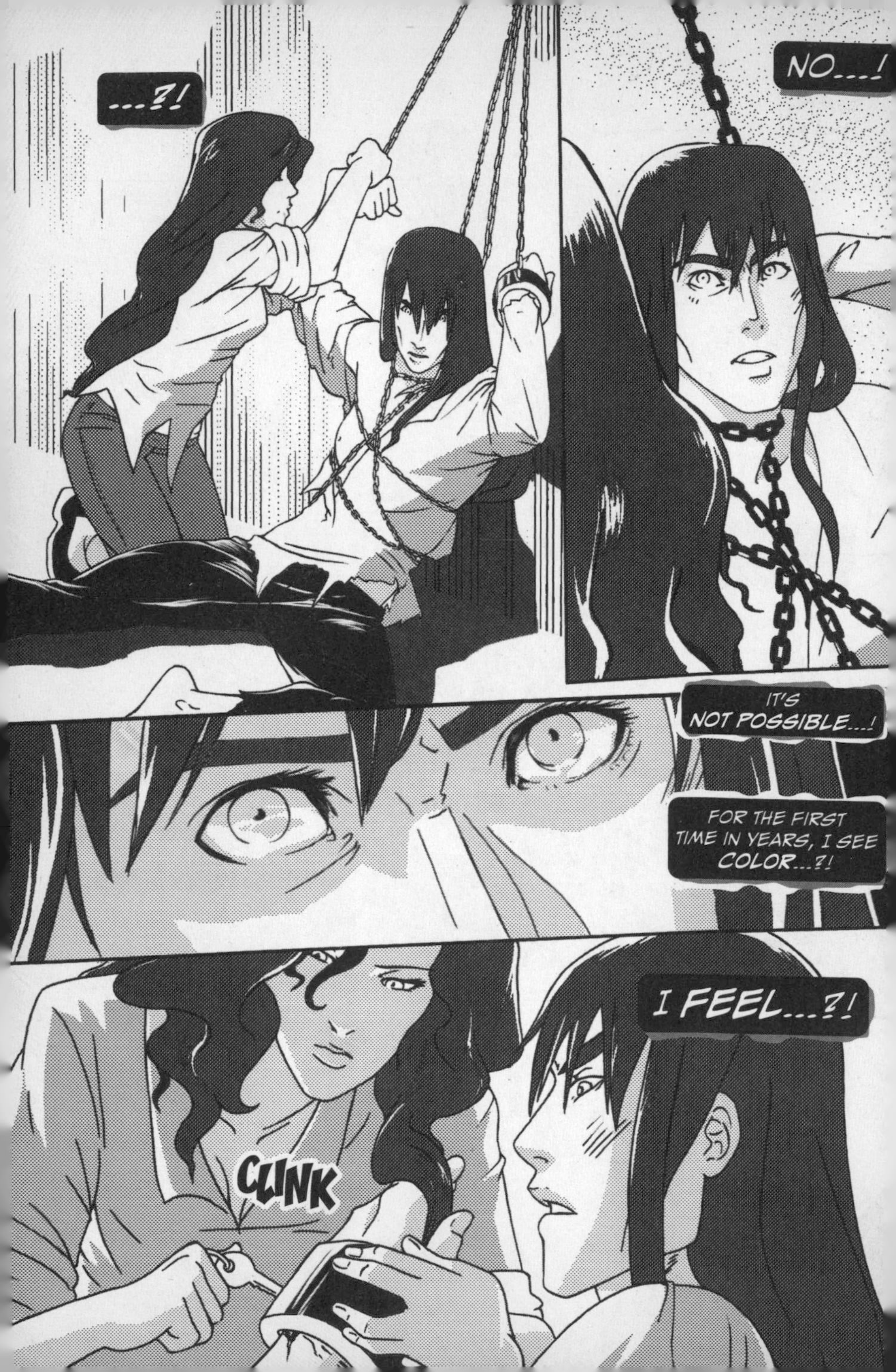
...?!
NO...!
IT'S NOT POSSIBLE...!
FOR THE FIRST TIME IN YEARS, I SEE COLOR...?!
I FEEL...?!
CLINK

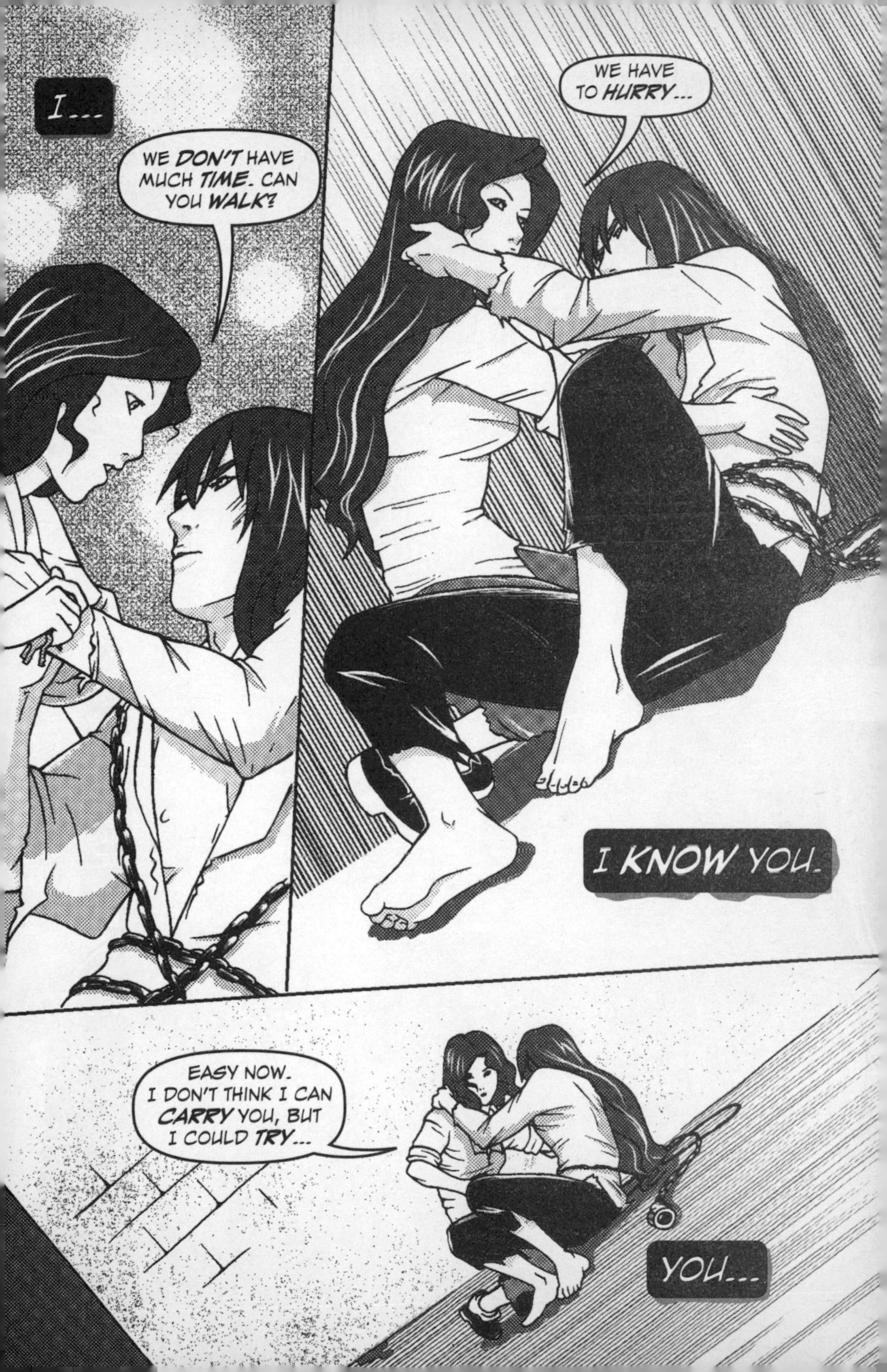
I...
WE DON'T HAVE MUCH TIME. CAN YOU WALK?
WE HAVE TO HURRY...
I KNOW YOU.
EASY NOW. I DON'T THINK I CAN CARRY YOU, BUT I COULD TRY...
YOU...

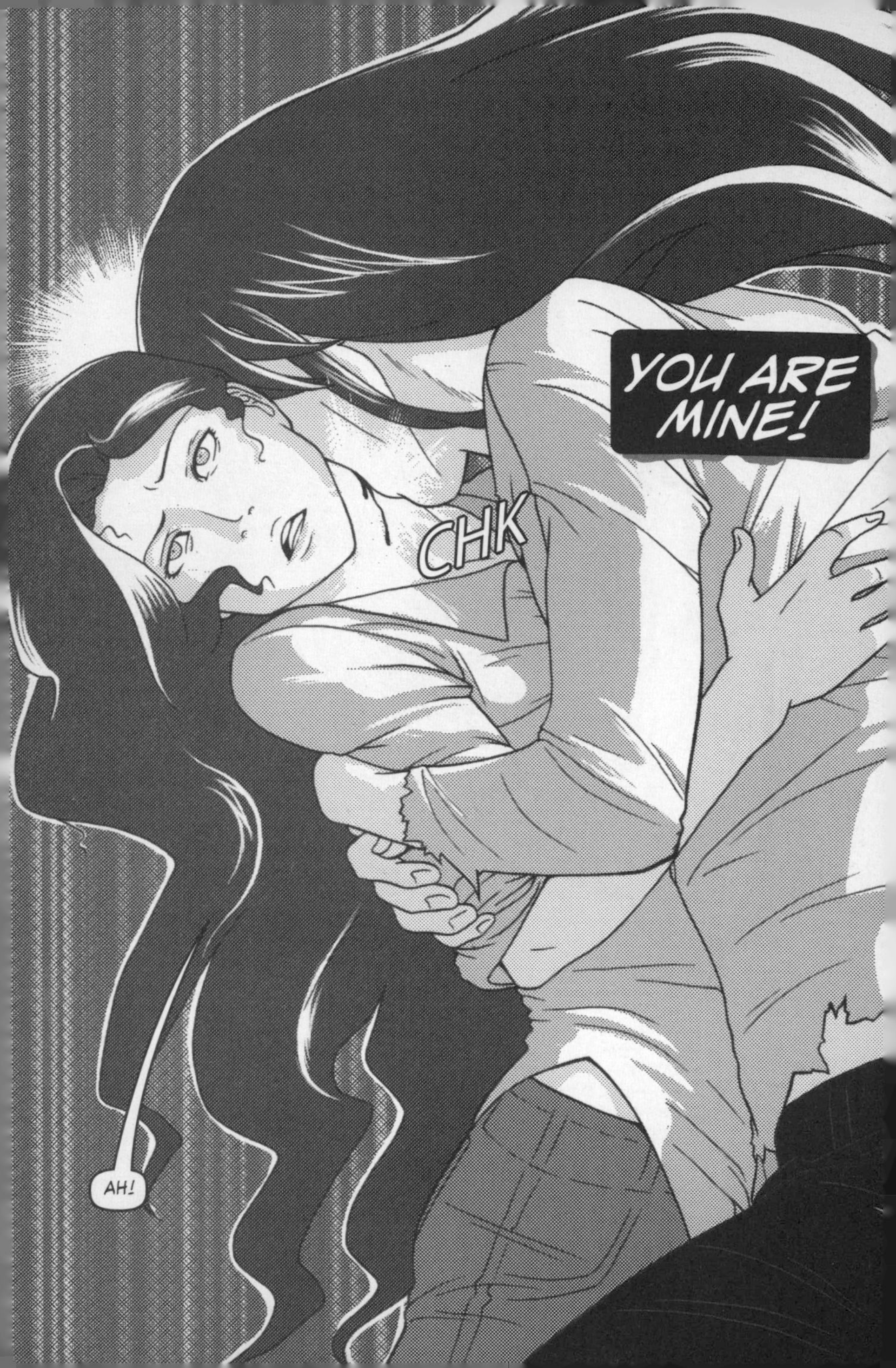
YOU ARE MINE!
CHK
AH!

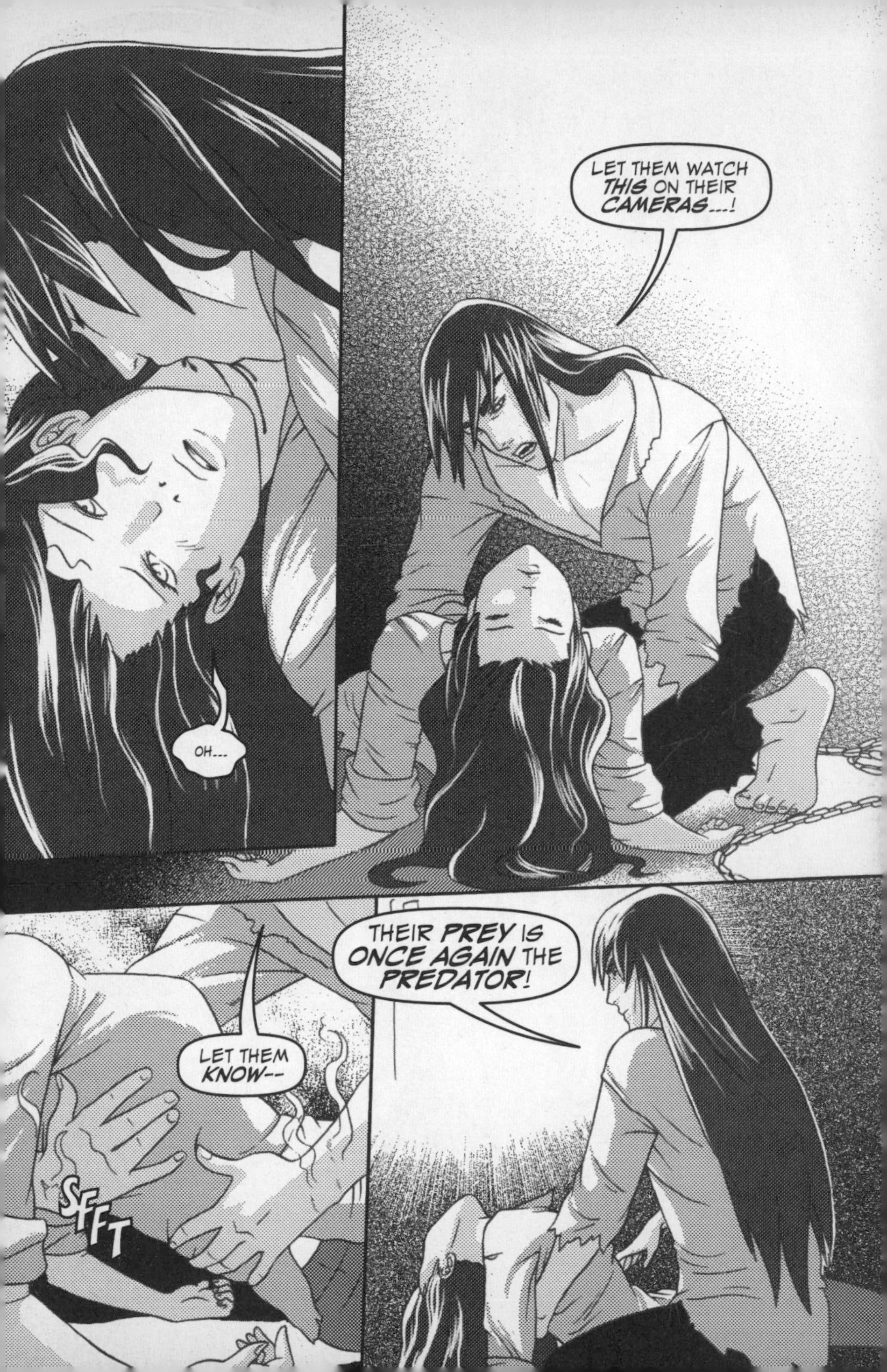
OH...
LET THEM WATCH THIS ON THEIR CAMERAS...!
LET THEM KNOW--
SFFT
THEIR PREY IS ONCE AGAIN THE PREDATOR!

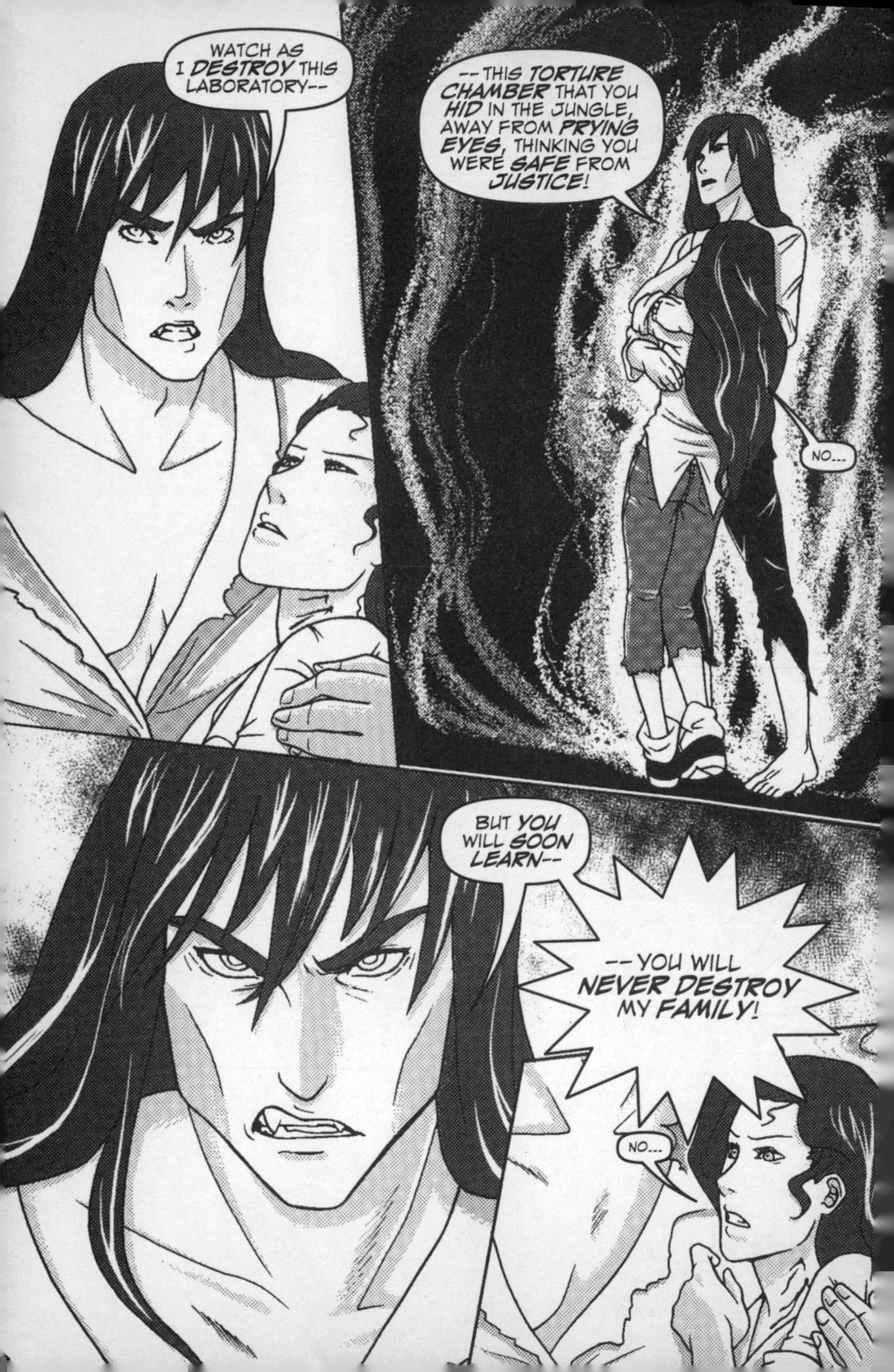
WATCH AS I DESTROY THIS LABORATORY--
--THIS TORTURE CHAMBER THAT YOU HID IN THE JUNGLE, AWAY FROM PRYING EYES, THINKING YOU WERE SAFE FROM JUSTICE!
NO...
BUT YOU WILL SOON LEARN--
--YOU WILL NEVER DESTROY MY FAMILY!
NO...

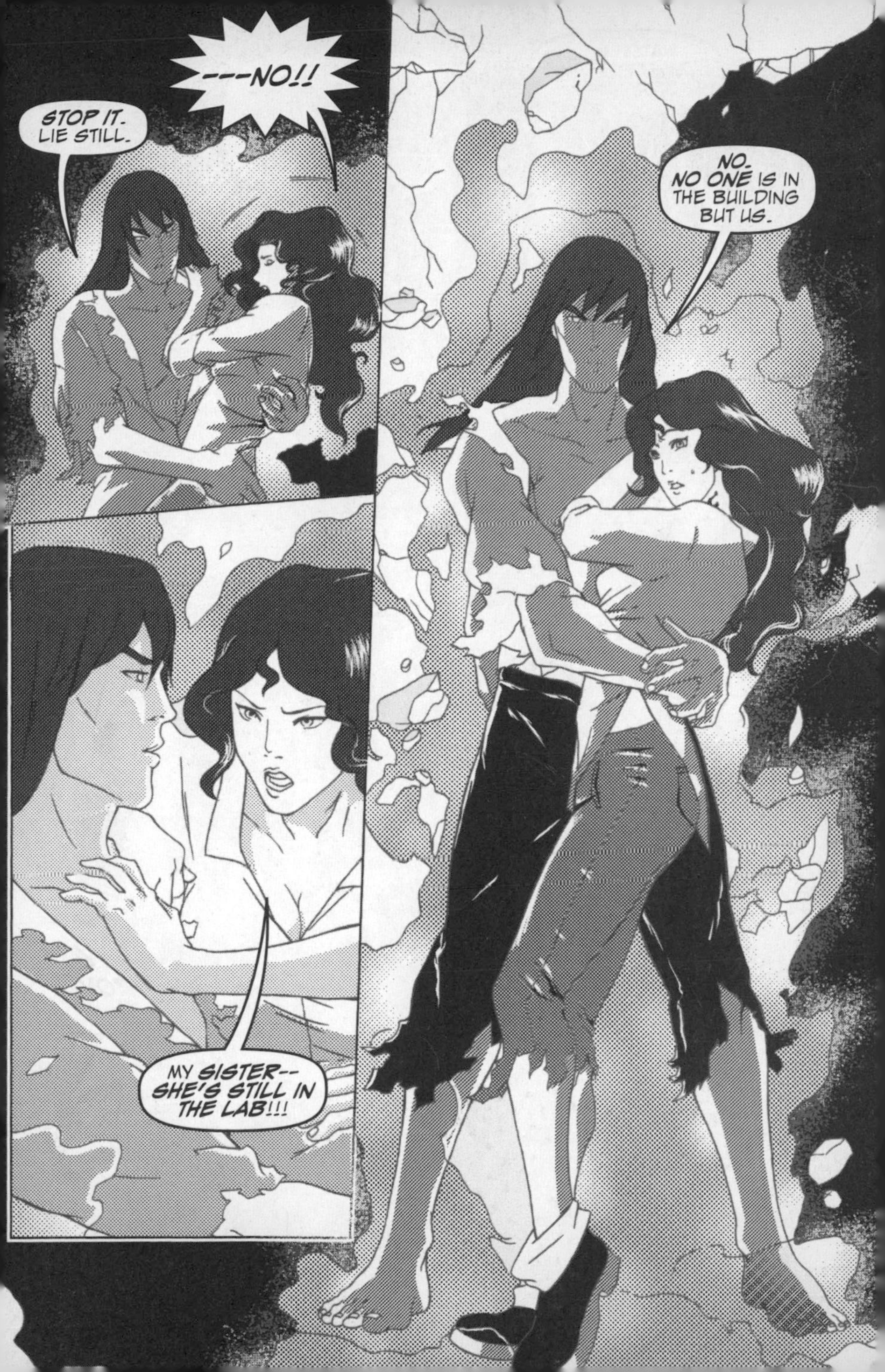
STOP IT. LIE STILL.
---NO!!
MY SISTER-- SHE'S STILL IN THE LAB!!!
NO. NO ONE IS IN THE BUILDING BUT US.

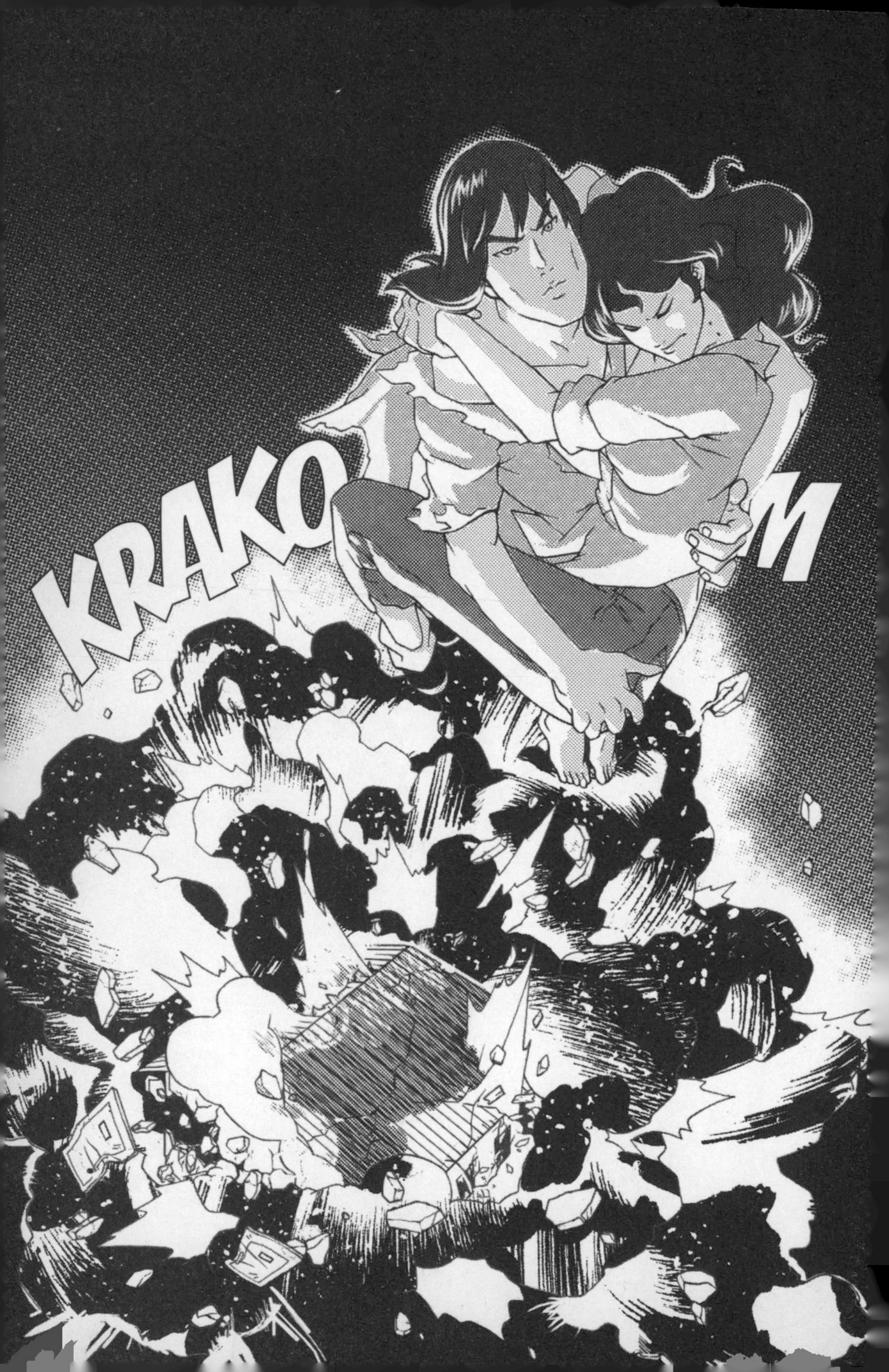
KRAKO M

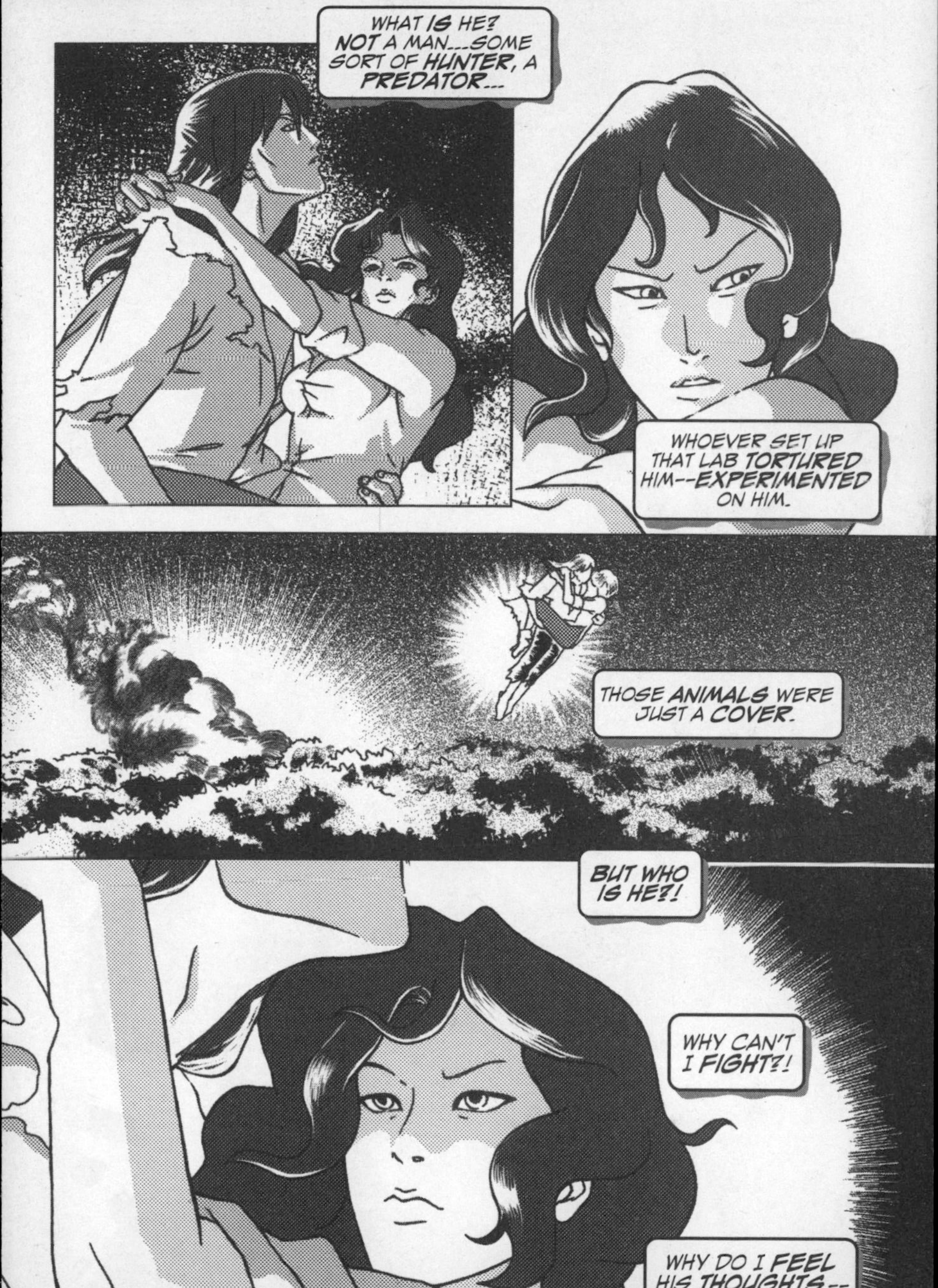
WHAT IS HE? NOT A MAN...SOME SORT OF HUNTER, A PREDATOR...
WHOEVER SET UP THAT LAB TORTURED HIM--EXPERIMENTED ON HIM.
THOSE ANIMALS WERE JUST A COVER.
BUT WHO IS HE?!
WHY CAN'T I FIGHT?!
WHY DO I FEEL HIS THOUGHTS--

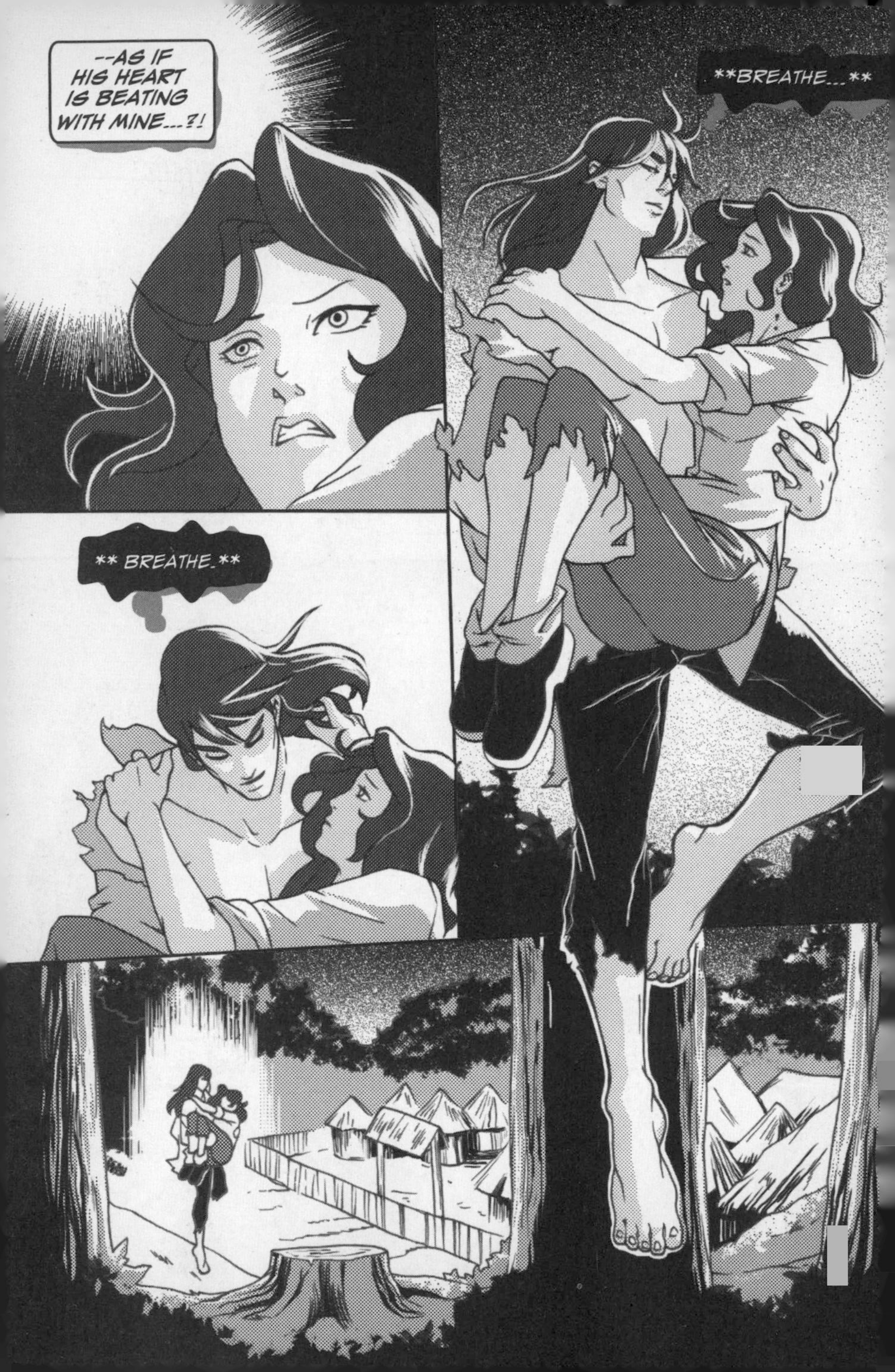
--AS IF HIS HEART IS BEATING WITH MINE...?!
BREATHE...
** BREATHE.**

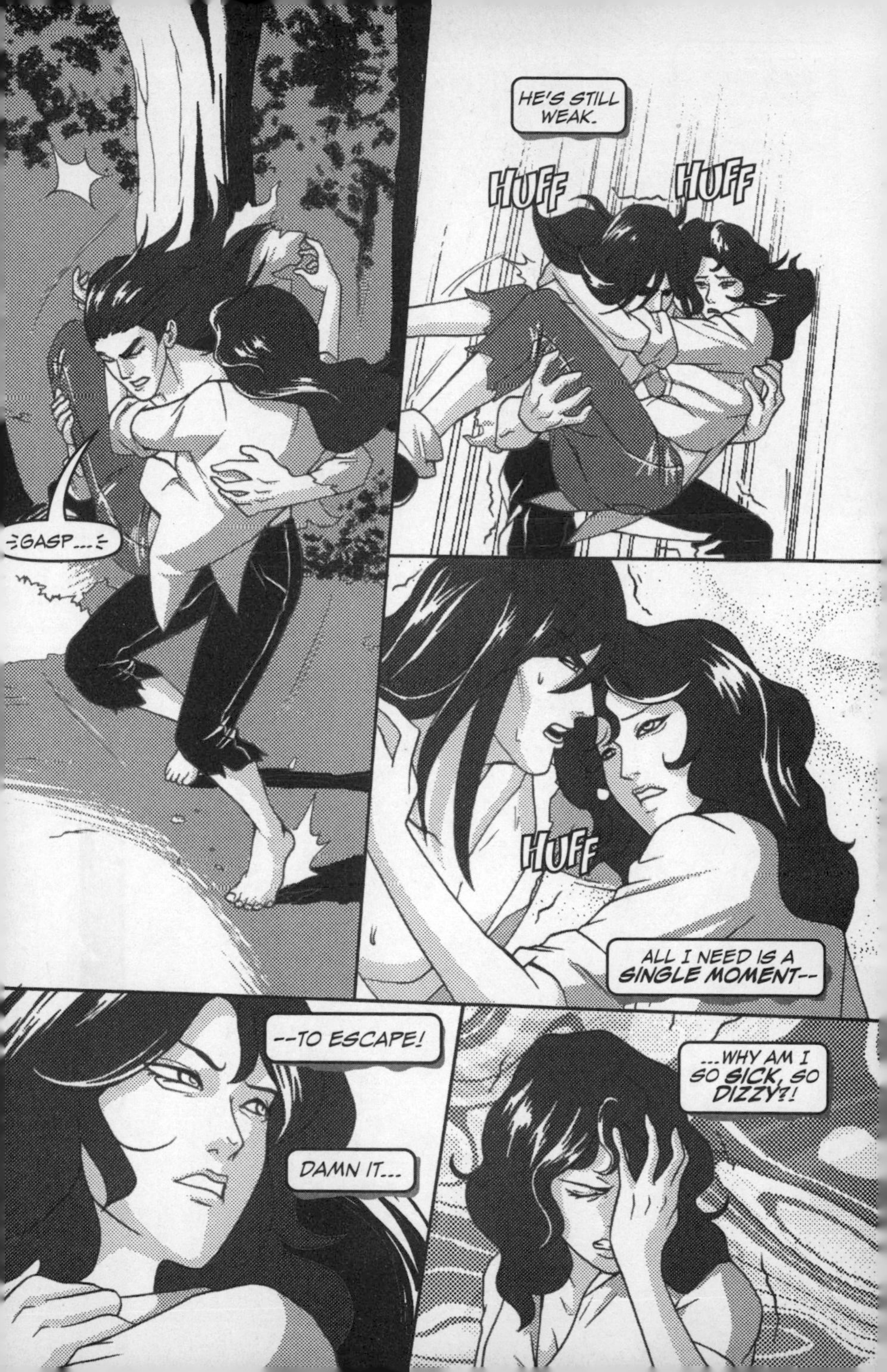
GASP...
HE'S STILL WEAK.
HUFF
HUFF
HUFF
ALL I NEED IS A SINGLE MOMENT--
--TO ESCAPE!
DAMN IT...
...WHY AM I SO SICK, SO DIZZY?!

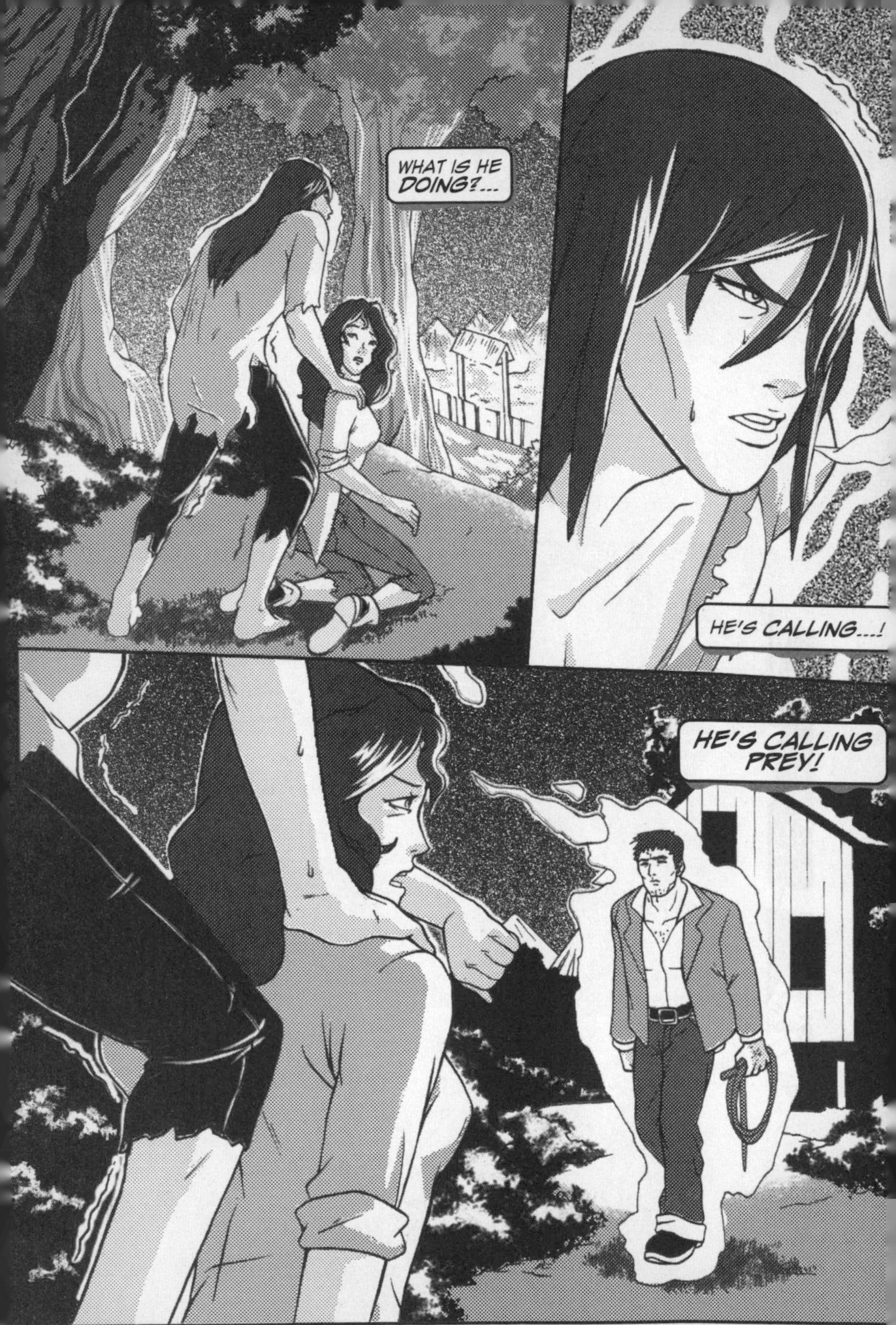
WHAT IS HE DOING?...
HE'S CALLING...!
HE'S CALLING PREY!

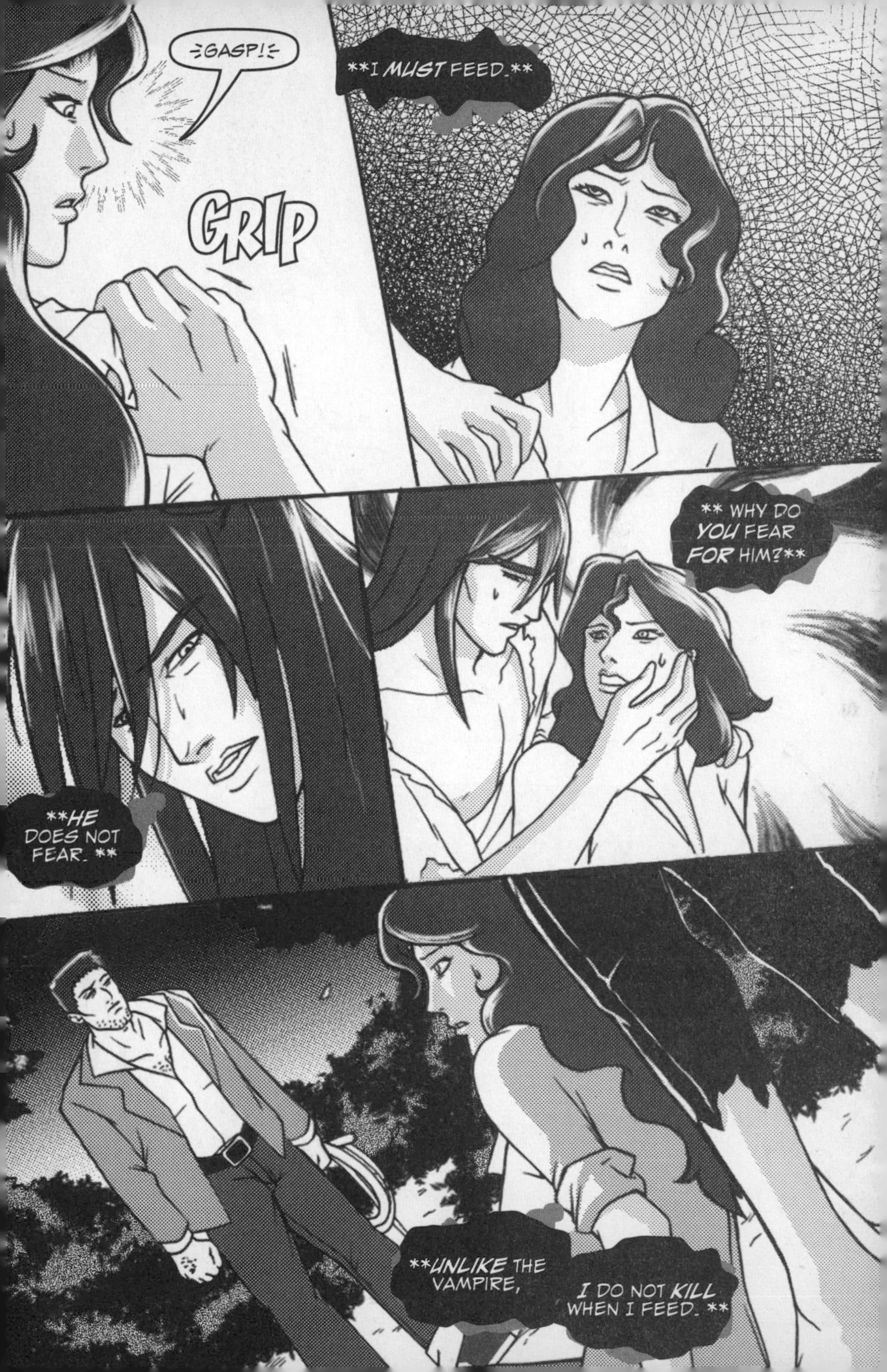

=GASP!=
GRIP
I MUST FEED.
HE DOES NOT FEAR.
** WHY DO YOU FEAR FOR HIM?**
**UNLIKE THE VAMPIRE,
I DO NOT KILL WHEN I FEED.**

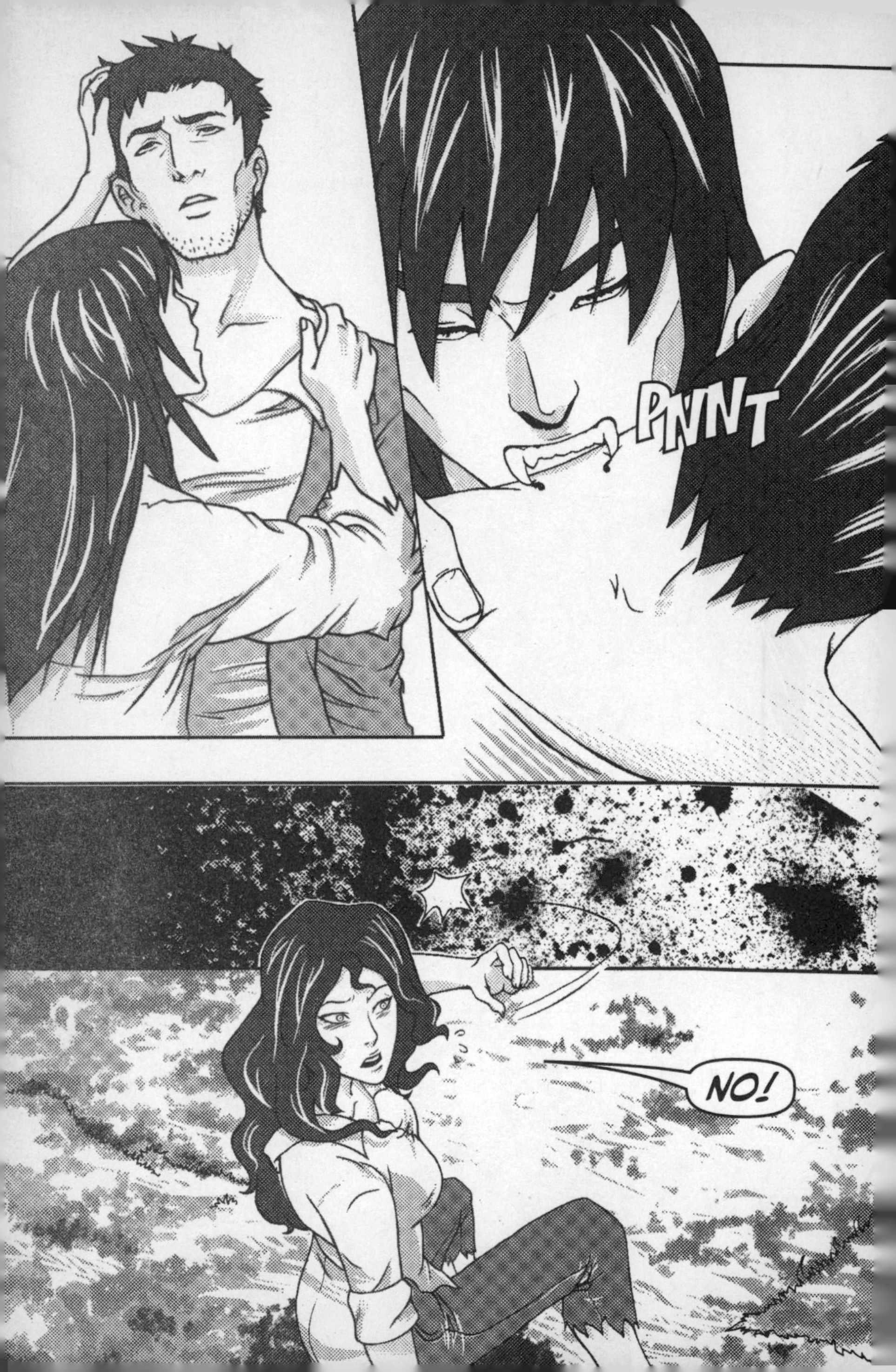
PNNT
NO!

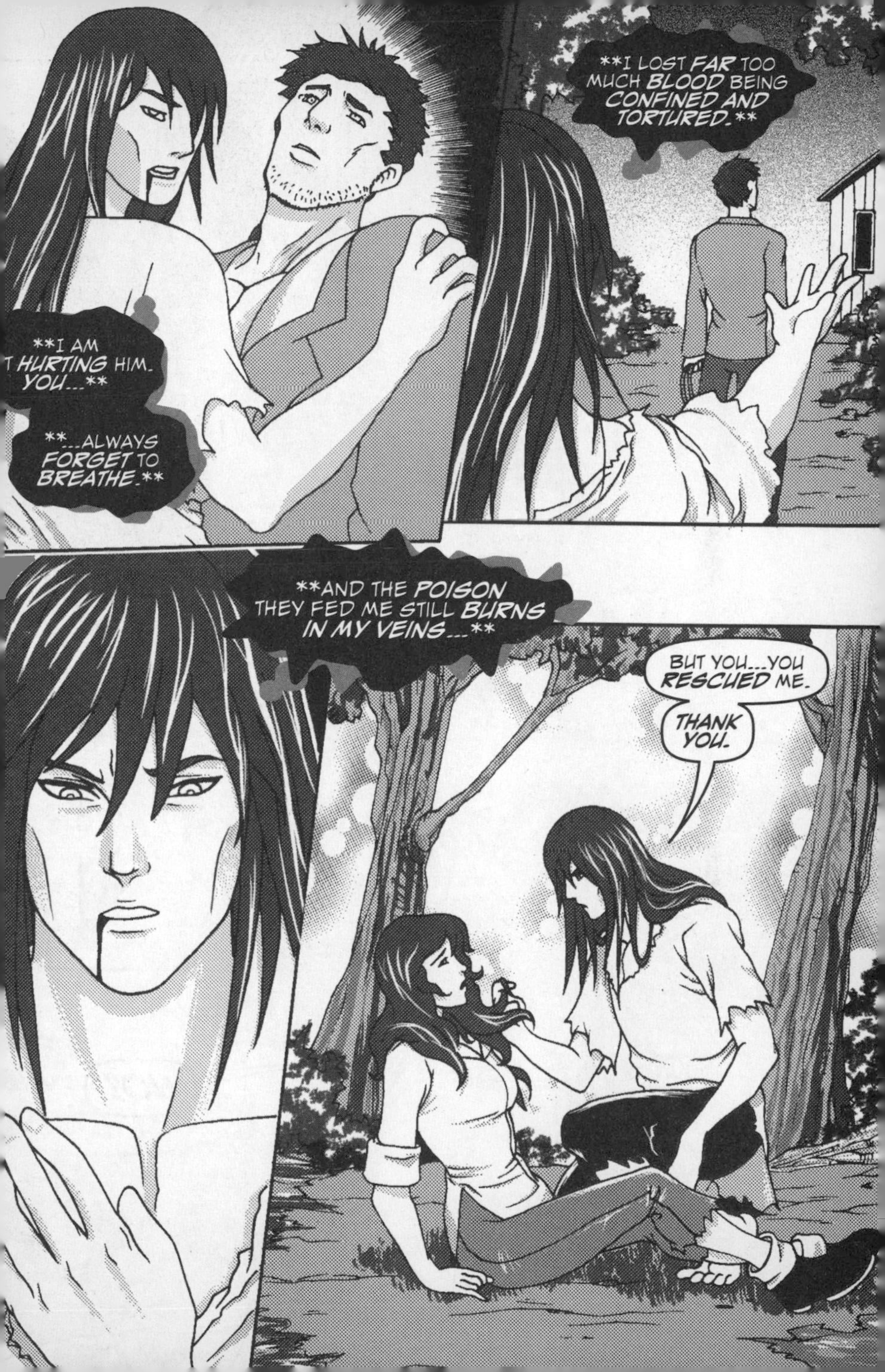
**I AM
T HURTING HIM.
YOU...**
...ALWAYS FORGET TO BREATHE.
I LOST FAR TOO MUCH BLOOD BEING CONFINED AND TORTURED.
AND THE POISON THEY FED ME STILL BURNS IN MY VEINS...
BUT YOU...YOU RESCUED ME.
THANK YOU.

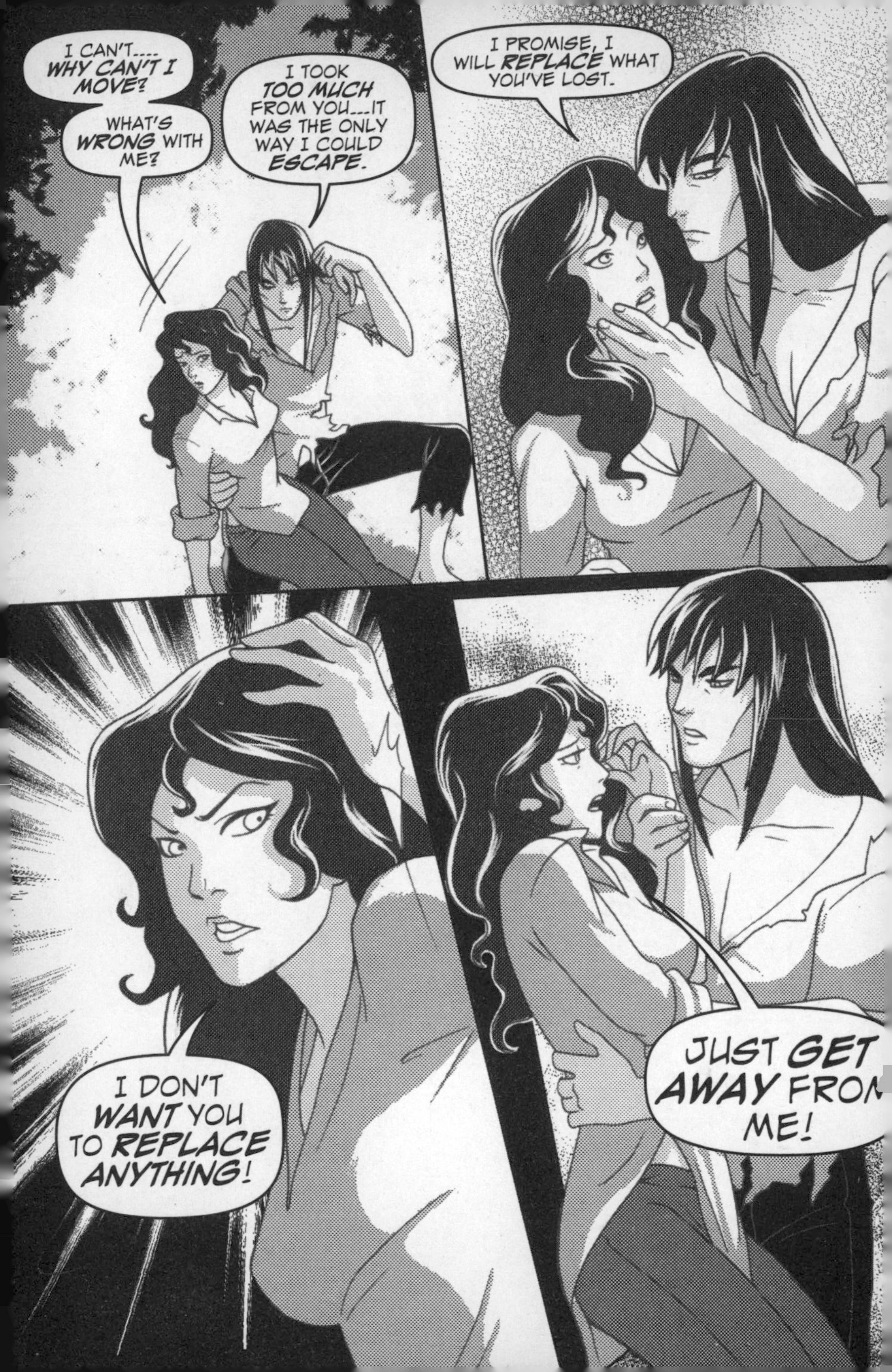
I CAN'T.... WHY CAN'T I MOVE?
WHAT'S WRONG WITH ME?
I TOOK TOO MUCH FROM YOU...IT WAS THE ONLY WAY I COULD ESCAPE.
I PROMISE, I WILL REPLACE WHAT YOU'VE LOST.
I DON'T WANT YOU TO REPLACE ANYTHING!
JUST GET AWAY FROM ME!

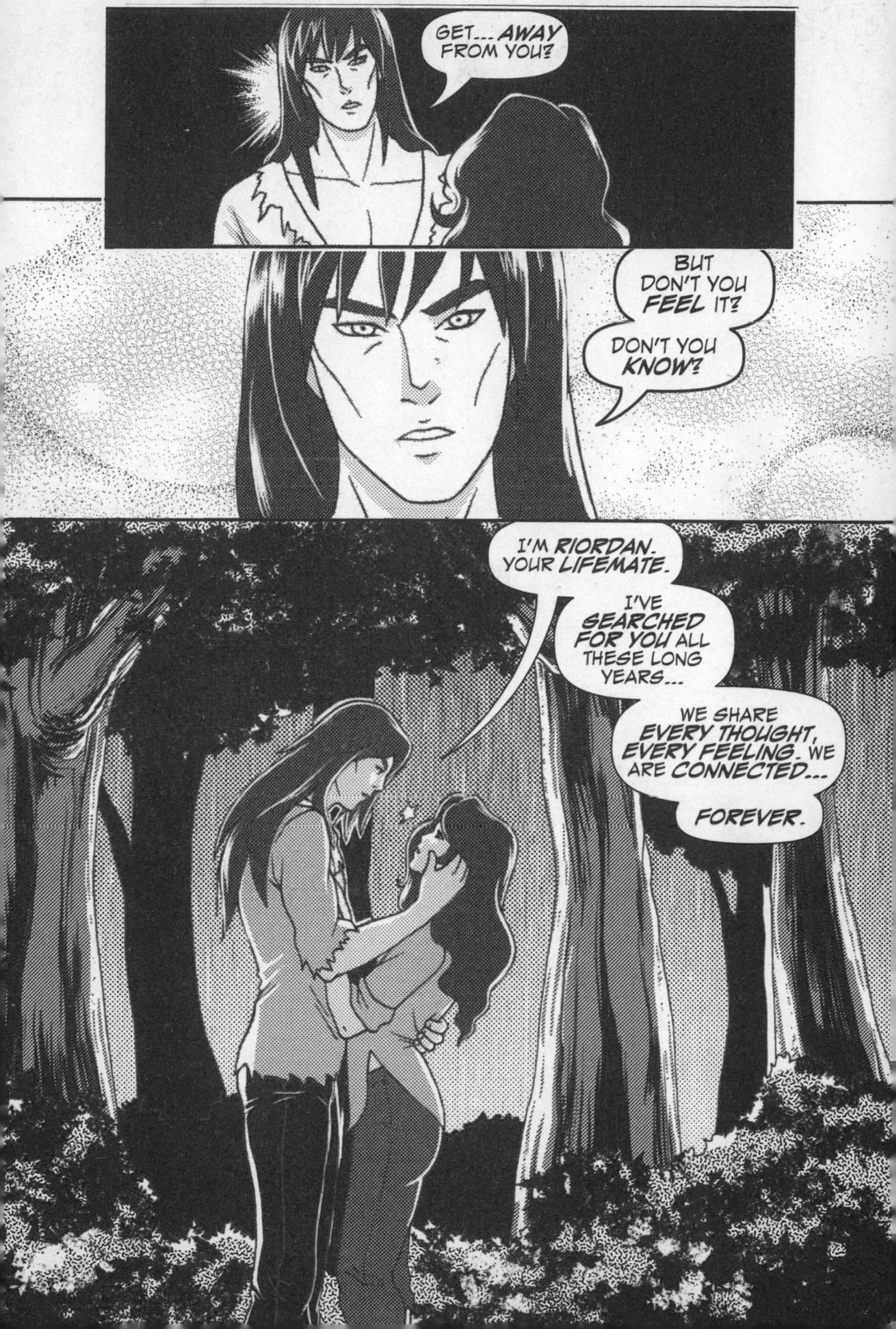
GET... AWAY FROM YOU?
BUT DON'T YOU FEEL IT?
DON'T YOU KNOW?
I'M RIORDAN. YOUR LIFEMATE.
I'VE SEARCHED FOR YOU ALL THESE LONG YEARS...
WE SHARE EVERY THOUGHT, EVERY FEELING. WE ARE CONNECTED...
FOREVER.

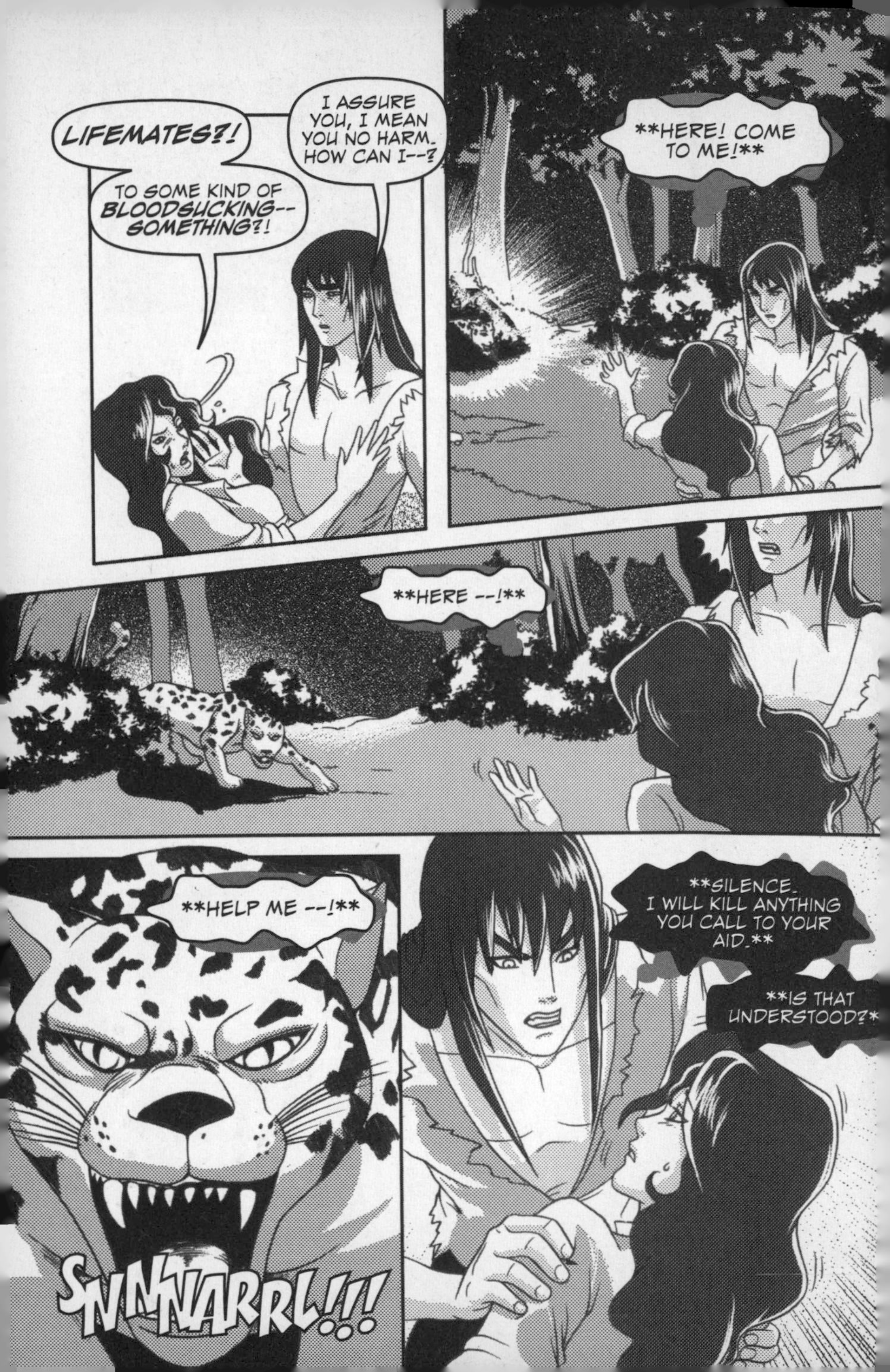
LIFEMATES?!
TO SOME KIND OF BLOODSUCKING-- SOMETHING?!
I ASSURE YOU, I MEAN YOU NO HARM. HOW CAN I--?
HERE! COME TO ME!
HERE --!
HELP ME --!
SNNNARRL!!!
SILENCE. I WILL KILL ANYTHING YOU CALL TO YOUR AID.
**IS THAT UNDERSTOOD?*

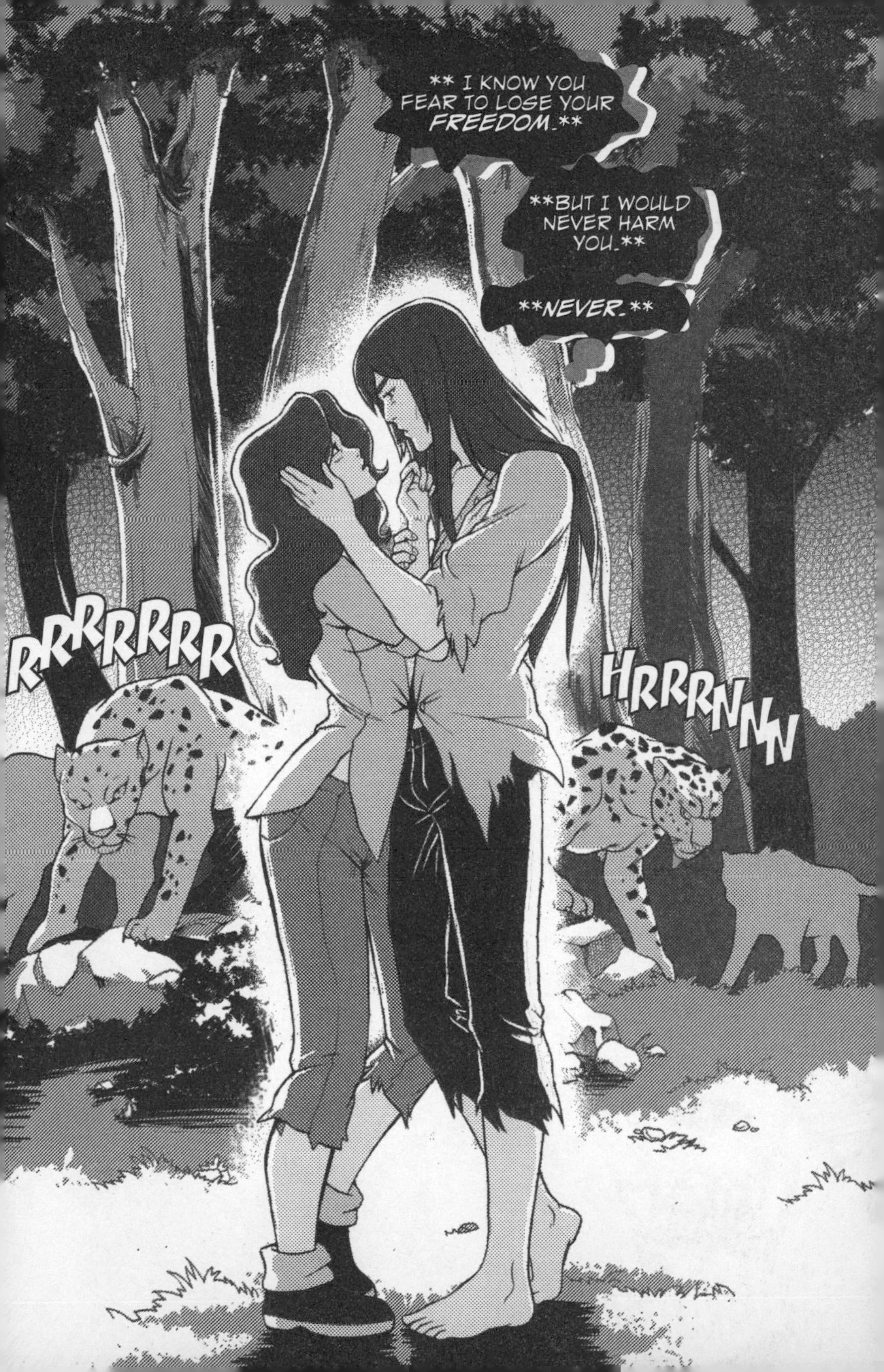
** I KNOW YOU FEAR TO LOSE YOUR FREEDOM.**
BUT I WOULD NEVER HARM YOU.
NEVER.
RRRRRRRR
HRRRRNNNN

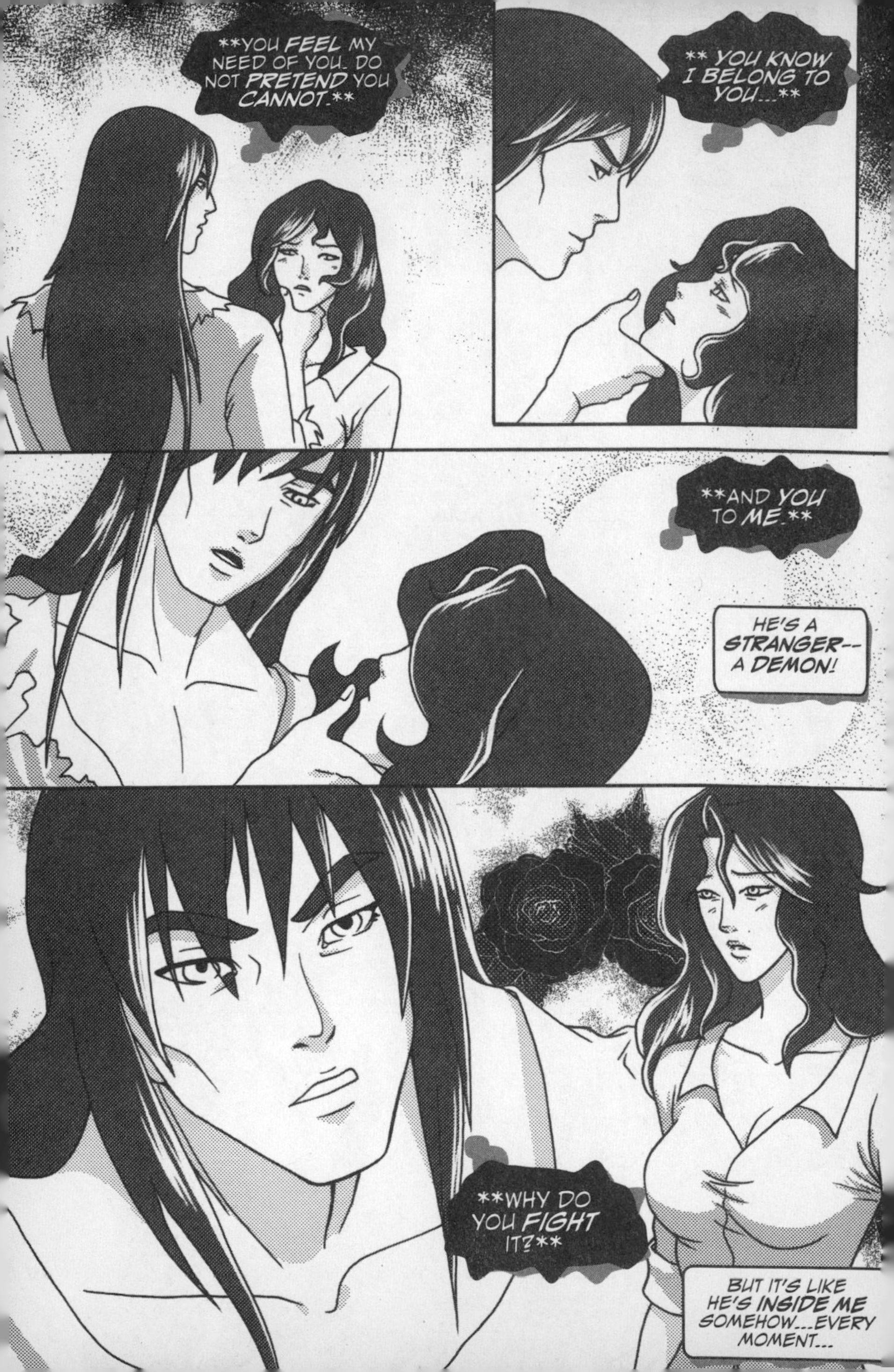
YOU FEEL MY NEED OF YOU. DO NOT PRETEND YOU CANNOT.
** YOU KNOW I BELONG TO YOU...**
AND YOU TO ME.
HE'S A STRANGER-- A DEMON!
WHY DO YOU FIGHT IT?
BUT IT'S LIKE HE'S INSIDE ME SOMEHOW...EVERY MOMENT...

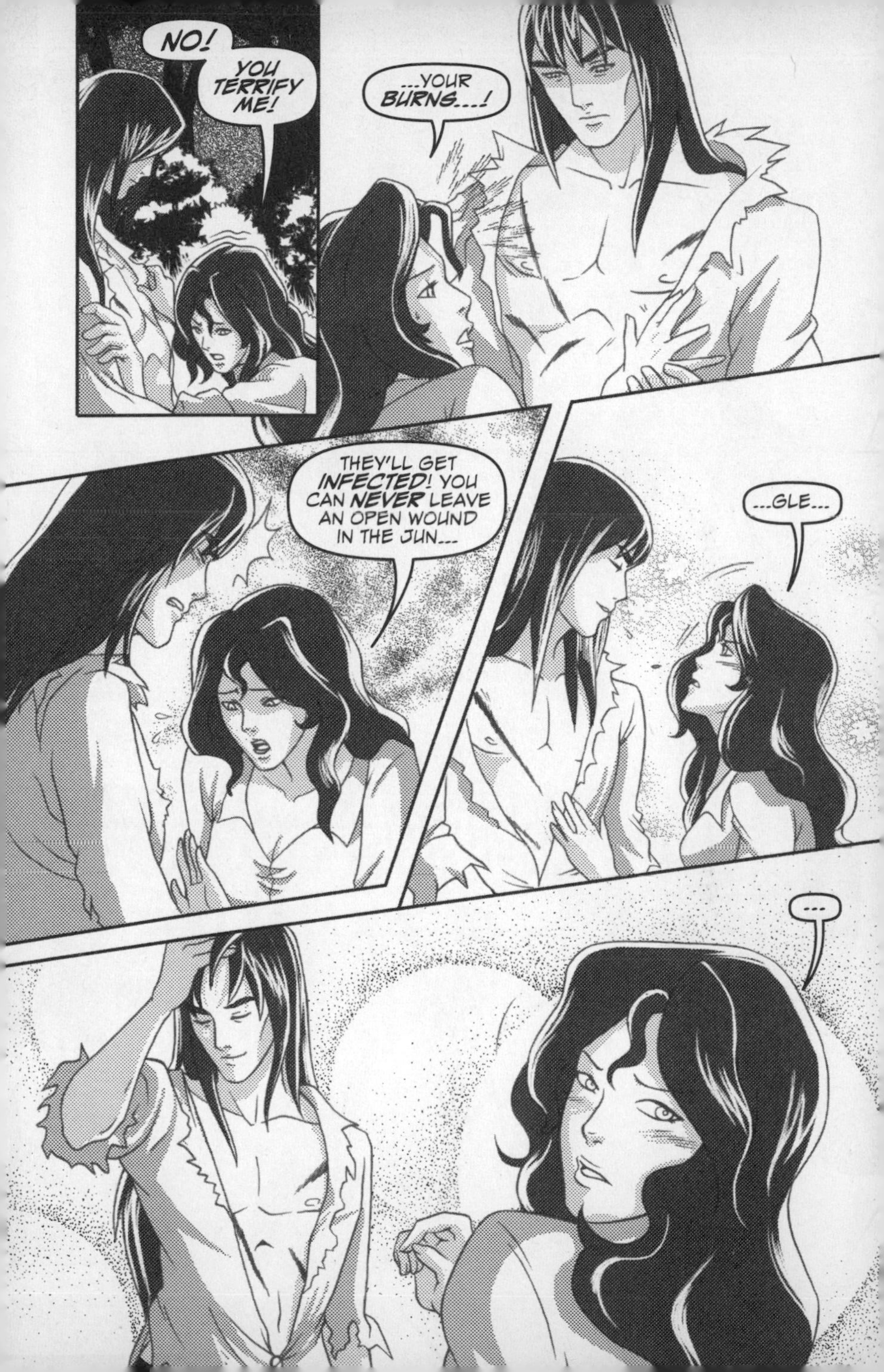
NO!
YOU TERRIFY ME!
...YOUR BURNS...!
THEY'LL GET INFECTED! YOU CAN NEVER LEAVE AN OPEN WOUND IN THE JUN...
...GLE...
...

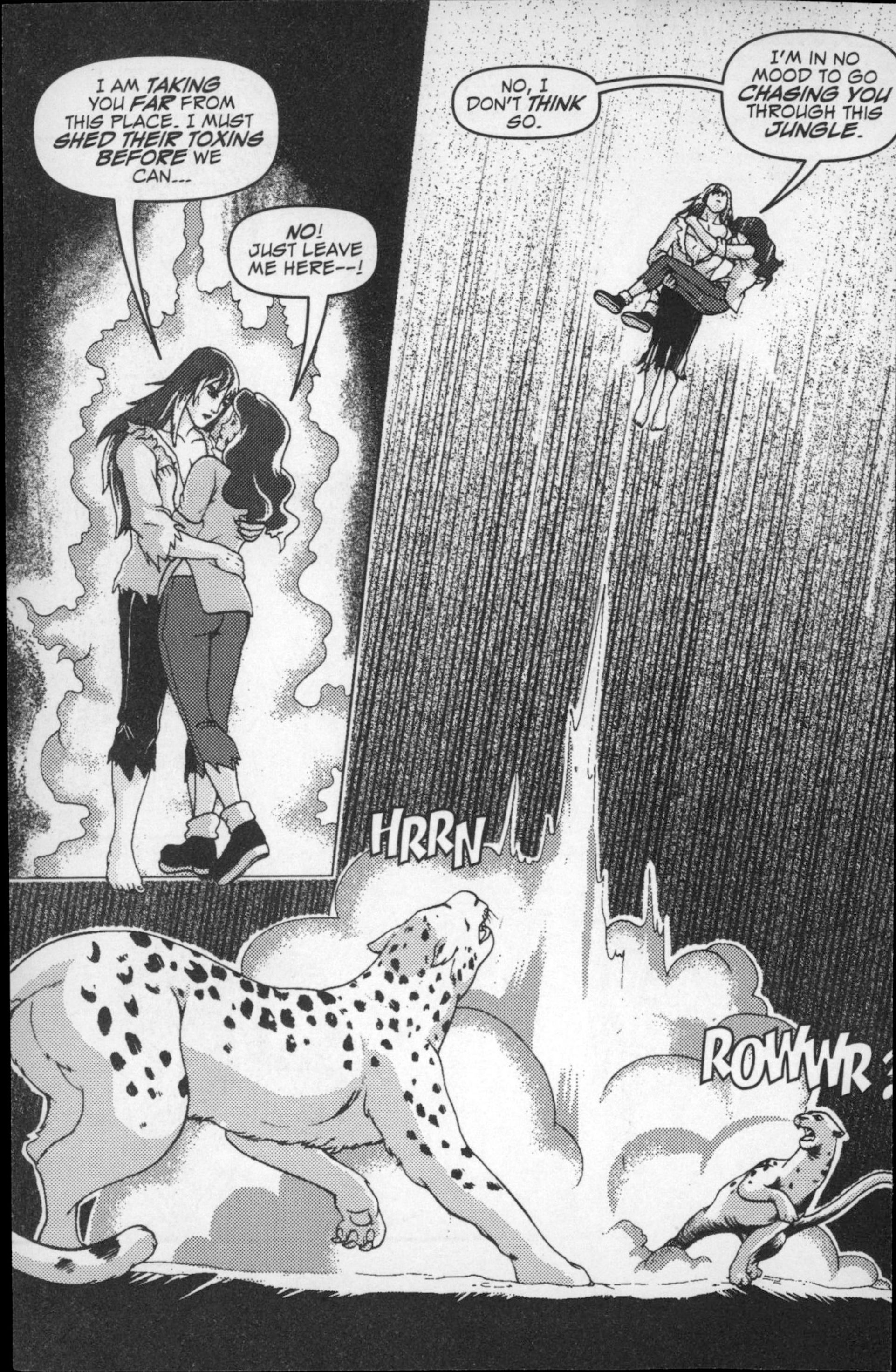
I AM TAKING YOU FAR FROM THIS PLACE. I MUST SHED THEIR TOXINS BEFORE WE CAN...
NO! JUST LEAVE ME HERE--!
NO, I DON'T THINK SO.
I'M IN NO MOOD TO GO CHASING YOU THROUGH THIS JUNGLE.
HRRN
ROWWR

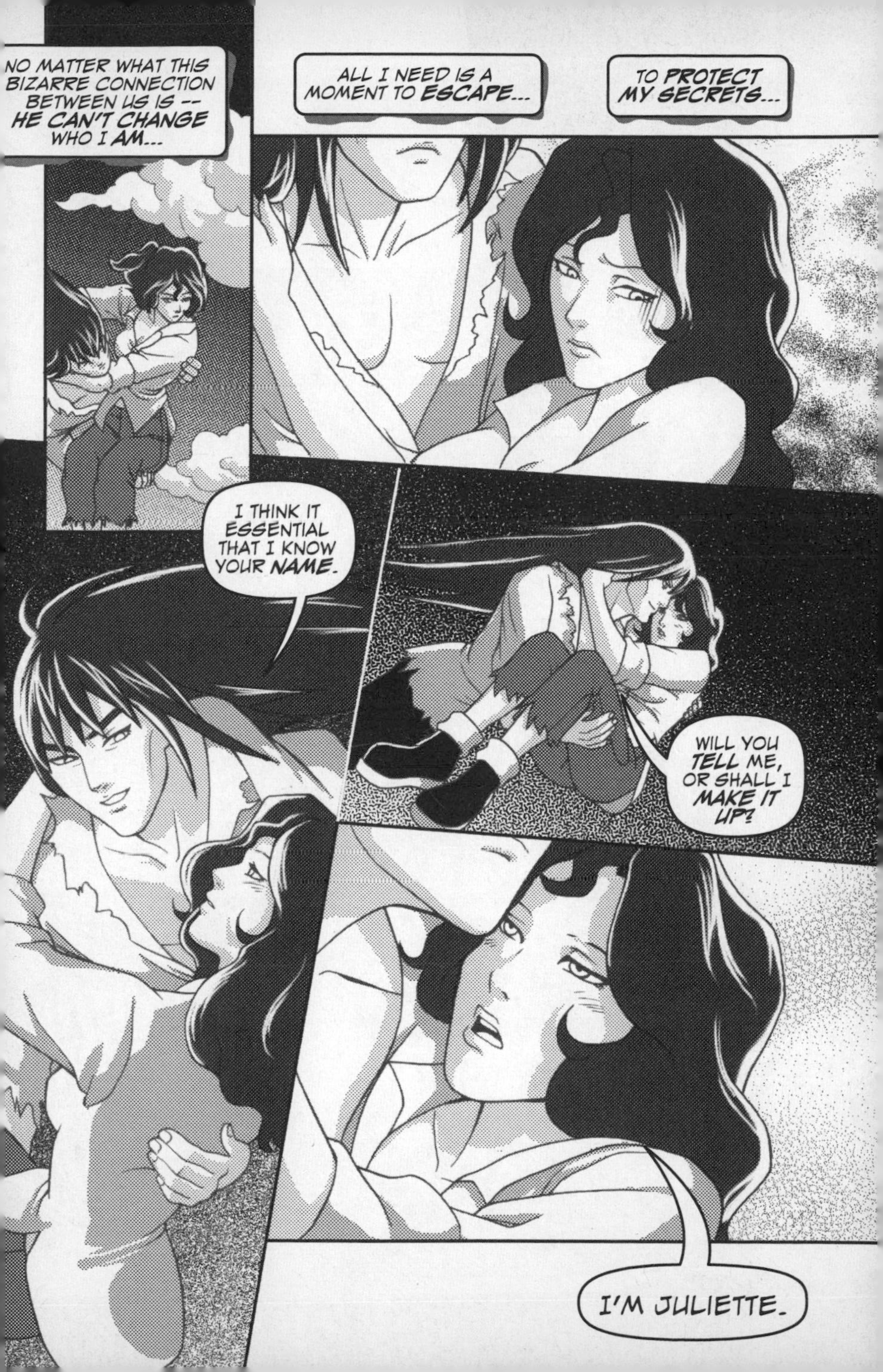

NO MATTER WHAT THIS BIZARRE CONNECTION BETWEEN US IS -- HE CAN'T CHANGE WHO I AM...
ALL I NEED IS A MOMENT TO ESCAPE...
TO PROTECT MY SECRETS...
I THINK IT ESSENTIAL THAT I KNOW YOUR NAME.
WILL YOU TELL ME, OR SHALL I MAKE IT UP?
I'M JULIETTE.

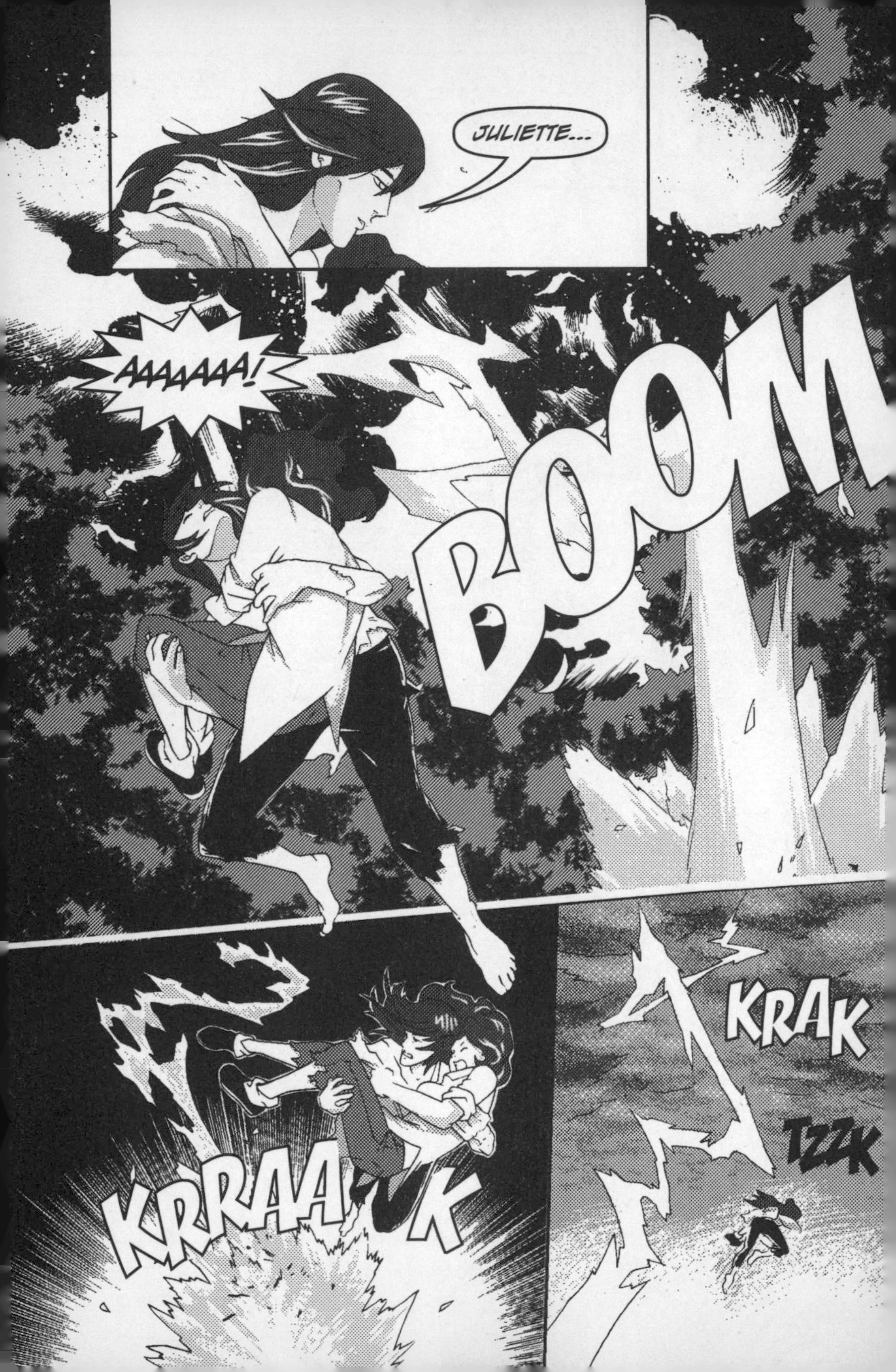
JULIETTE...
AAAAAAA!
BOOM
KRRAAK
KRAK
TZZK

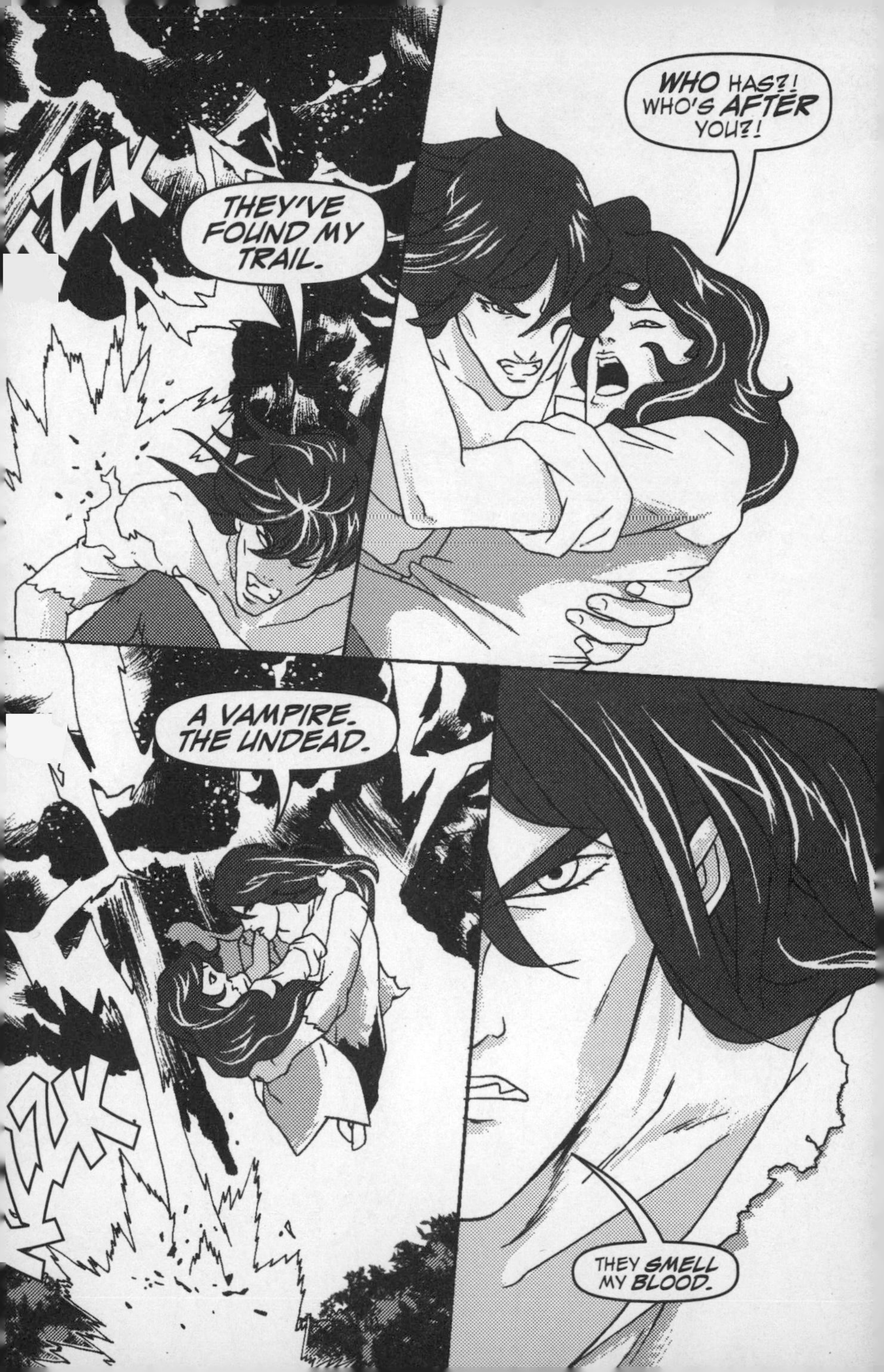
THEY'VE FOUND MY TRAIL.
WHO HAS?! WHO'S AFTER YOU?!
A VAMPIRE. THE UNDEAD.
THEY SMELL MY BLOOD.

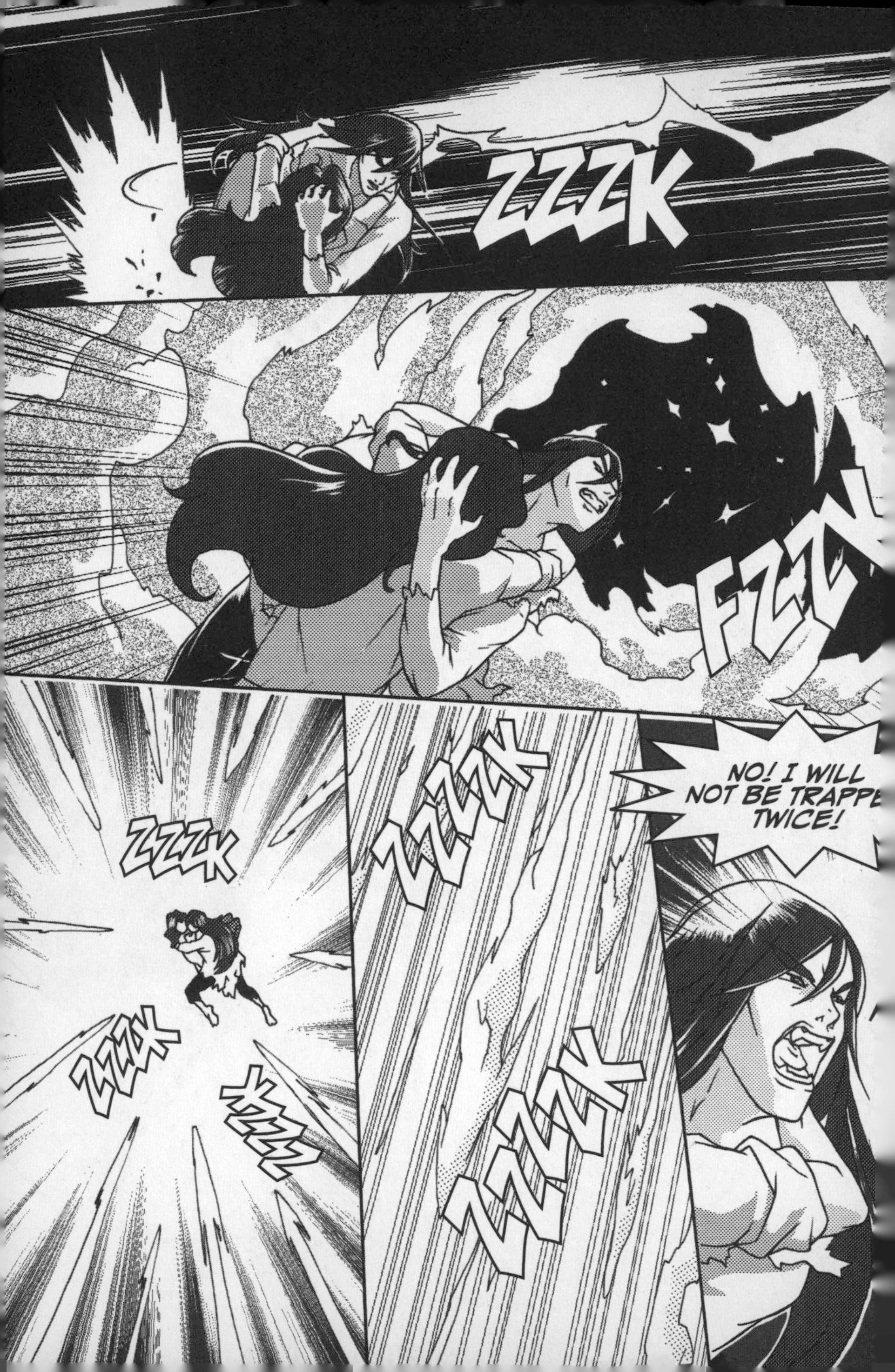

ZZZK
FZZZ
ZZZK
ZZZK
ZZZK
ZZZZK
ZZZZK
NO! I WILL NOT BE TRAPPE TWICE!

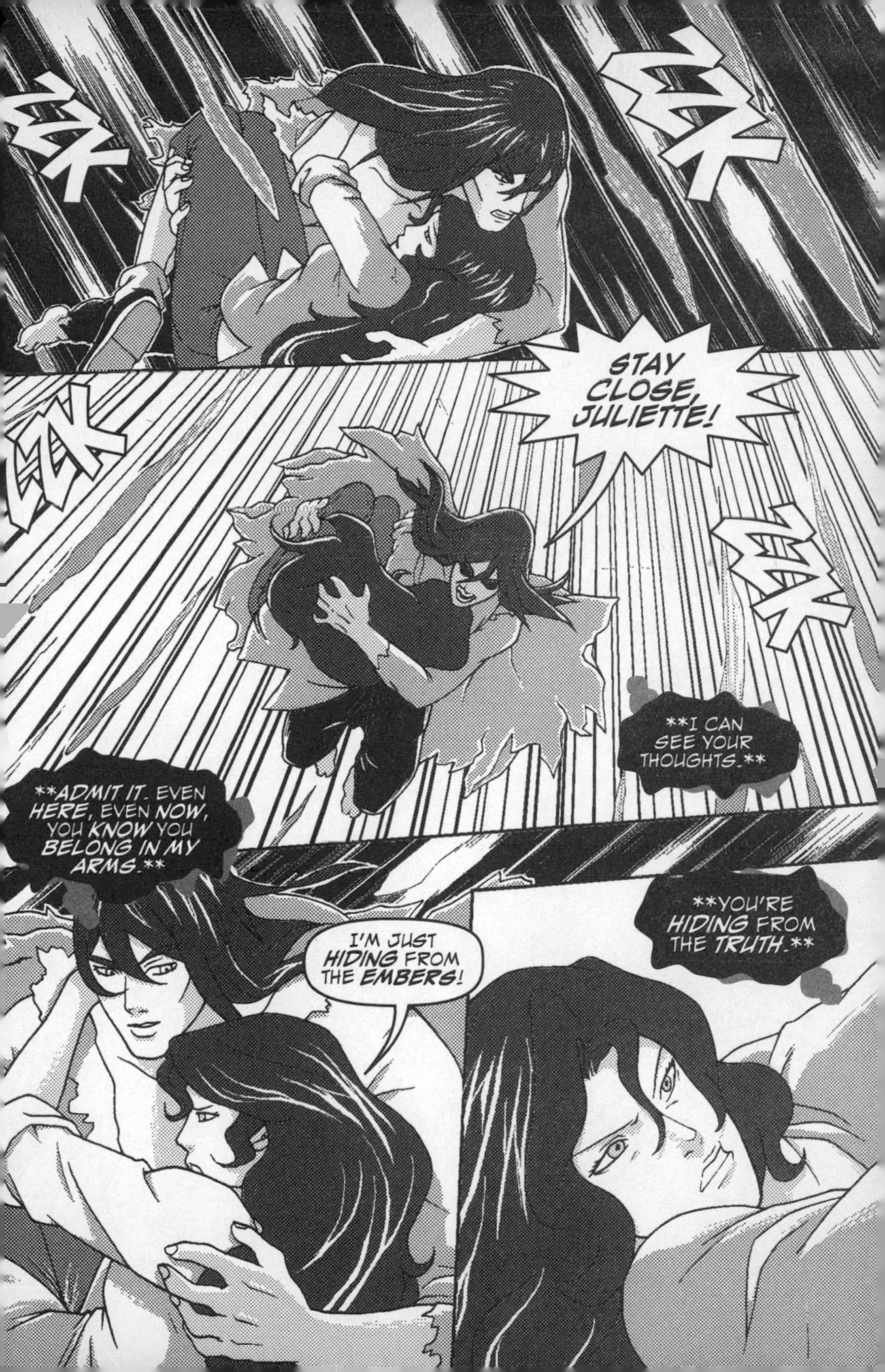
STAY CLOSE, JULIETTE!
I CAN SEE YOUR THOUGHTS.
ADMIT IT. EVEN HERE, EVEN NOW, YOU KNOW YOU BELONG IN MY ARMS.
I'M JUST HIDING FROM THE EMBERS!
YOU'RE HIDING FROM THE TRUTH.

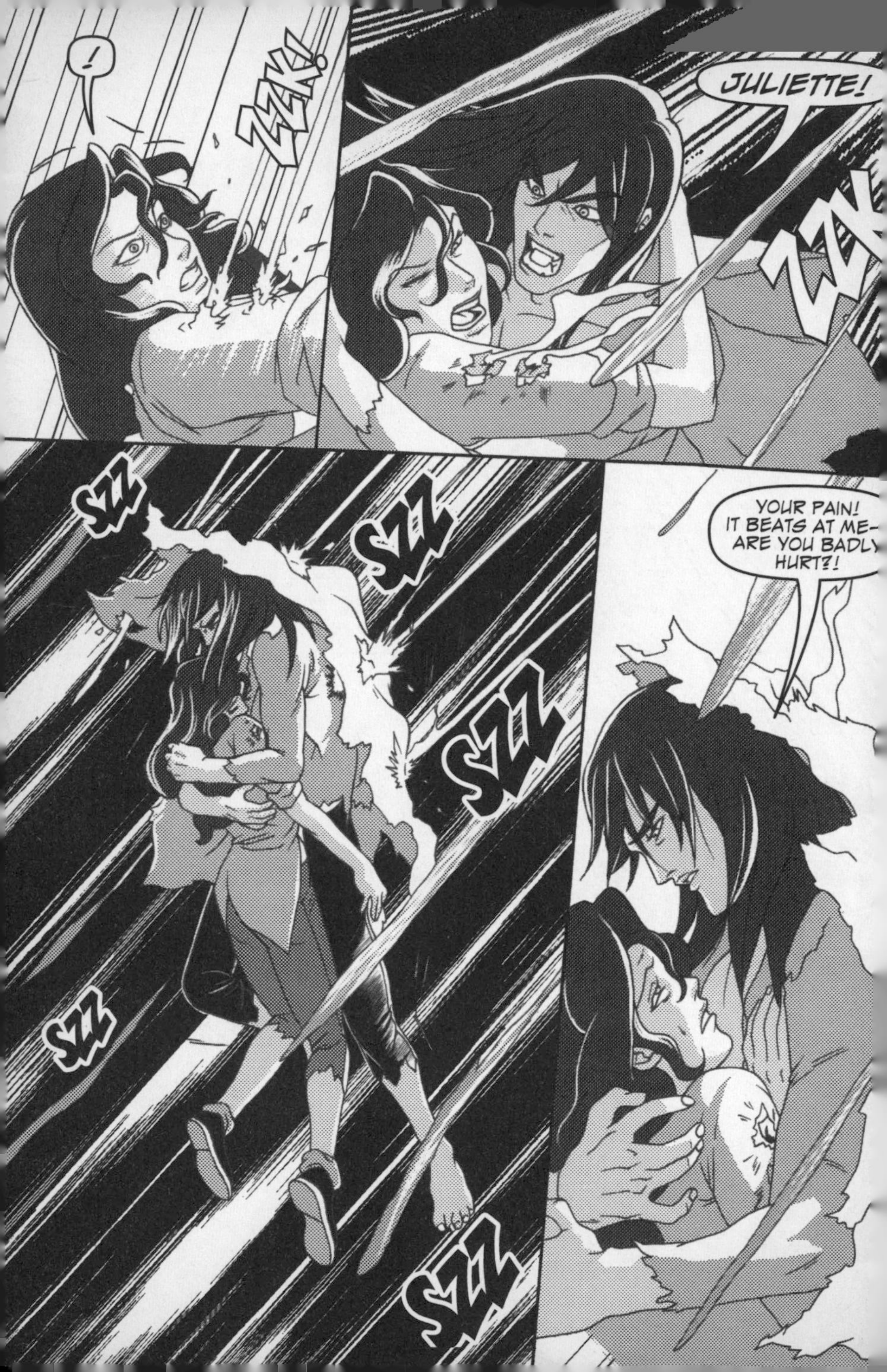
!
ZZZK!
JULIETTE!
ZZZK
SZZ
SZZ
SZZ
SZZ
SZZ
YOUR PAIN!
IT BEATS AT ME-
ARE YOU BADLY
HURT?!

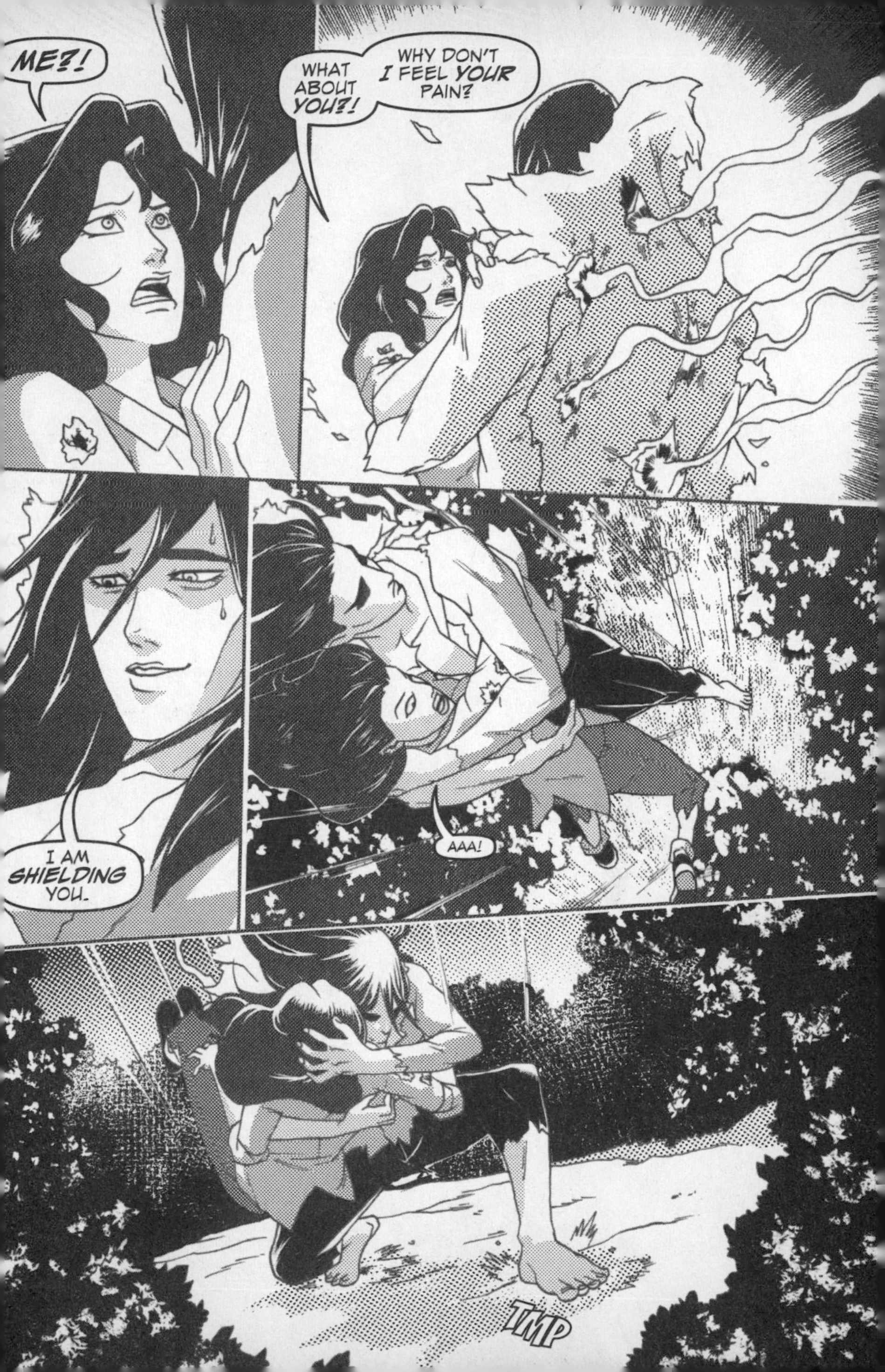
ME?!
WHAT ABOUT YOU?!
WHY DON'T I FEEL YOUR PAIN?
I AM SHIELDING YOU.
AAA!
TMP

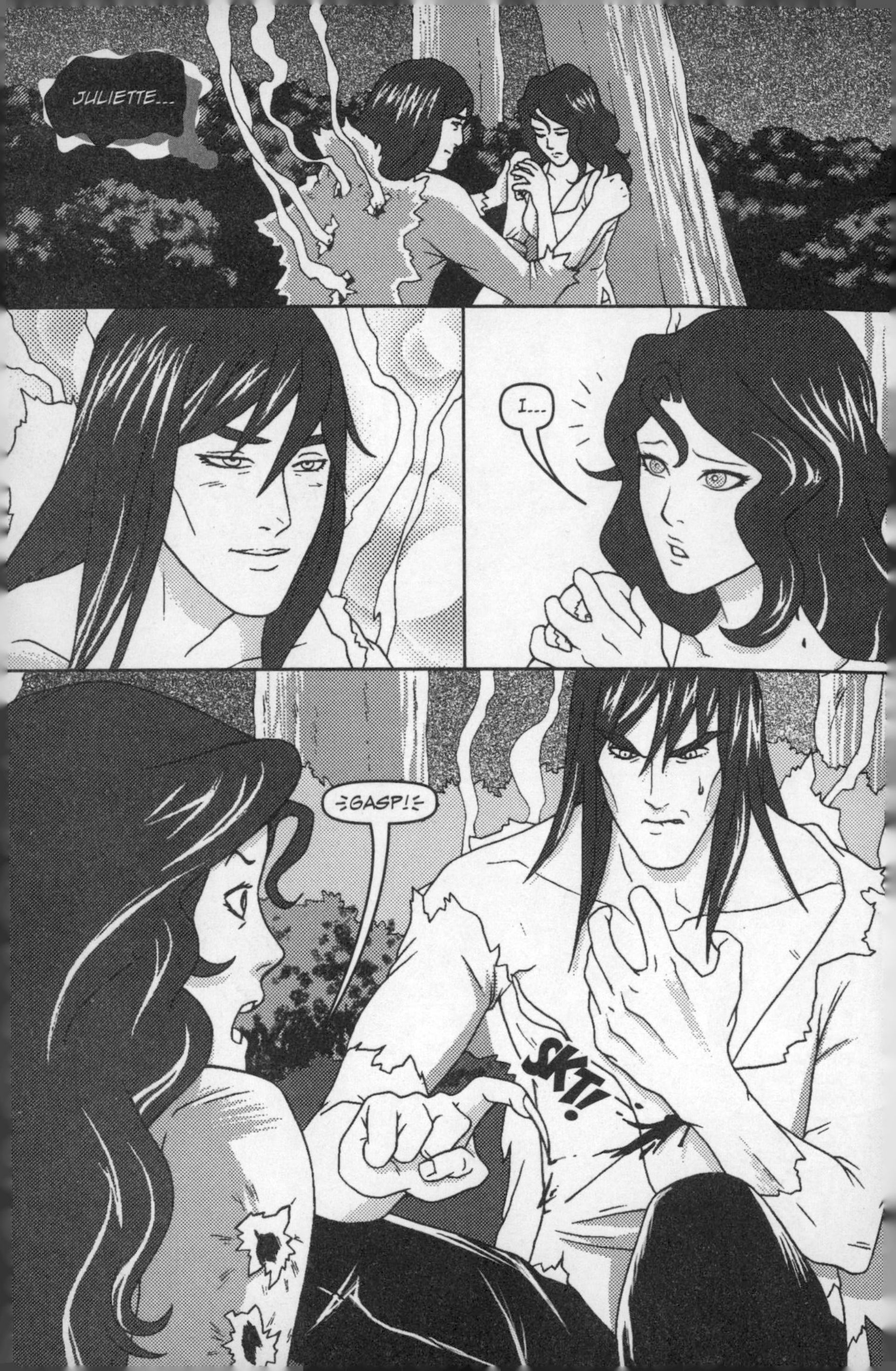
JULIETTE...
I...
GASP!
SKT!

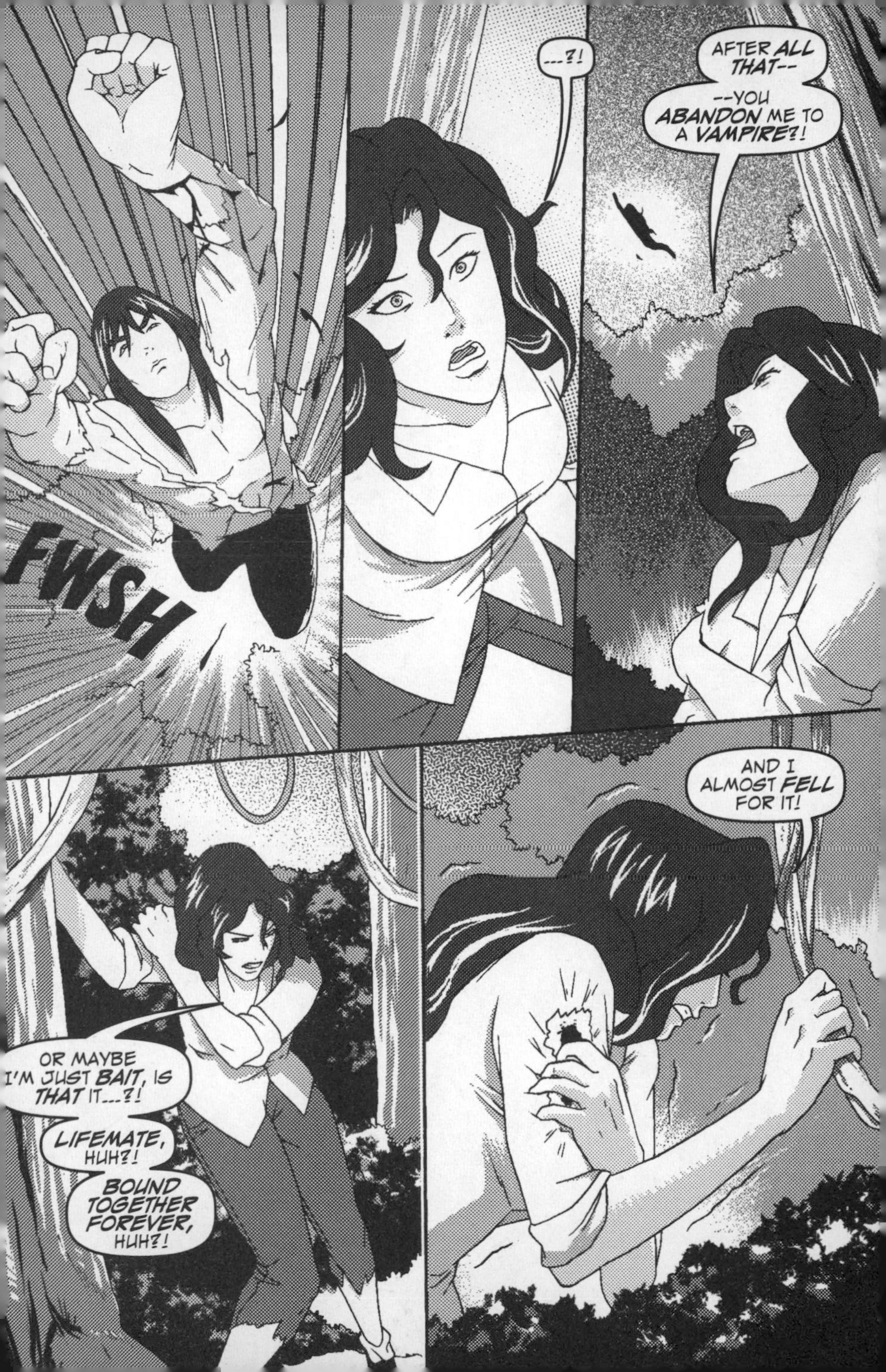
FWSH
---?!
AFTER ALL THAT--
--YOU ABANDON ME TO A VAMPIRE?!
OR MAYBE I'M JUST BAIT, IS THAT IT---?!
LIFEMATE, HUH?!
BOUND TOGETHER FOREVER, HUH?!
AND I ALMOST FELL FOR IT!

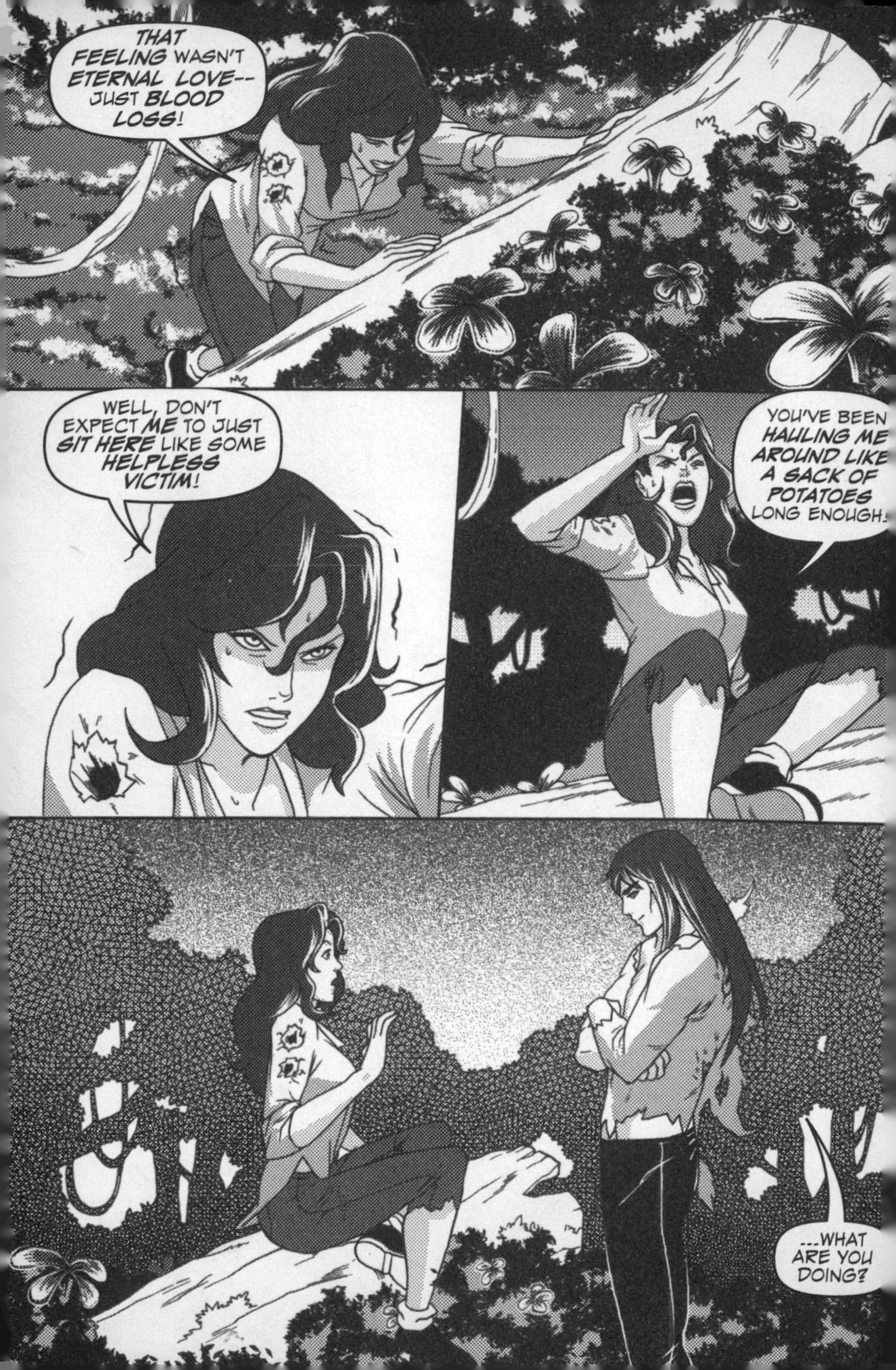
THAT FEELING WASN'T ETERNAL LOVE-- JUST BLOOD LOSS!
WELL, DON'T EXPECT ME TO JUST SIT HERE LIKE SOME HELPLESS VICTIM!
YOU'VE BEEN HAULING ME AROUND LIKE A SACK OF POTATOES LONG ENOUGH!
...WHAT ARE YOU DOING?

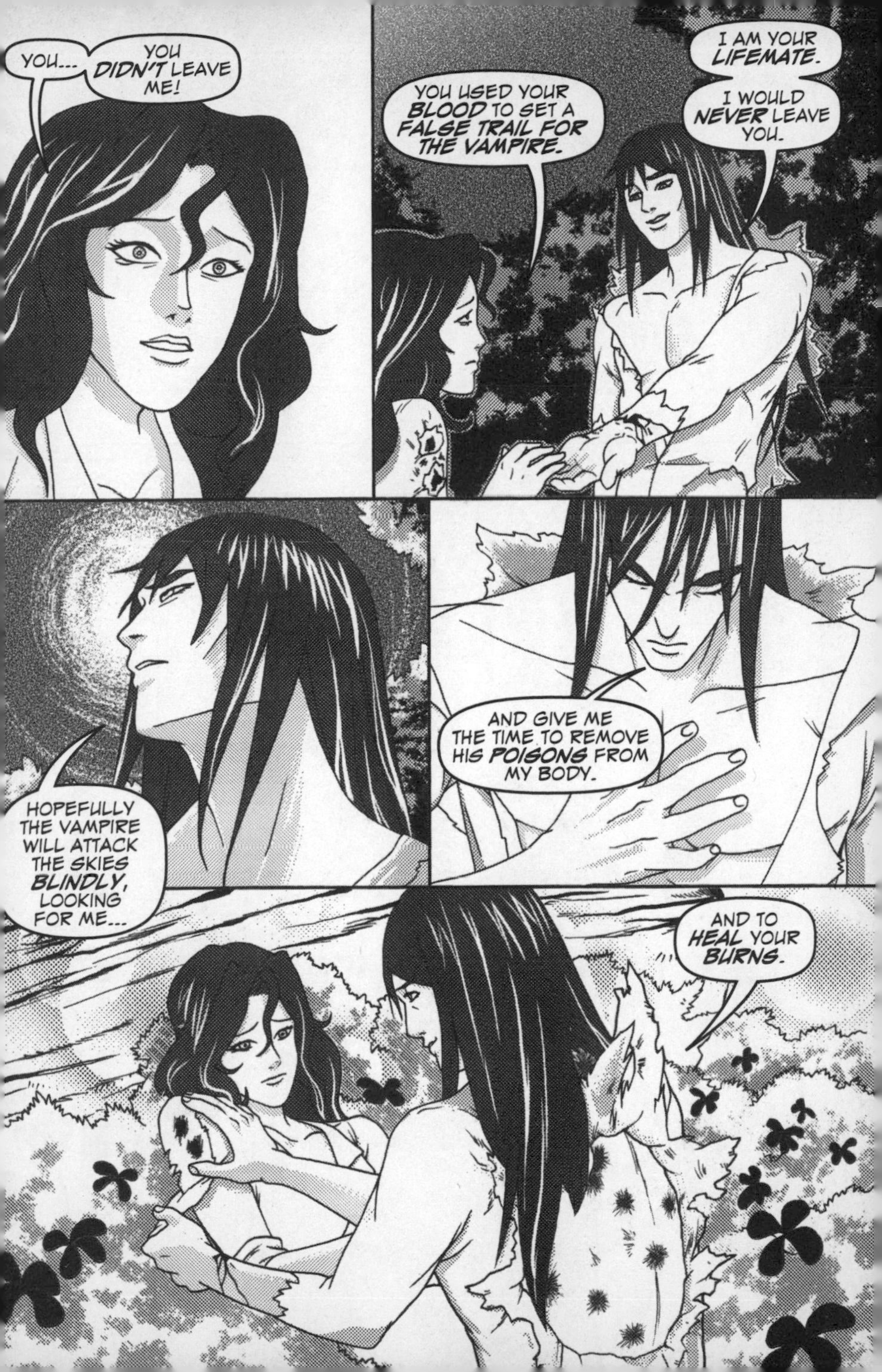
YOU...
YOU DIDN'T LEAVE ME!
YOU USED YOUR BLOOD TO SET A FALSE TRAIL FOR THE VAMPIRE.
I AM YOUR LIFEMATE.
I WOULD NEVER LEAVE YOU.
HOPEFULLY THE VAMPIRE WILL ATTACK THE SKIES BLINDLY, LOOKING FOR ME...
AND GIVE ME THE TIME TO REMOVE HIS POISONS FROM MY BODY.
AND TO HEAL YOUR BURNS.

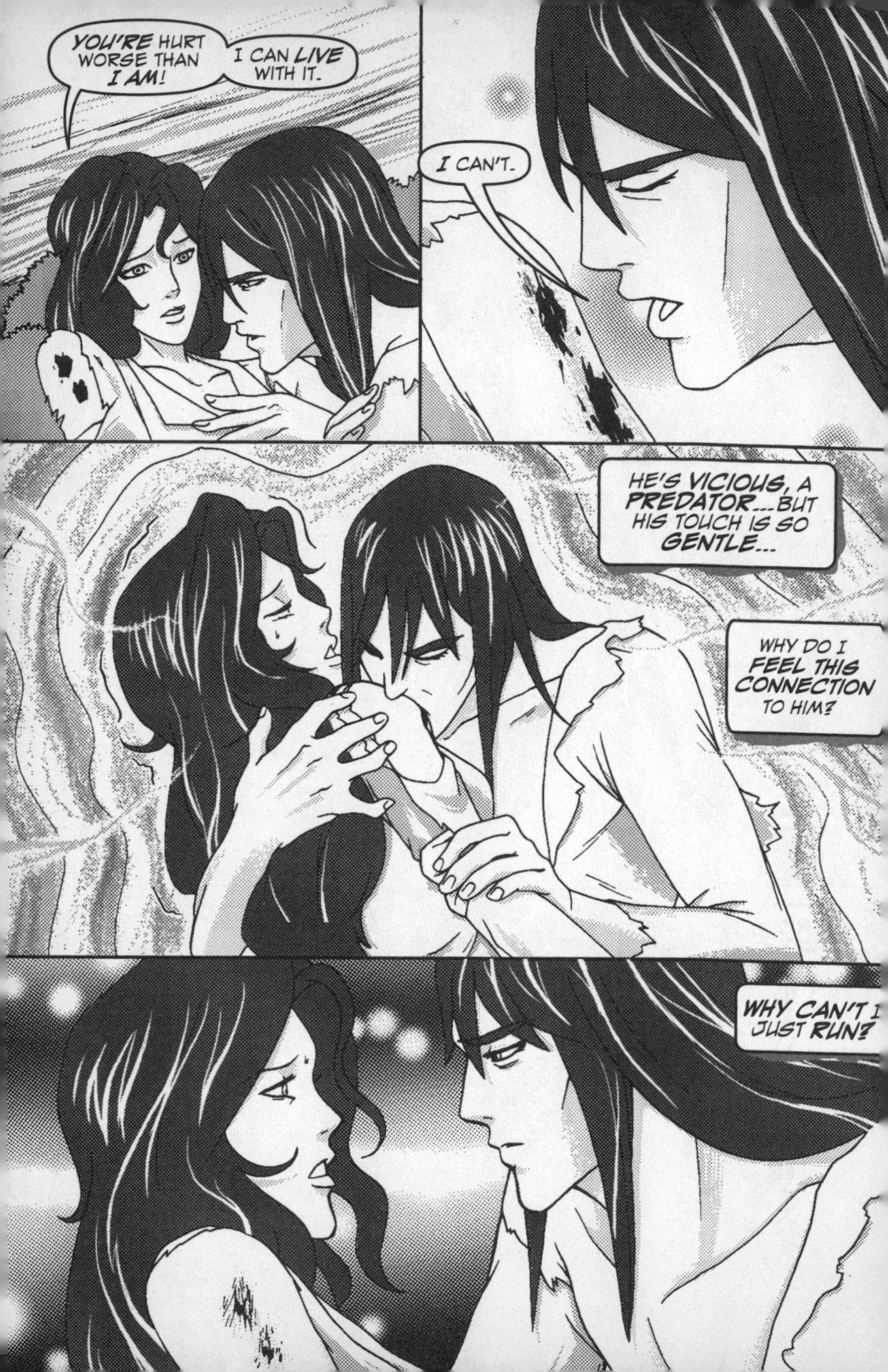
YOU'RE HURT WORSE THAN I AM!
I CAN LIVE WITH IT.
I CAN'T.
HE'S VICIOUS, A PREDATOR... BUT HIS TOUCH IS SO GENTLE...
WHY DO I FEEL THIS CONNECTION TO HIM?
WHY CAN'T I JUST RUN?

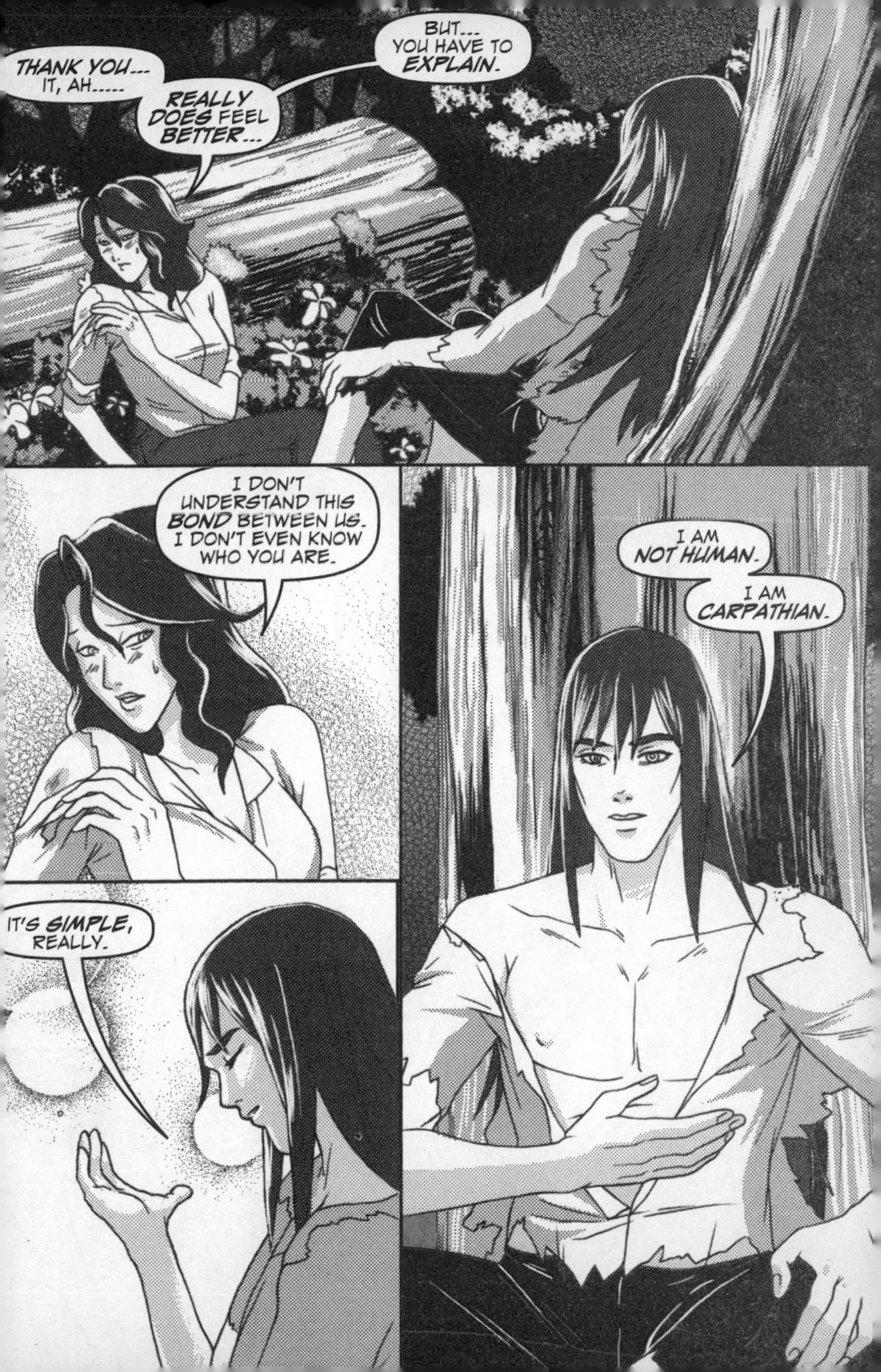
THANK YOU... IT, AH.....
REALLY DOES FEEL BETTER...
BUT... YOU HAVE TO EXPLAIN.
I DON'T UNDERSTAND THIS BOND BETWEEN US. I DON'T EVEN KNOW WHO YOU ARE.
I AM NOT HUMAN.
I AM CARPATHIAN.
IT'S SIMPLE, REALLY.

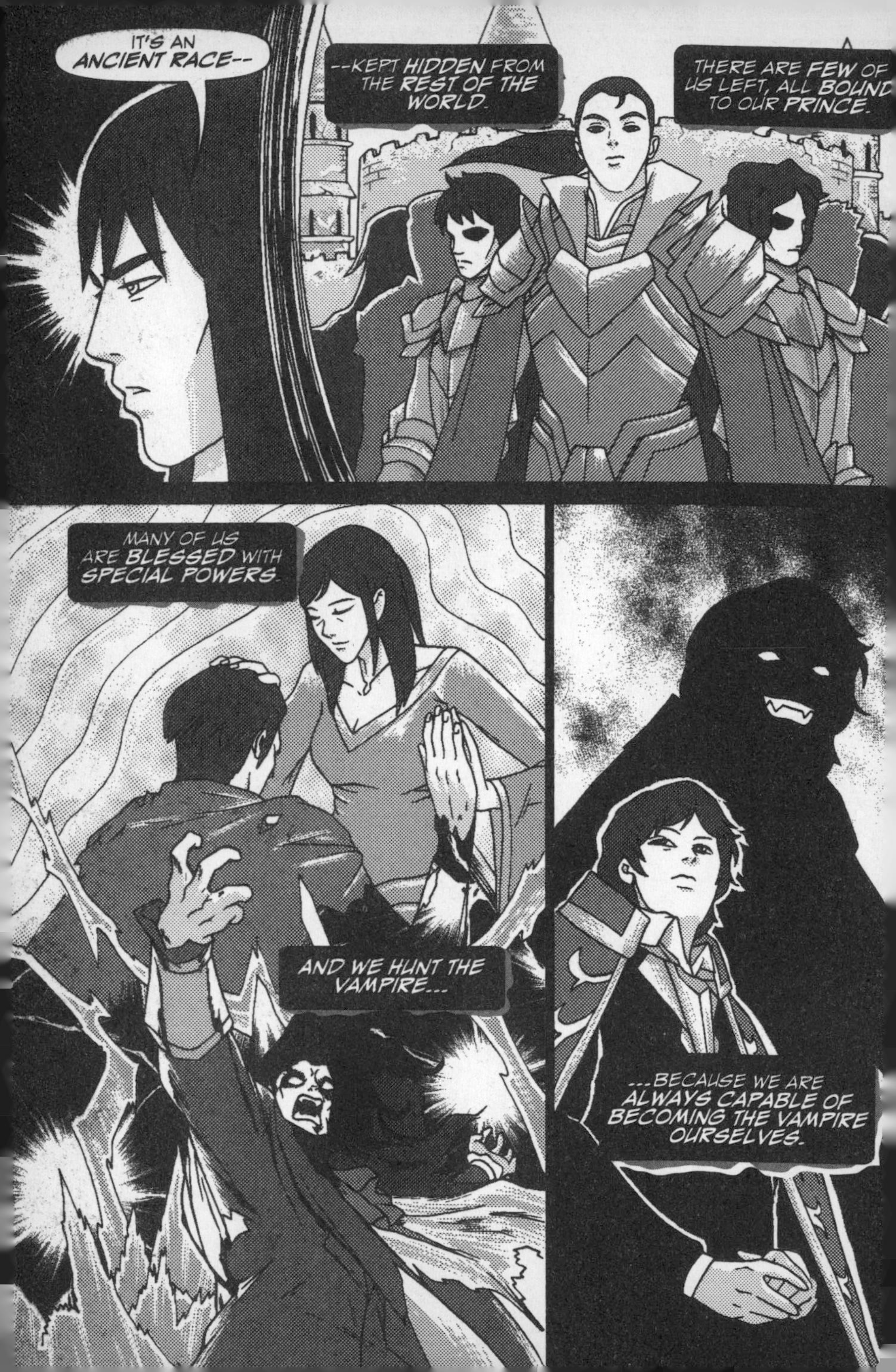
IT'S AN ANCIENT RACE--
--KEPT HIDDEN FROM THE REST OF THE WORLD.
THERE ARE FEW OF US LEFT, ALL BOUND TO OUR PRINCE.
MANY OF US ARE BLESSED WITH SPECIAL POWERS.
AND WE HUNT THE VAMPIRE...
...BECAUSE WE ARE ALWAYS CAPABLE OF BECOMING THE VAMPIRE OURSELVES.

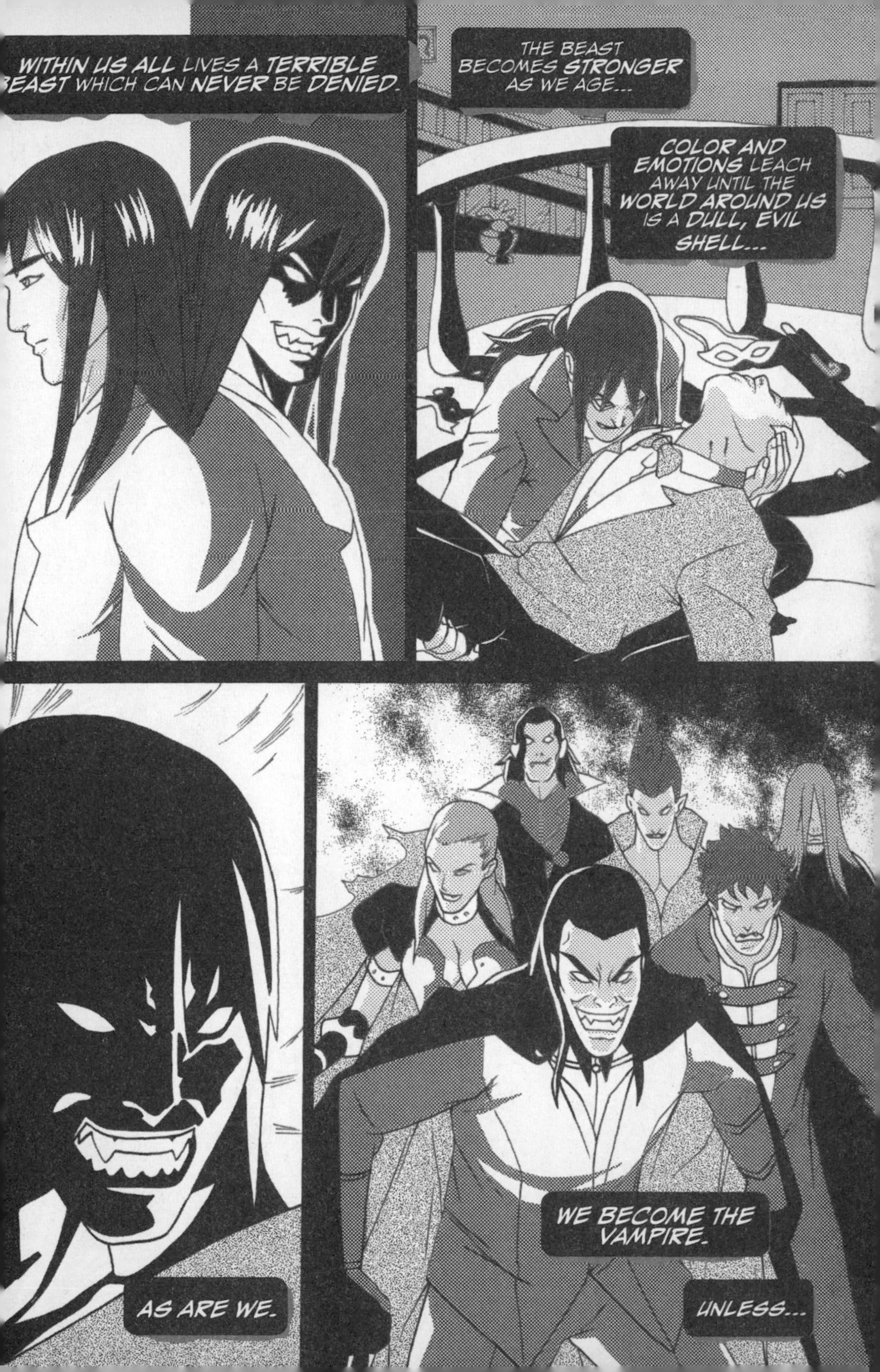
WITHIN US ALL LIVES A TERRIBLE BEAST WHICH CAN NEVER BE DENIED.
THE BEAST BECOMES STRONGER AS WE AGE...
COLOR AND EMOTIONS LEACH AWAY UNTIL THE WORLD AROUND US IS A DULL, EVIL SHELL...
AS ARE WE.
WE BECOME THE VAMPIRE.
UNLESS...

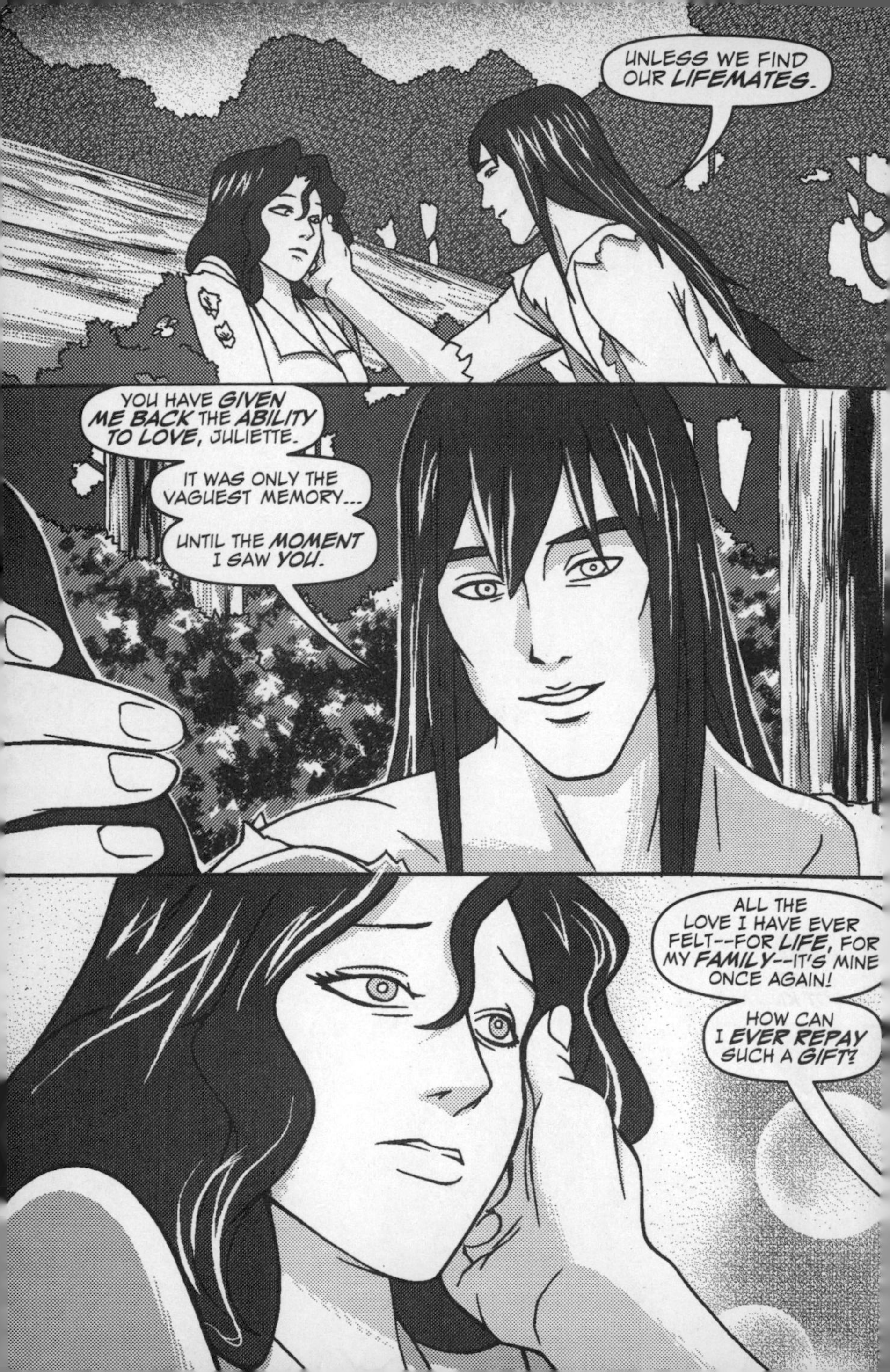
UNLESS WE FIND OUR LIFEMATES.
YOU HAVE GIVEN ME BACK THE ABILITY TO LOVE, JULIETTE.
IT WAS ONLY THE VAGUEST MEMORY...
UNTIL THE MOMENT I SAW YOU.
ALL THE LOVE I HAVE EVER FELT--FOR LIFE, FOR MY FAMILY--IT'S MINE ONCE AGAIN!
HOW CAN I EVER REPAY SUCH A GIFT?

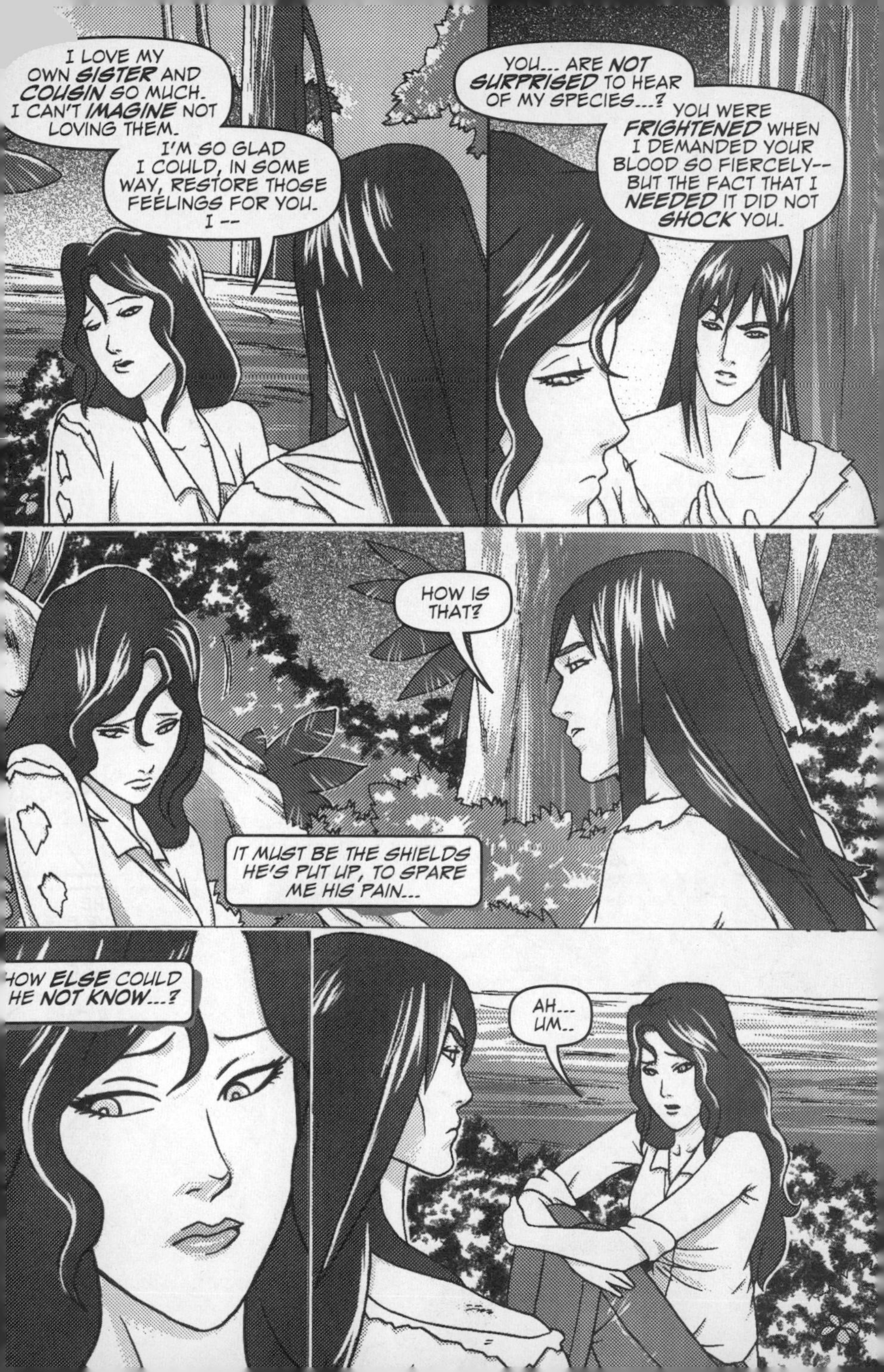
I LOVE MY OWN SISTER AND COUSIN SO MUCH. I CAN'T IMAGINE NOT LOVING THEM.
I'M SO GLAD I COULD, IN SOME WAY, RESTORE THOSE FEELINGS FOR YOU. I --
YOU... ARE NOT SURPRISED TO HEAR OF MY SPECIES...?
YOU WERE FRIGHTENED WHEN I DEMANDED YOUR BLOOD SO FIERCELY-- BUT THE FACT THAT I NEEDED IT DID NOT SHOCK YOU.
HOW IS THAT?
IT MUST BE THE SHIELDS HE'S PUT UP, TO SPARE ME HIS PAIN...
HOW ELSE COULD HE NOT KNOW...?
AH... UM..

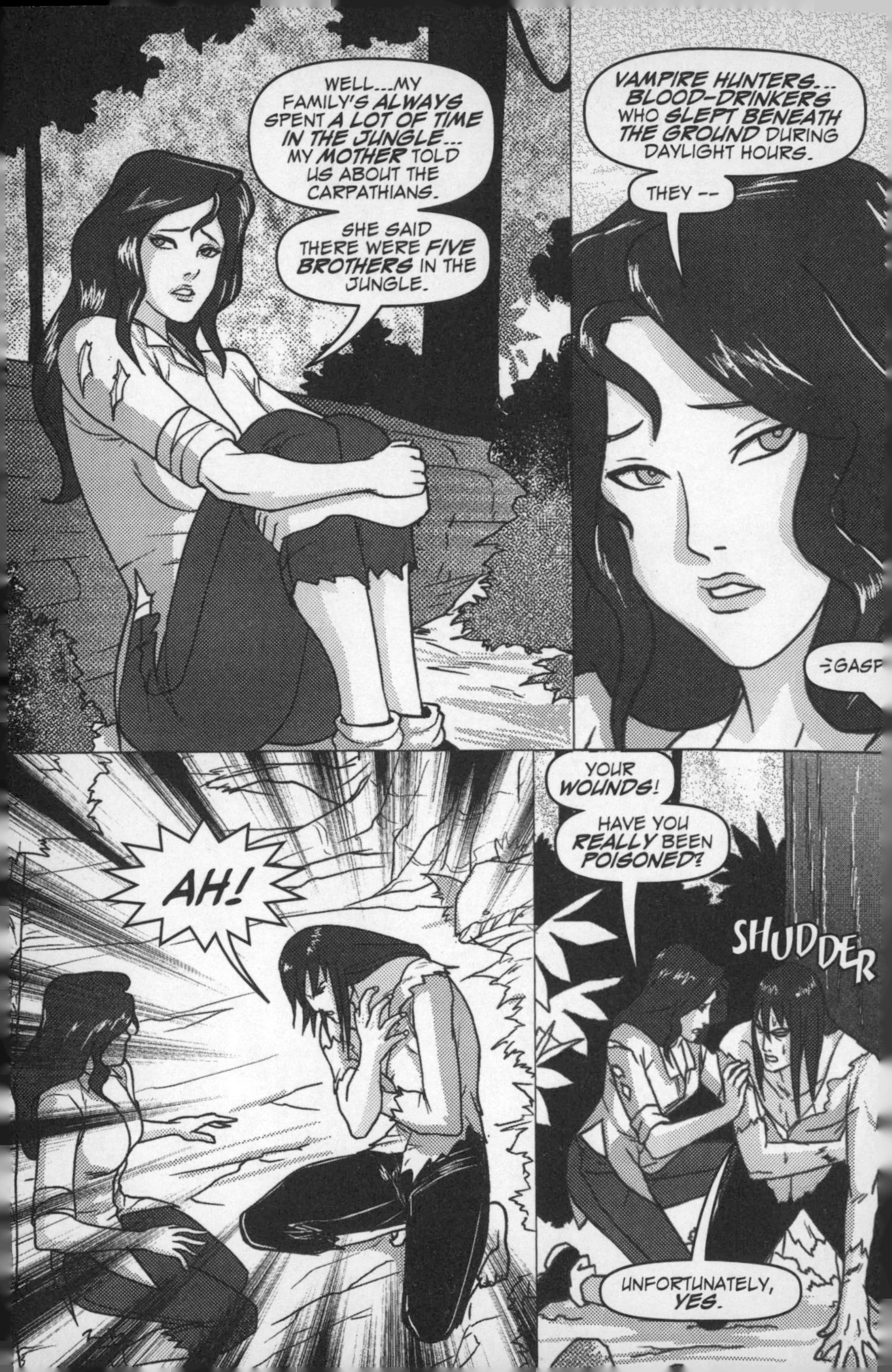
WELL...MY FAMILY'S ALWAYS SPENT A LOT OF TIME IN THE JUNGLE... MY MOTHER TOLD US ABOUT THE CARPATHIANS.
SHE SAID THERE WERE FIVE BROTHERS IN THE JUNGLE.
VAMPIRE HUNTERS... BLOOD-DRINKERS WHO SLEPT BENEATH THE GROUND DURING DAYLIGHT HOURS.
THEY --
GASP
AH!
YOUR WOUNDS!
HAVE YOU REALLY BEEN POISONED?
SHUDDER
UNFORTUNATELY, YES.

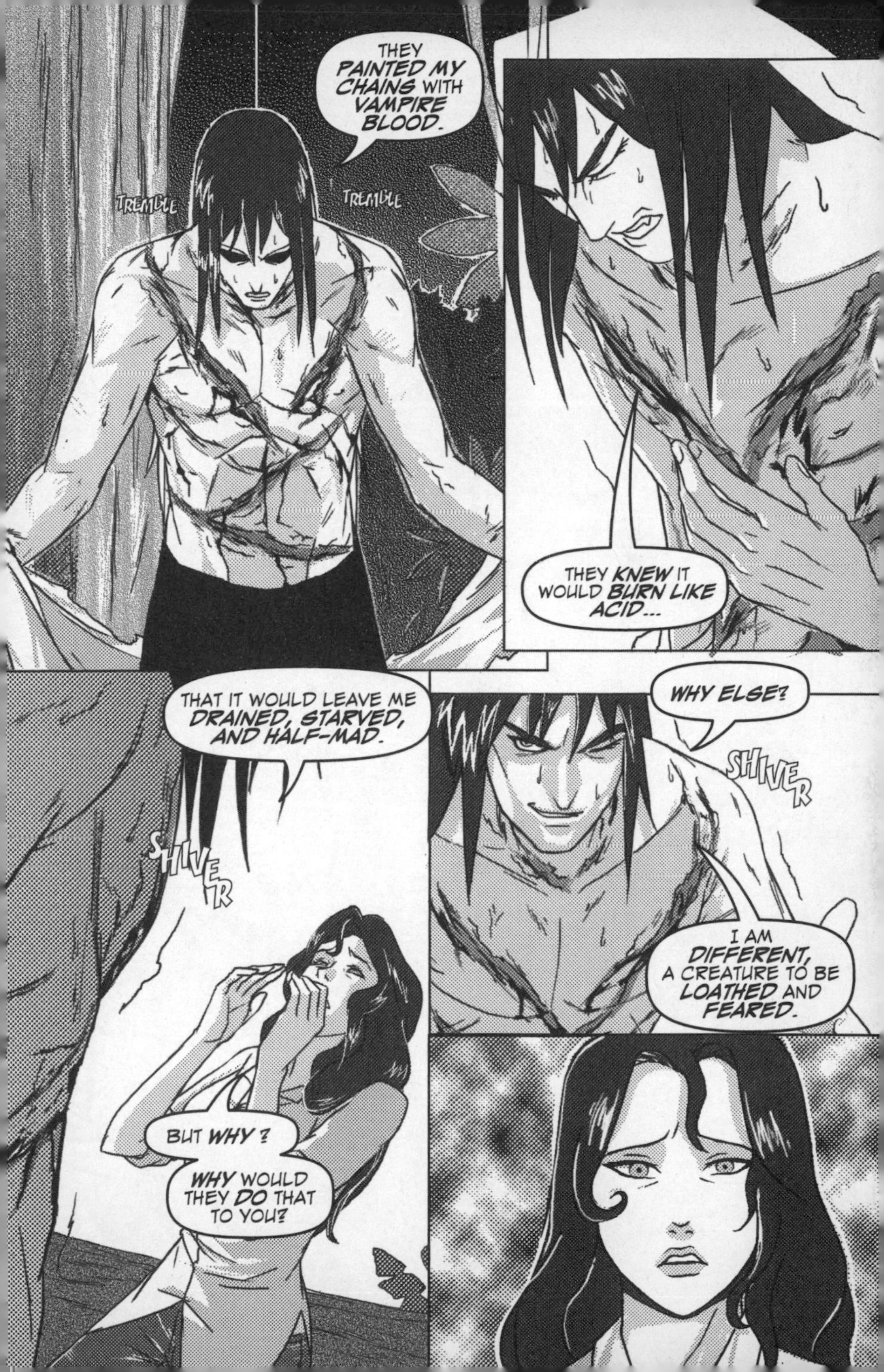
THEY PAINTED MY CHAINS WITH VAMPIRE BLOOD.
TREMBLE
TREMBLE
THEY KNEW IT WOULD BURN LIKE ACID...
THAT IT WOULD LEAVE ME DRAINED, STARVED, AND HALF-MAD.
SHIVER
BUT WHY?
WHY WOULD THEY DO THAT TO YOU?
WHY ELSE?
SHIVER
I AM DIFFERENT, A CREATURE TO BE LOATHED AND FEARED.

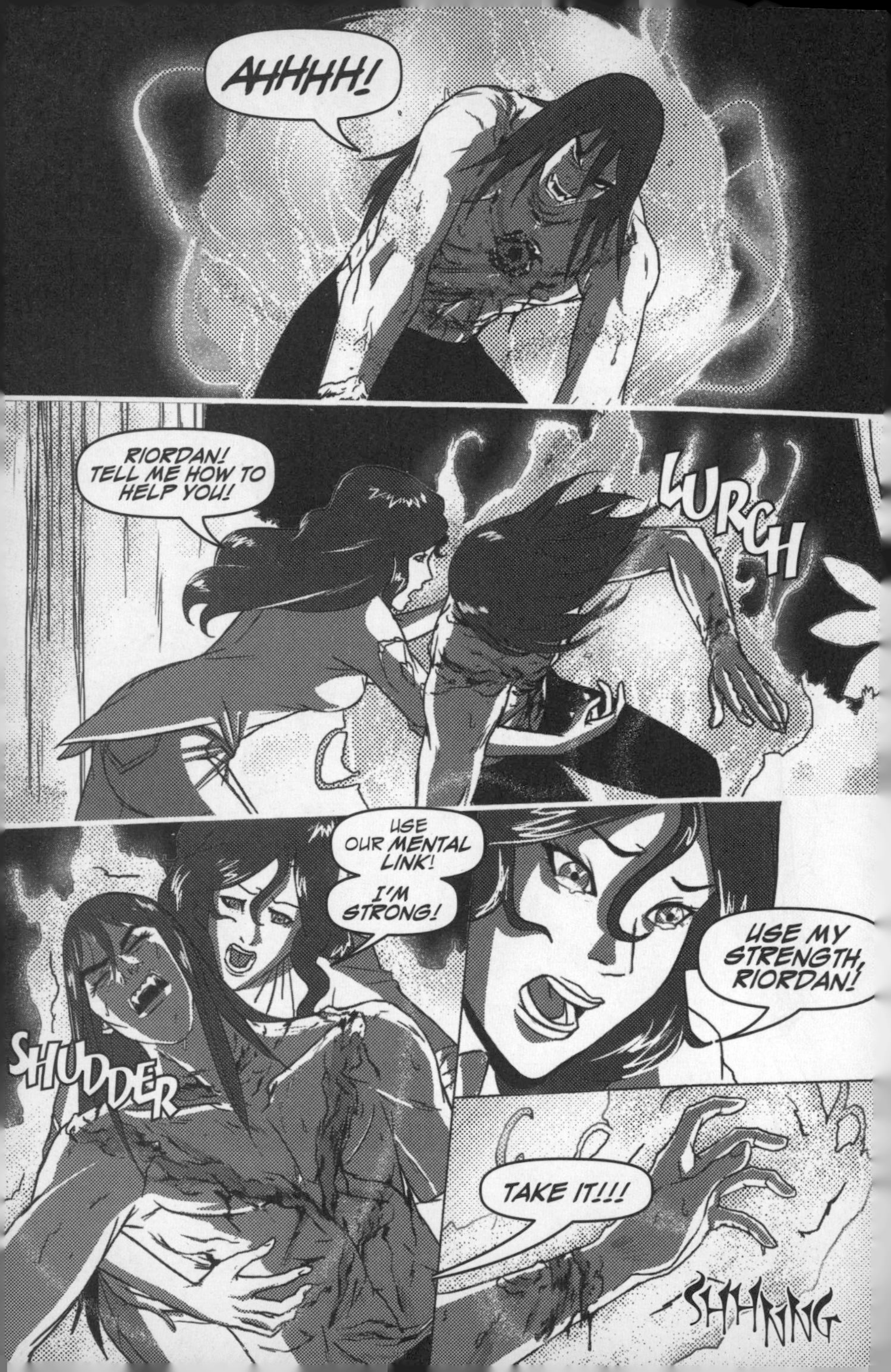
AHHHH!
RIORDAN! TELL ME HOW TO HELP YOU!
LURCH
USE OUR MENTAL LINK!
I'M STRONG!
SHUDDER
USE MY STRENGTH, RIORDAN!
TAKE IT!!!
SHHRING

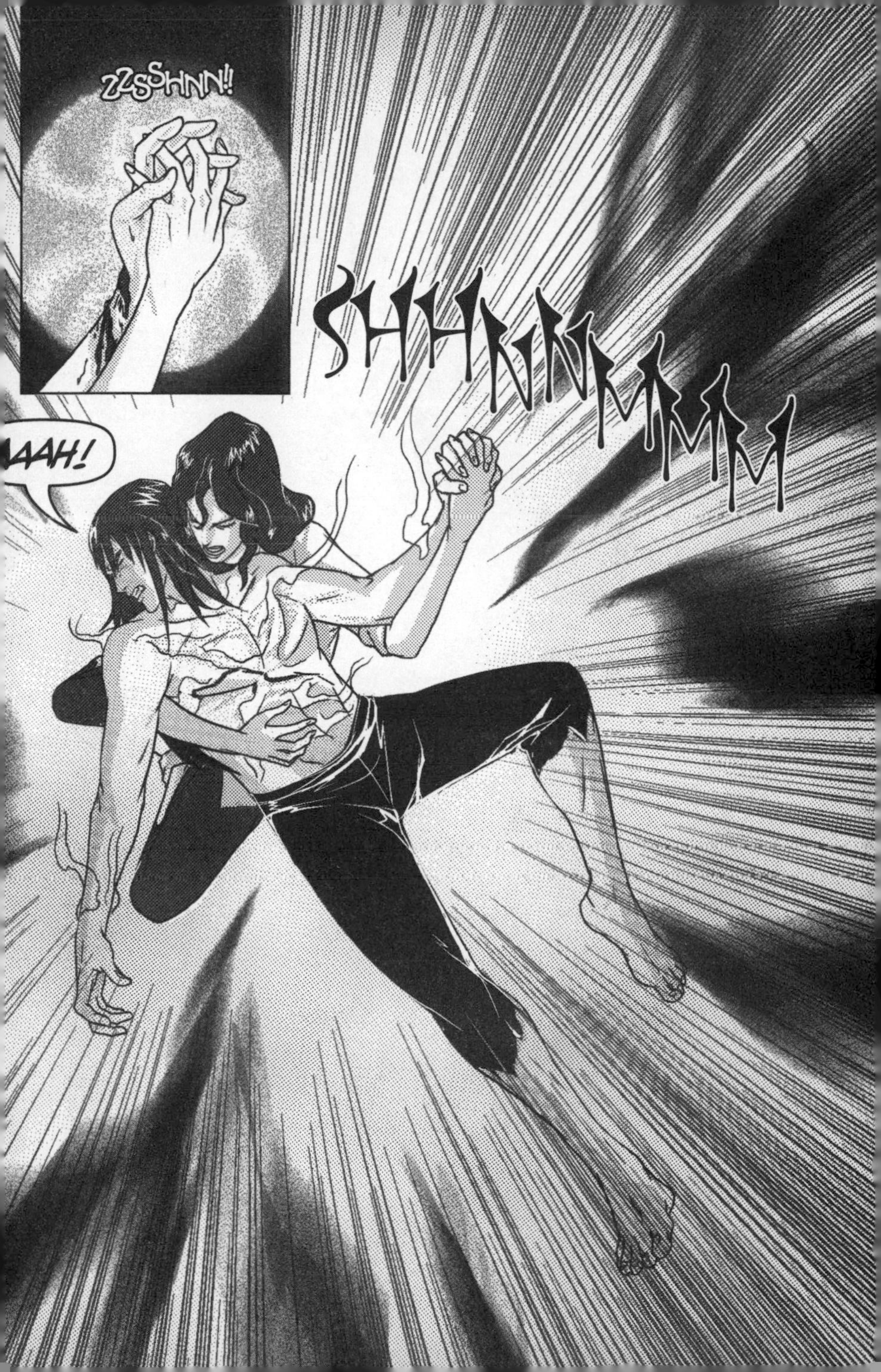
ZZSSHNN!!
AAAH!
SHHRNNMMMM

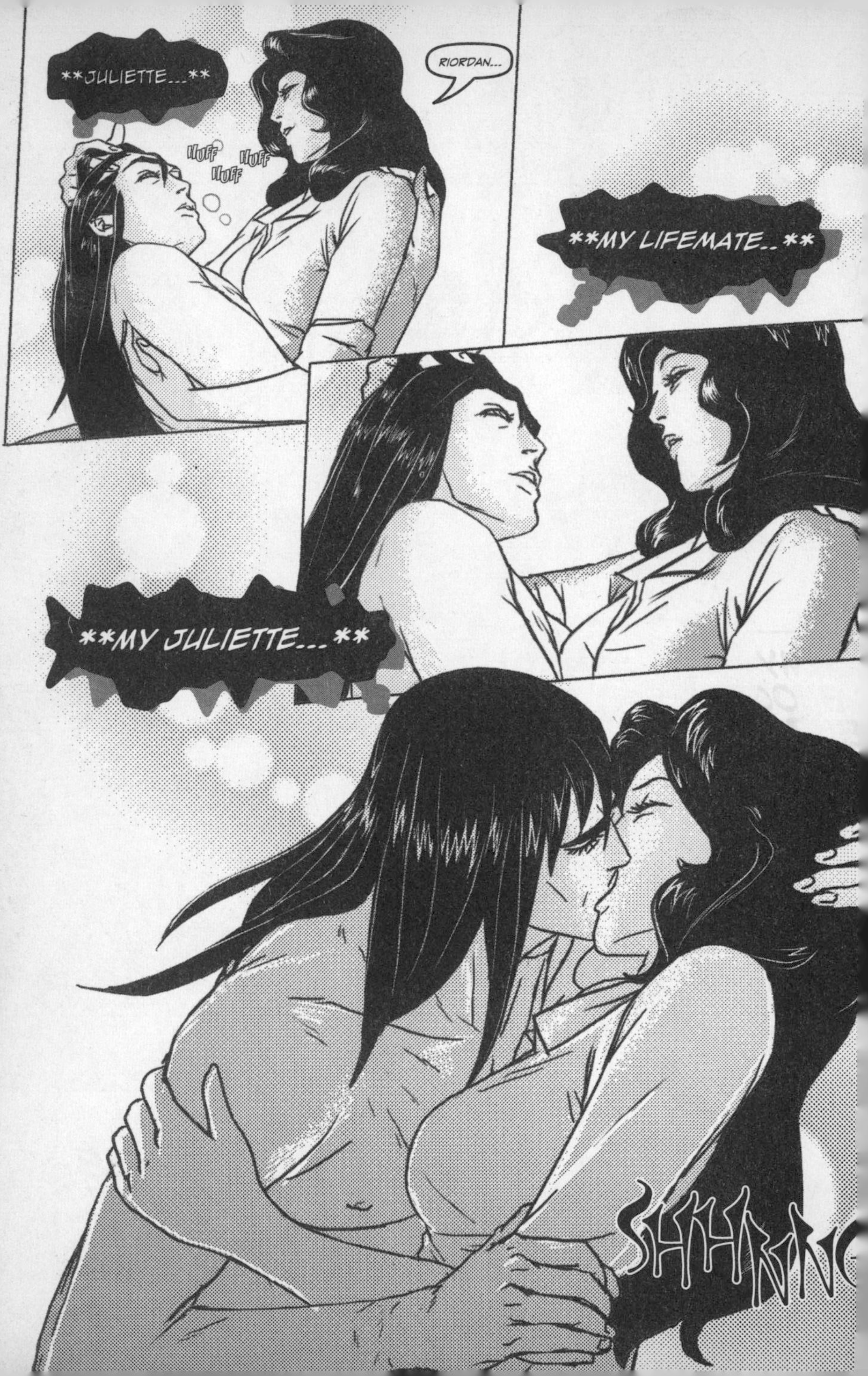
JULIETTE...
HUFF
HUFF
HUFF
RIORDAN...
MY LIFEMATE...
MY JULIETTE...
SHHHING

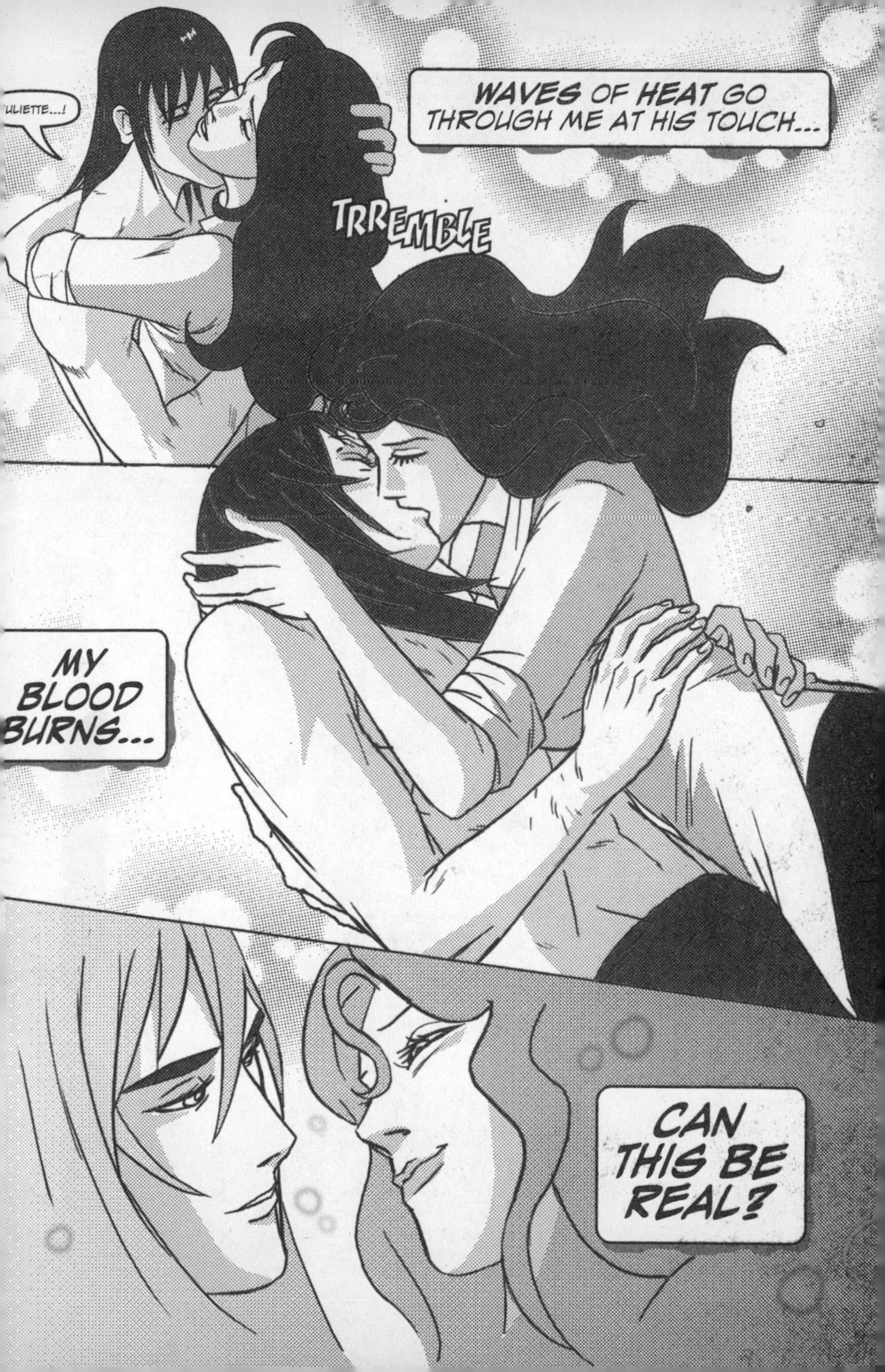
ULIETTE...!
WAVES OF HEAT GO THROUGH ME AT HIS TOUCH...
TRREMBLE
MY BLOOD BURNS...
CAN THIS BE REAL?

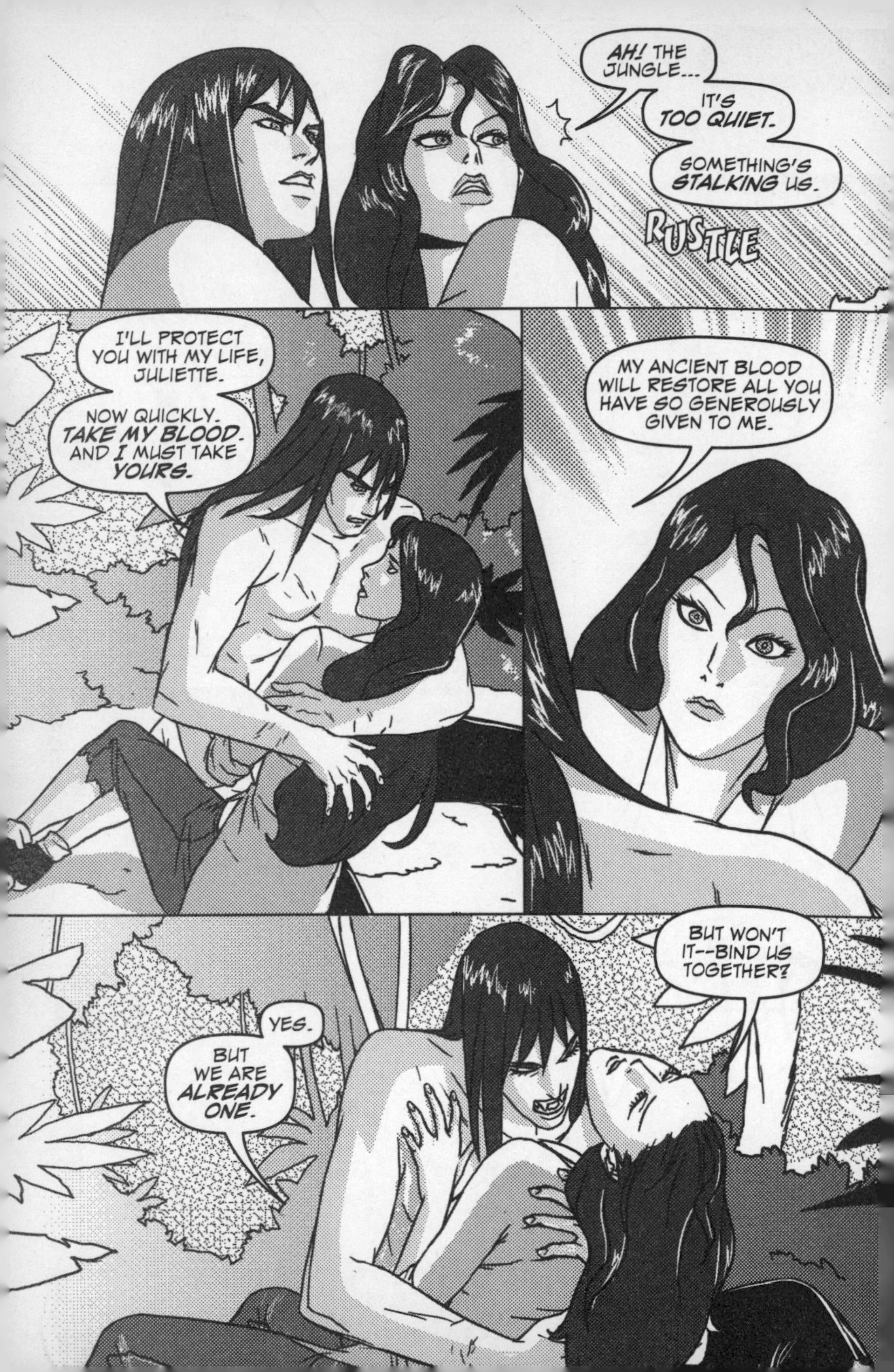
AH! THE JUNGLE...
IT'S TOO QUIET.
SOMETHING'S STALKING US.
RUSTLE
I'LL PROTECT YOU WITH MY LIFE, JULIETTE.
NOW QUICKLY. TAKE MY BLOOD. AND I MUST TAKE YOURS.
MY ANCIENT BLOOD WILL RESTORE ALL YOU HAVE SO GENEROUSLY GIVEN TO ME.
BUT WON'T IT--BIND US TOGETHER?
YES.
BUT WE ARE ALREADY ONE.

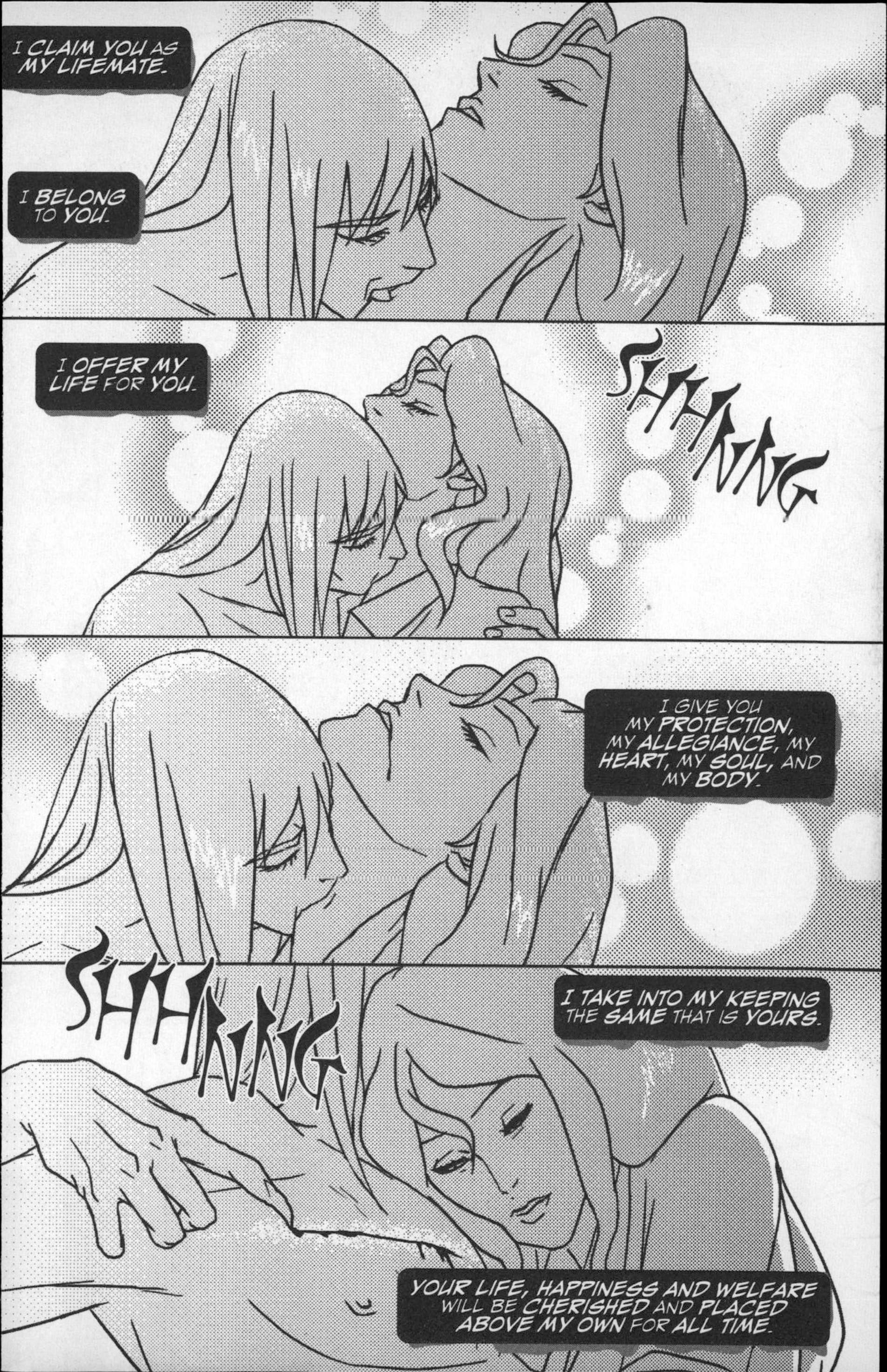
I CLAIM YOU AS MY LIFEMATE.
I BELONG TO YOU.
I OFFER MY LIFE FOR YOU.
SHHRRG
I GIVE YOU MY PROTECTION, MY ALLEGIANCE, MY HEART, MY SOUL, AND MY BODY.
SHHRRG
I TAKE INTO MY KEEPING THE SAME THAT IS YOURS.
YOUR LIFE, HAPPINESS AND WELFARE WILL BE CHERISHED AND PLACED ABOVE MY OWN FOR ALL TIME.

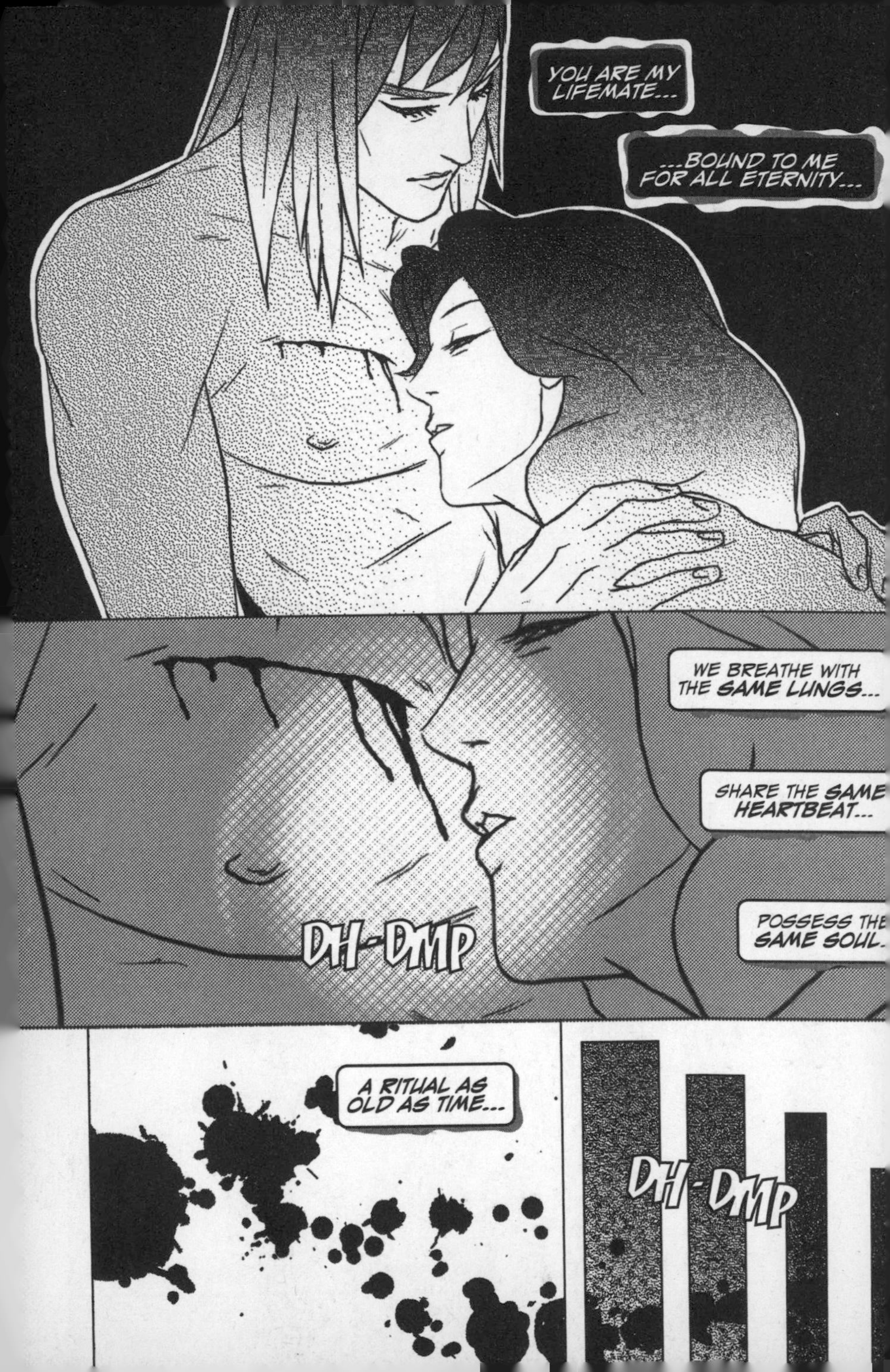
YOU ARE MY LIFEMATE...
...BOUND TO ME FOR ALL ETERNITY...
WE BREATHE WITH THE SAME LUNGS...
SHARE THE SAME HEARTBEAT...
POSSESS THE SAME SOUL...
DH-DMP
A RITUAL AS OLD AS TIME...
DH-DMP

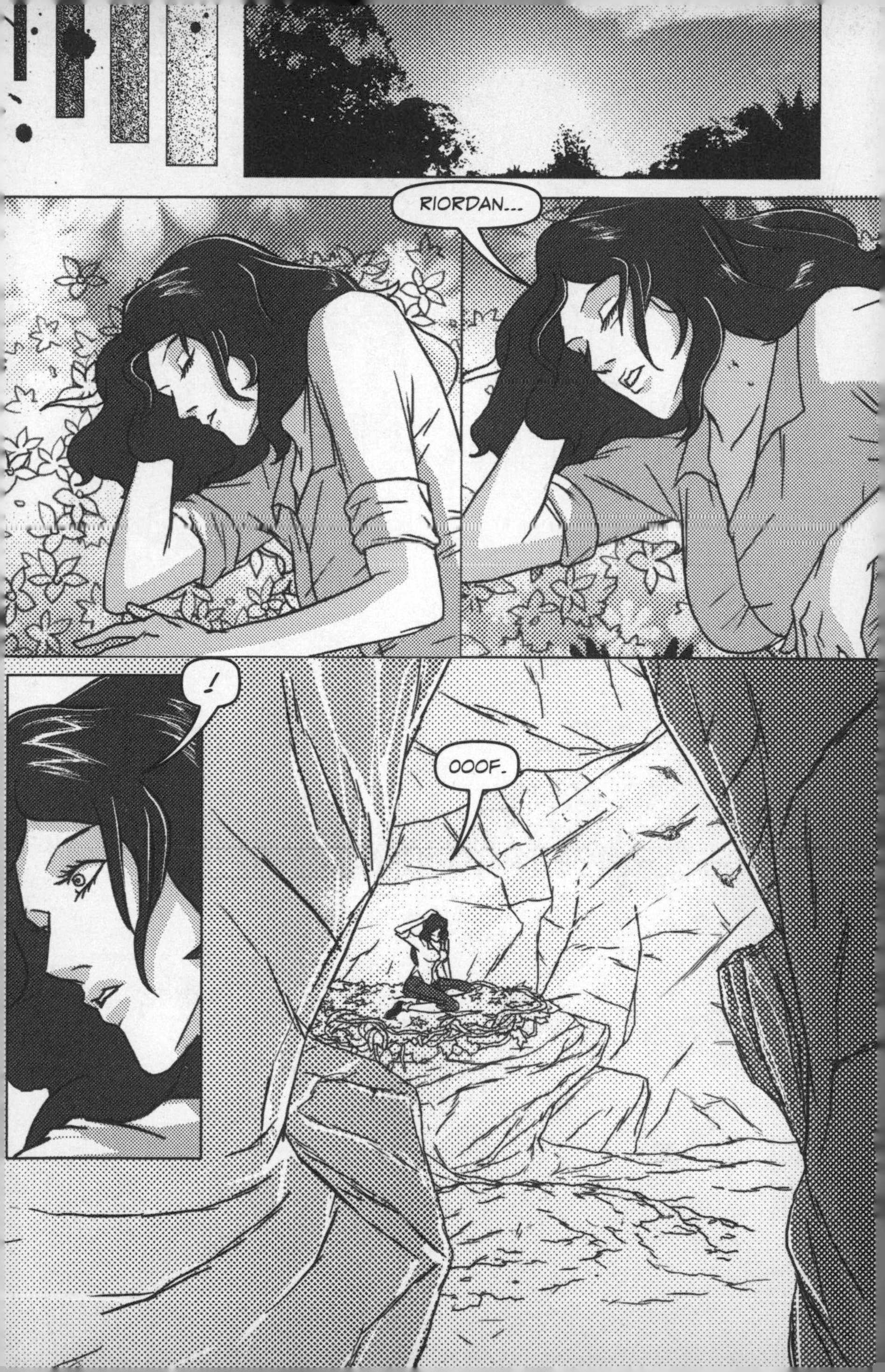
RIORDAN...
!
OOOF.

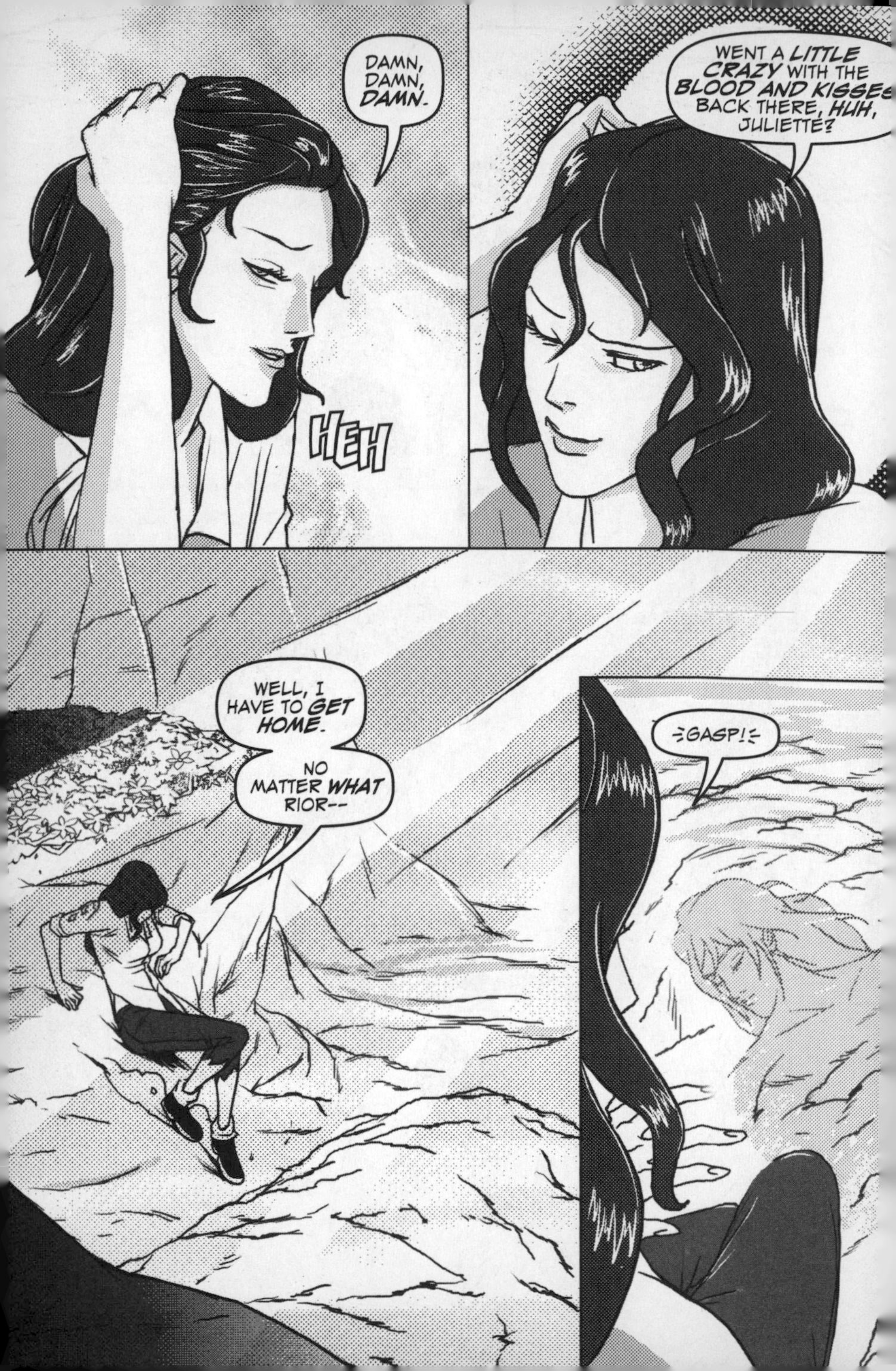
DAMN, DAMN, DAMN.
HEH
WENT A LITTLE CRAZY WITH THE BLOOD AND KISSES BACK THERE, HUH, JULIETTE?
WELL, I HAVE TO GET HOME.
NO MATTER WHAT RIOR--
GASP!

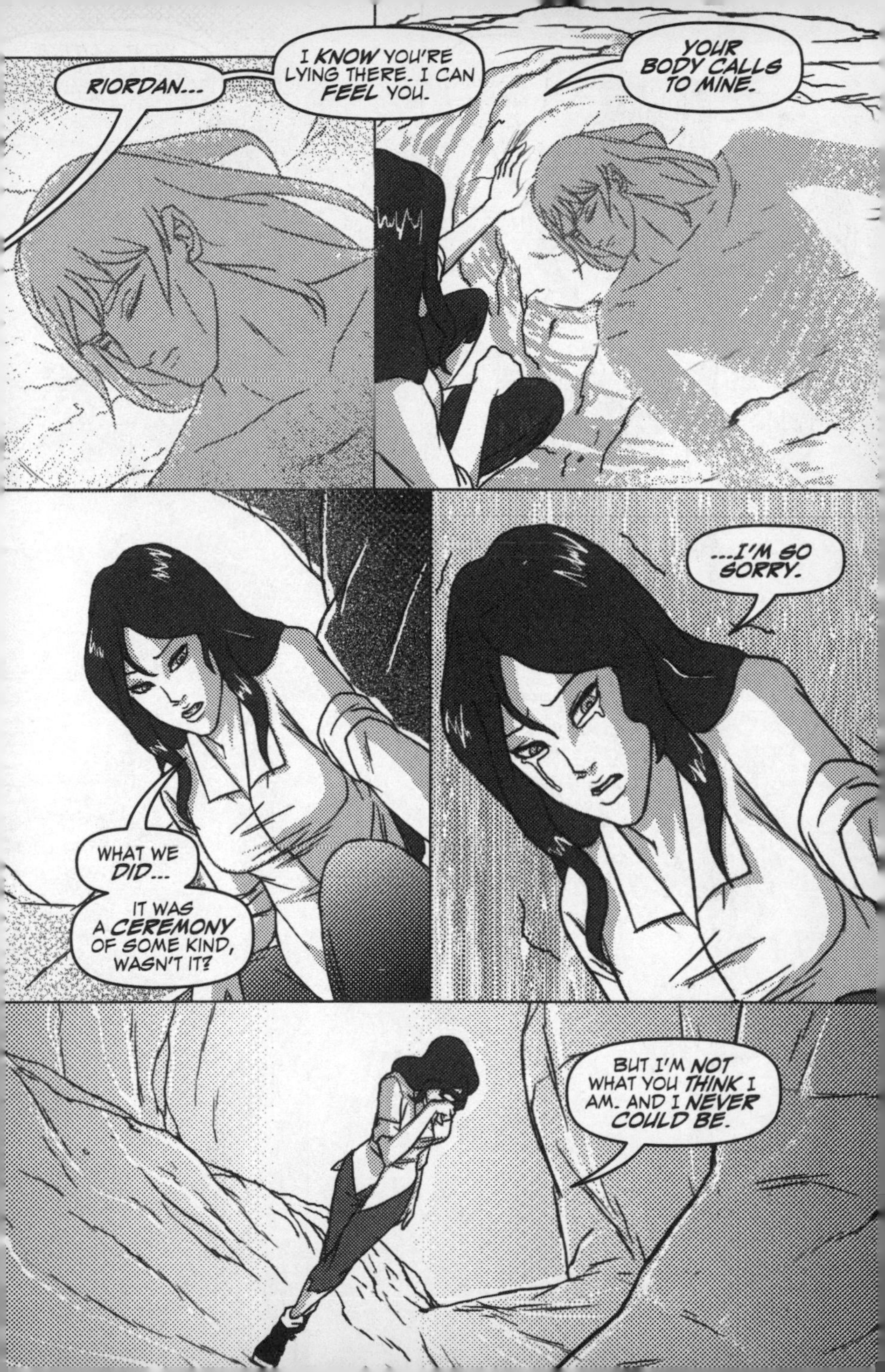
RIORDAN...
I KNOW YOU'RE LYING THERE. I CAN FEEL YOU.
YOUR BODY CALLS TO MINE.
WHAT WE DID...
IT WAS A CEREMONY OF SOME KIND, WASN'T IT?
...I'M SO SORRY.
BUT I'M NOT WHAT YOU THINK I AM. AND I NEVER COULD BE.

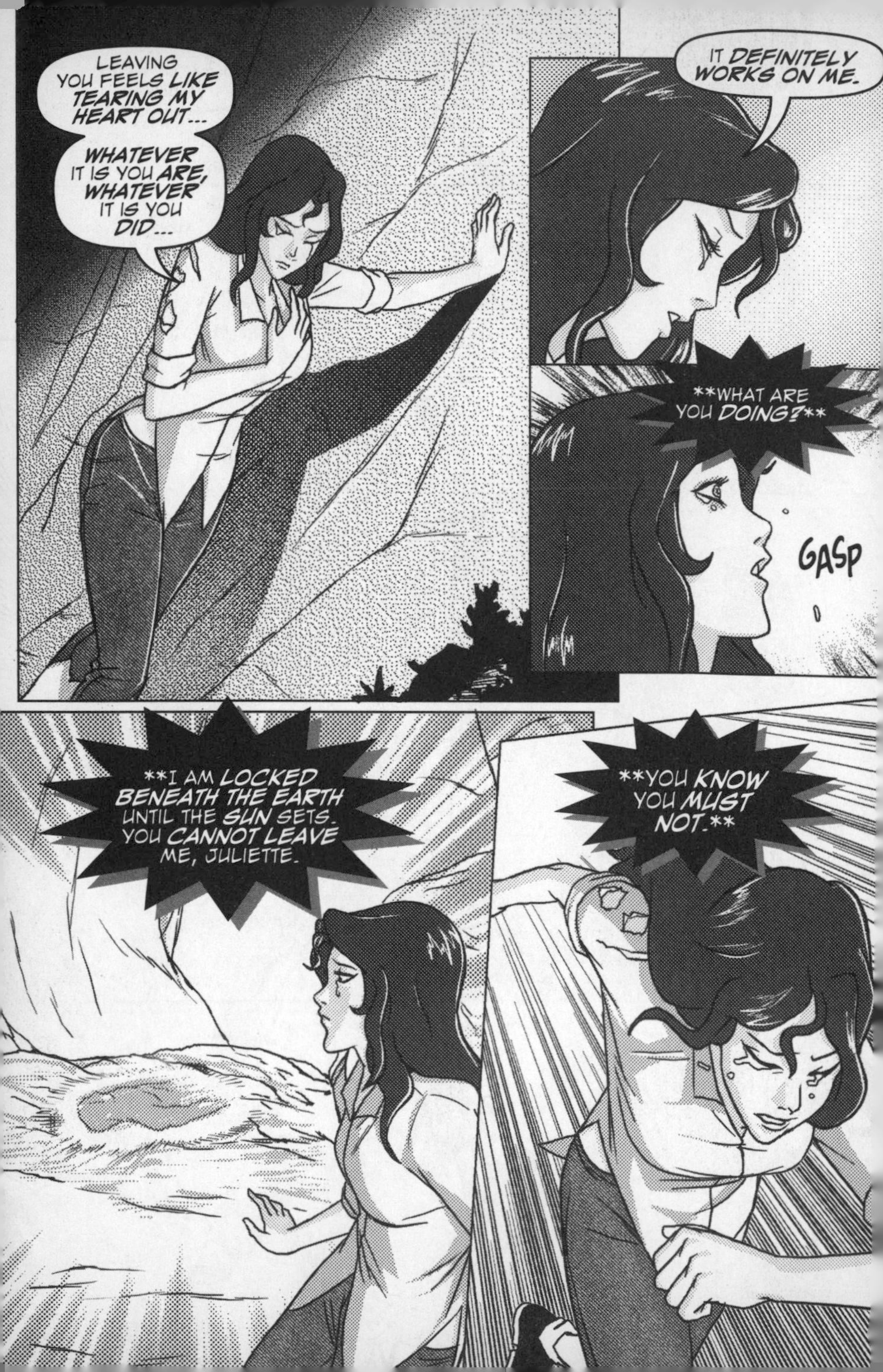
LEAVING YOU FEELS LIKE TEARING MY HEART OUT...
WHATEVER IT IS YOU ARE, WHATEVER IT IS YOU DID...
IT DEFINITELY WORKS ON ME.
WHAT ARE YOU DOING?
GASP
**I AM LOCKED BENEATH THE EARTH UNTIL THE SUN SETS. YOU CANNOT LEAVE ME, JULIETTE.
YOU KNOW YOU MUST NOT.

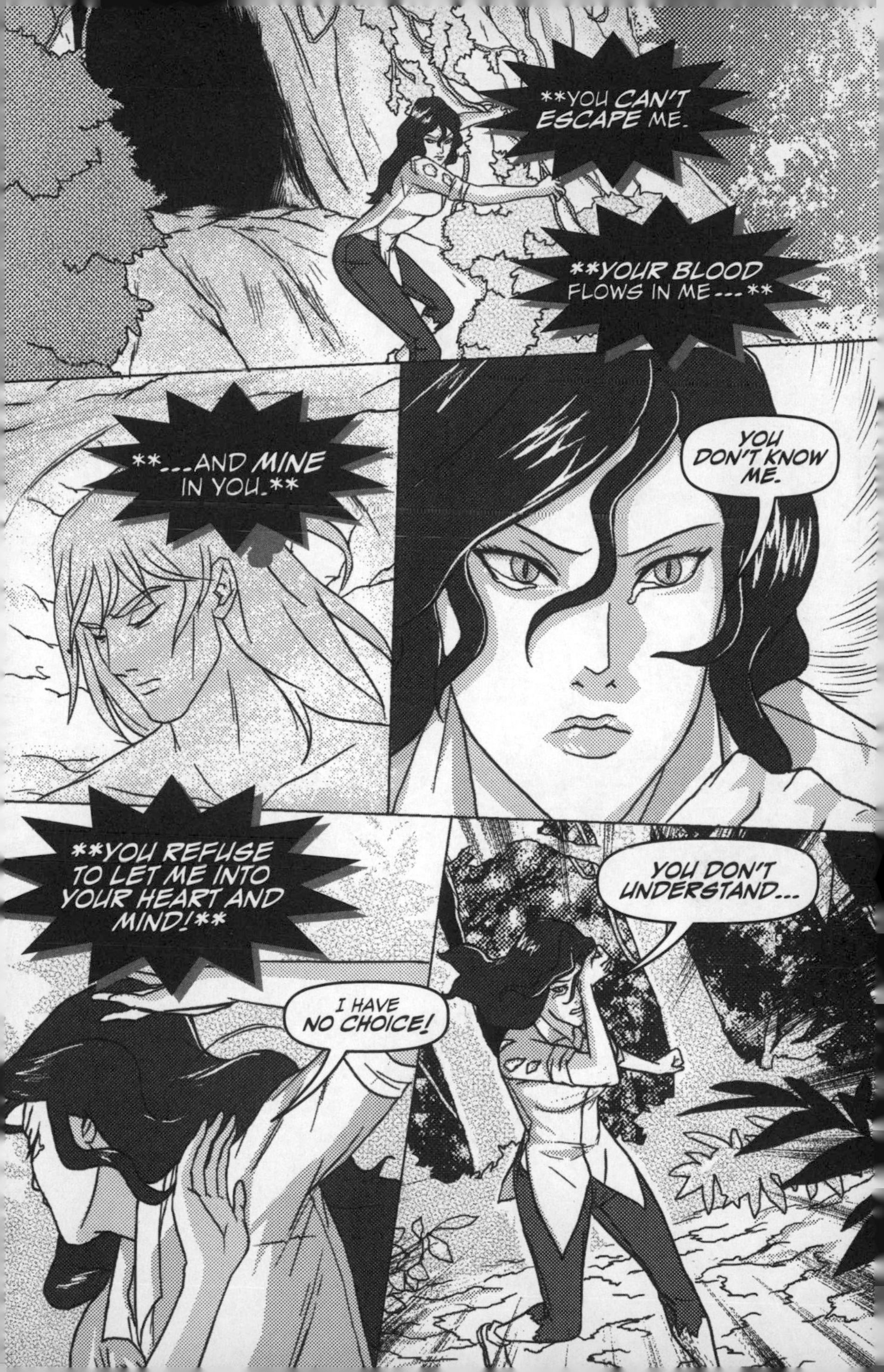
**YOU CAN'T ESCAPE ME.
YOUR BLOOD FLOWS IN ME---
---AND MINE IN YOU.
YOU DON'T KNOW ME.
YOU REFUSE TO LET ME INTO YOUR HEART AND MIND!
I HAVE NO CHOICE!
YOU DON'T UNDERSTAND...

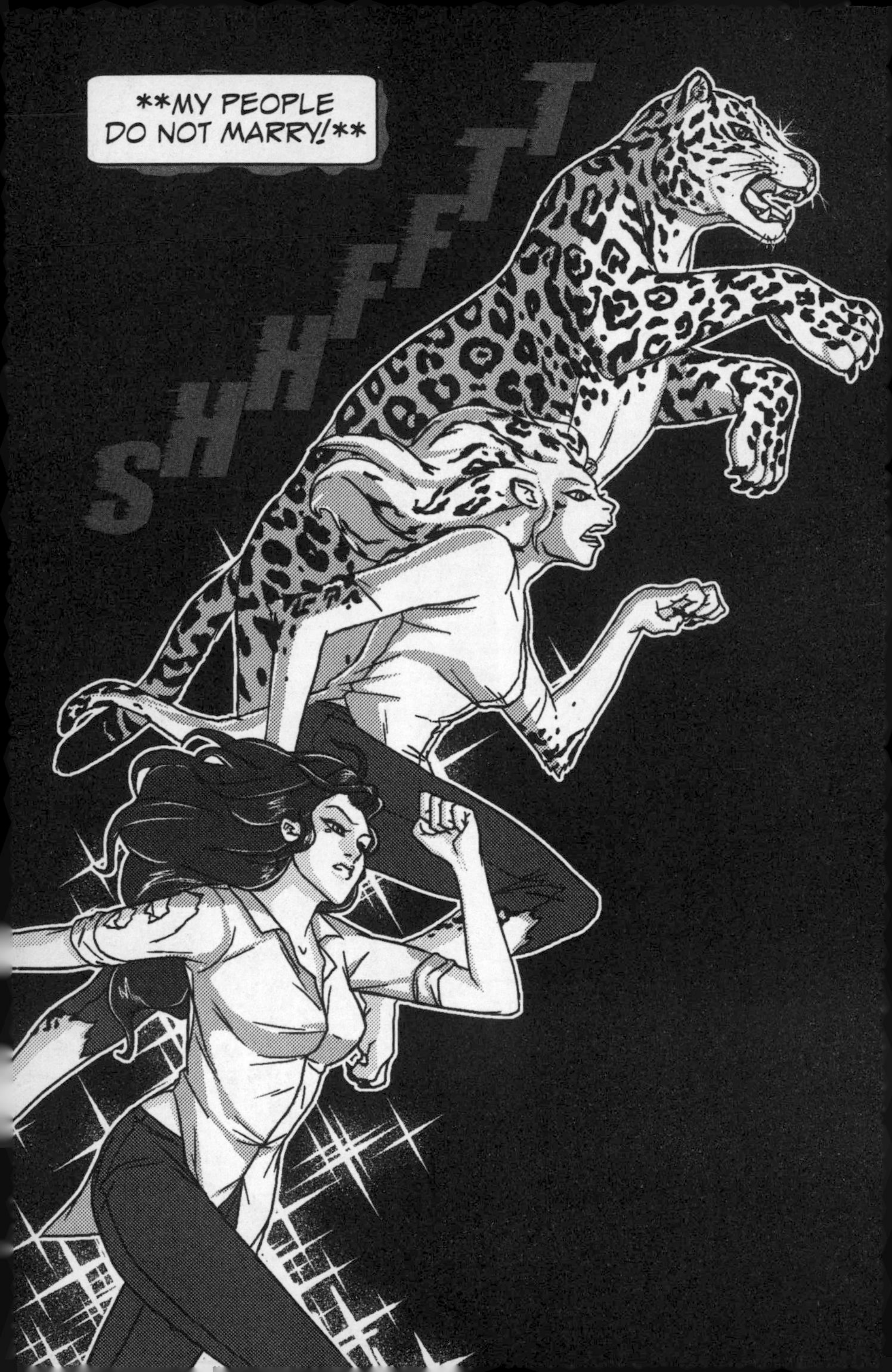
**MY PEOPLE
DO NOT MARRY!**
SHHFFFTTT

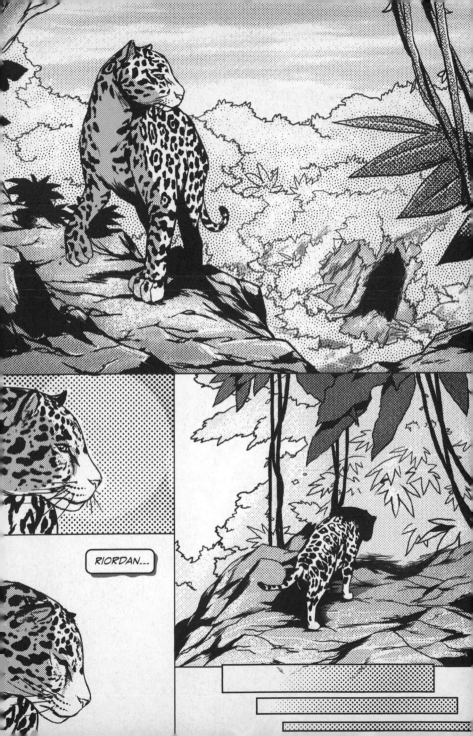

RIORDAN...

SHHFFTT

THE SUN'S
SETTING...

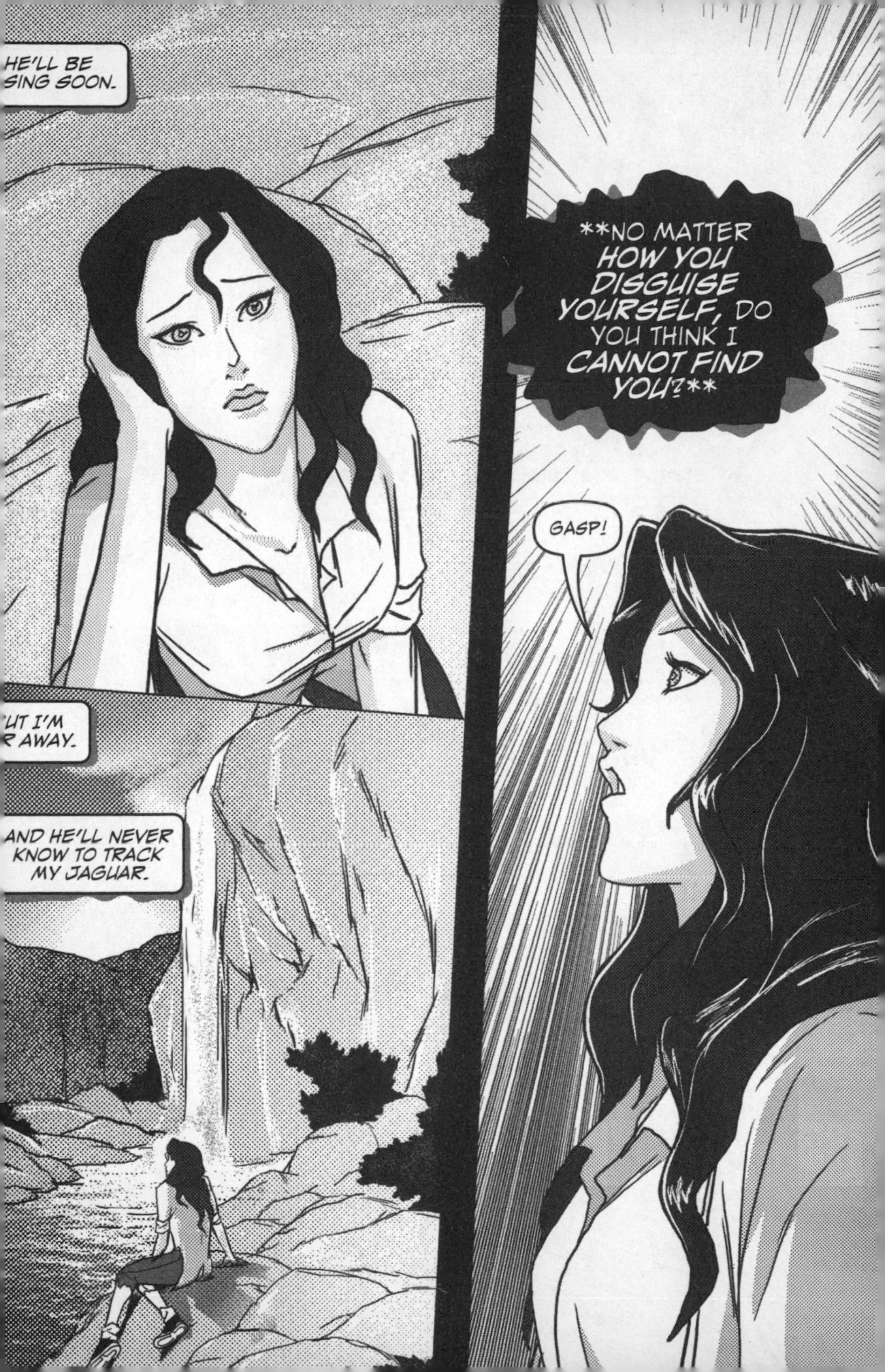
HE'LL BE SING SOON.
UT I'M R AWAY.
AND HE'LL NEVER KNOW TO TRACK MY JAGUAR.
NO MATTER HOW YOU DISGUISE YOURSELF, DO YOU THINK I CANNOT FIND YOU?
GASP!

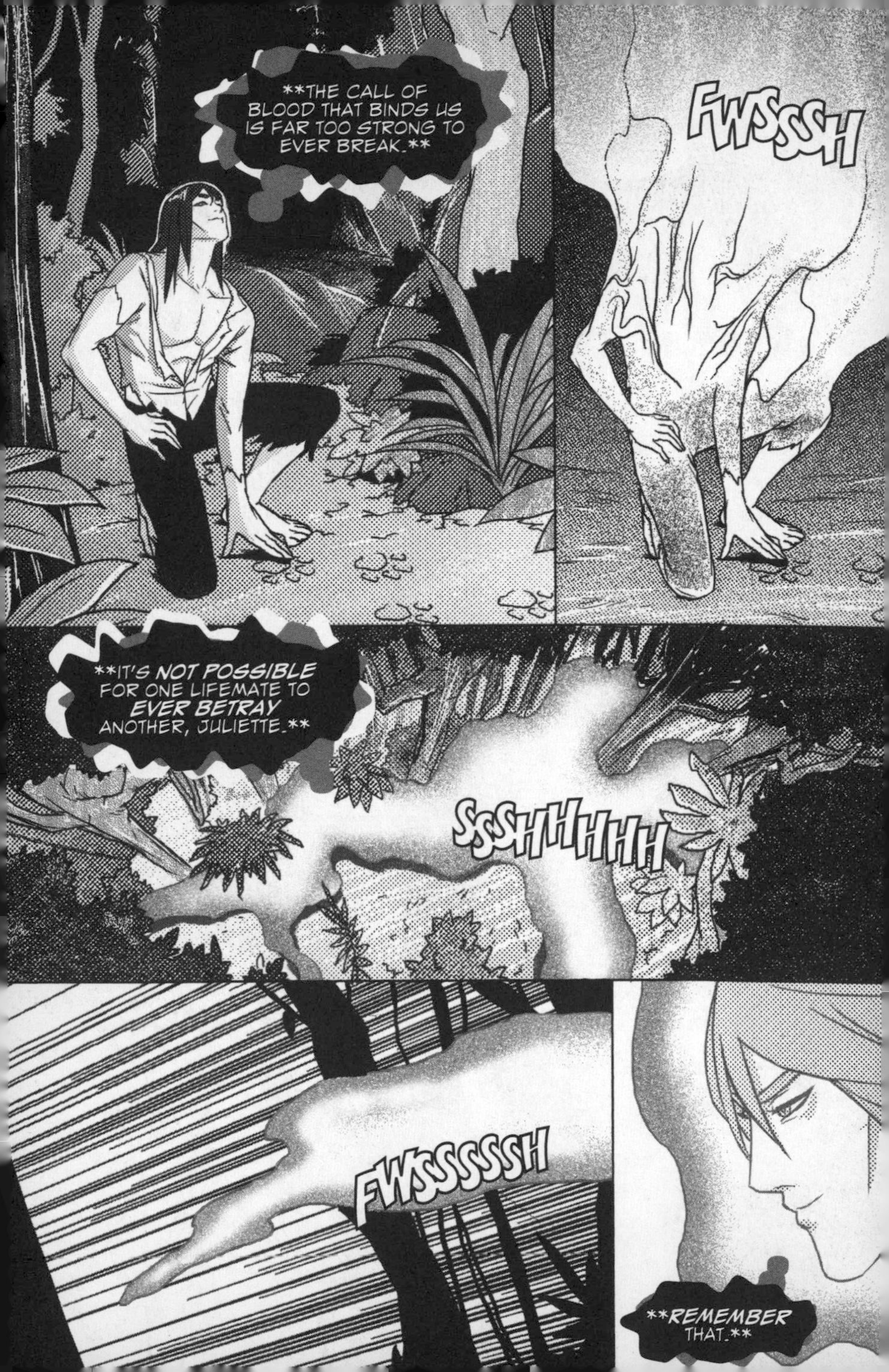
THE CALL OF BLOOD THAT BINDS US IS FAR TOO STRONG TO EVER BREAK.
FWSSSH
IT'S NOT POSSIBLE FOR ONE LIFEMATE TO EVER BETRAY ANOTHER, JULIETTE.
SSSHHHHHH
FWSSSSSH
REMEMBER THAT.

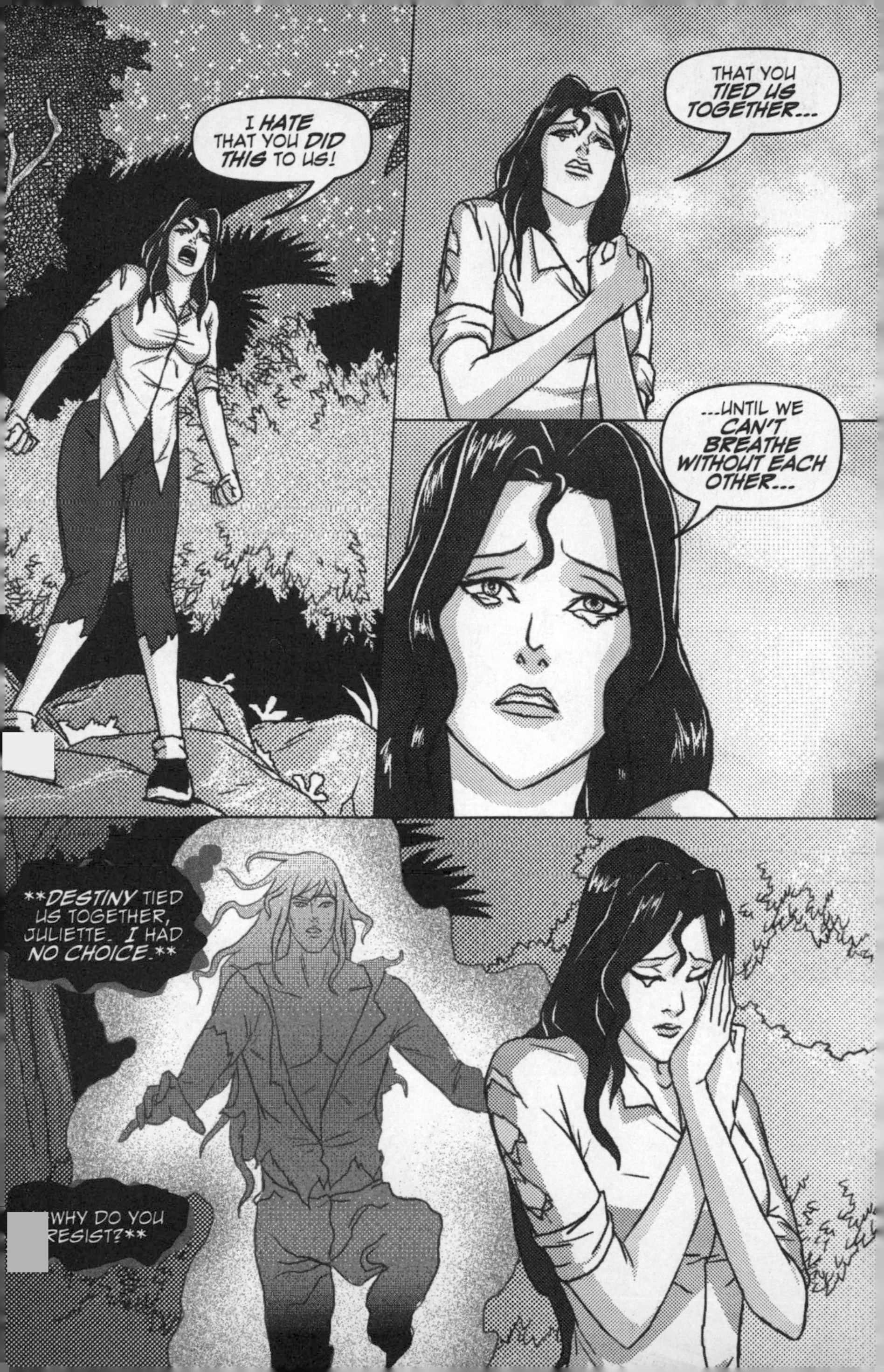

I HATE THAT YOU DID THIS TO US!
THAT YOU TIED US TOGETHER...
...UNTIL WE CAN'T BREATHE WITHOUT EACH OTHER...
DESTINY TIED US TOGETHER, JULIETTE. I HAD NO CHOICE.
WHY DO YOU RESIST?**

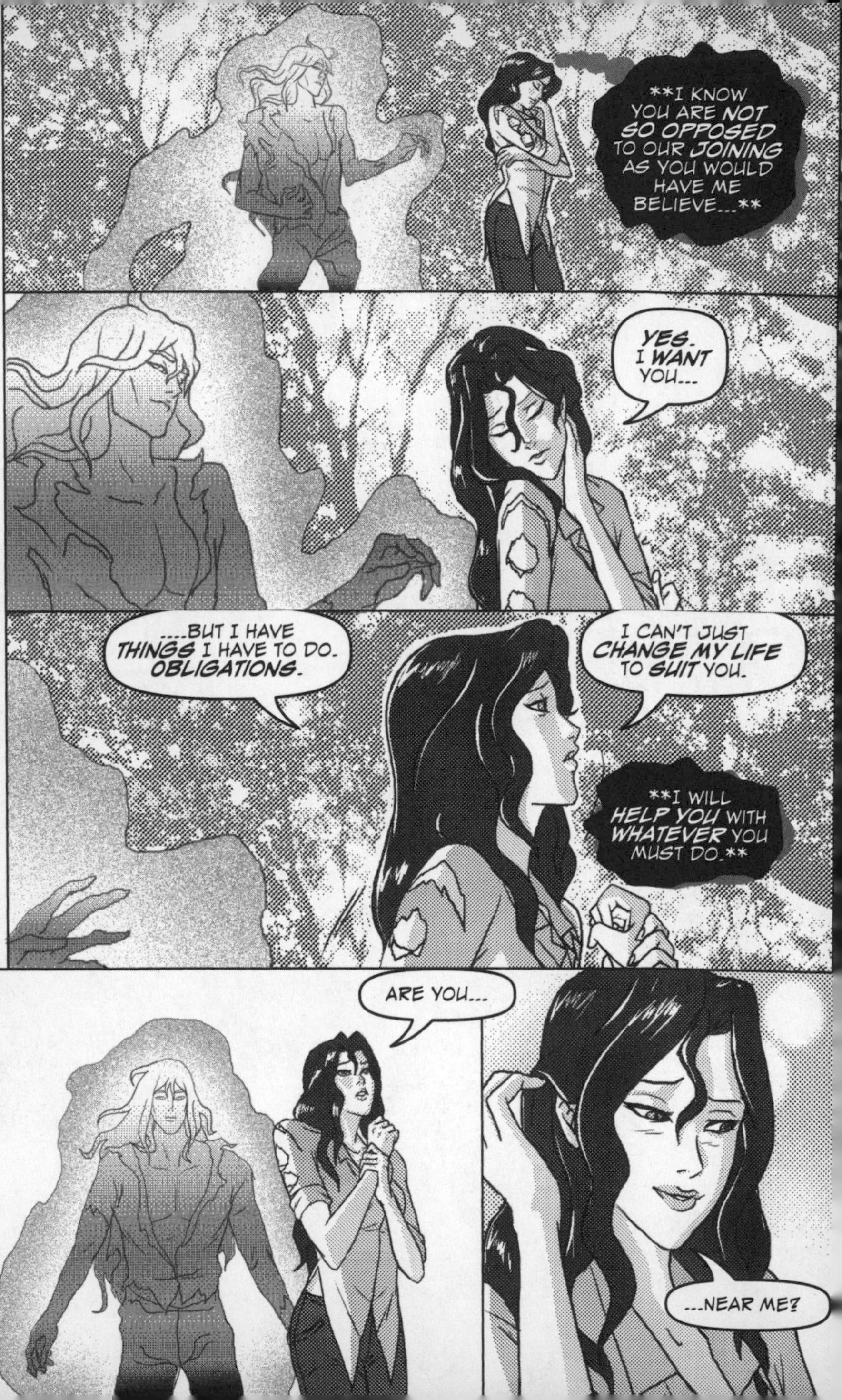
I KNOW YOU ARE NOT SO OPPOSED TO OUR JOINING AS YOU WOULD HAVE ME BELIEVE...
YES. I WANT YOU...
....BUT I HAVE THINGS I HAVE TO DO. OBLIGATIONS.
I CAN'T JUST CHANGE MY LIFE TO SUIT YOU.
I WILL HELP YOU WITH WHATEVER YOU MUST DO.
ARE YOU...
...NEAR ME?

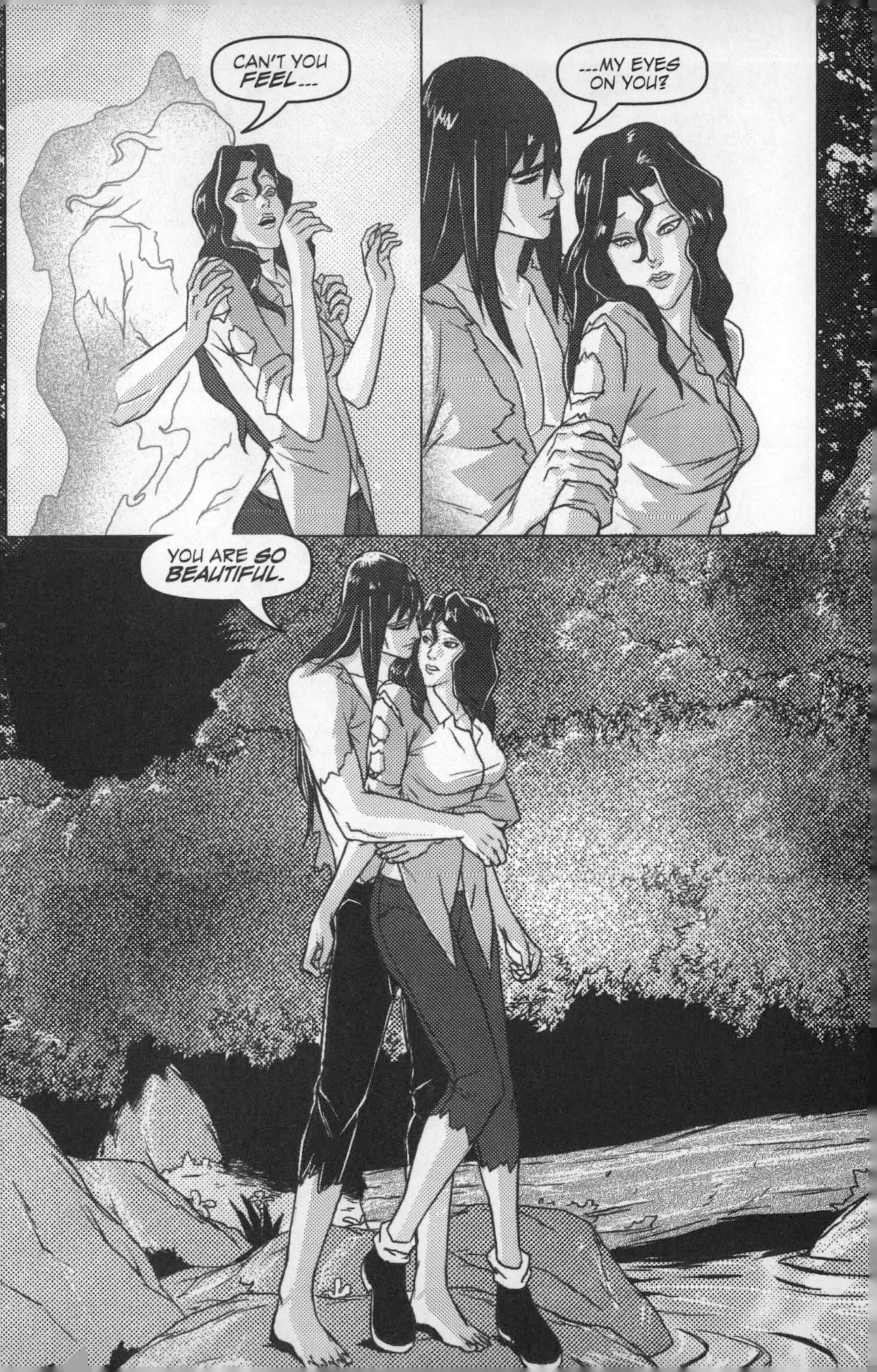
CAN'T YOU FEEL...
...MY EYES ON YOU?
YOU ARE SO BEAUTIFUL.

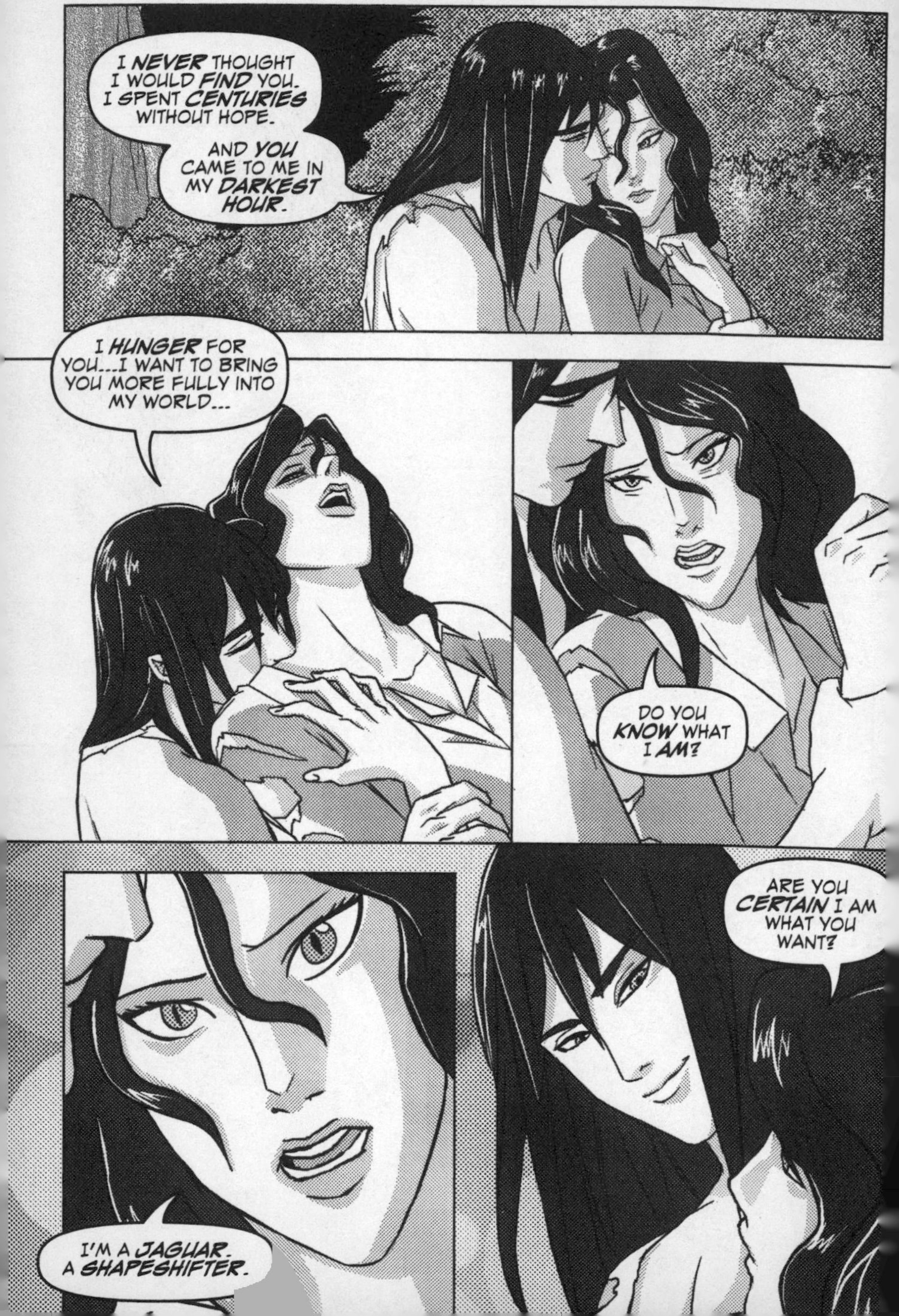
I NEVER THOUGHT I WOULD FIND YOU. I SPENT CENTURIES WITHOUT HOPE.
AND YOU CAME TO ME IN MY DARKEST HOUR.
I HUNGER FOR YOU...I WANT TO BRING YOU MORE FULLY INTO MY WORLD...
DO YOU KNOW WHAT I AM?
I'M A JAGUAR. A SHAPESHIFTER.
ARE YOU CERTAIN I AM WHAT YOU WANT?

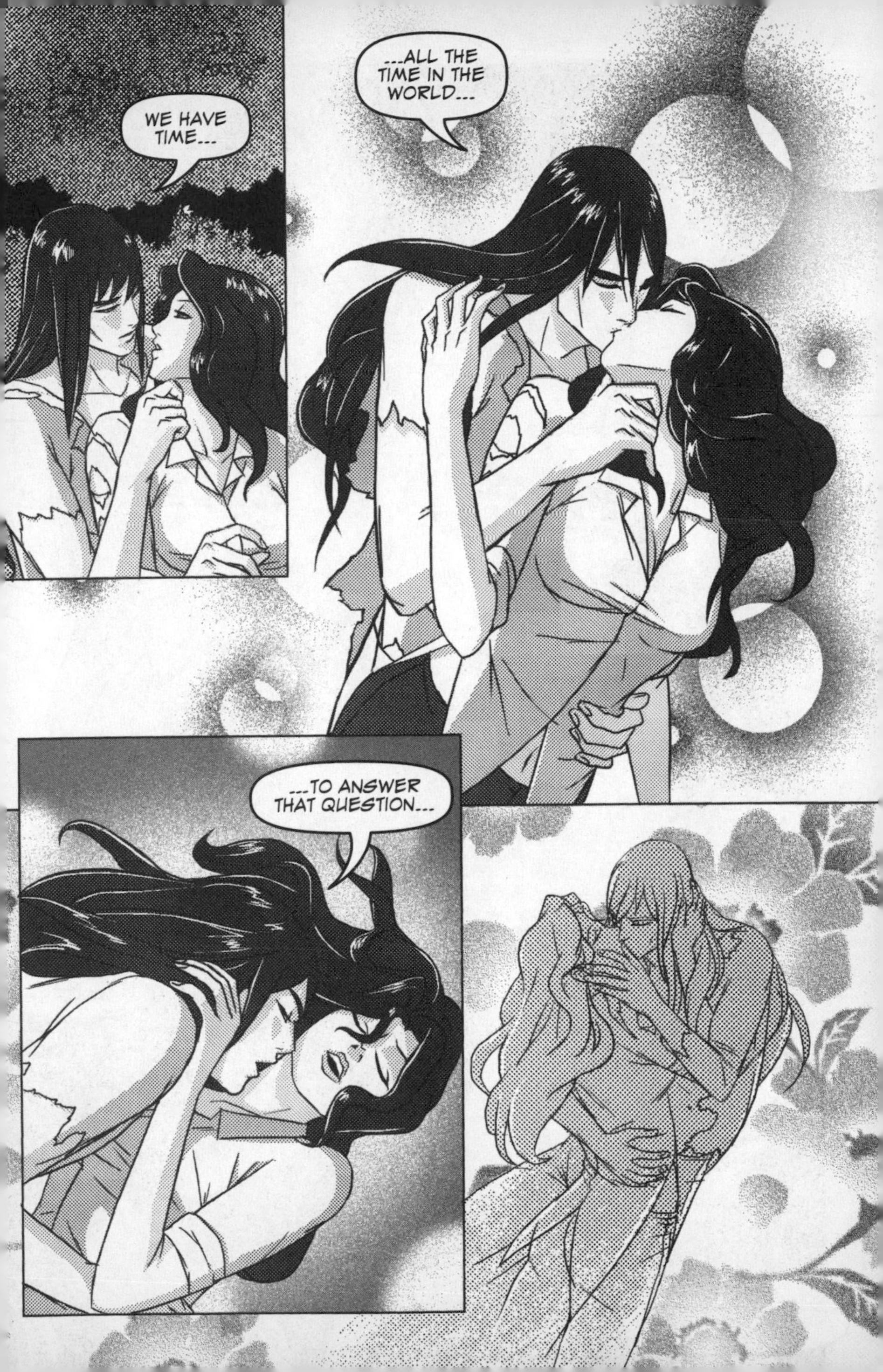
WE HAVE TIME...
...ALL THE TIME IN THE WORLD...
...TO ANSWER THAT QUESTION...

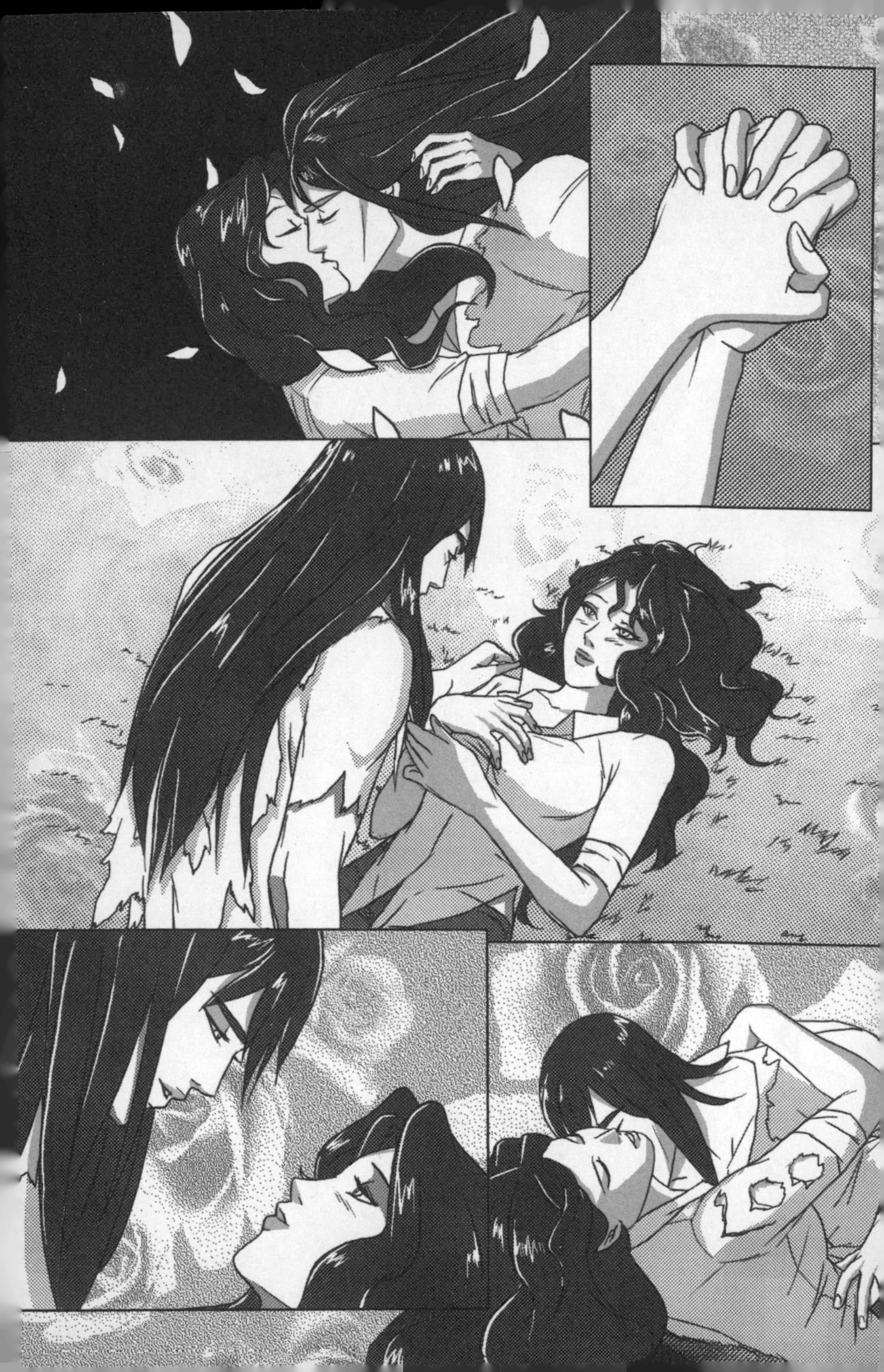

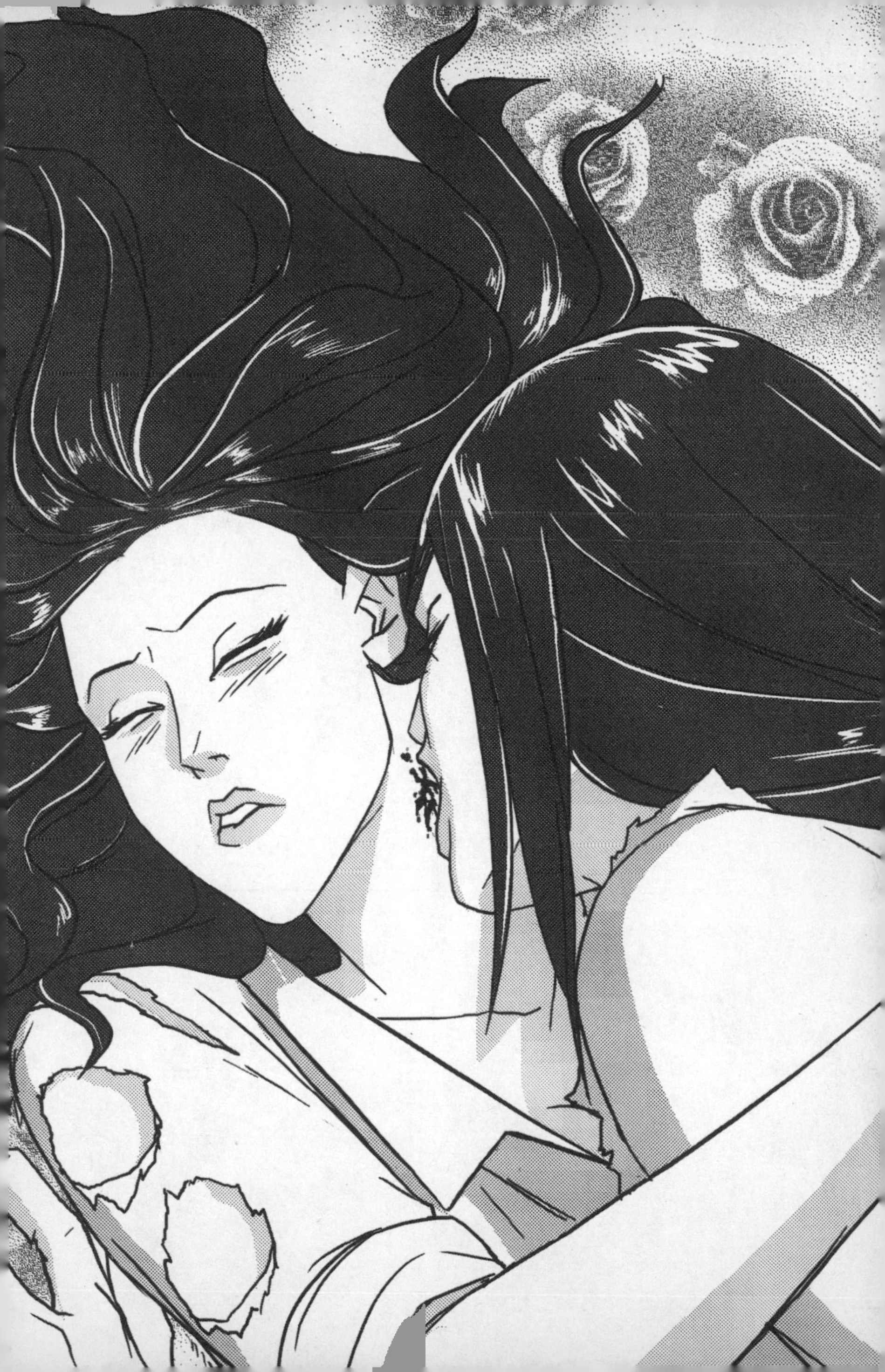

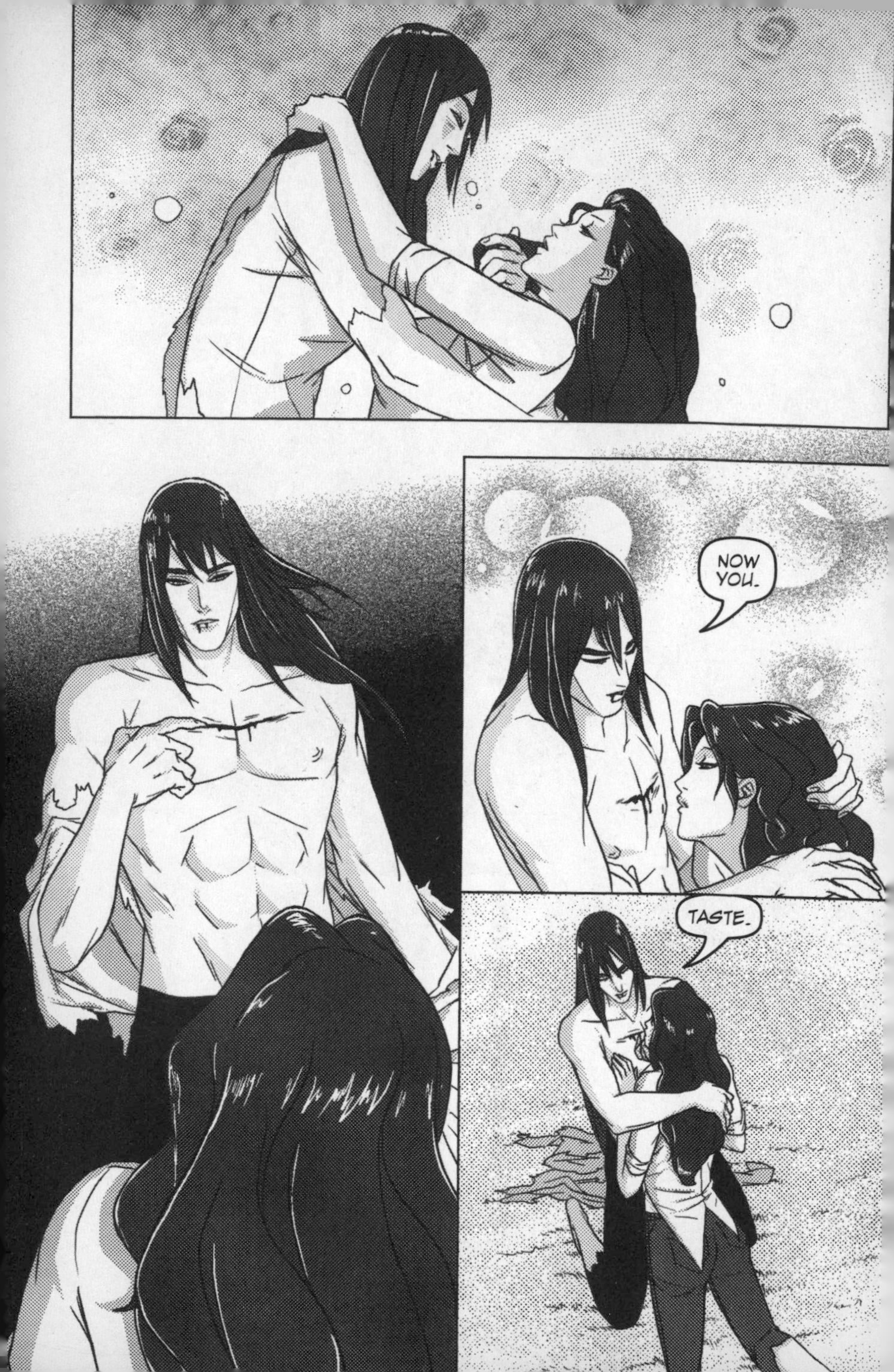
NOW YOU.
TASTE.

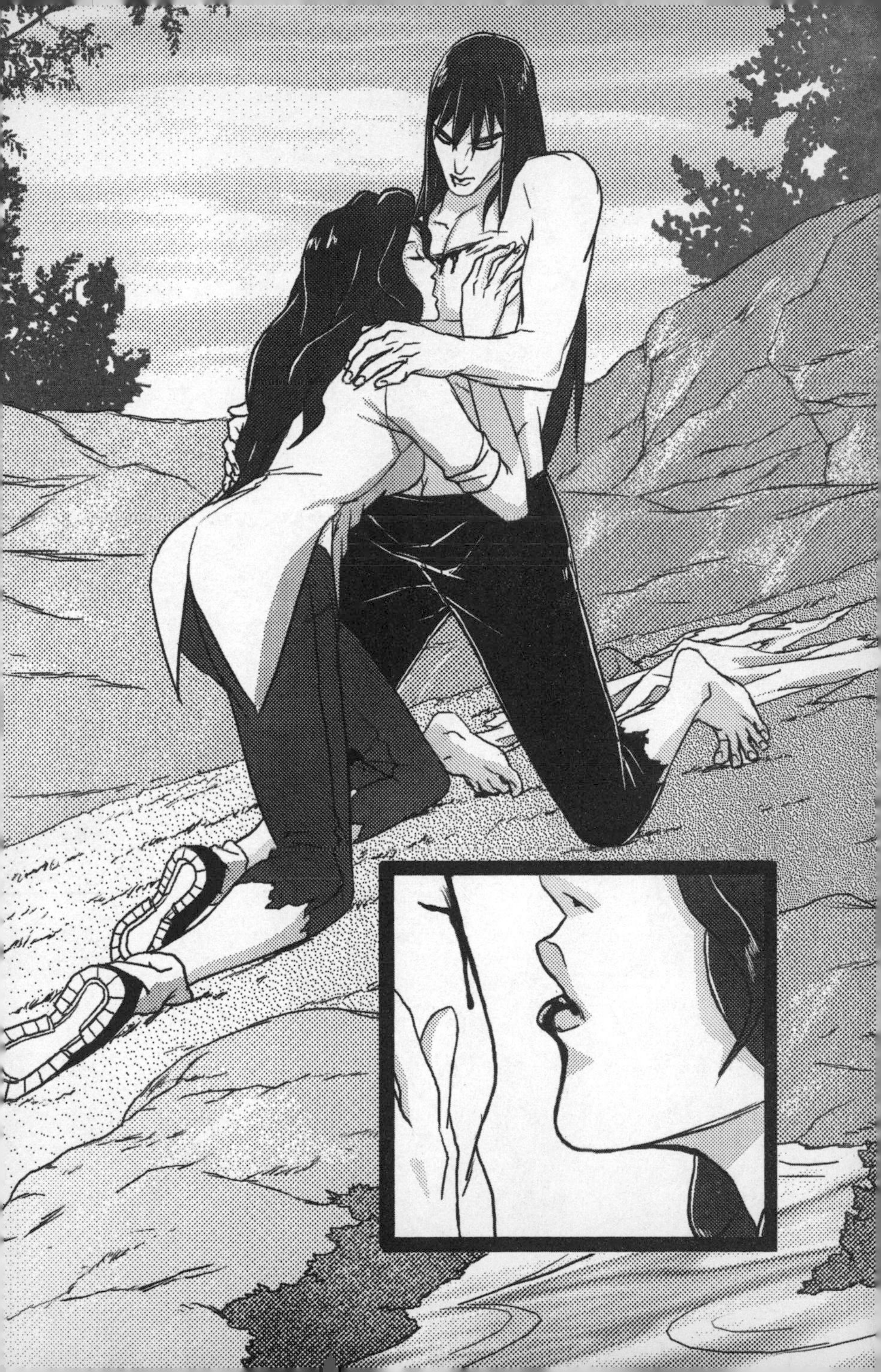

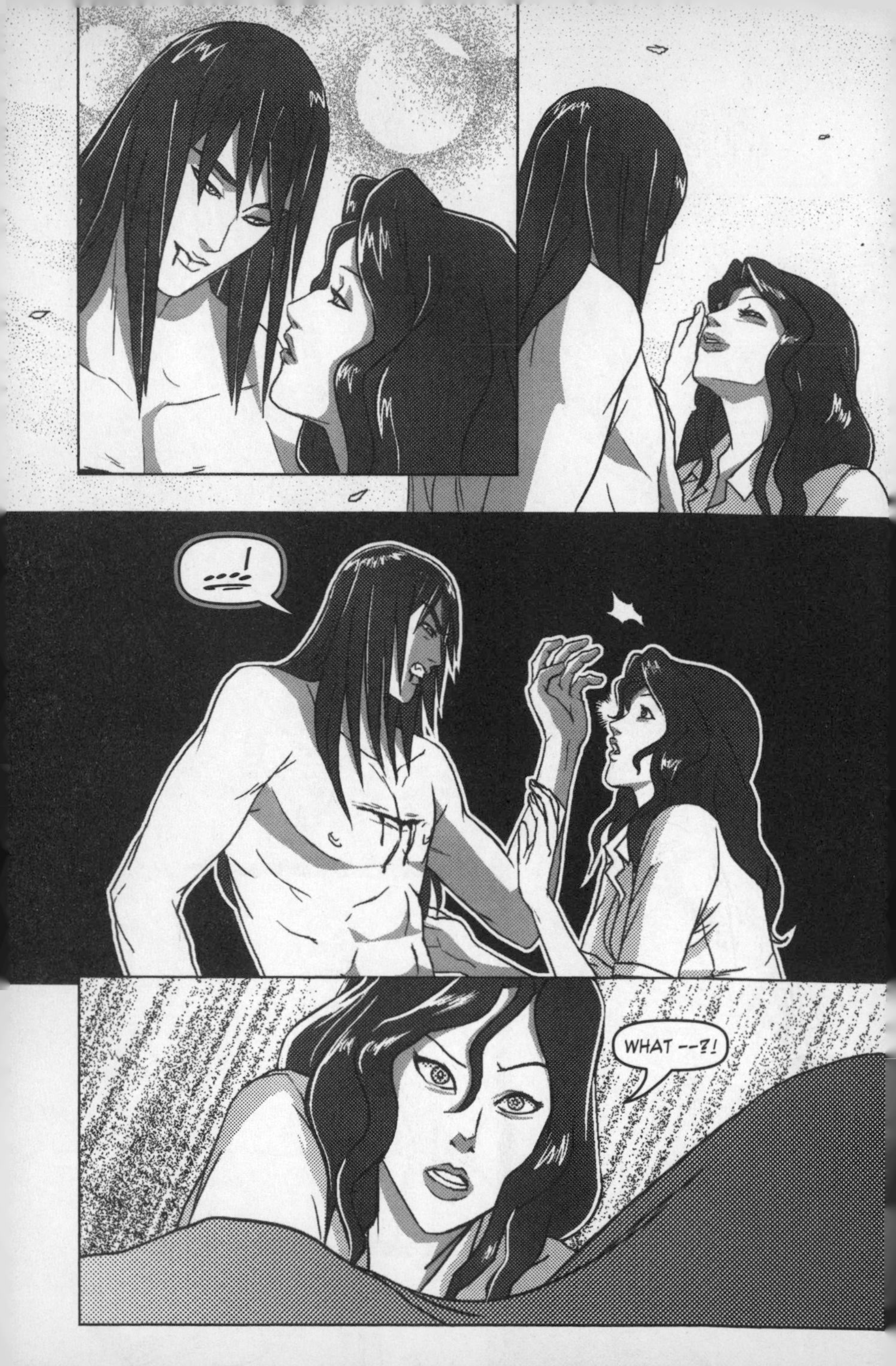

....!
WHAT --?!

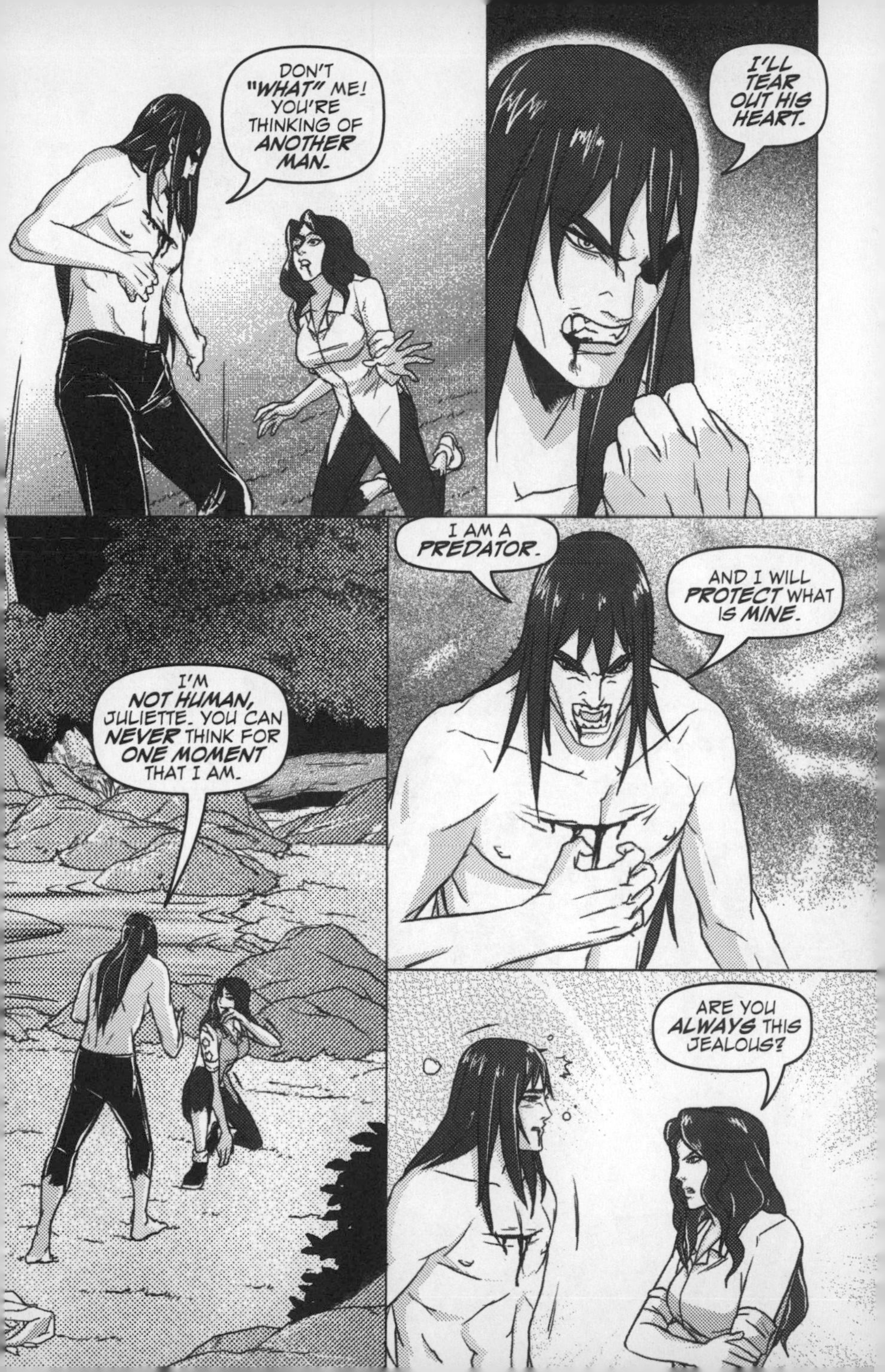
DON'T "WHAT" ME! YOU'RE THINKING OF ANOTHER MAN.
I'LL TEAR OUT HIS HEART.
I'M NOT HUMAN, JULIETTE. YOU CAN NEVER THINK FOR ONE MOMENT THAT I AM.
I AM A PREDATOR.
AND I WILL PROTECT WHAT IS MINE.
ARE YOU ALWAYS THIS JEALOUS?

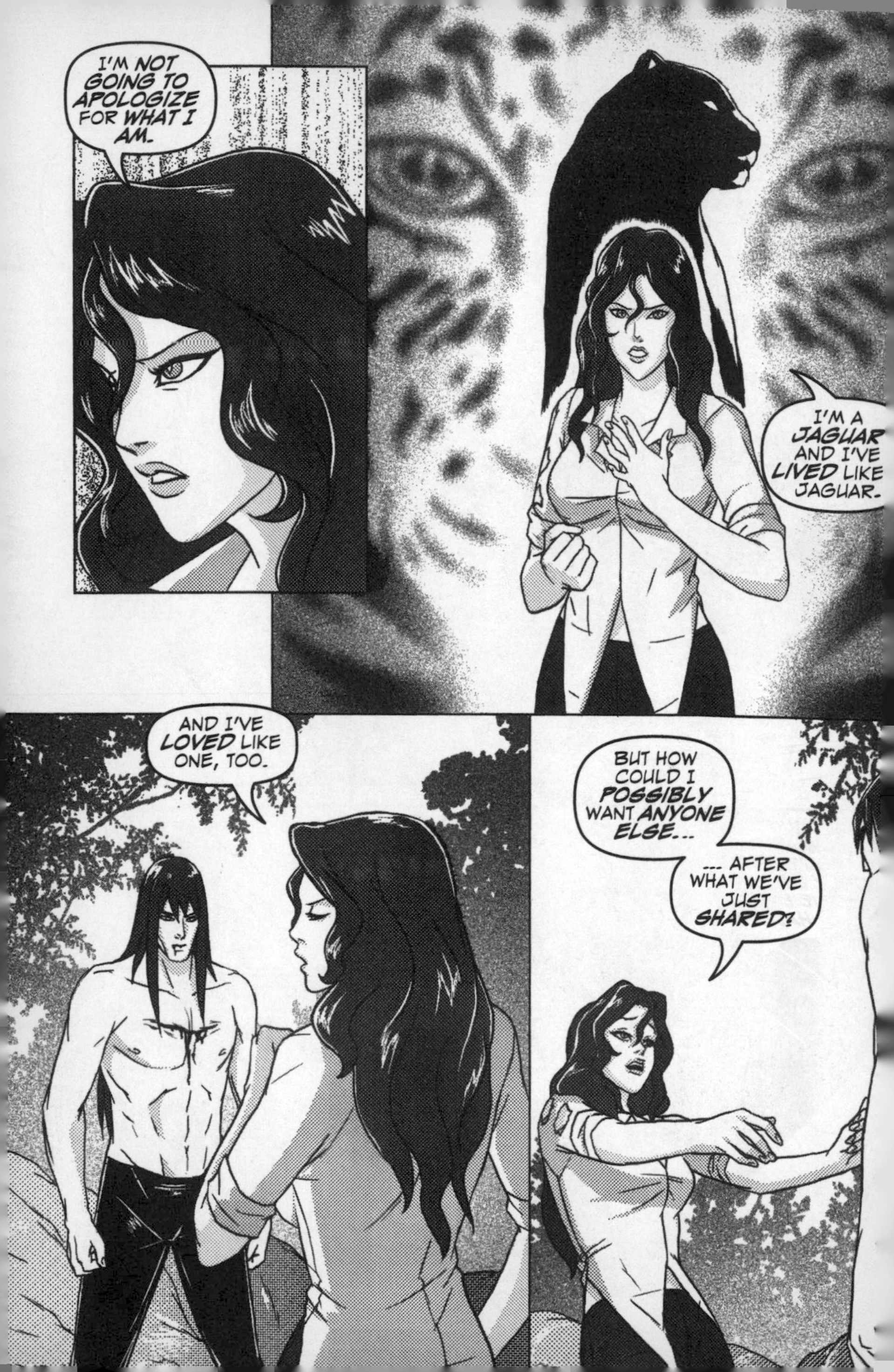
I'M NOT GOING TO APOLOGIZE FOR WHAT I AM.
I'M A JAGUAR AND I'VE LIVED LIKE JAGUAR.
AND I'VE LOVED LIKE ONE, TOO.
BUT HOW COULD I POSSIBLY WANT ANYONE ELSE...
... AFTER WHAT WE'VE JUST SHARED?

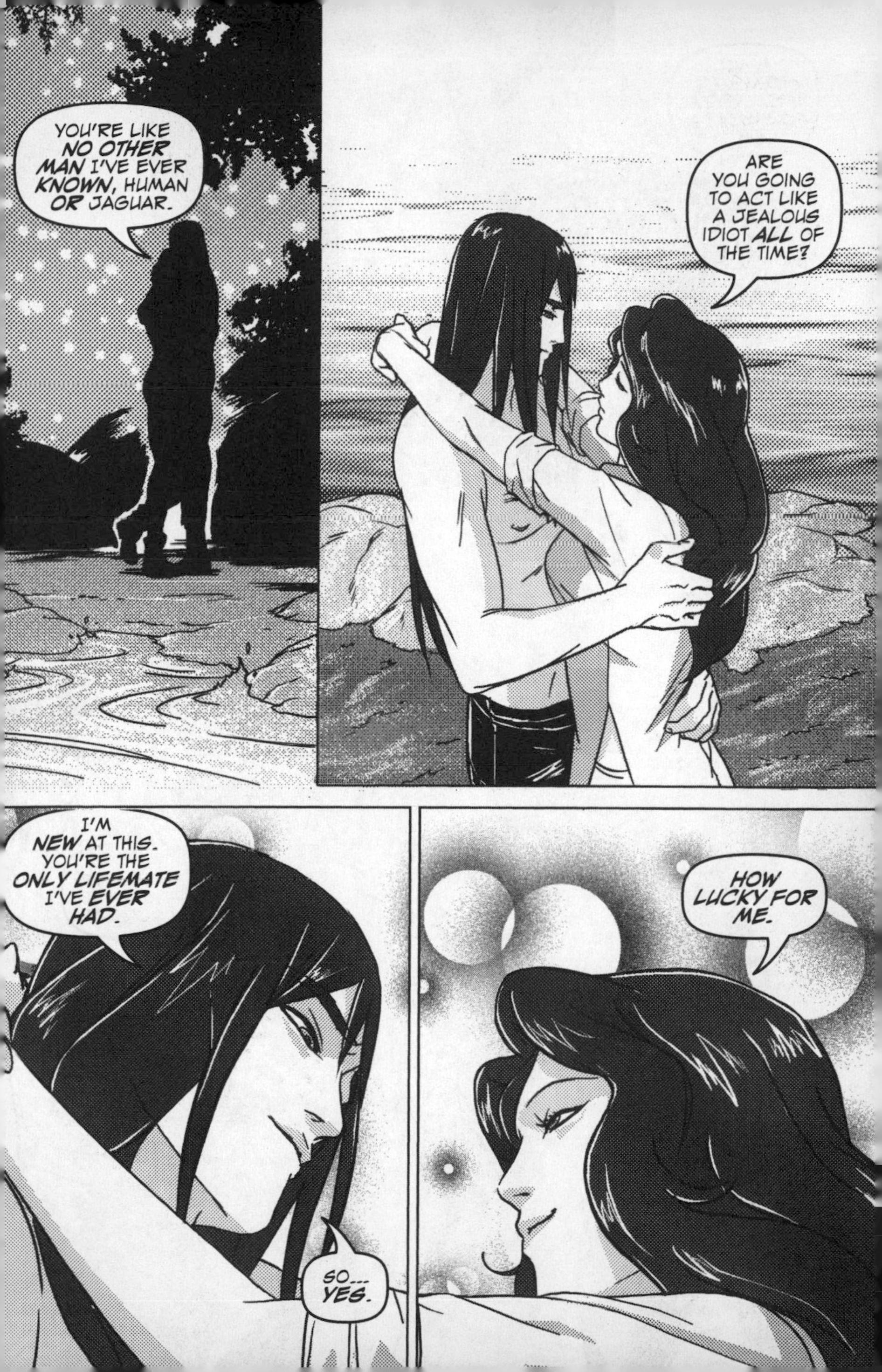
YOU'RE LIKE NO OTHER MAN I'VE EVER KNOWN, HUMAN OR JAGUAR.
ARE YOU GOING TO ACT LIKE A JEALOUS IDIOT ALL OF THE TIME?
I'M NEW AT THIS. YOU'RE THE ONLY LIFEMATE I'VE EVER HAD.
SO... YES.
HOW LUCKY FOR ME.

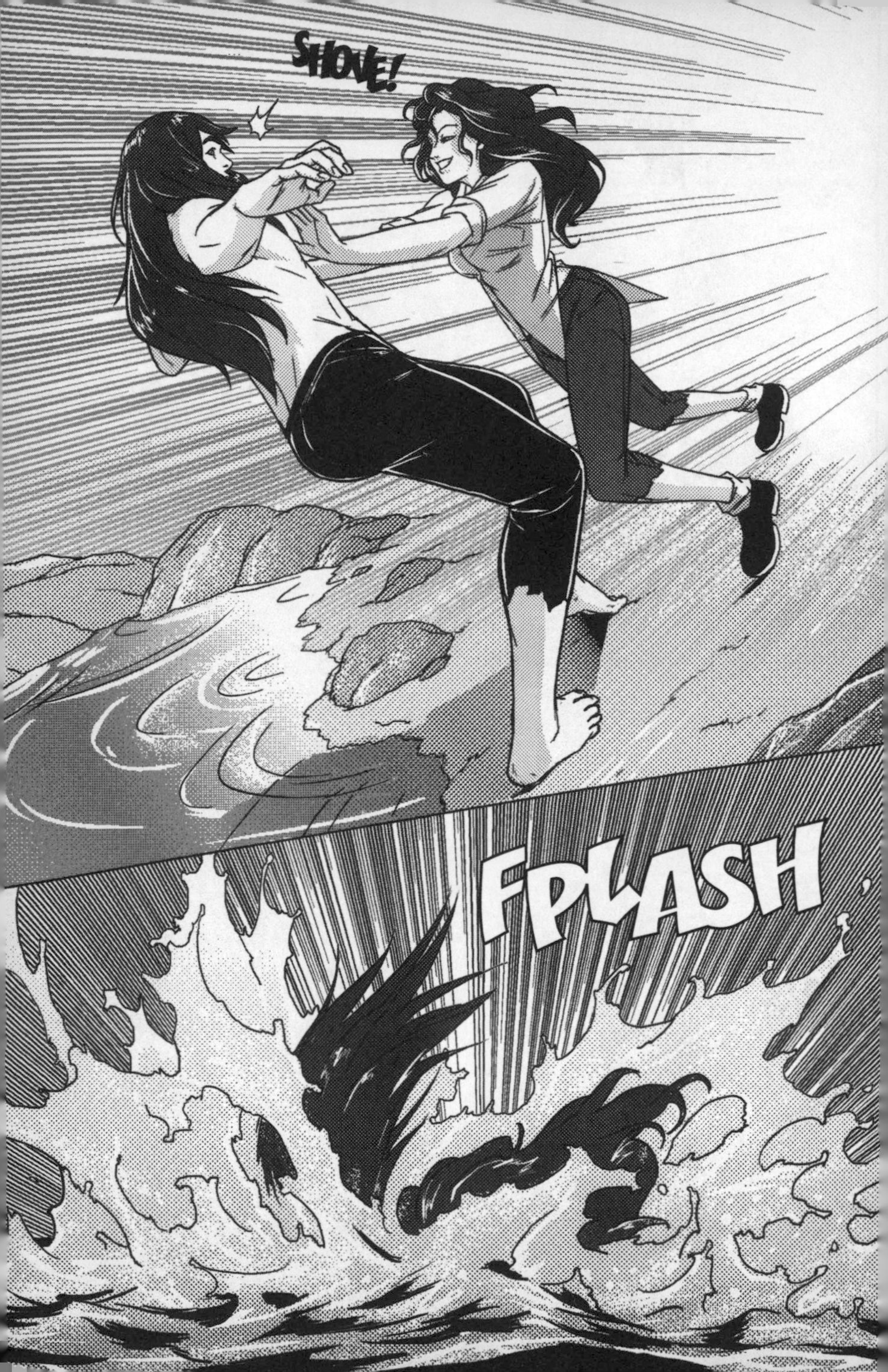
SHOVE!
FPLASH

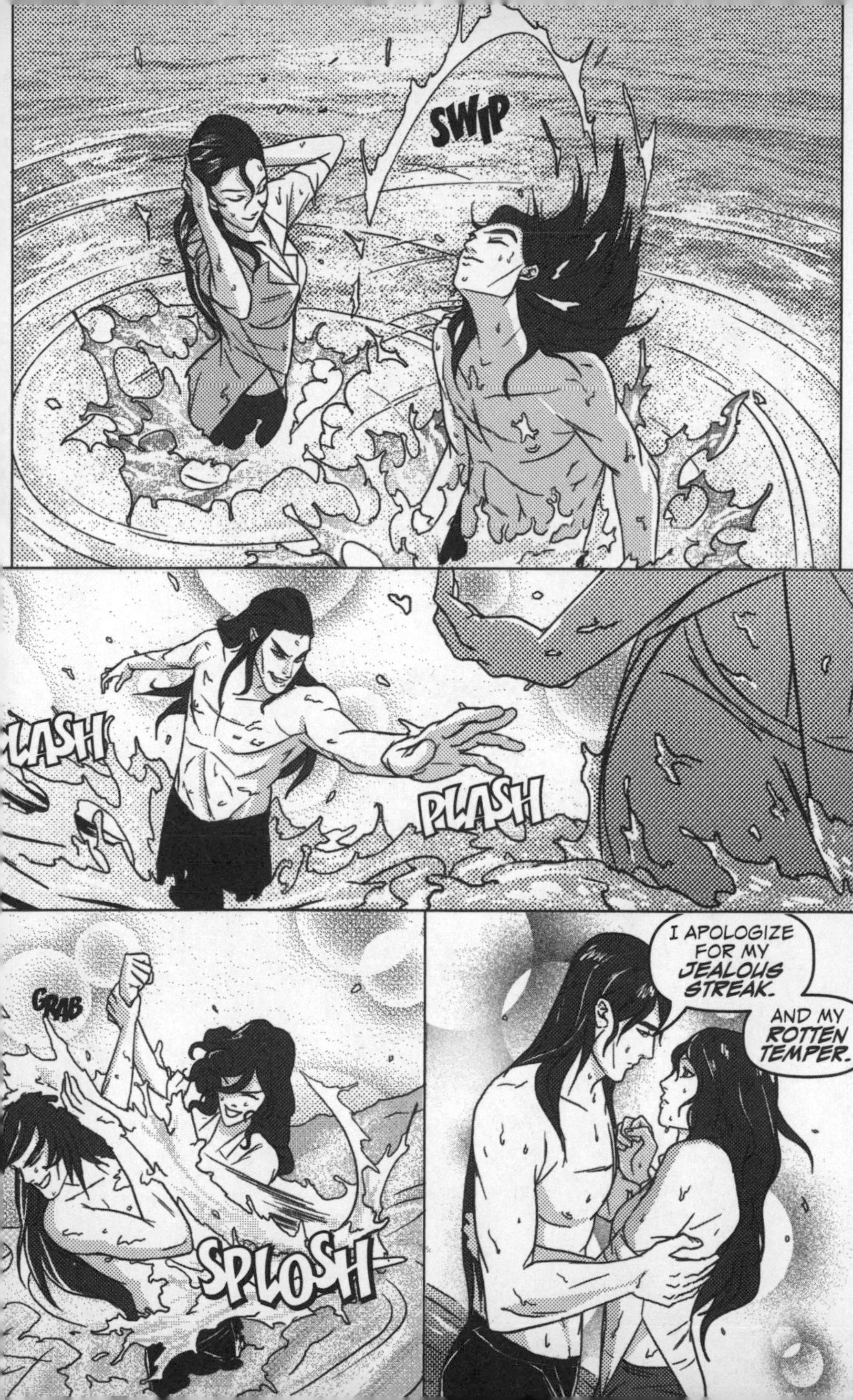
SWIP
PLASH
PLASH
GRAB
SPLOSH
I APOLOGIZE FOR MY JEALOUS STREAK.
AND MY ROTTEN TEMPER.

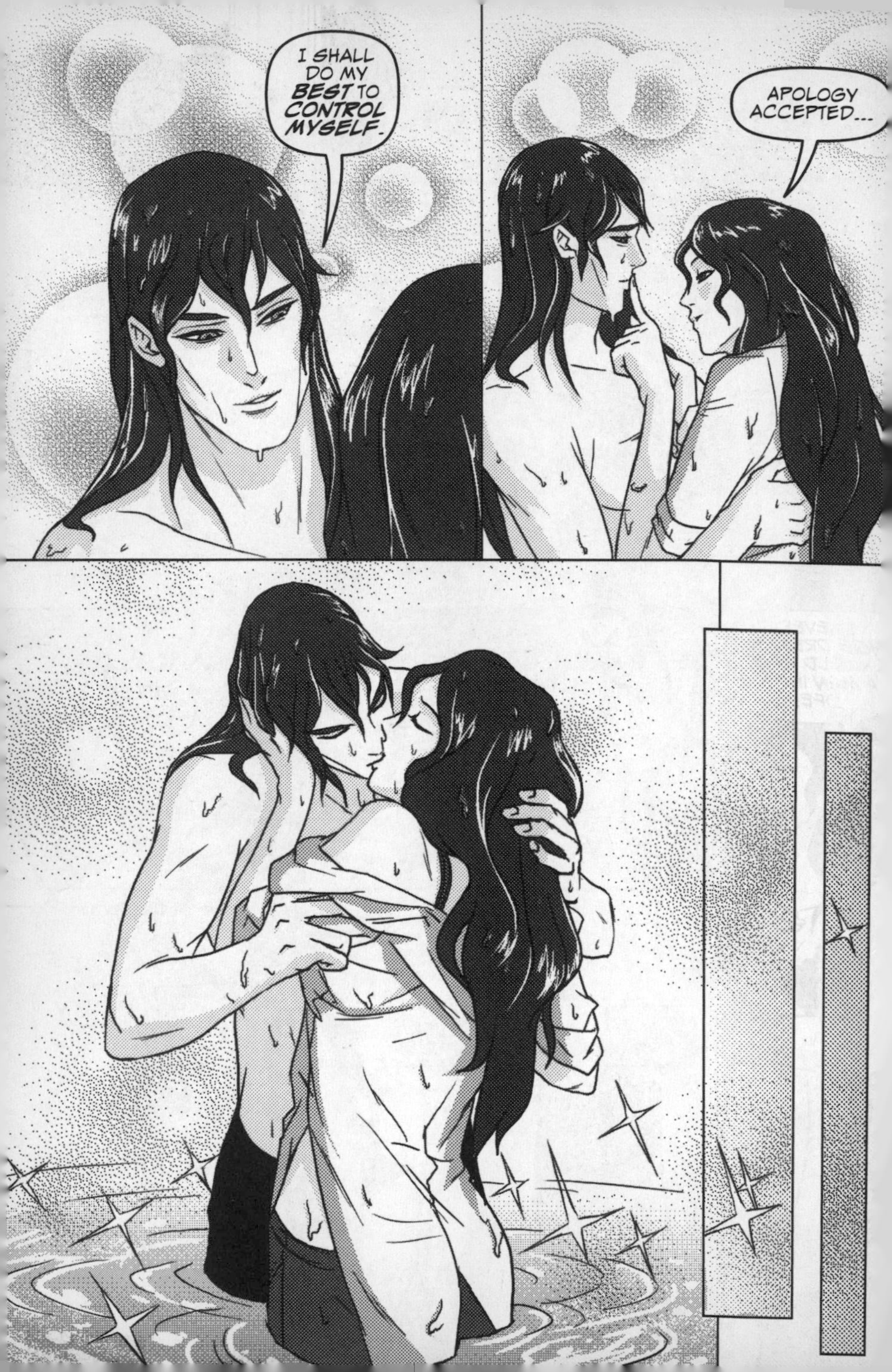
I SHALL DO MY **BEST** TO CONTROL MYSELF.
APOLOGY ACCEPTED...

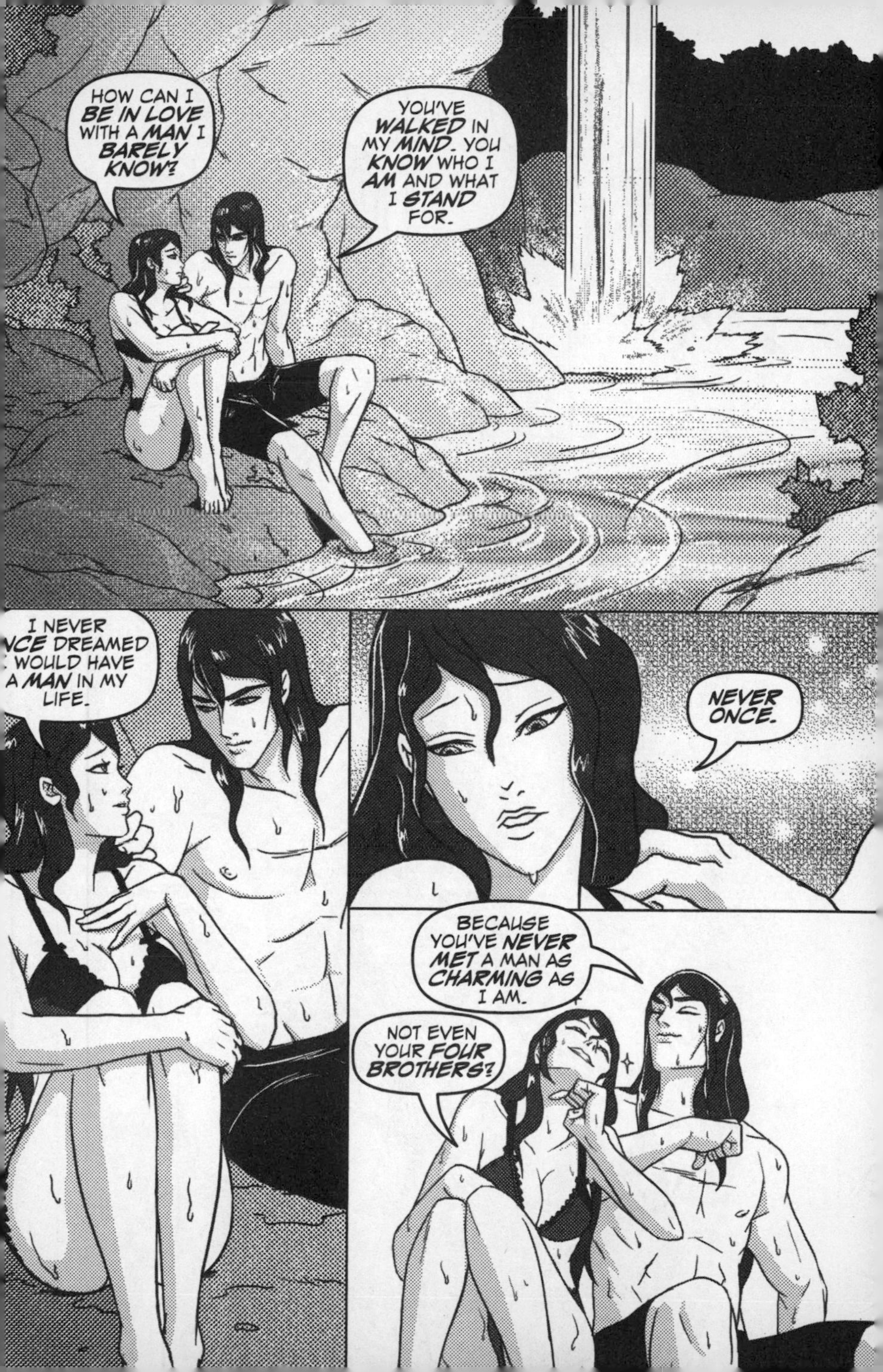
HOW CAN I BE IN LOVE WITH A MAN I BARELY KNOW?
YOU'VE WALKED IN MY MIND. YOU KNOW WHO I AM AND WHAT I STAND FOR.
I NEVER NCE DREAMED WOULD HAVE A MAN IN MY LIFE.
NEVER ONCE.
BECAUSE YOU'VE NEVER MET A MAN AS CHARMING AS I AM.
NOT EVEN YOUR FOUR BROTHERS?

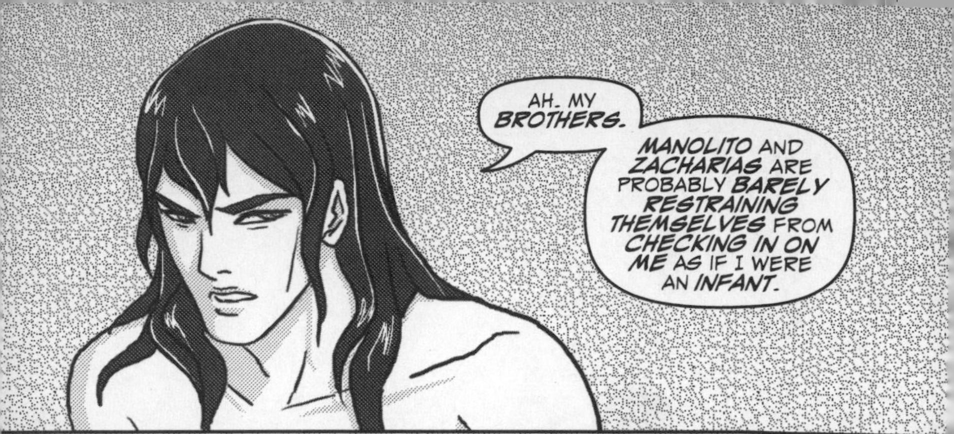
AH. MY BROTHERS.
MANOLITO AND ZACHARIAS ARE PROBABLY BARELY RESTRAINING THEMSELVES FROM CHECKING IN ON ME AS IF I WERE AN INFANT.

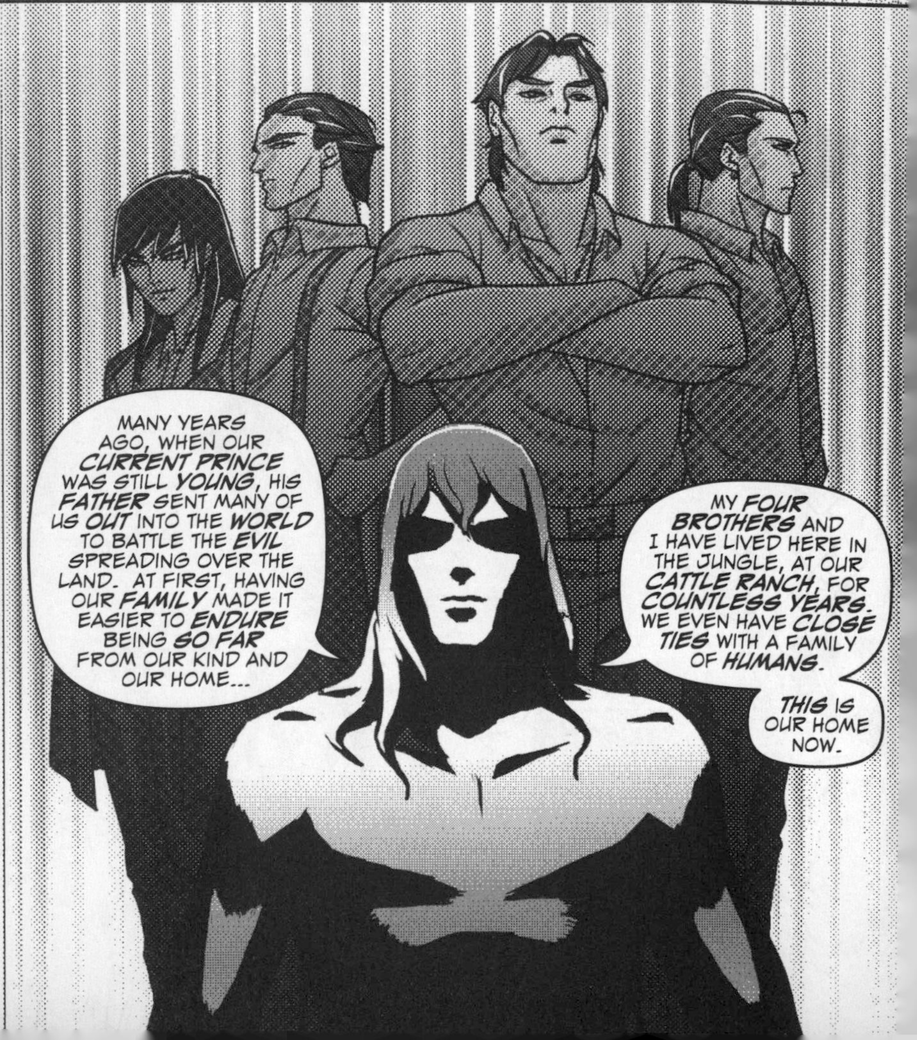
MANY YEARS AGO, WHEN OUR CURRENT PRINCE WAS STILL YOUNG, HIS FATHER SENT MANY OF US OUT INTO THE WORLD TO BATTLE THE EVIL SPREADING OVER THE LAND. AT FIRST, HAVING OUR FAMILY MADE IT EASIER TO ENDURE BEING SO FAR FROM OUR KIND AND OUR HOME...
MY FOUR BROTHERS AND I HAVE LIVED HERE IN THE JUNGLE, AT OUR CATTLE RANCH, FOR COUNTLESS YEARS. WE EVEN HAVE CLOSE TIES WITH A FAMILY OF HUMANS.
THIS IS OUR HOME NOW.

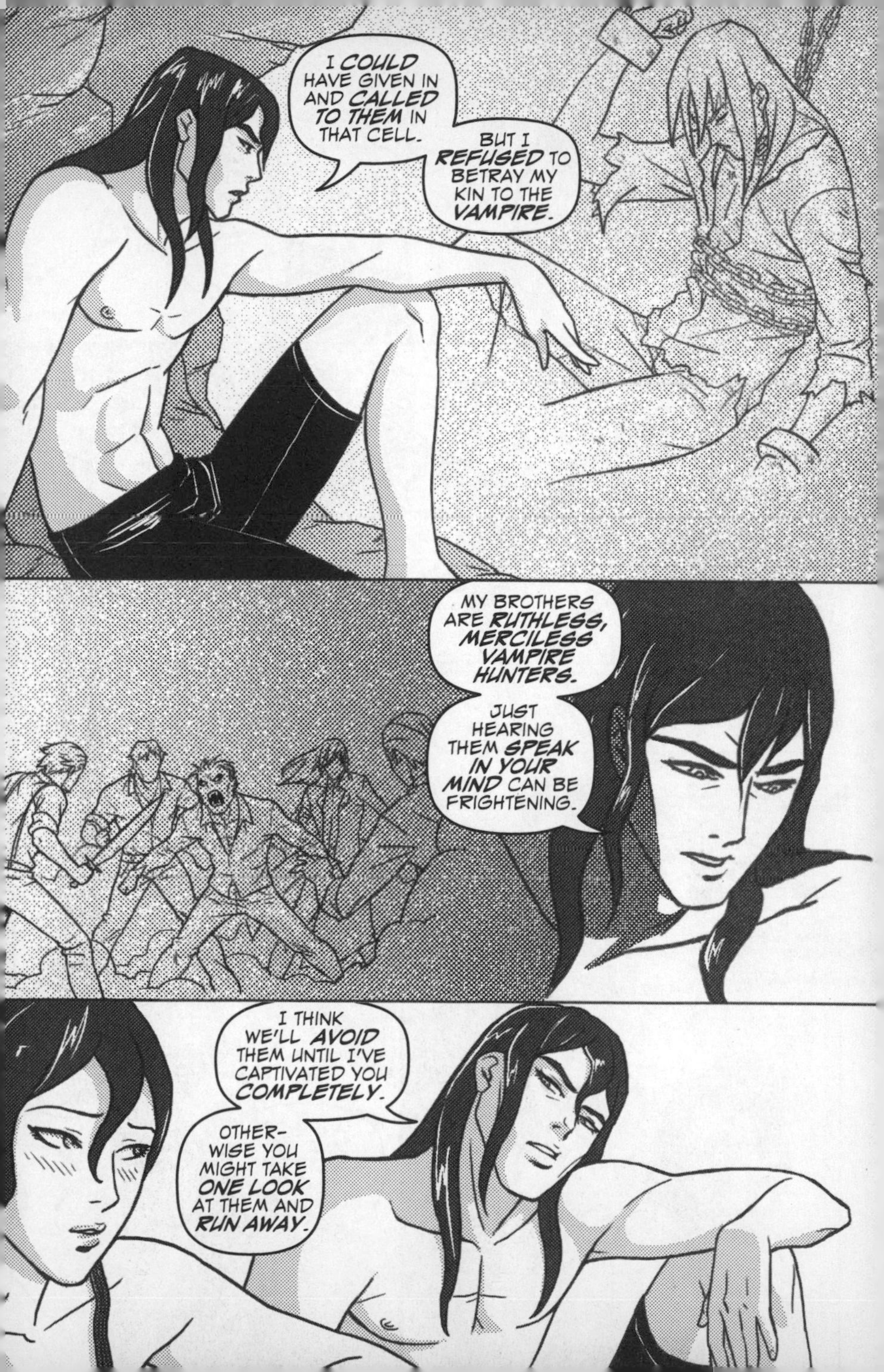
I COULD HAVE GIVEN IN AND CALLED TO THEM IN THAT CELL.
BUT I REFUSED TO BETRAY MY KIN TO THE VAMPIRE.
MY BROTHERS ARE RUTHLESS, MERCILESS VAMPIRE HUNTERS.
JUST HEARING THEM SPEAK IN YOUR MIND CAN BE FRIGHTENING.
I THINK WE'LL AVOID THEM UNTIL I'VE CAPTIVATED YOU COMPLETELY.
OTHER-WISE YOU MIGHT TAKE ONE LOOK AT THEM AND RUN AWAY.

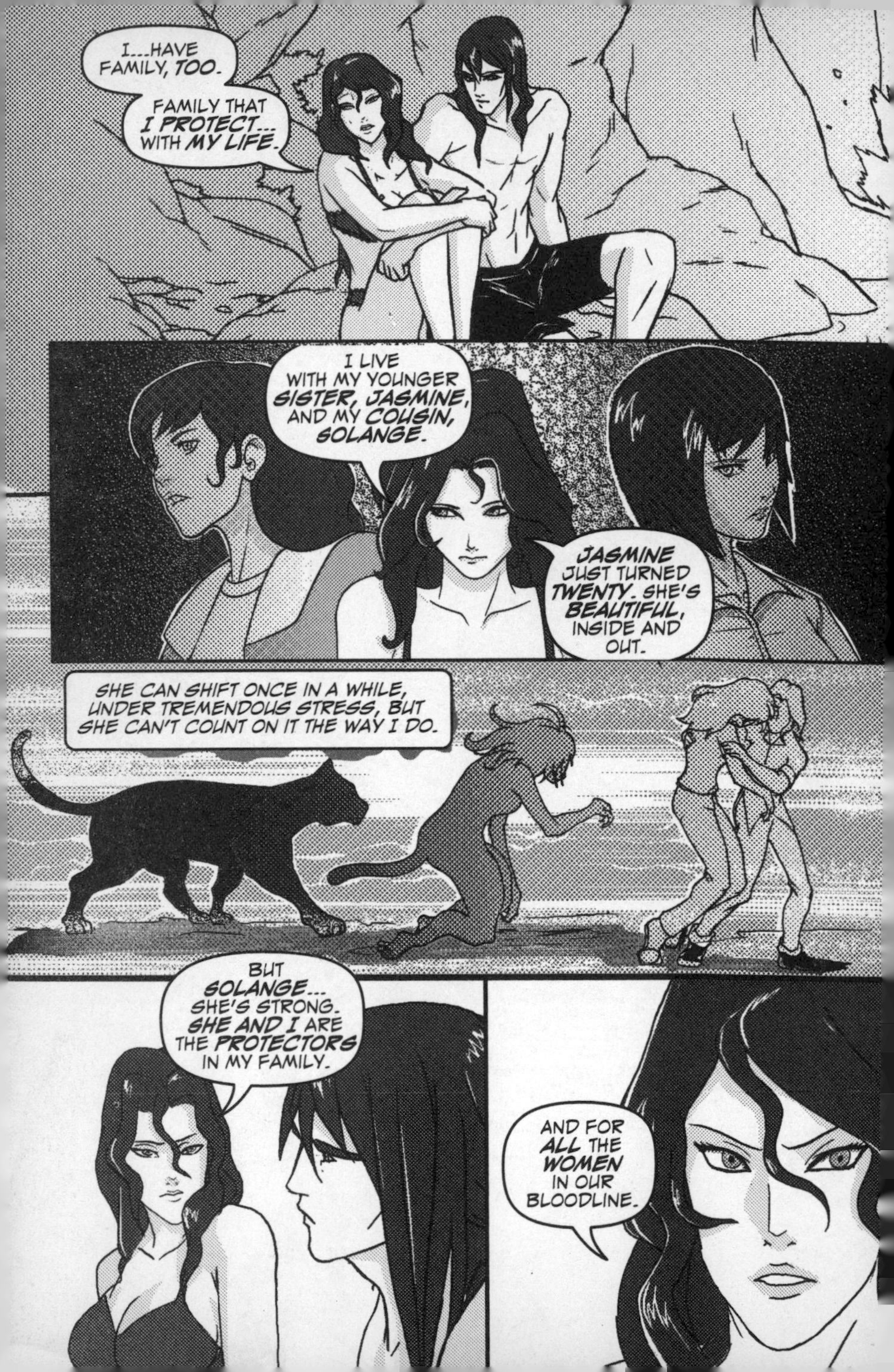

I...HAVE FAMILY, TOO.
FAMILY THAT I PROTECT... WITH MY LIFE.
I LIVE WITH MY YOUNGER SISTER, JASMINE, AND MY COUSIN, SOLANGE.
JASMINE JUST TURNED TWENTY. SHE'S BEAUTIFUL, INSIDE AND OUT.
SHE CAN SHIFT ONCE IN A WHILE, UNDER TREMENDOUS STRESS, BUT SHE CAN'T COUNT ON IT THE WAY I DO.
BUT SOLANGE... SHE'S STRONG. SHE AND I ARE THE PROTECTORS IN MY FAMILY.
AND FOR ALL THE WOMEN IN OUR BLOODLINE.

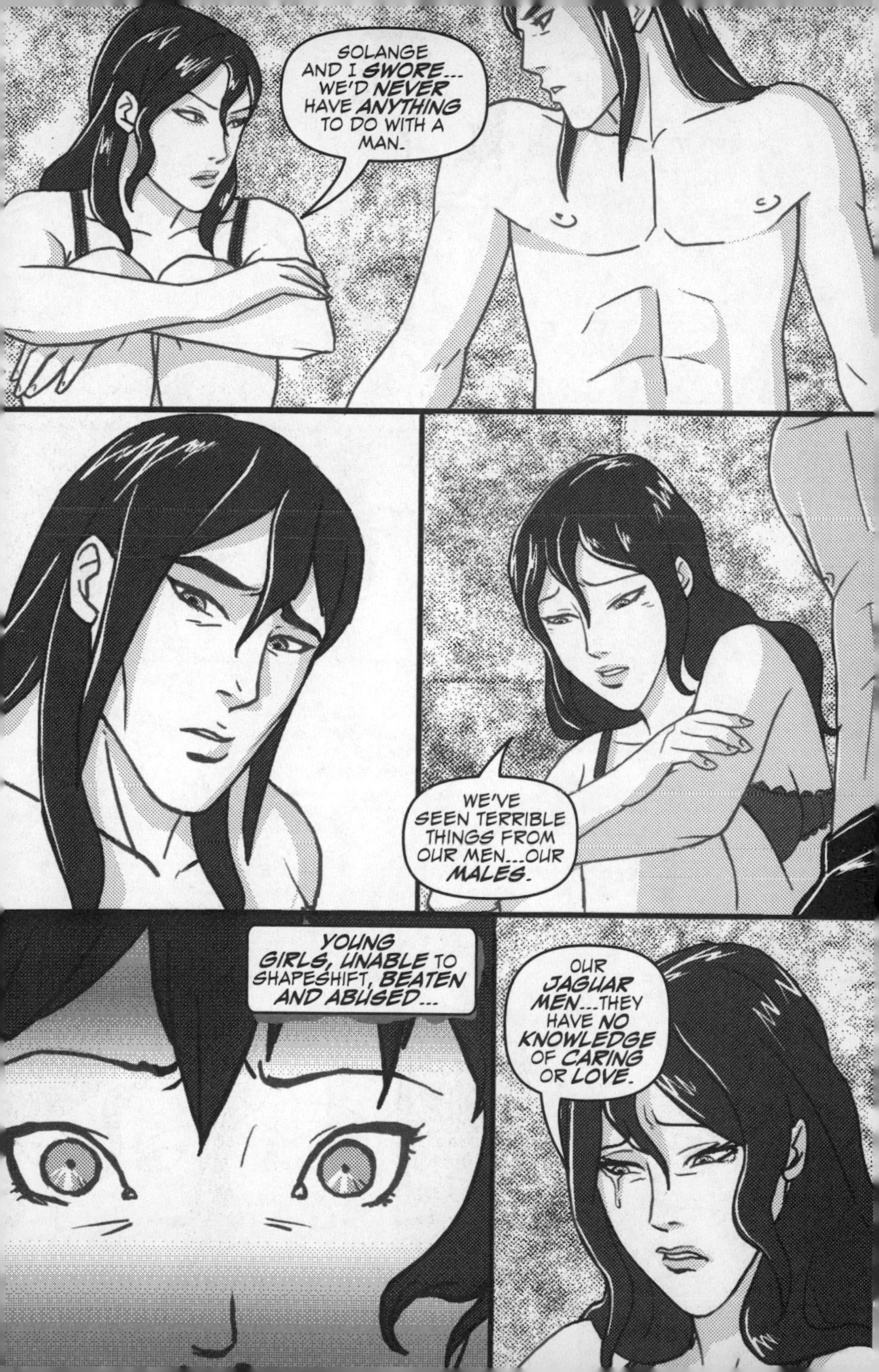
SOLANGE AND I SWORE... WE'D NEVER HAVE ANYTHING TO DO WITH A MAN.
WE'VE SEEN TERRIBLE THINGS FROM OUR MEN...OUR MALES.
YOUNG GIRLS, UNABLE TO SHAPESHIFT, BEATEN AND ABUSED...
OUR JAGUAR MEN...THEY HAVE NO KNOWLEDGE OF CARING OR LOVE.

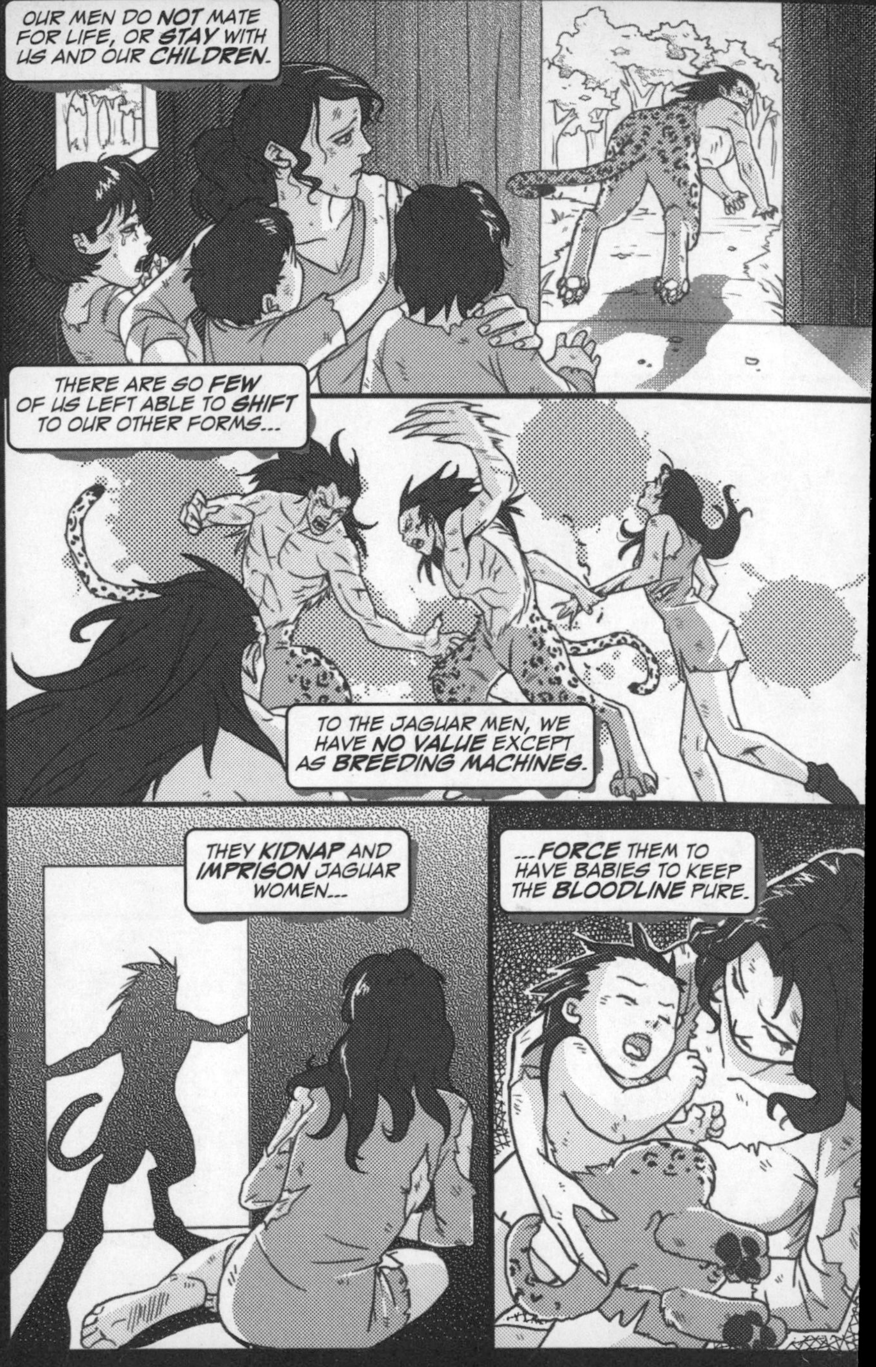
OUR MEN DO NOT MATE FOR LIFE, OR STAY WITH US AND OUR CHILDREN.
THERE ARE SO FEW OF US LEFT ABLE TO SHIFT TO OUR OTHER FORMS...
TO THE JAGUAR MEN, WE HAVE NO VALUE EXCEPT AS BREEDING MACHINES.
THEY KIDNAP AND IMPRISON JAGUAR WOMEN...
...FORCE THEM TO HAVE BABIES TO KEEP THE BLOODLINE PURE.

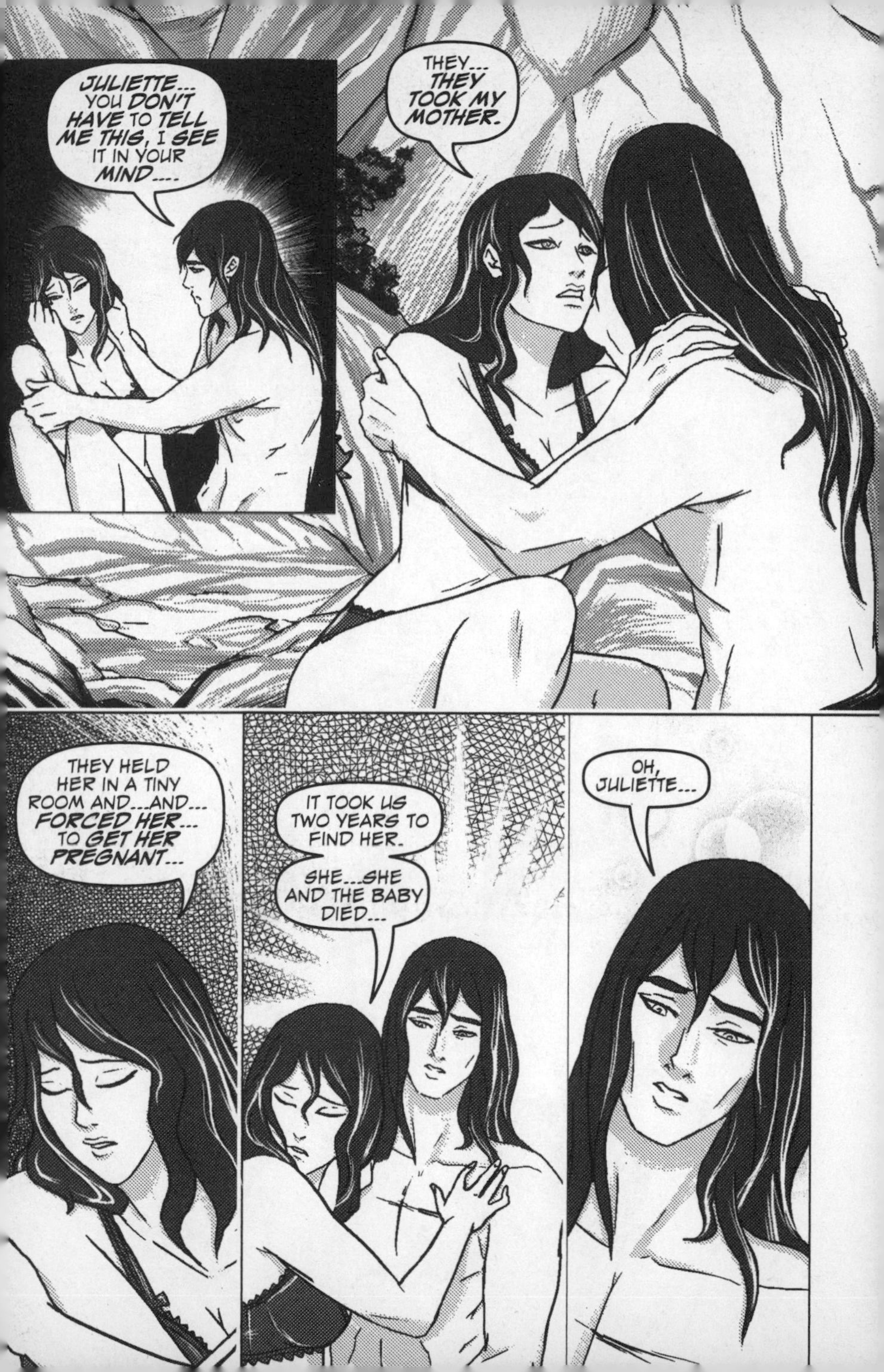
JULIETTE... YOU DON'T HAVE TO TELL ME THIS, I SEE IT IN YOUR MIND....
THEY... THEY TOOK MY MOTHER.
THEY HELD HER IN A TINY ROOM AND...AND... FORCED HER... TO GET HER PREGNANT...
IT TOOK US TWO YEARS TO FIND HER.
SHE...SHE AND THE BABY DIED...
OH, JULIETTE...

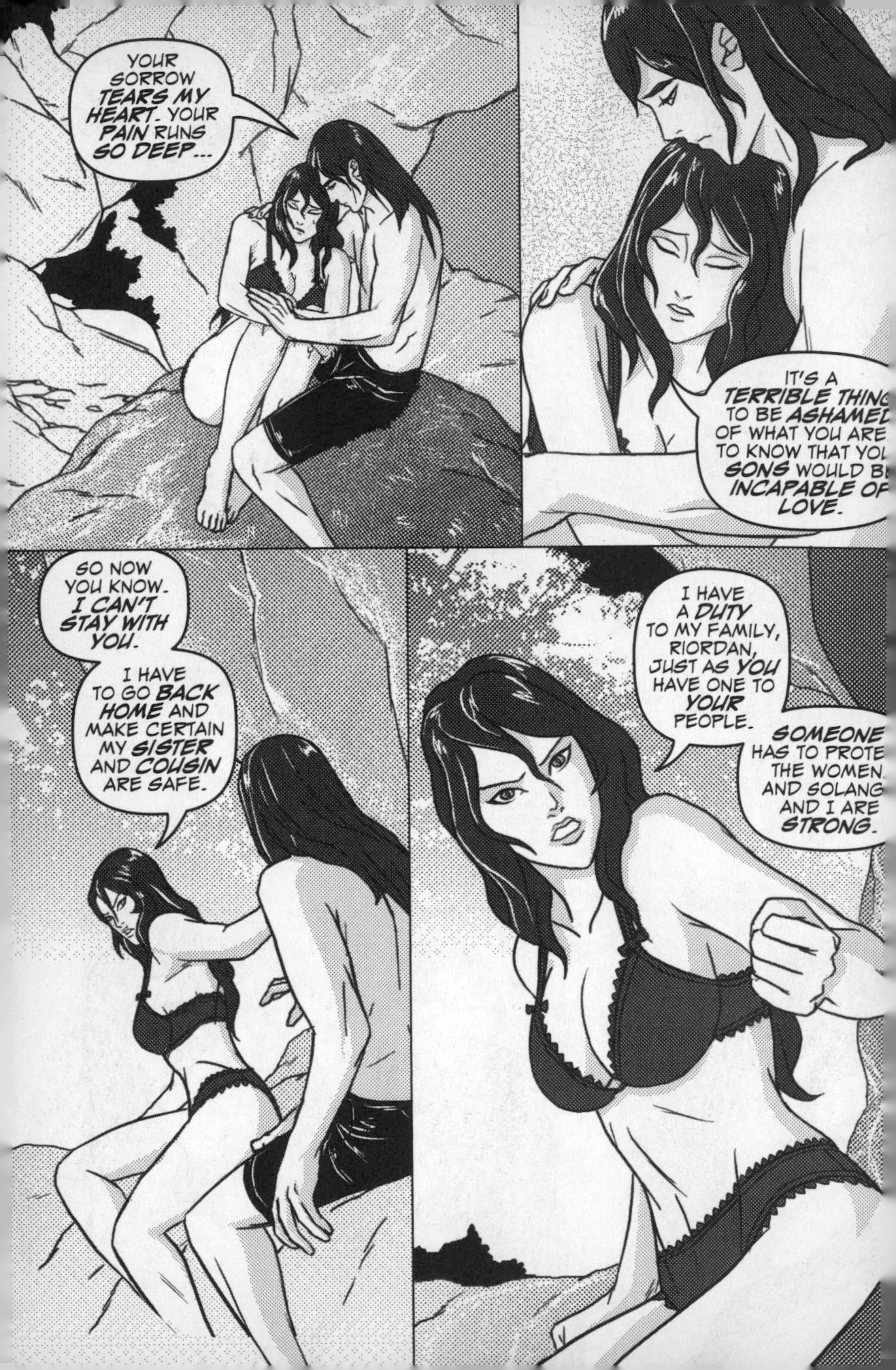
YOUR SORROW TEARS MY HEART. YOUR PAIN RUNS SO DEEP...
IT'S A TERRIBLE THING TO BE ASHAMED OF WHAT YOU ARE, TO KNOW THAT YOUR SONS WOULD BE INCAPABLE OF LOVE.
SO NOW YOU KNOW. I CAN'T STAY WITH YOU.
I HAVE TO GO BACK HOME AND MAKE CERTAIN MY SISTER AND COUSIN ARE SAFE.
I HAVE A DUTY TO MY FAMILY, RIORDAN, JUST AS YOU HAVE ONE TO YOUR PEOPLE.
SOMEONE HAS TO PROTE THE WOMEN. AND SOLANG AND I ARE STRONG.

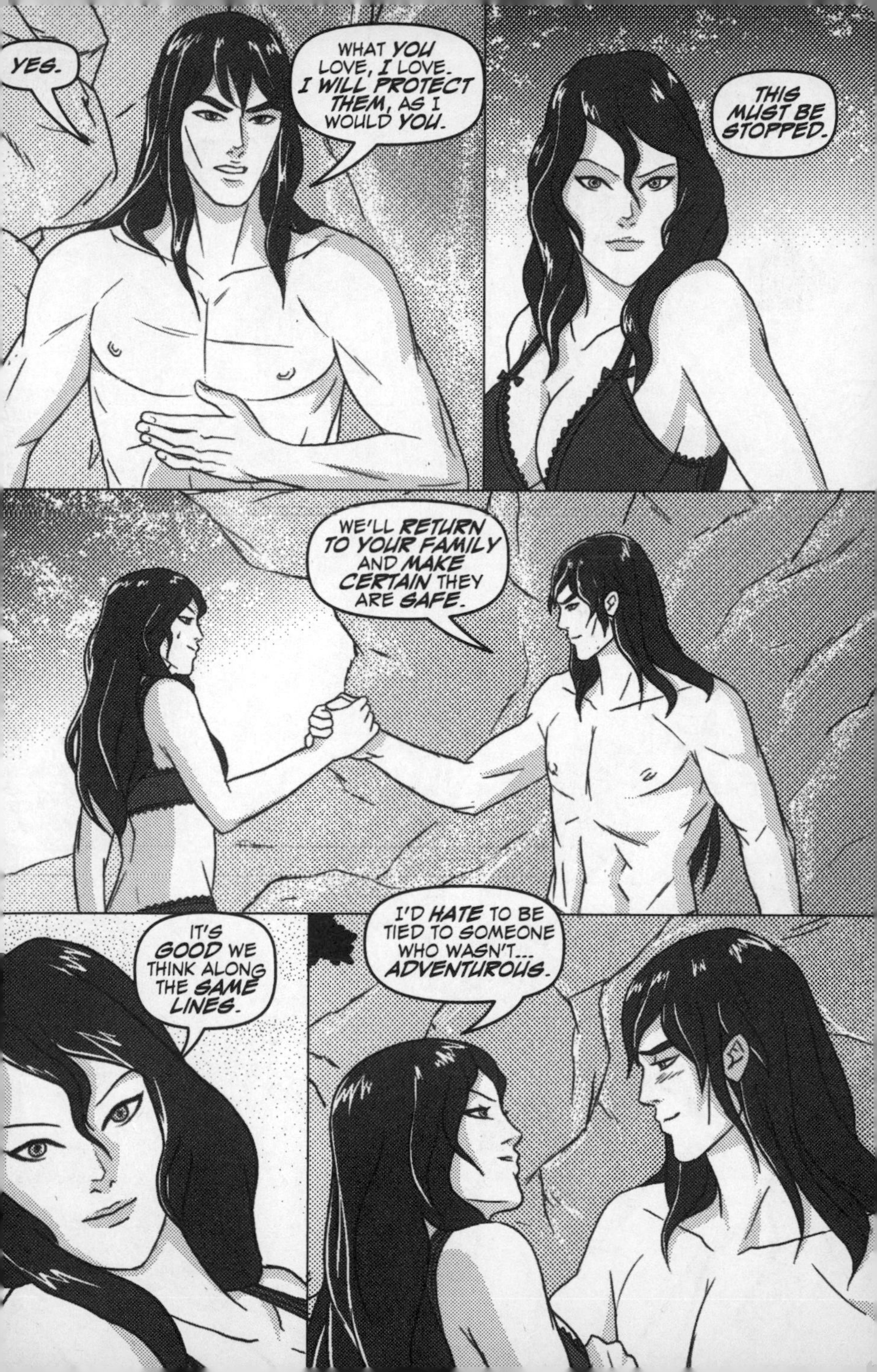
YES.
WHAT YOU LOVE, I LOVE. I WILL PROTECT THEM, AS I WOULD YOU.
THIS MUST BE STOPPED.
WE'LL RETURN TO YOUR FAMILY AND MAKE CERTAIN THEY ARE SAFE.
IT'S GOOD WE THINK ALONG THE SAME LINES.
I'D HATE TO BE TIED TO SOMEONE WHO WASN'T... ADVENTUROUS.

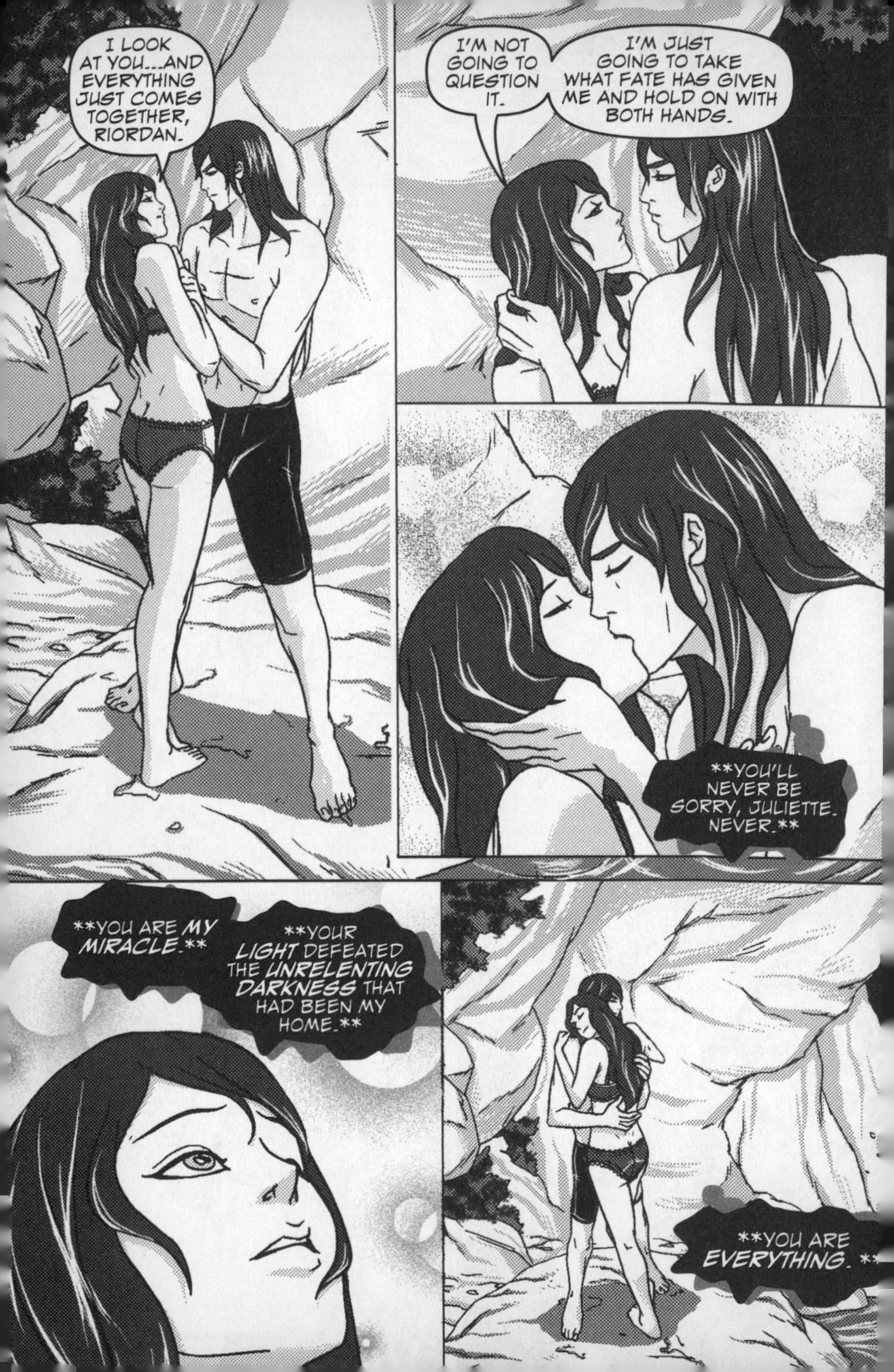
I LOOK AT YOU...AND EVERYTHING JUST COMES TOGETHER, RIORDAN.
I'M NOT GOING TO QUESTION IT.
I'M JUST GOING TO TAKE WHAT FATE HAS GIVEN ME AND HOLD ON WITH BOTH HANDS.
YOU'LL NEVER BE SORRY, JULIETTE. NEVER.
YOU ARE MY MIRACLE.
YOUR LIGHT DEFEATED THE UNRELENTING DARKNESS THAT HAD BEEN MY HOME.
YOU ARE EVERYTHING.

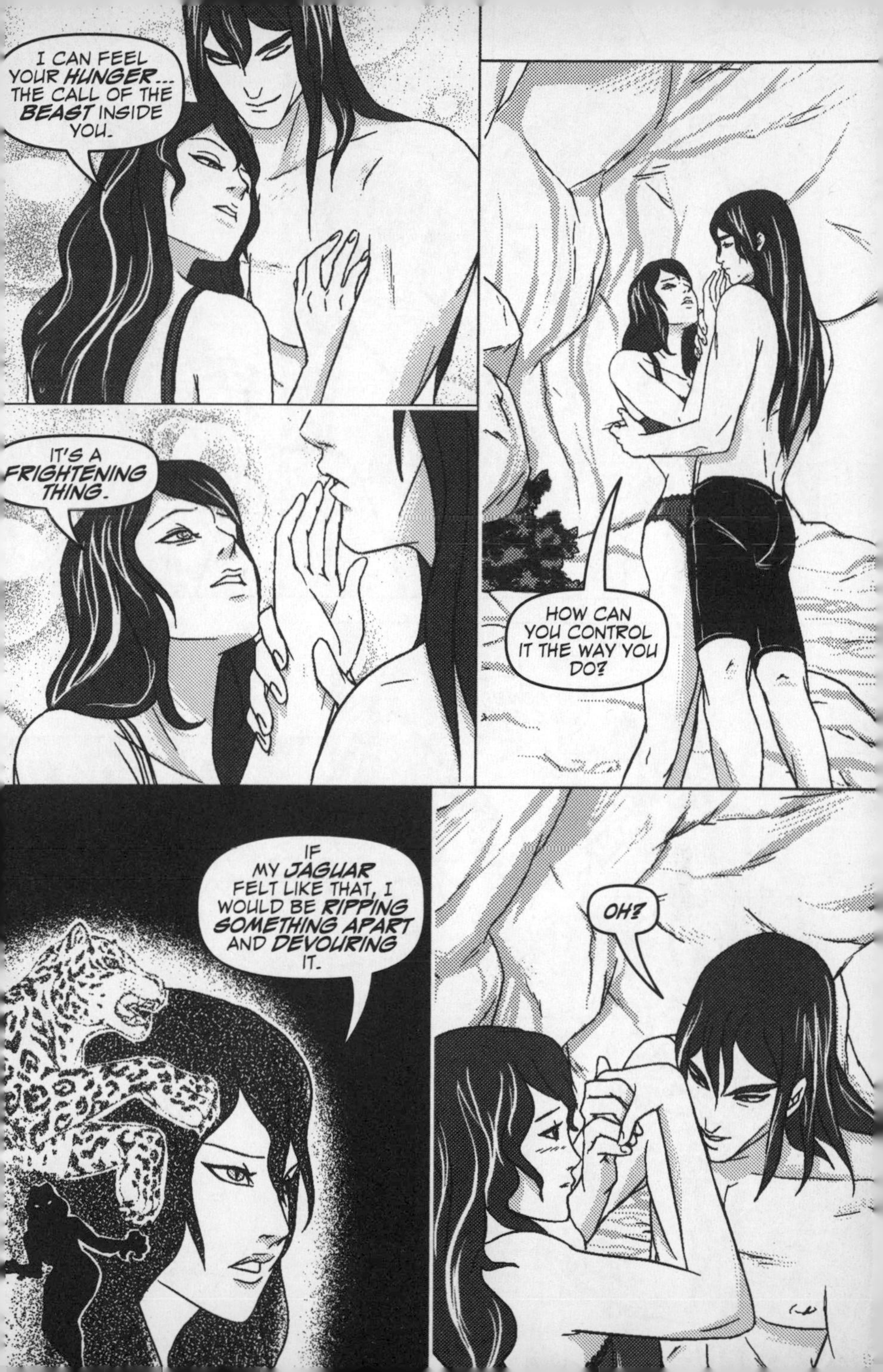
I CAN FEEL YOUR HUNGER... THE CALL OF THE BEAST INSIDE YOU.
IT'S A FRIGHTENING THING.
HOW CAN YOU CONTROL IT THE WAY YOU DO?
IF MY JAGUAR FELT LIKE THAT, I WOULD BE RIPPING SOMETHING APART AND DEVOURING IT.
OH?

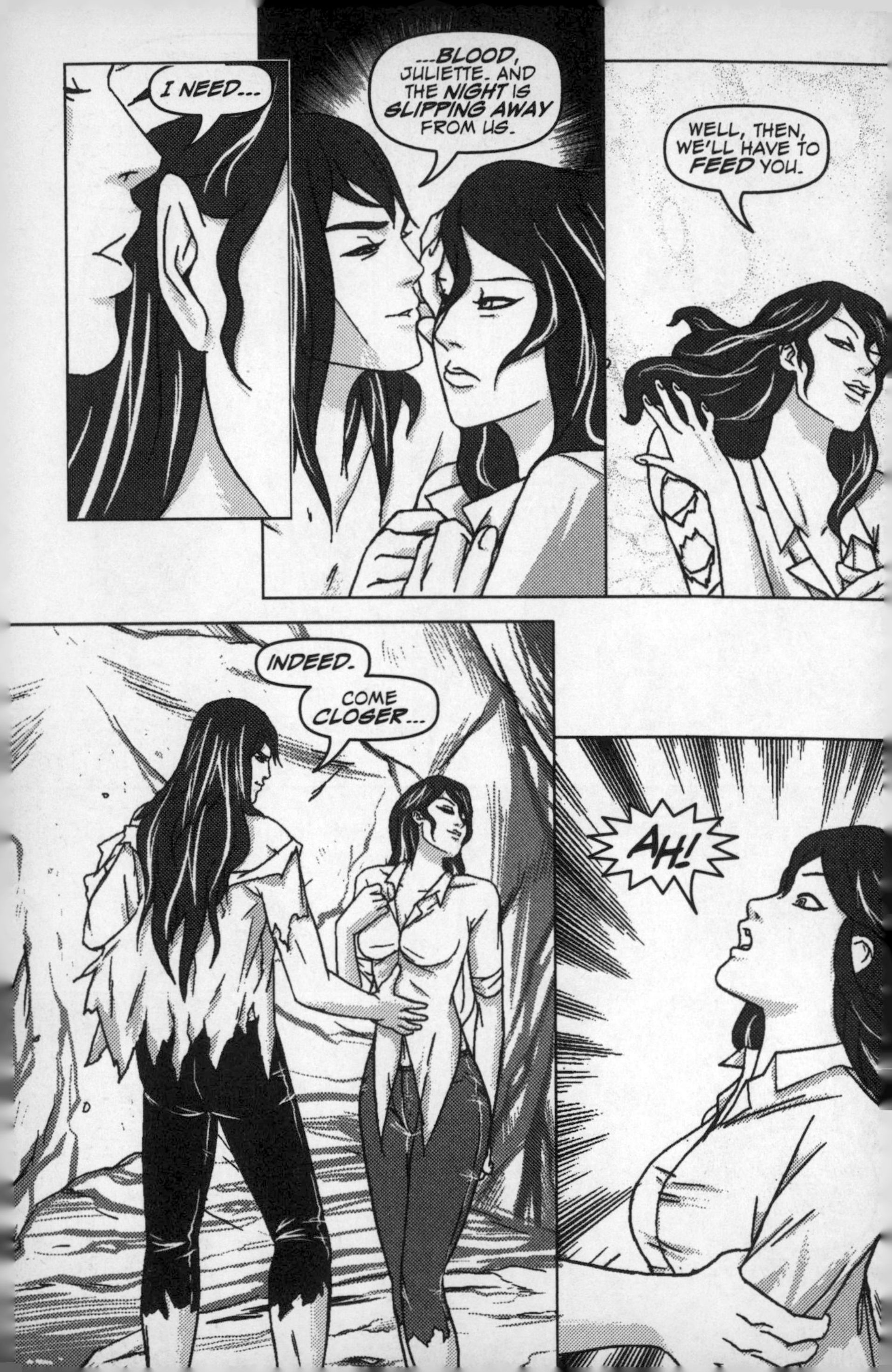
I NEED...
...BLOOD, JULIETTE. AND THE NIGHT IS SLIPPING AWAY FROM US.
WELL, THEN, WE'LL HAVE TO FEED YOU.
INDEED.
COME CLOSER...
AH!

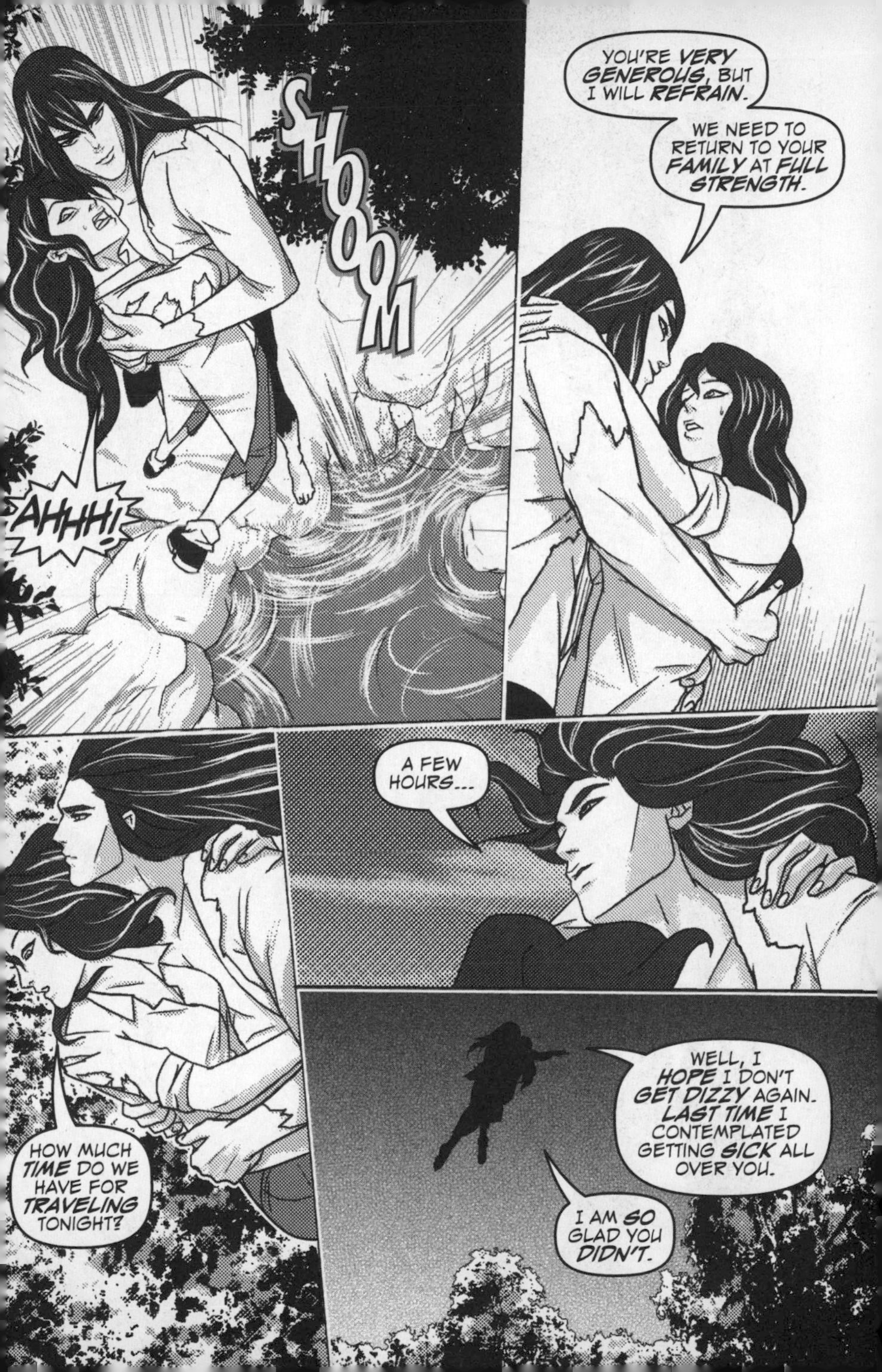
SHOOOOM
AHHH!
YOU'RE VERY GENEROUS, BUT I WILL REFRAIN.
WE NEED TO RETURN TO YOUR FAMILY AT FULL STRENGTH.
HOW MUCH TIME DO WE HAVE FOR TRAVELING TONIGHT?
A FEW HOURS...
WELL, I HOPE I DON'T GET DIZZY AGAIN. LAST TIME I CONTEMPLATED GETTING SICK ALL OVER YOU.
I AM SO GLAD YOU DIDN'T.

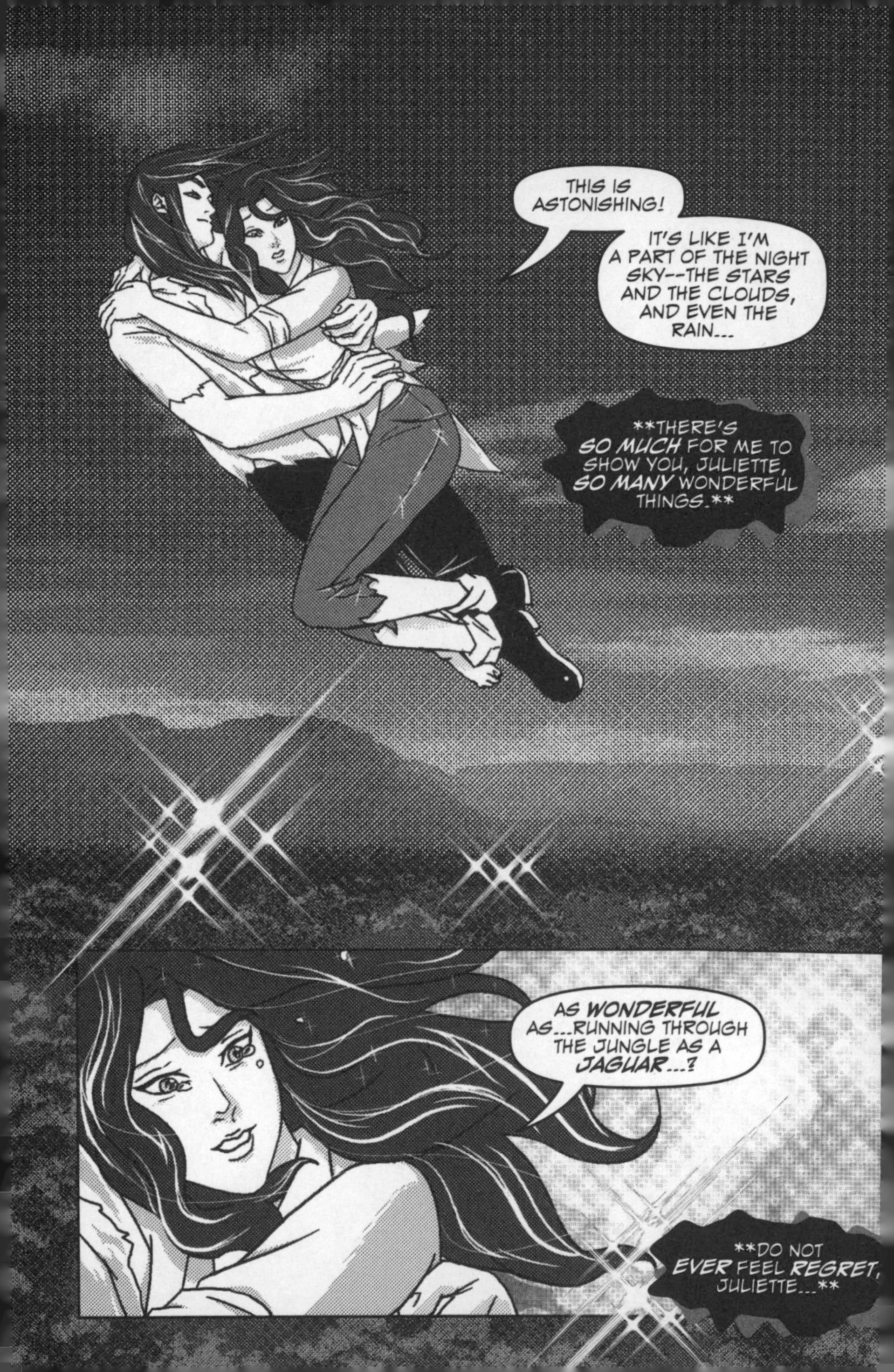
THIS IS ASTONISHING!
IT'S LIKE I'M A PART OF THE NIGHT SKY--THE STARS AND THE CLOUDS, AND EVEN THE RAIN...
THERE'S SO MUCH FOR ME TO SHOW YOU, JULIETTE, SO MANY WONDERFUL THINGS.
AS WONDERFUL AS...RUNNING THROUGH THE JUNGLE AS A JAGUAR...?
DO NOT EVER FEEL REGRET, JULIETTE...

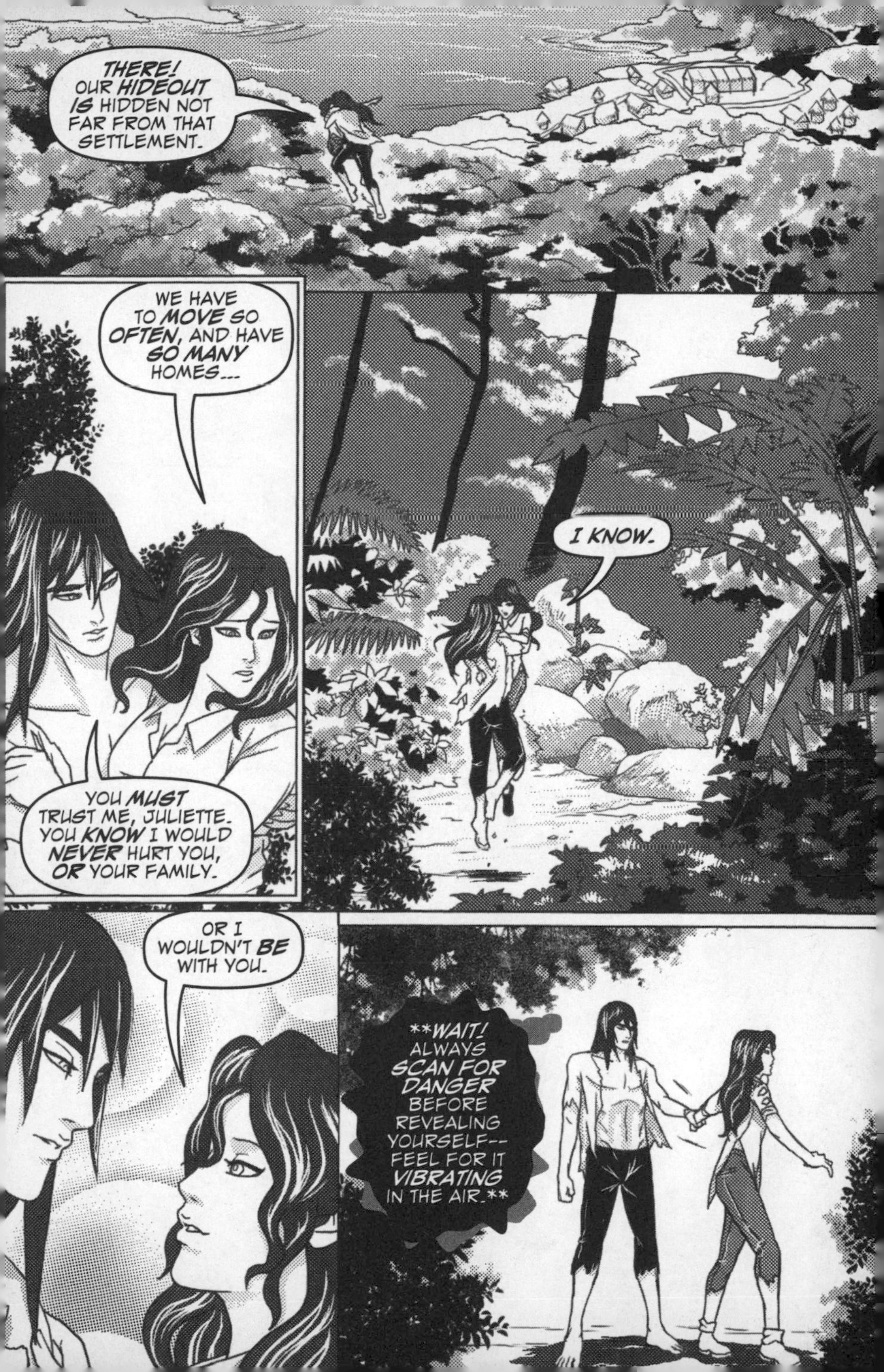
THERE! OUR HIDEOUT IS HIDDEN NOT FAR FROM THAT SETTLEMENT.
WE HAVE TO MOVE SO OFTEN, AND HAVE SO MANY HOMES...
YOU MUST TRUST ME, JULIETTE. YOU KNOW I WOULD NEVER HURT YOU, OR YOUR FAMILY.
I KNOW.
OR I WOULDN'T BE WITH YOU.
WAIT! ALWAYS SCAN FOR DANGER BEFORE REVEALING YOURSELF--FEEL FOR IT VIBRATING IN THE AIR.

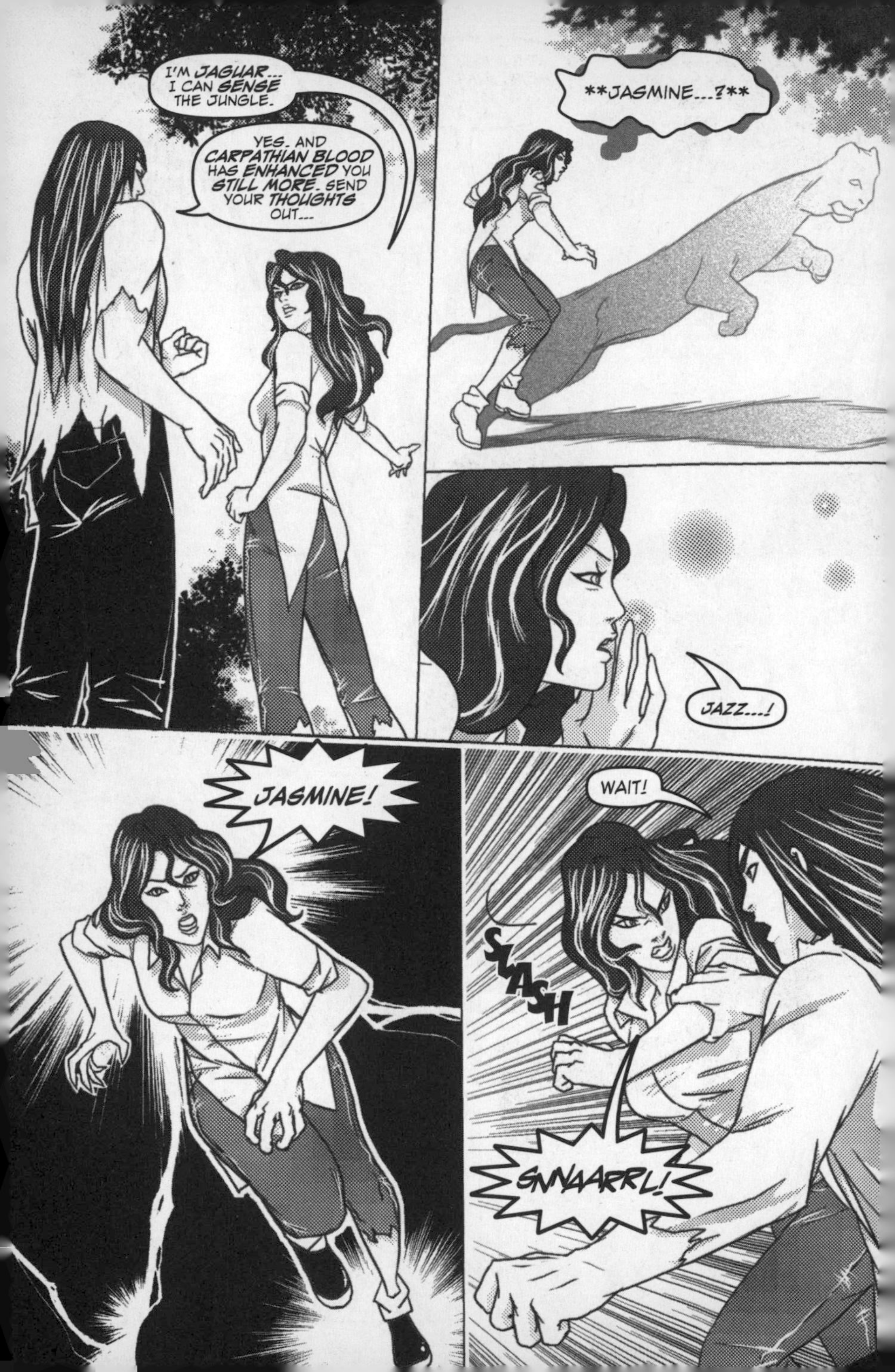

I'M JAGUAR... I CAN SENSE THE JUNGLE.
YES. AND CARPATHIAN BLOOD HAS ENHANCED YOU STILL MORE. SEND YOUR THOUGHTS OUT...
JASMINE...?
JAZZ...!
JASMINE!
WAIT!
SLASH
GNNAARRL!

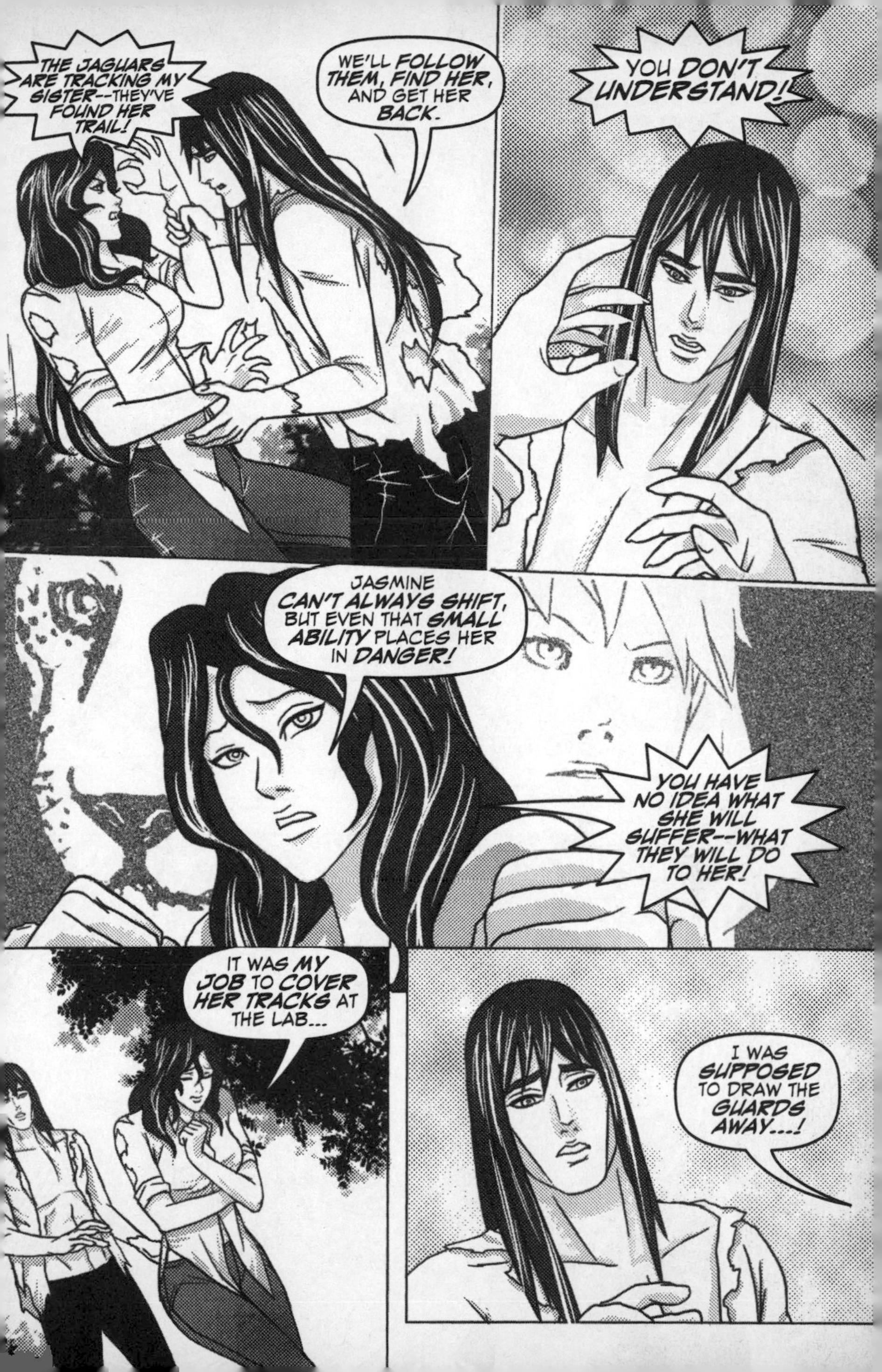
THE JAGUARS ARE TRACKING MY SISTER--THEY'VE FOUND HER TRAIL!
WE'LL FOLLOW THEM, FIND HER, AND GET HER BACK.
YOU DON'T UNDERSTAND!
JASMINE CAN'T ALWAYS SHIFT, BUT EVEN THAT SMALL ABILITY PLACES HER IN DANGER!
YOU HAVE NO IDEA WHAT SHE WILL SUFFER--WHAT THEY WILL DO TO HER!
IT WAS MY JOB TO COVER HER TRACKS AT THE LAB...
I WAS SUPPOSED TO DRAW THE GUARDS AWAY...!

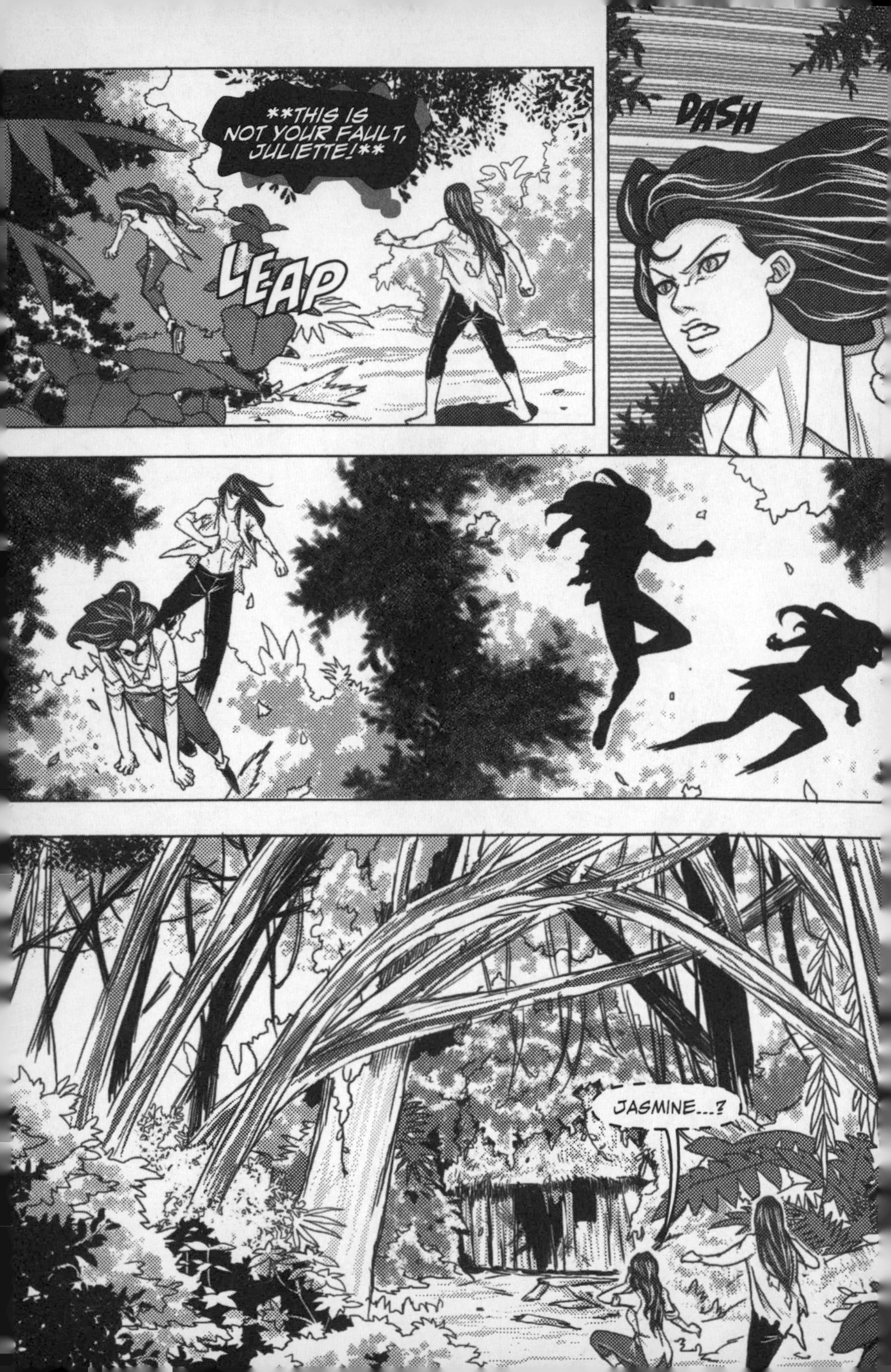
THIS IS NOT YOUR FAULT, JULIETTE!
LEAP
DASH
JASMINE...?

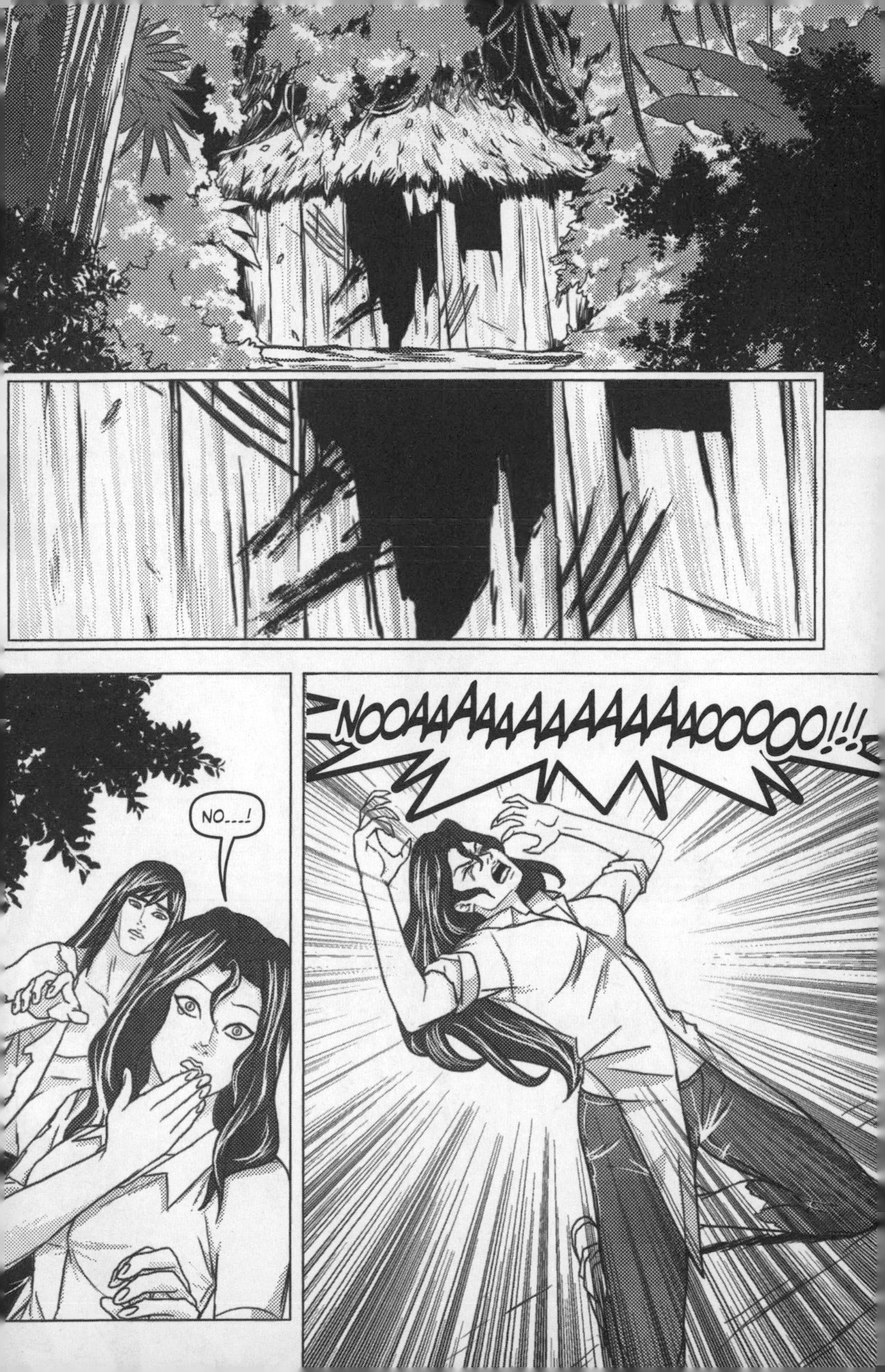
NO...!
NOOAAAAAAAAAAAAOOOOOO!!!

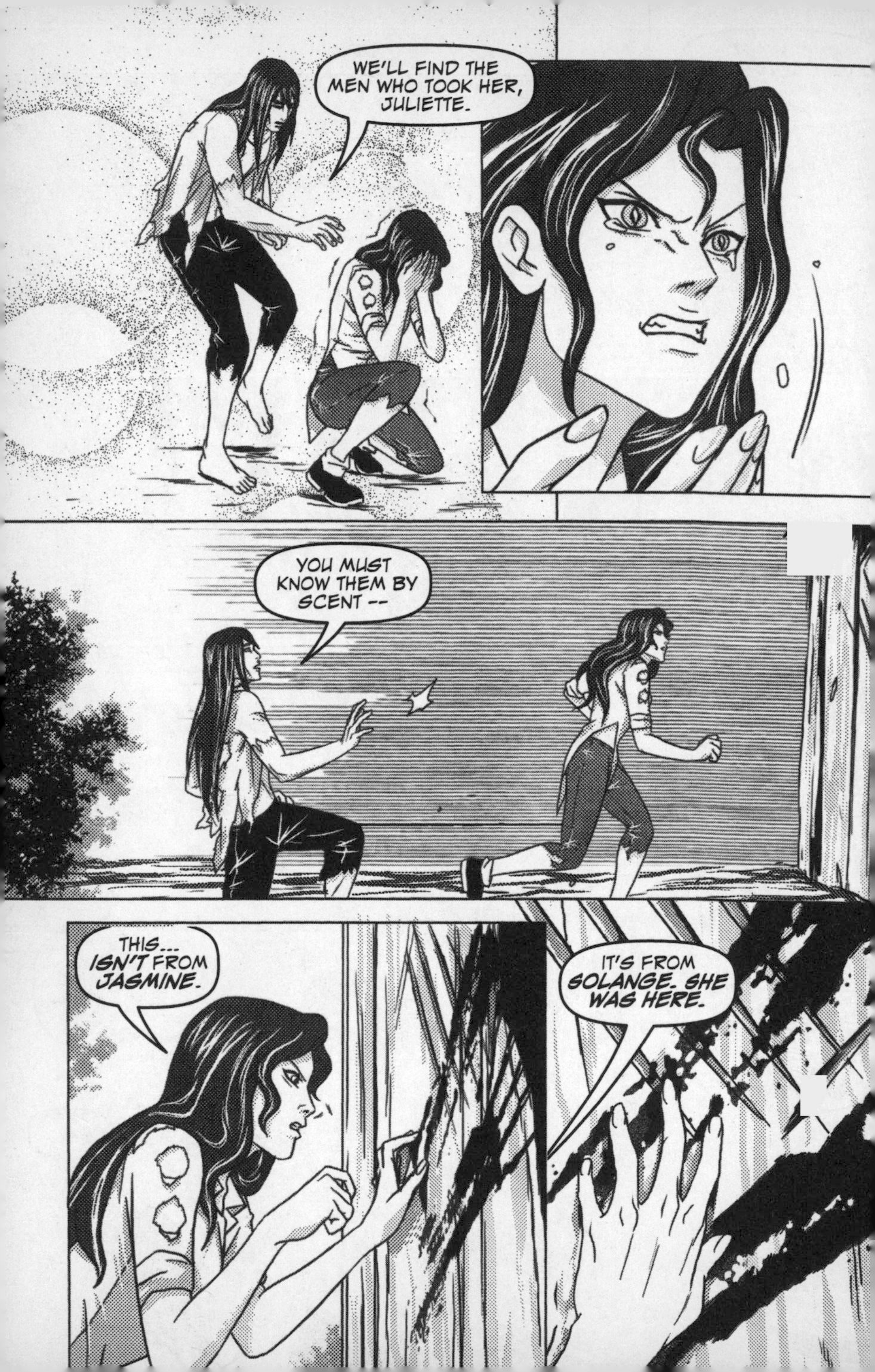
WE'LL FIND THE MEN WHO TOOK HER, JULIETTE.
YOU MUST KNOW THEM BY SCENT --
THIS... *ISN'T* FROM *JASMINE*.
IT'S FROM *SOLANGE. SHE WAS HERE.*

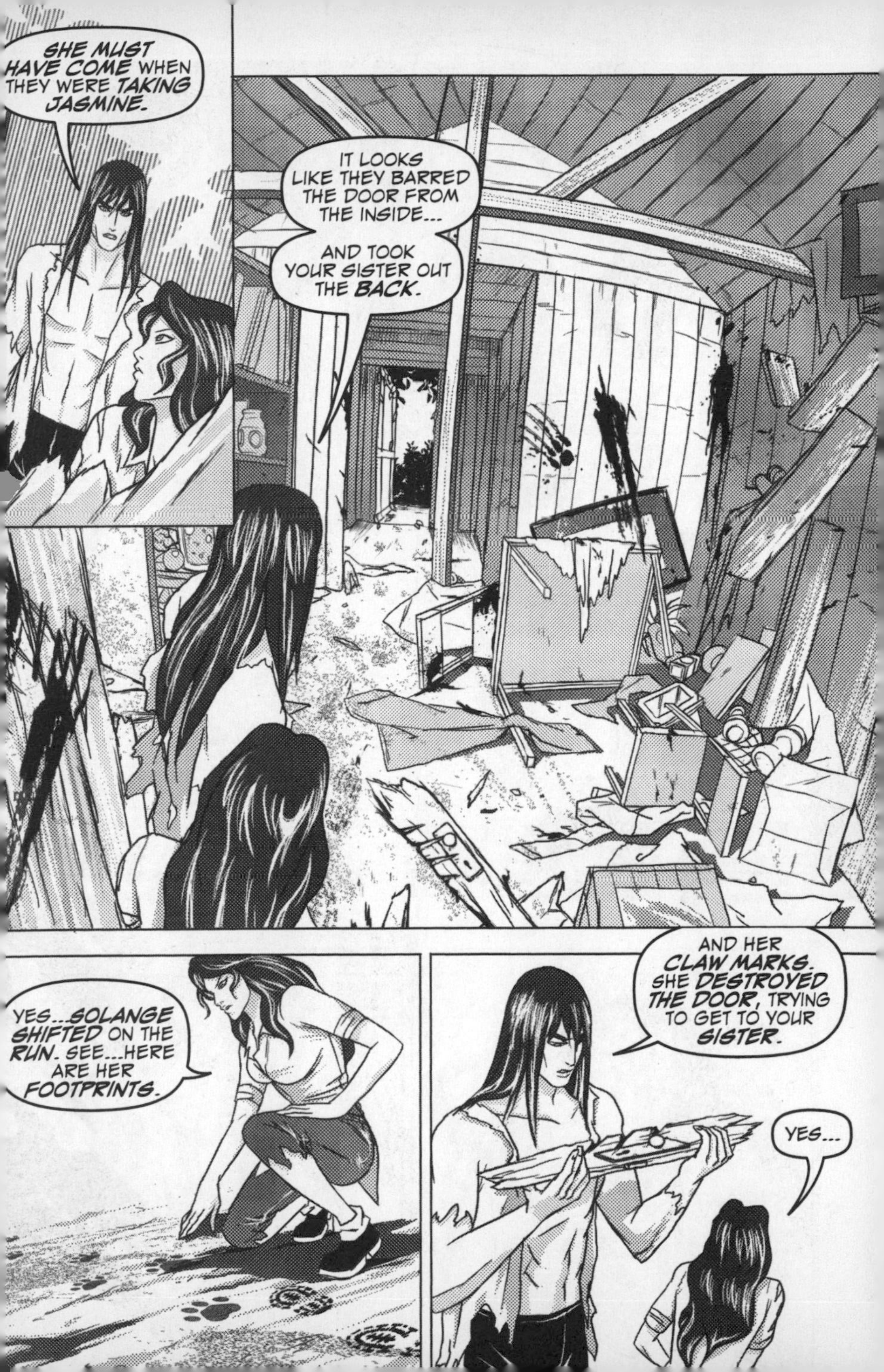
SHE MUST HAVE COME WHEN THEY WERE TAKING JASMINE.
IT LOOKS LIKE THEY BARRED THE DOOR FROM THE INSIDE...
AND TOOK YOUR SISTER OUT THE BACK.
YES...SOLANGE SHIFTED ON THE RUN. SEE...HERE ARE HER FOOTPRINTS.
AND HER CLAW MARKS. SHE DESTROYED THE DOOR, TRYING TO GET TO YOUR SISTER.
YES...

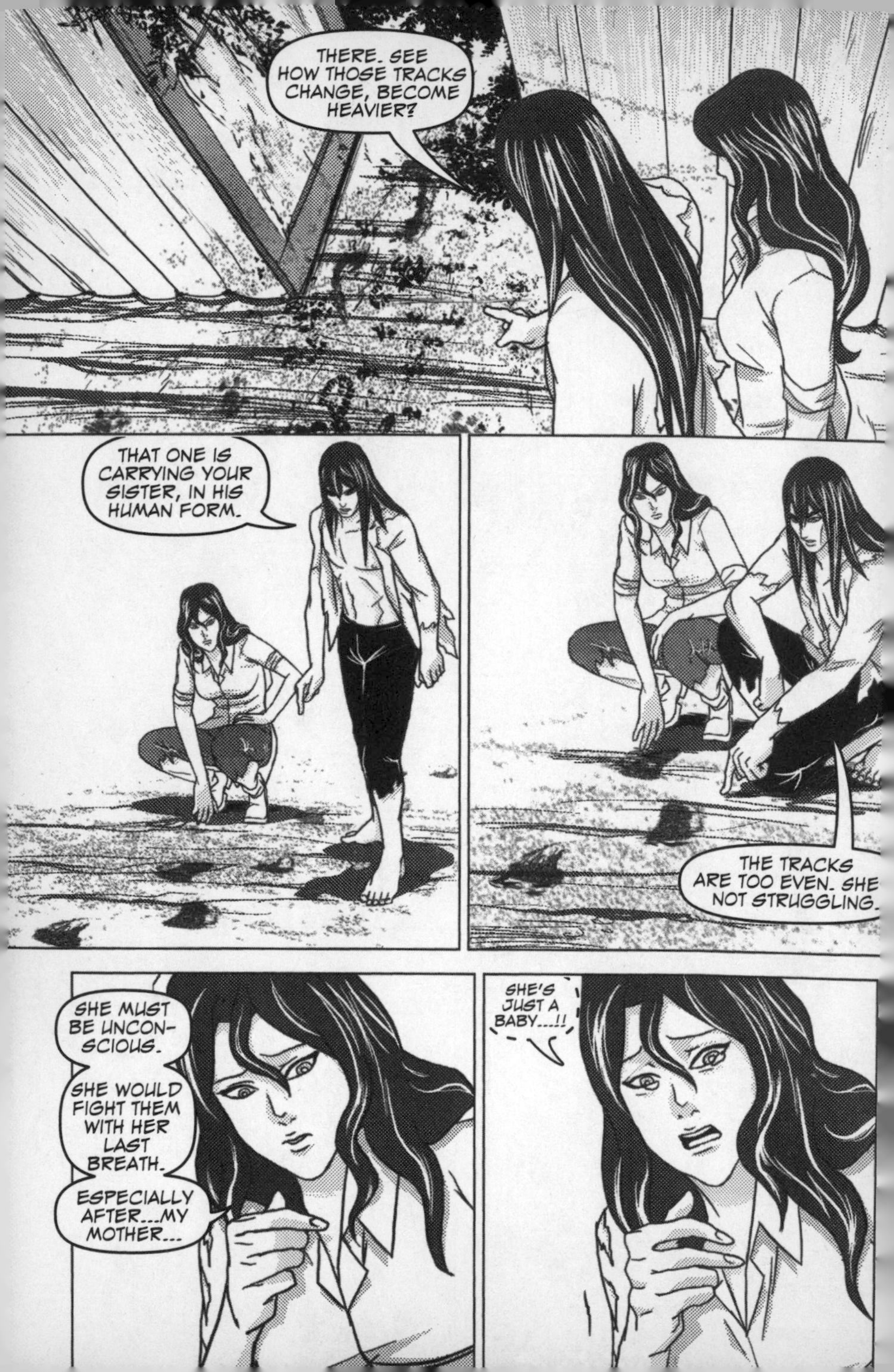

THERE. SEE HOW THOSE TRACKS CHANGE, BECOME HEAVIER?
THAT ONE IS CARRYING YOUR SISTER, IN HIS HUMAN FORM.
THE TRACKS ARE TOO EVEN. SHE NOT STRUGGLING.
SHE MUST BE UNCON-SCIOUS.
SHE WOULD FIGHT THEM WITH HER LAST BREATH.
ESPECIALLY AFTER...MY MOTHER...
SHE'S JUST A BABY...!!

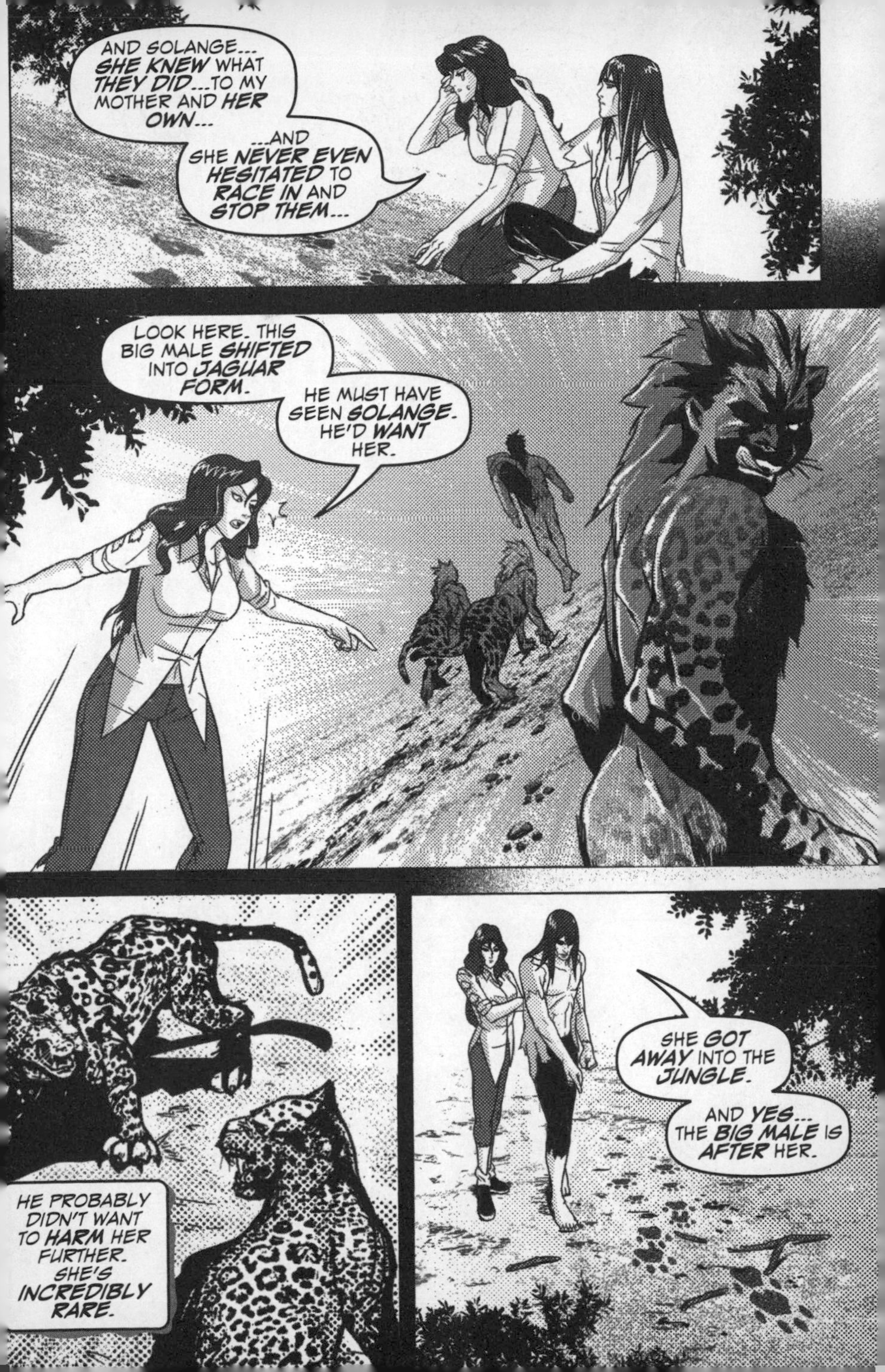
AND SOLANGE... SHE KNEW WHAT THEY DID...TO MY MOTHER AND HER OWN...
...AND SHE NEVER EVEN HESITATED TO RACE IN AND STOP THEM...
LOOK HERE. THIS BIG MALE SHIFTED INTO JAGUAR FORM.
HE MUST HAVE SEEN SOLANGE. HE'D WANT HER.
HE PROBABLY DIDN'T WANT TO HARM HER FURTHER. SHE'S INCREDIBLY RARE.
SHE GOT AWAY INTO THE JUNGLE.
AND YES... THE BIG MALE IS AFTER HER.

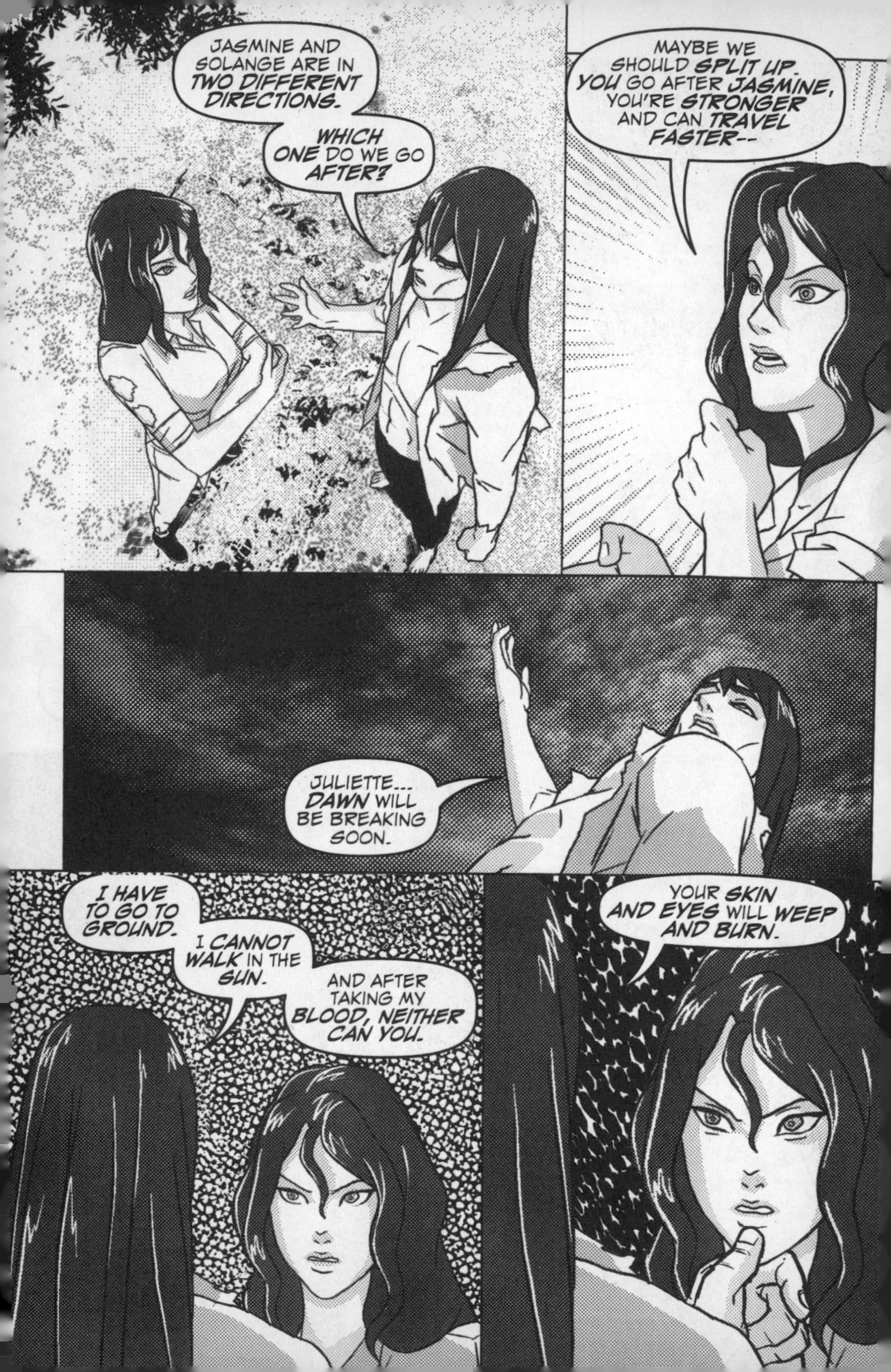
JASMINE AND SOLANGE ARE IN TWO DIFFERENT DIRECTIONS.
WHICH ONE DO WE GO AFTER?
MAYBE WE SHOULD SPLIT UP. YOU GO AFTER JASMINE, YOU'RE STRONGER AND CAN TRAVEL FASTER--
JULIETTE... DAWN WILL BE BREAKING SOON.
I HAVE TO GO TO GROUND.
I CANNOT WALK IN THE SUN.
AND AFTER TAKING MY BLOOD, NEITHER CAN YOU.
YOUR SKIN AND EYES WILL WEEP AND BURN.

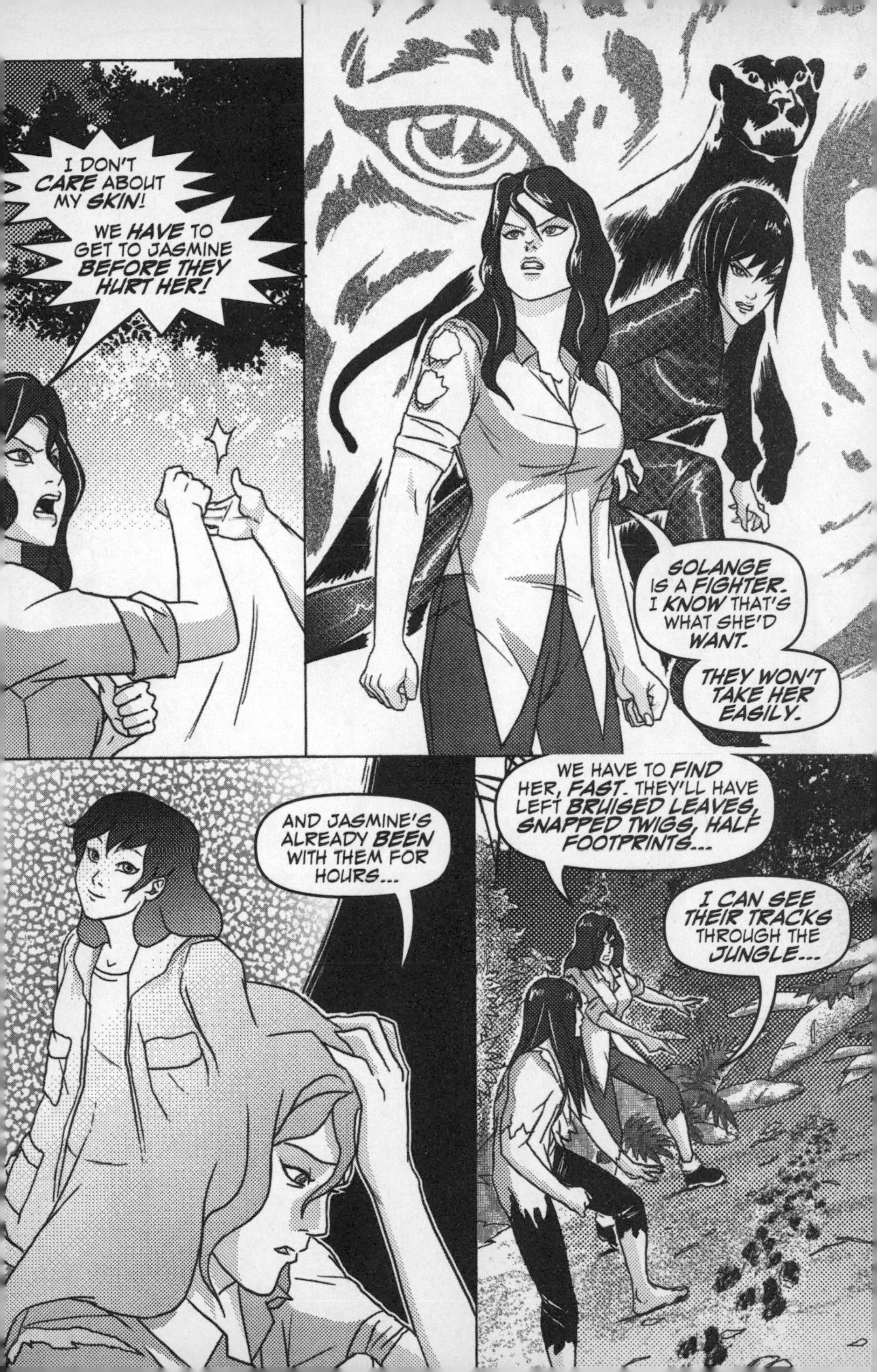
I DON'T CARE ABOUT MY SKIN!
WE HAVE TO GET TO JASMINE BEFORE THEY HURT HER!
SOLANGE IS A FIGHTER. I KNOW THAT'S WHAT SHE'D WANT.
THEY WON'T TAKE HER EASILY.
AND JASMINE'S ALREADY BEEN WITH THEM FOR HOURS...
WE HAVE TO FIND HER, FAST. THEY'LL HAVE LEFT BRUISED LEAVES, SNAPPED TWIGS, HALF FOOTPRINTS...
I CAN SEE THEIR TRACKS THROUGH THE JUNGLE...

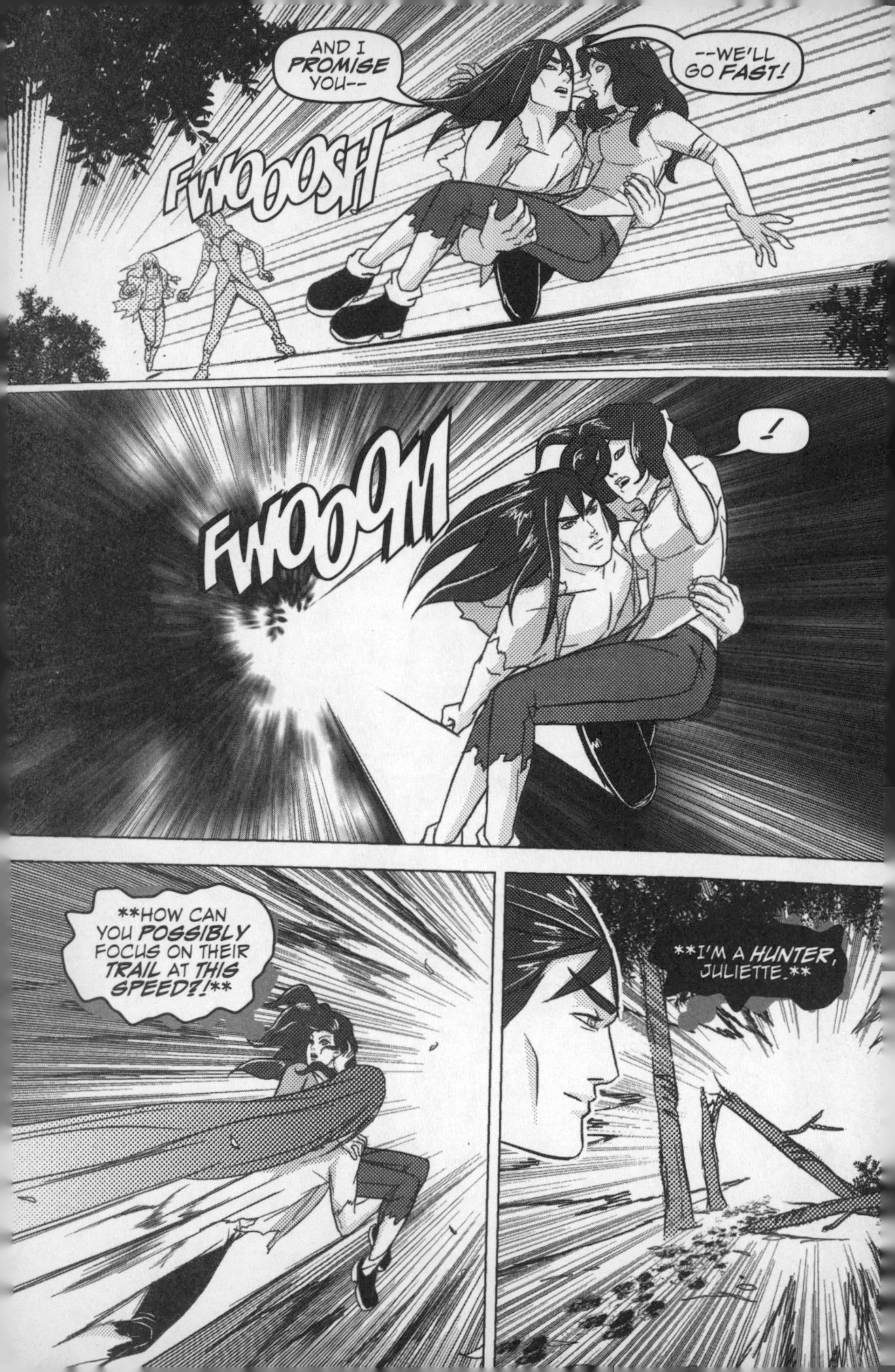
AND I PROMISE YOU--
--WE'LL GO FAST!
FWOOOSH
FWOOOM
!
HOW CAN YOU POSSIBLY FOCUS ON THEIR TRAIL AT THIS SPEED?!
I'M A HUNTER, JULIETTE.

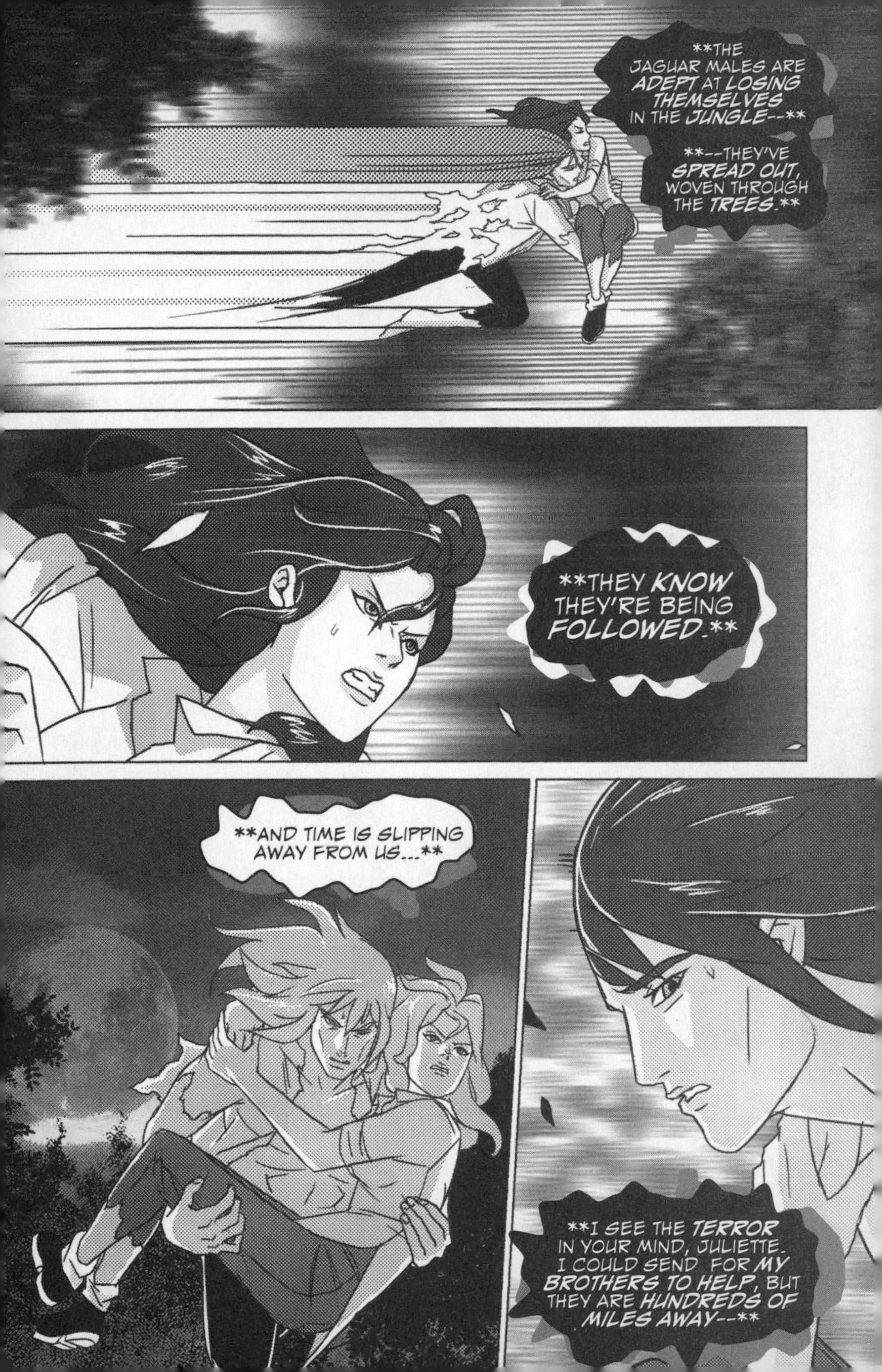
THE JAGUAR MALES ARE ADEPT AT LOSING THEMSELVES IN THE JUNGLE--
--THEY'VE SPREAD OUT, WOVEN THROUGH THE TREES.
THEY KNOW THEY'RE BEING FOLLOWED.
AND TIME IS SLIPPING AWAY FROM US...
I SEE THE TERROR IN YOUR MIND, JULIETTE. I COULD SEND FOR MY BROTHERS TO HELP, BUT THEY ARE HUNDREDS OF MILES AWAY--

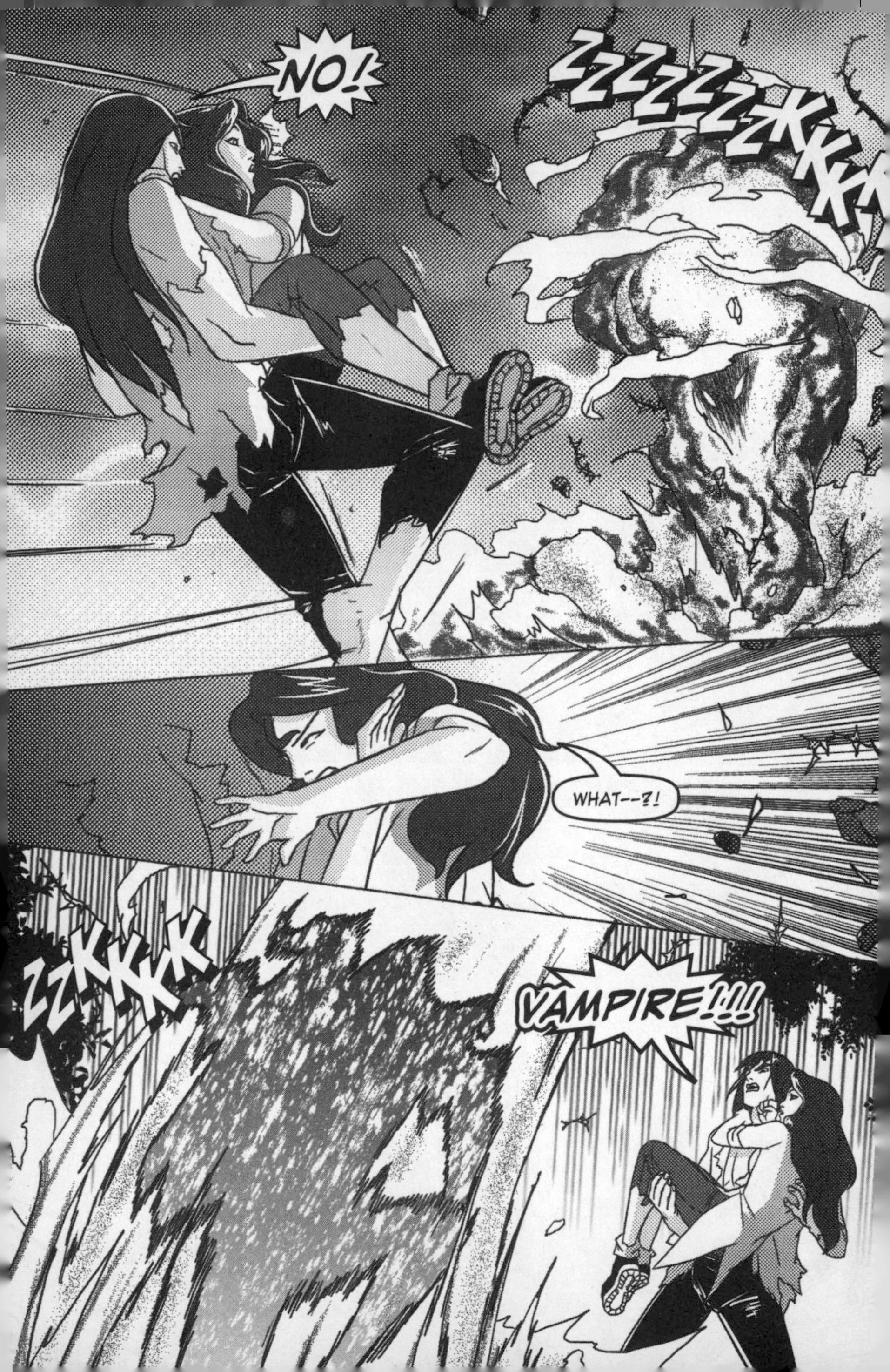
NO!
ZZZZZZZKKKK
WHAT--?!
ZZKKKK
VAMPIRE!!!!

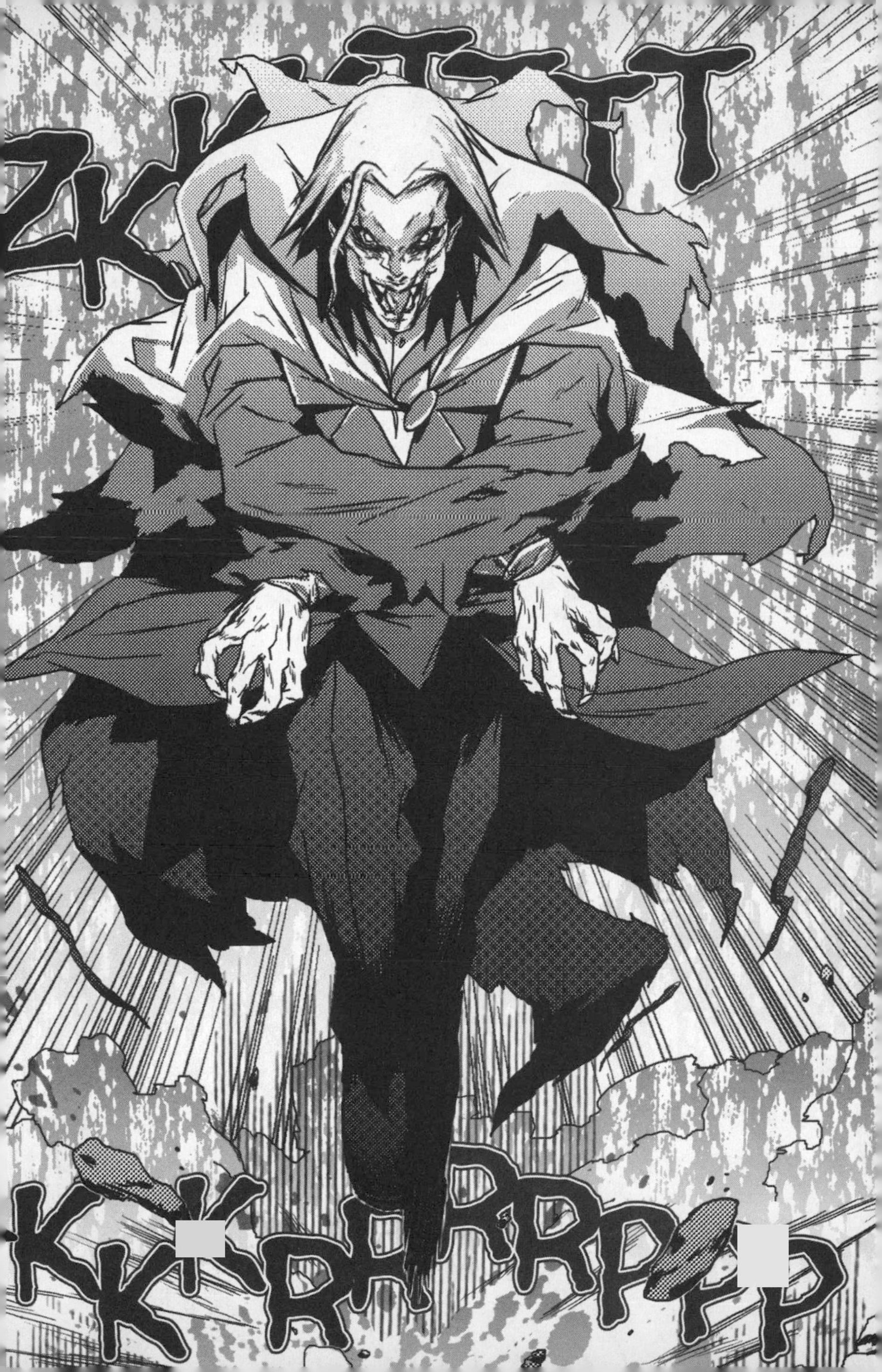

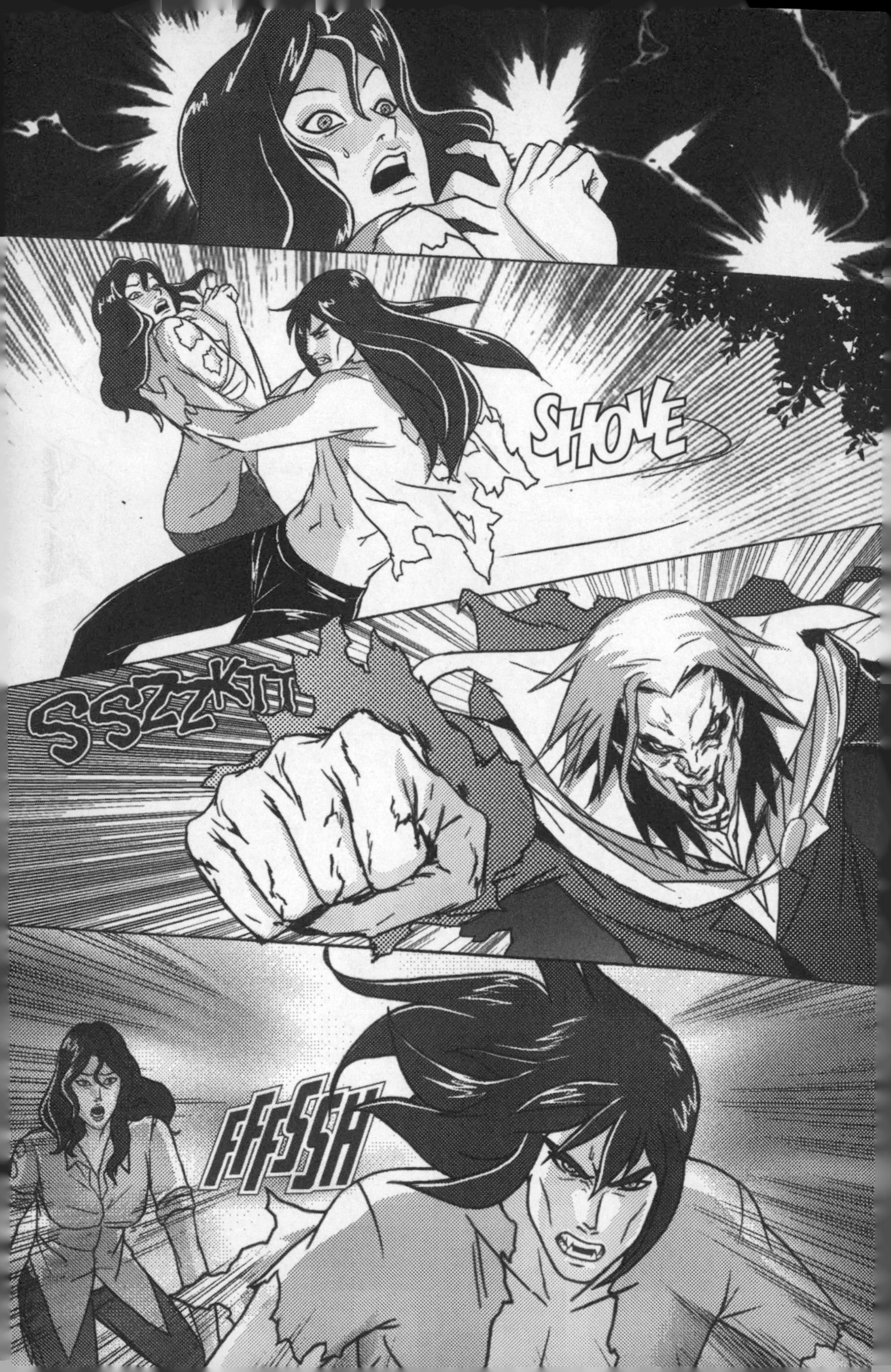
SHOVE
SSZZKTT
FFSSH

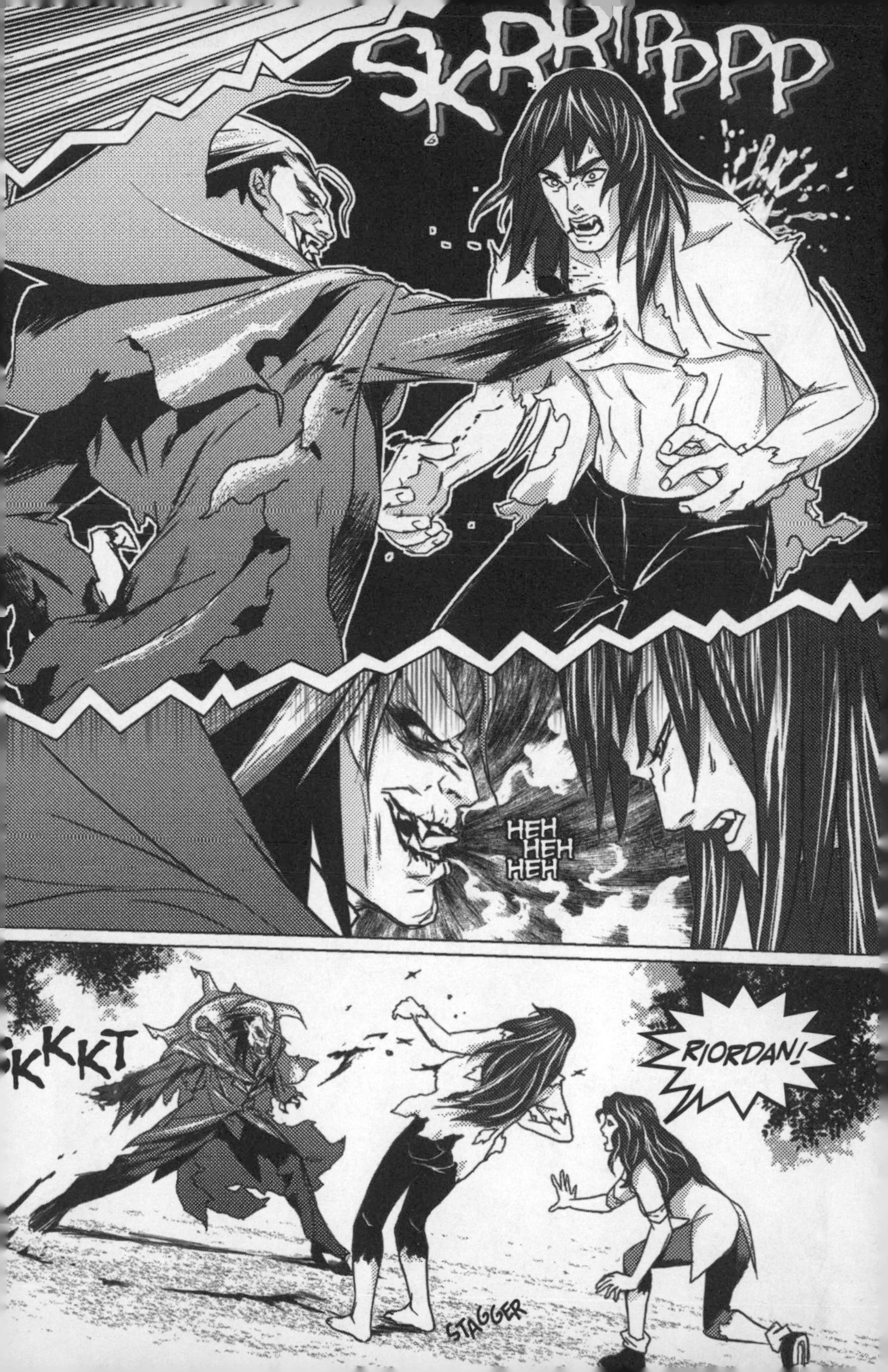
SKRRRIPPPP
HEH
HEH
HEH
KKKT
RIORDAN!
STAGGER

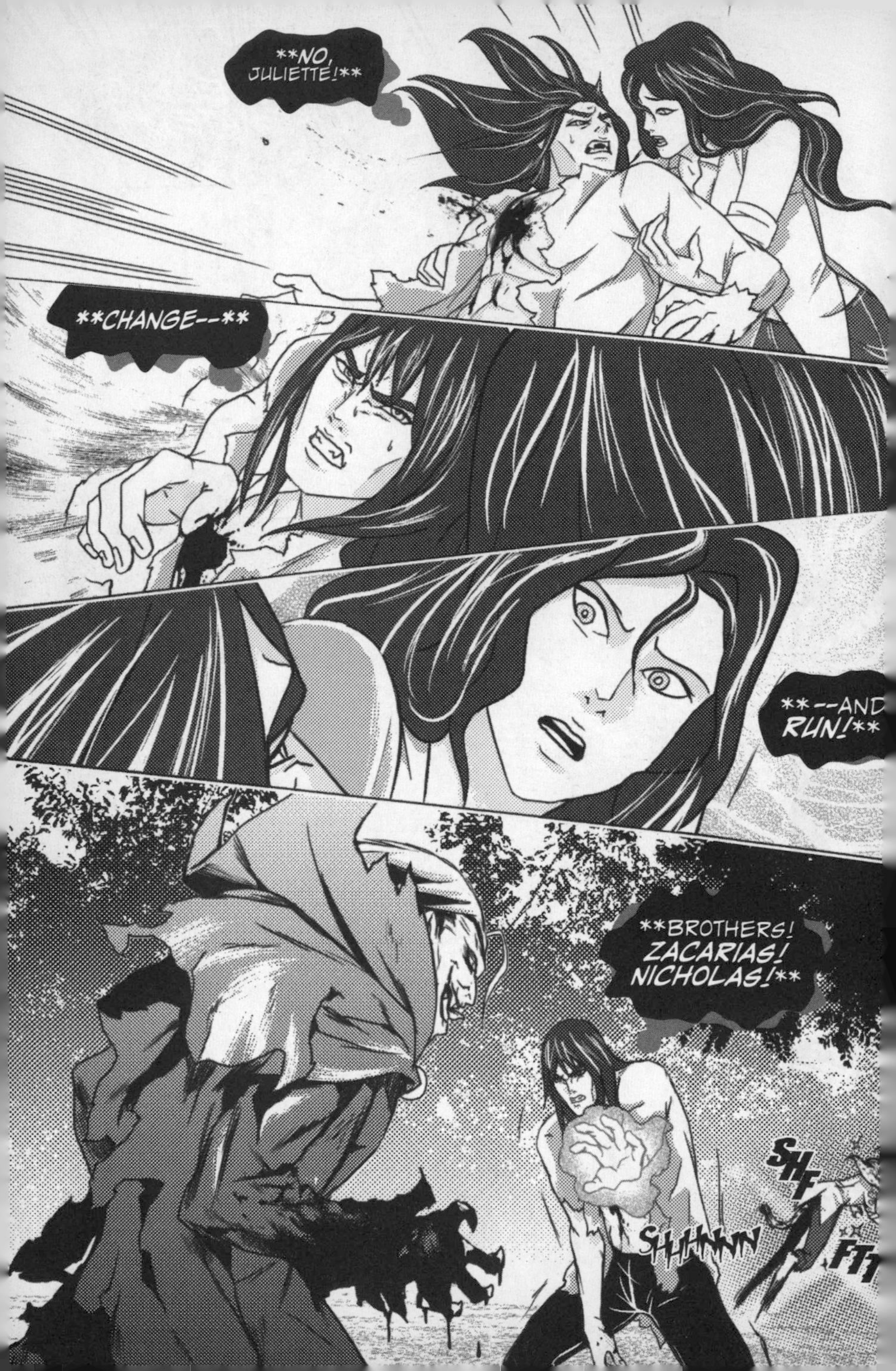
NO, JULIETTE!
CHANGE--
--AND RUN!
BROTHERS! ZACARIAS! NICHOLAS!
SHF
SHHHNN
FTT

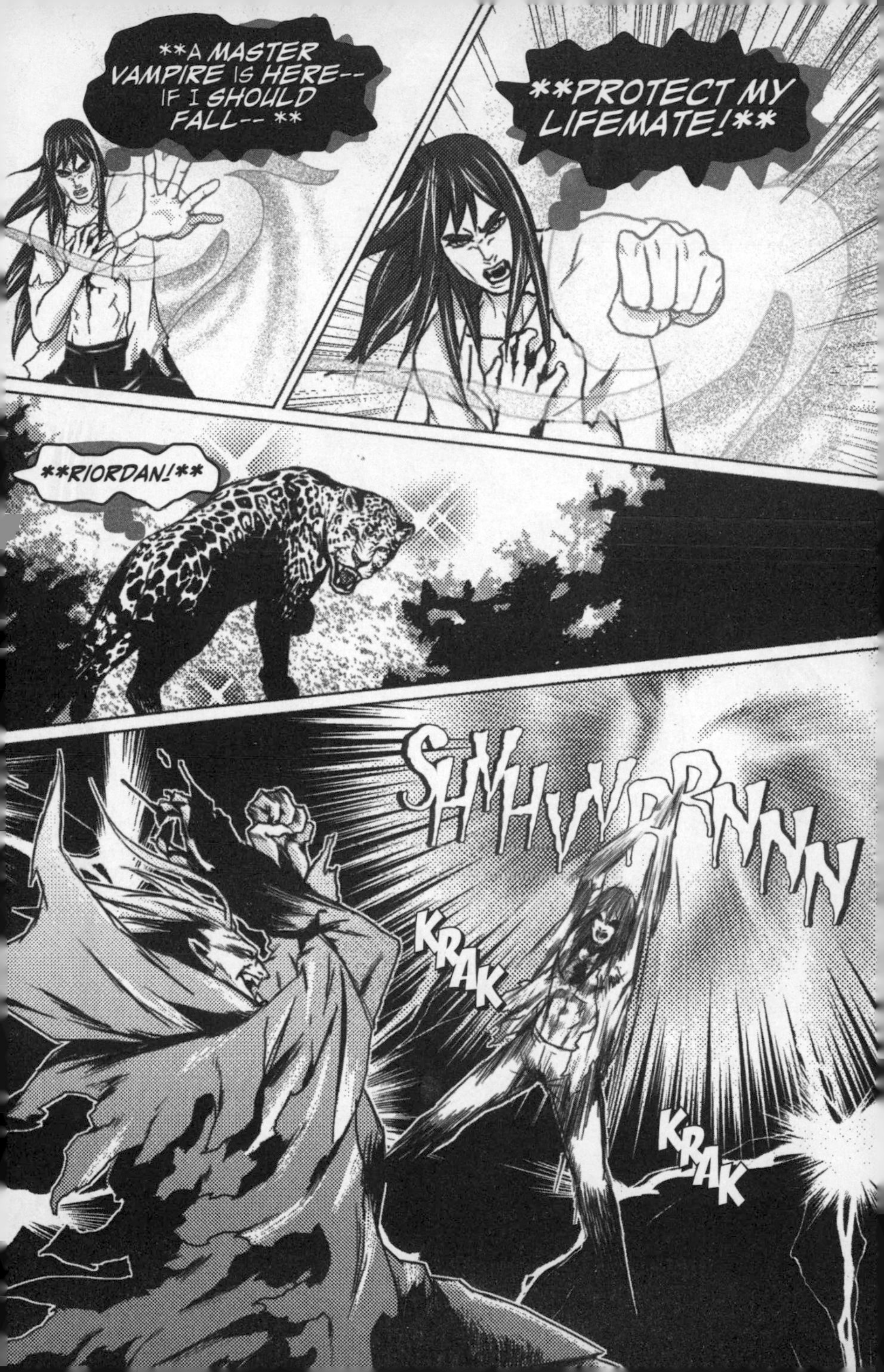
**A MASTER VAMPIRE IS HERE-- IF I SHOULD FALL-- **
PROTECT MY LIFEMATE!
RIORDAN!
SHHVVRNNNN
KRAK
KRAK

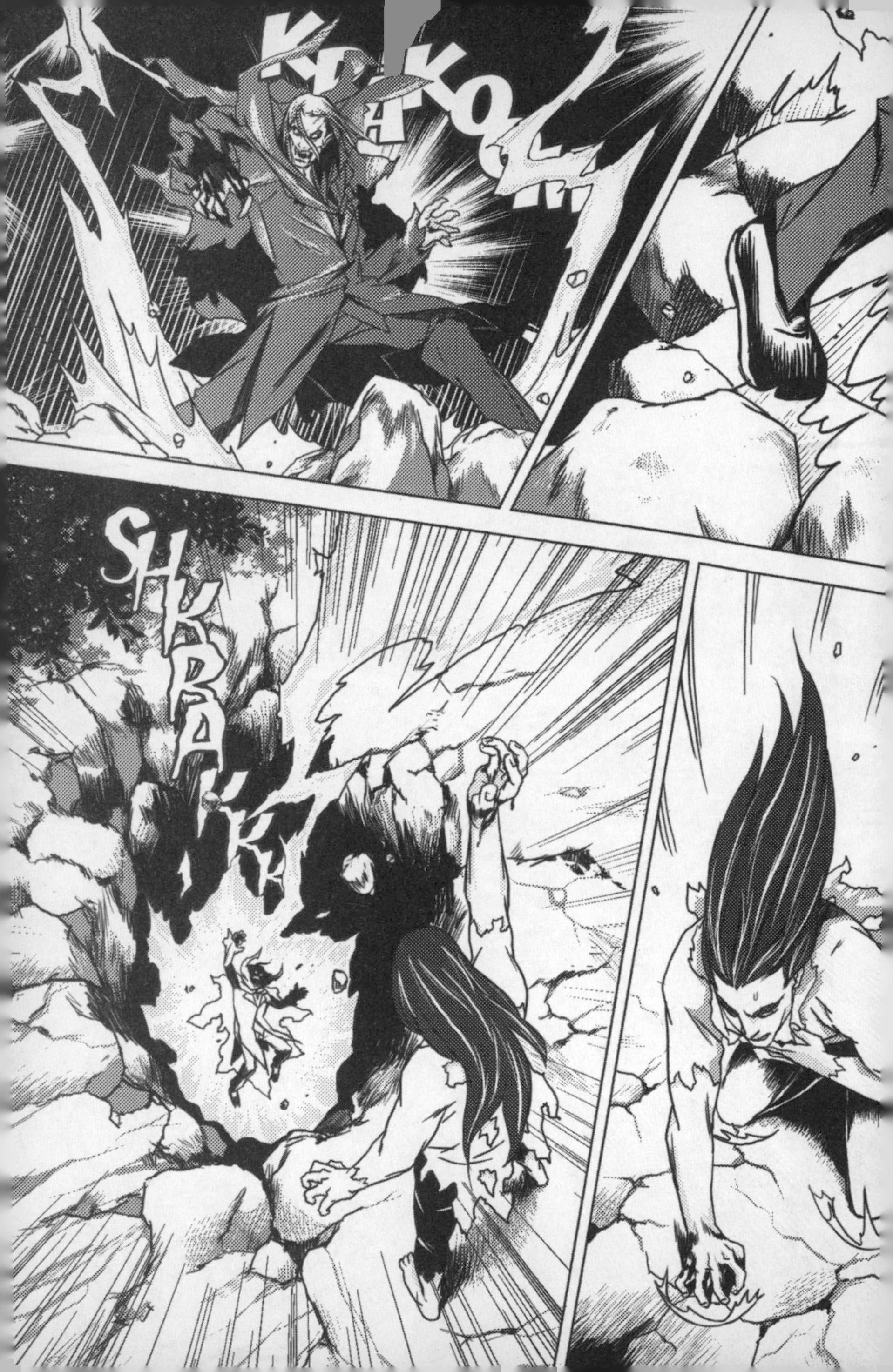
SHKRAKK

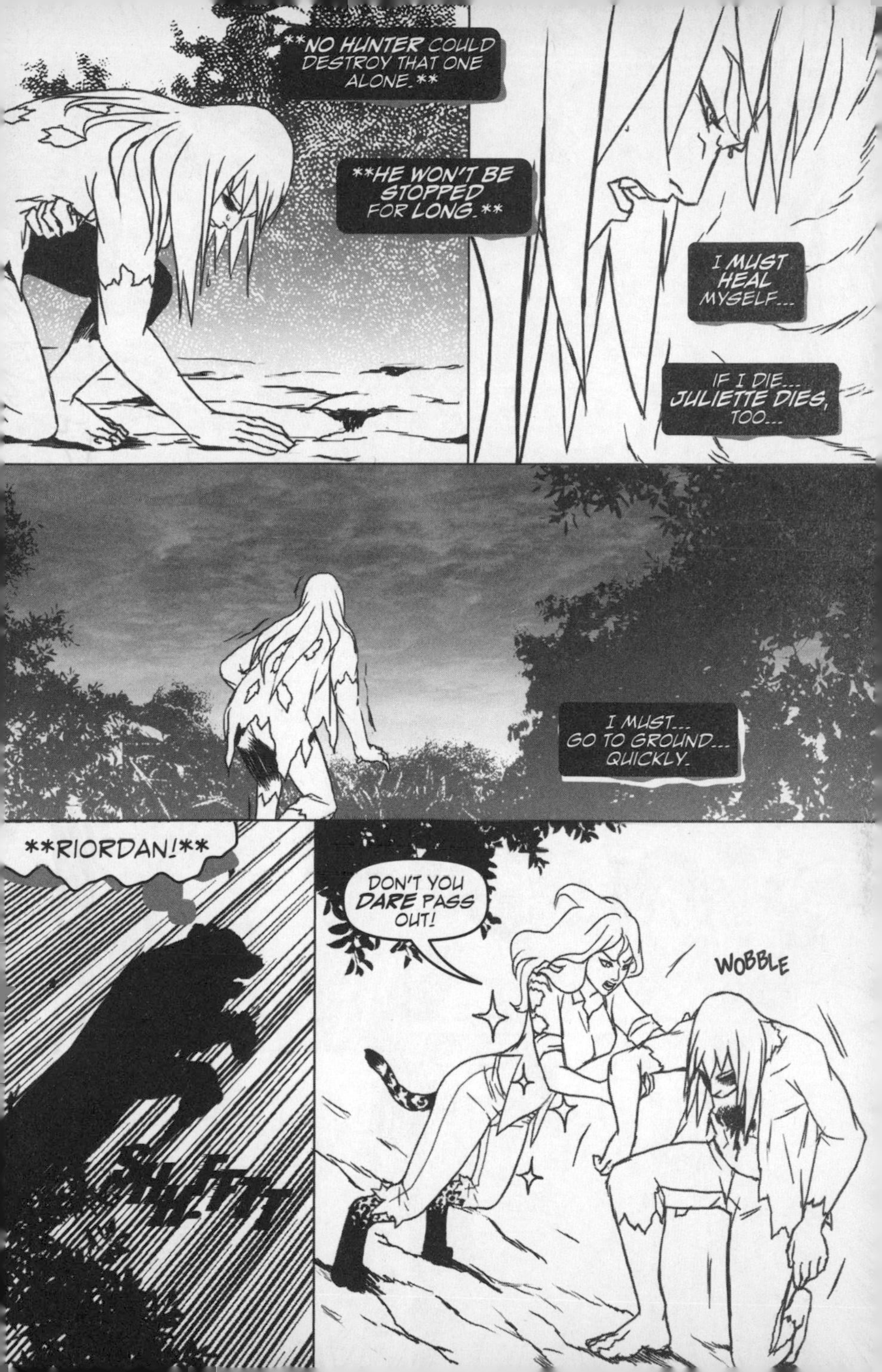
NO HUNTER COULD DESTROY THAT ONE ALONE.
HE WON'T BE STOPPED FOR LONG.
I MUST HEAL MYSELF...
IF I DIE... JULIETTE DIES, TOO...
I MUST... GO TO GROUND... QUICKLY.
RIORDAN!
DON'T YOU DARE PASS OUT!
WOBBLE

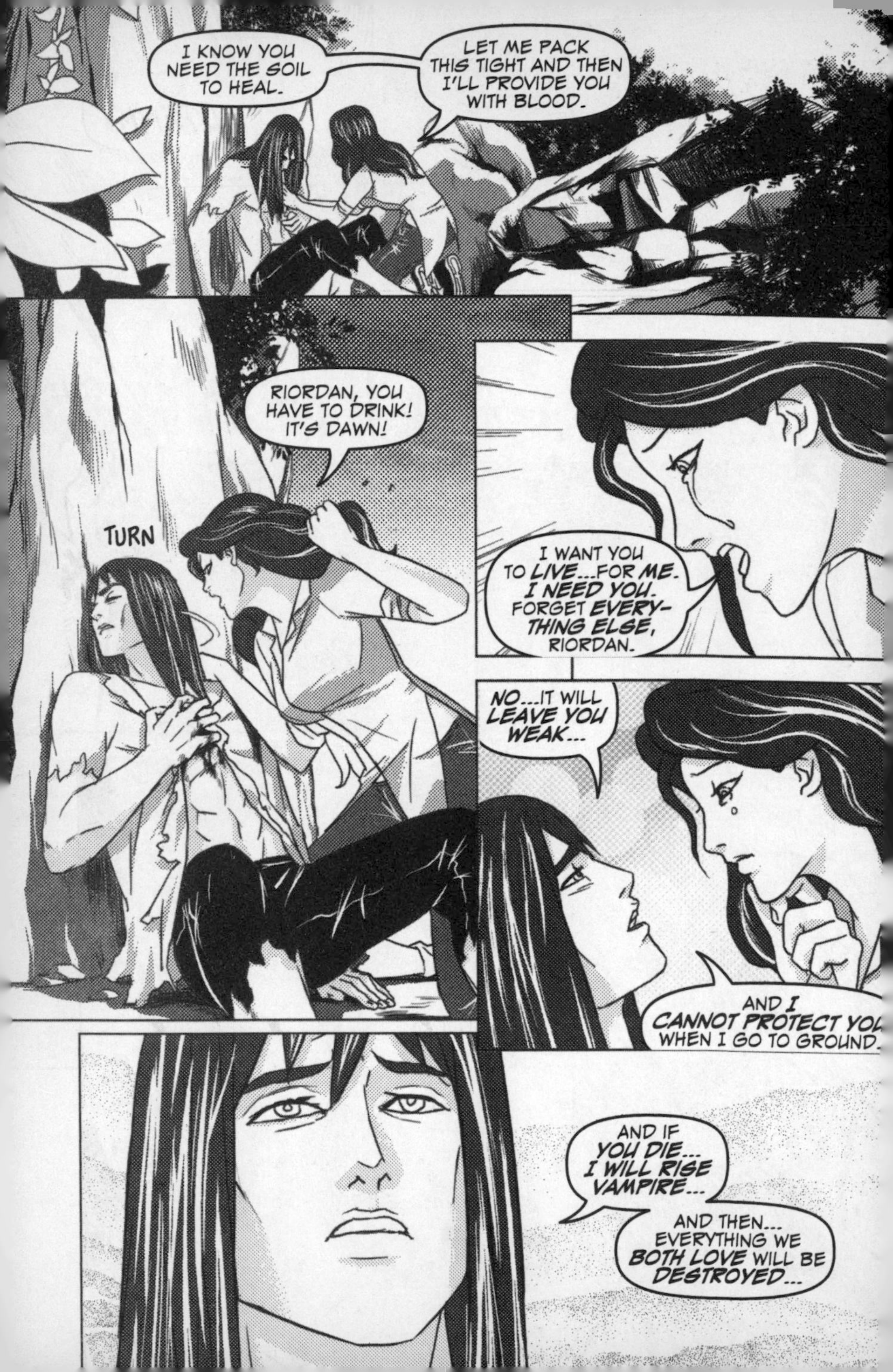
I KNOW YOU NEED THE SOIL TO HEAL.
LET ME PACK THIS TIGHT AND THEN I'LL PROVIDE YOU WITH BLOOD.
RIORDAN, YOU HAVE TO DRINK! IT'S DAWN!
TURN
I WANT YOU TO *LIVE*...FOR *ME*. *I NEED YOU.* FORGET *EVERY-THING ELSE,* RIORDAN.
NO...IT WILL *LEAVE YOU WEAK*...
AND *I CANNOT PROTECT YOU* WHEN I GO TO GROUND.
AND IF *YOU DIE*... *I WILL RISE VAMPIRE*...
AND THEN... EVERYTHING WE *BOTH LOVE* WILL BE *DESTROYED*...

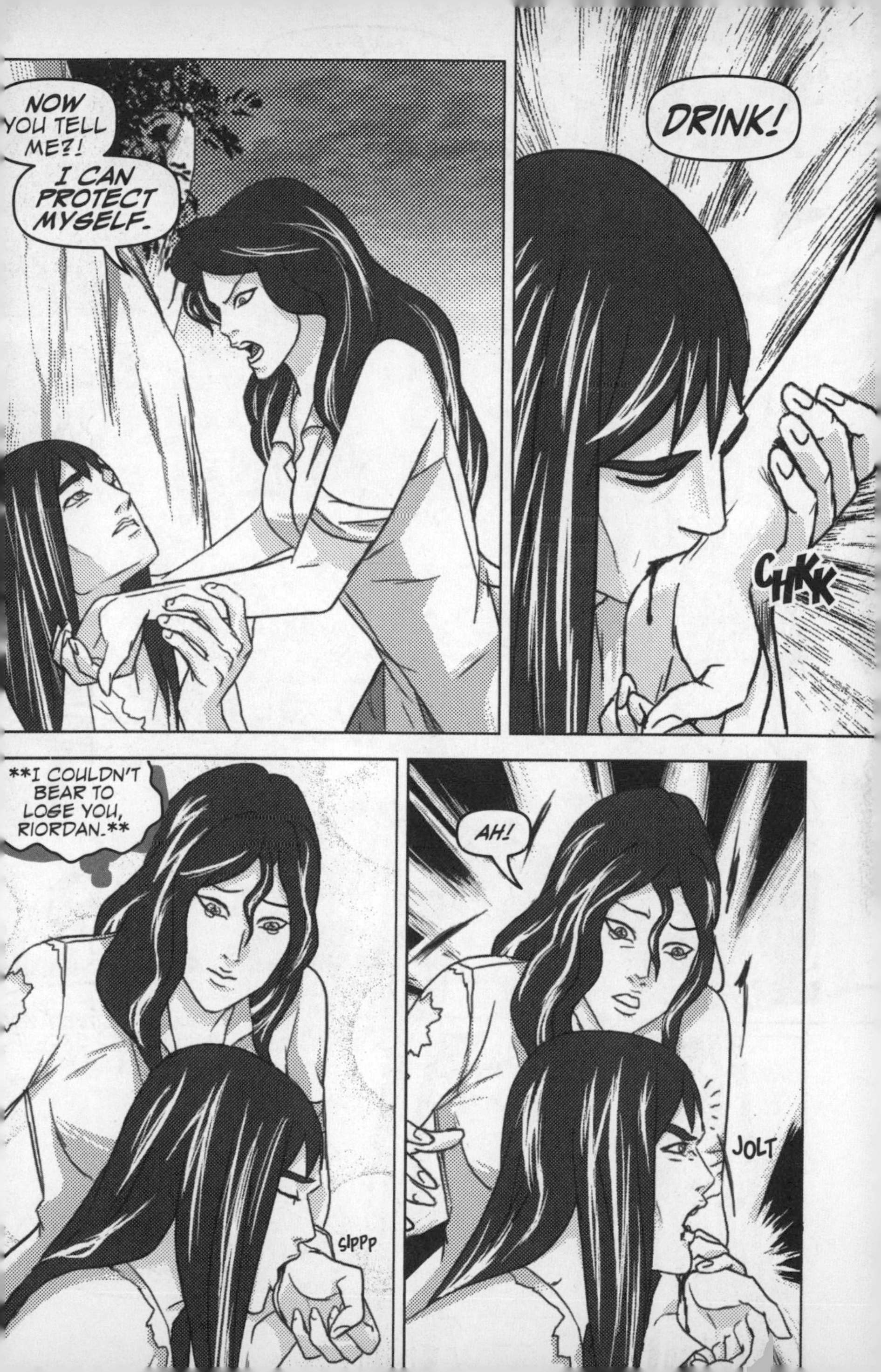
NOW YOU TELL ME?!
I CAN PROTECT MYSELF.
DRINK!
CHKKK
I COULDN'T BEAR TO LOSE YOU, RIORDAN.
SIPPP
AH!
JOLT

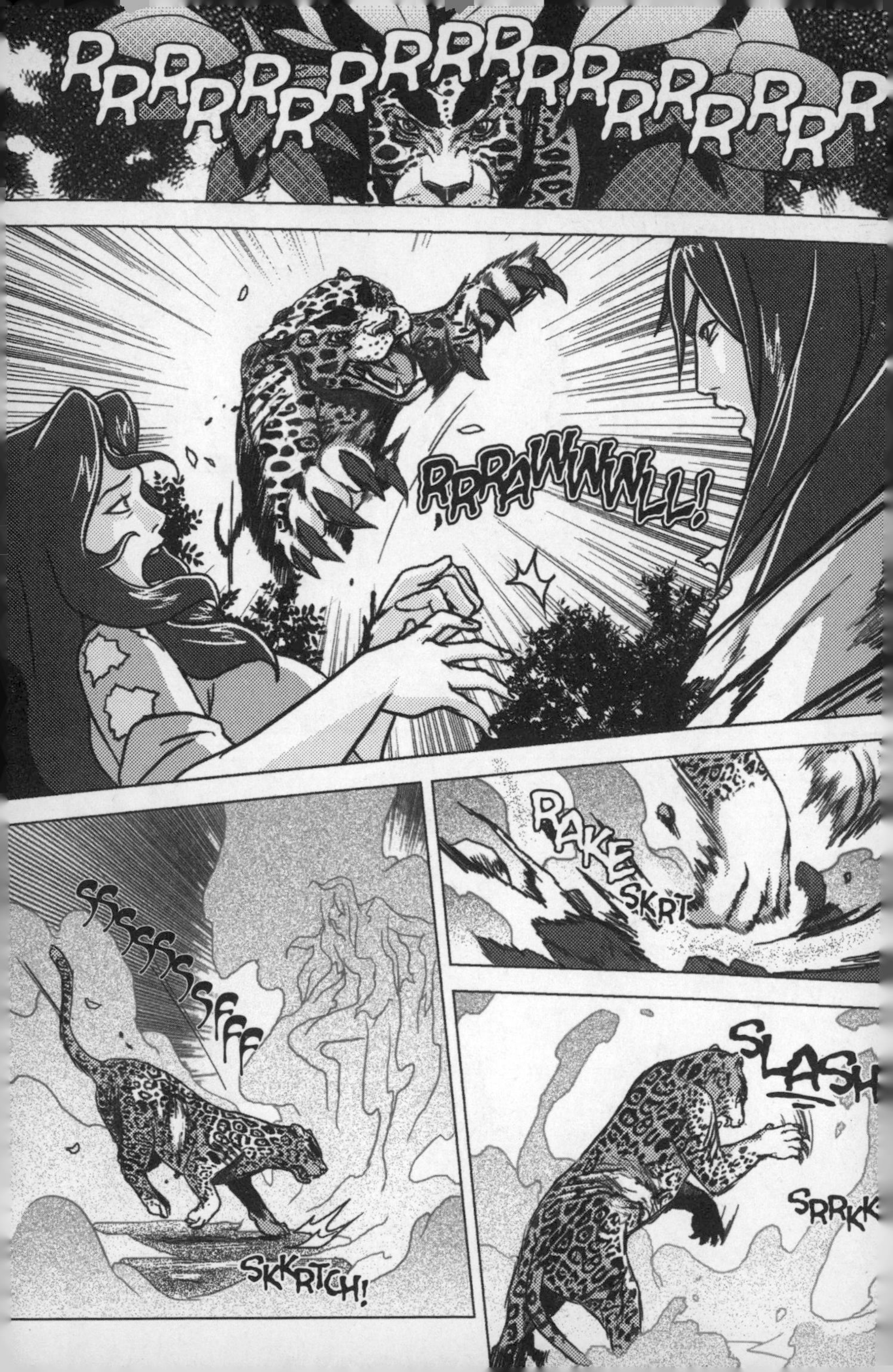
RRRRRRRRRRRRRRRRRRRR
RRRRAWWWLLL!
SFSSFSSSFFF
SKKRTCH!
RAKE
SKRT
SLASH
SRRKK

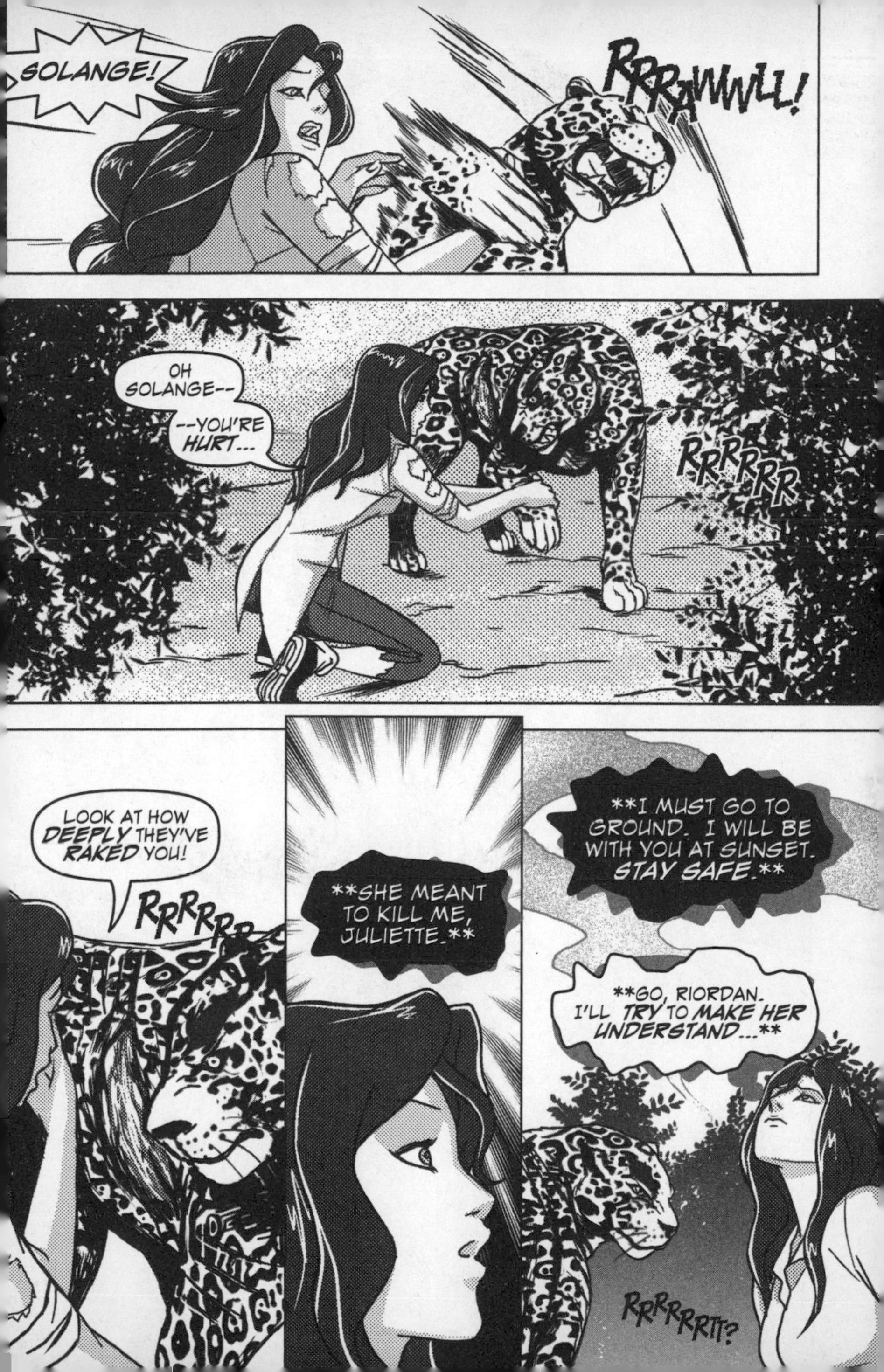
SOLANGE!
RRRAWWLL!
OH SOLANGE--
--YOU'RE HURT...
RRRRRR
LOOK AT HOW DEEPLY THEY'VE RAKED YOU!
RRRR
SHE MEANT TO KILL ME, JULIETTE.
I MUST GO TO GROUND. I WILL BE WITH YOU AT SUNSET. STAY SAFE.
GO, RIORDAN. I'LL TRY TO MAKE HER UNDERSTAND...
RRRRRRTT?

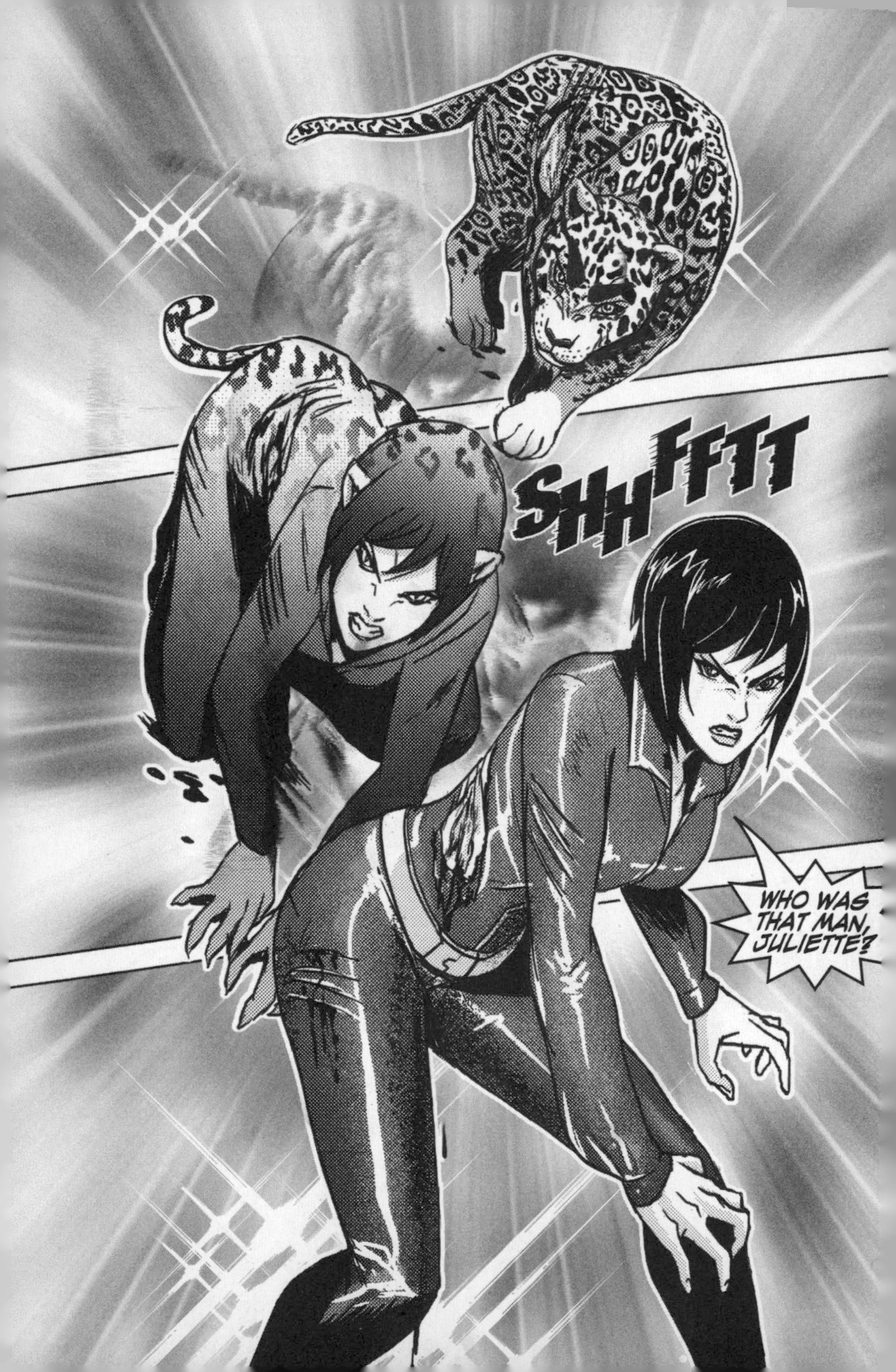
SHHFFTT
WHO WAS THAT MAN, JULIETTE?

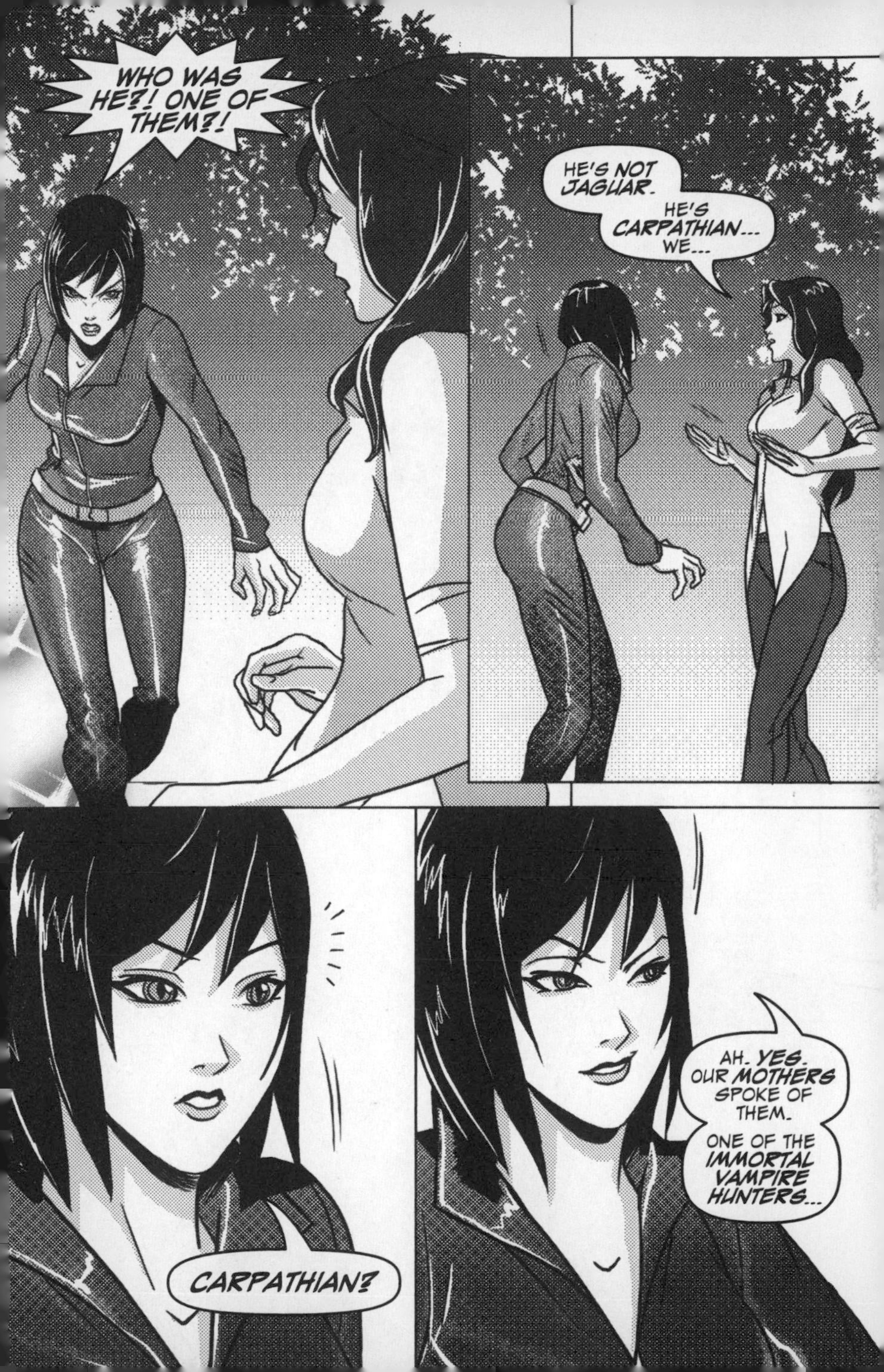
WHO WAS HE?! ONE OF THEM?!
HE'S NOT JAGUAR.
HE'S CARPATHIAN... WE...
CARPATHIAN?
AH. YES. OUR MOTHERS SPOKE OF THEM.
ONE OF THE IMMORTAL VAMPIRE HUNTERS...

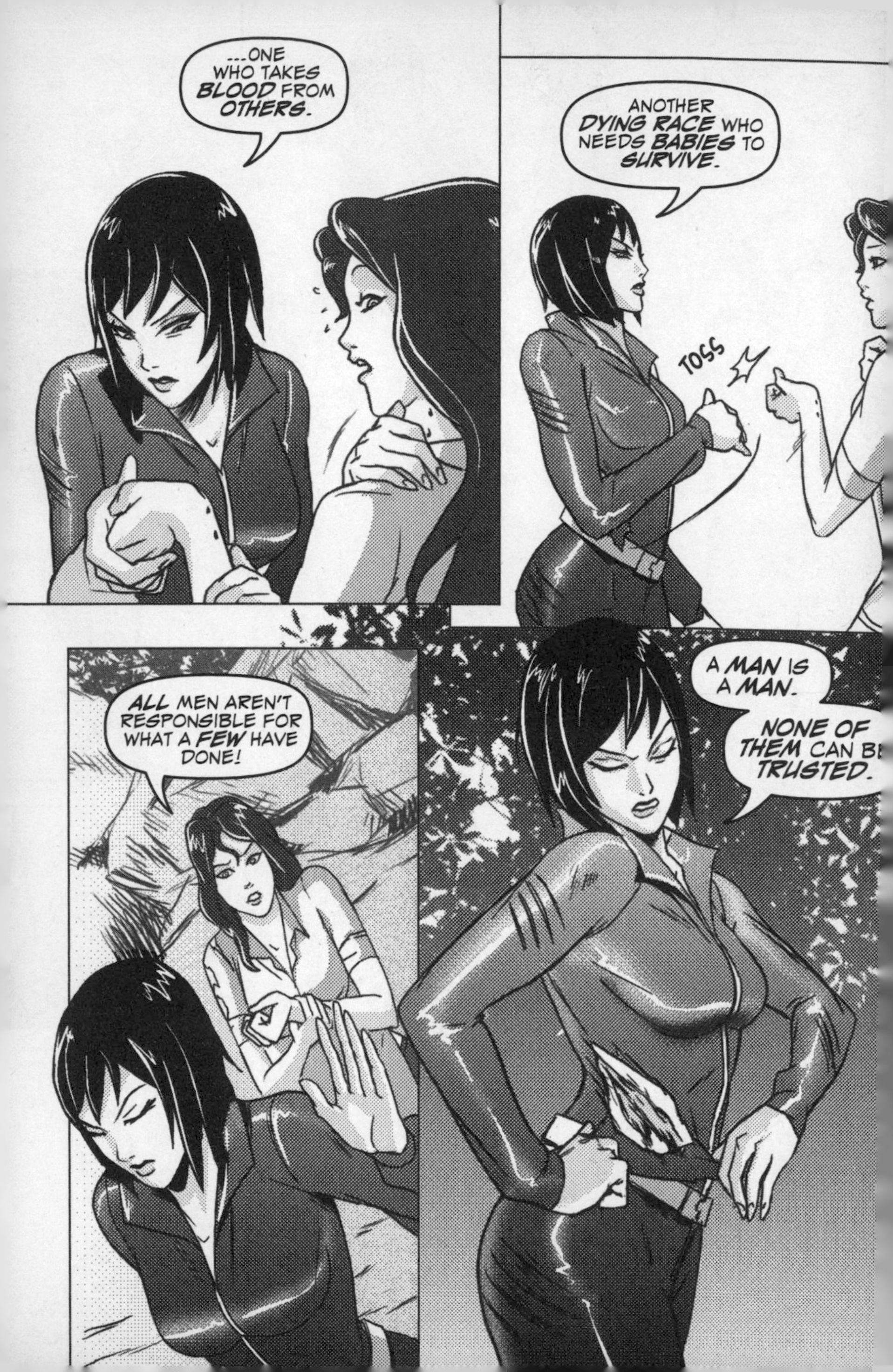
...ONE WHO TAKES BLOOD FROM OTHERS.
ANOTHER DYING RACE WHO NEEDS BABIES TO SURVIVE.
TOSS
ALL MEN AREN'T RESPONSIBLE FOR WHAT A FEW HAVE DONE!
A MAN IS A MAN.
NONE OF THEM CAN BE TRUSTED.

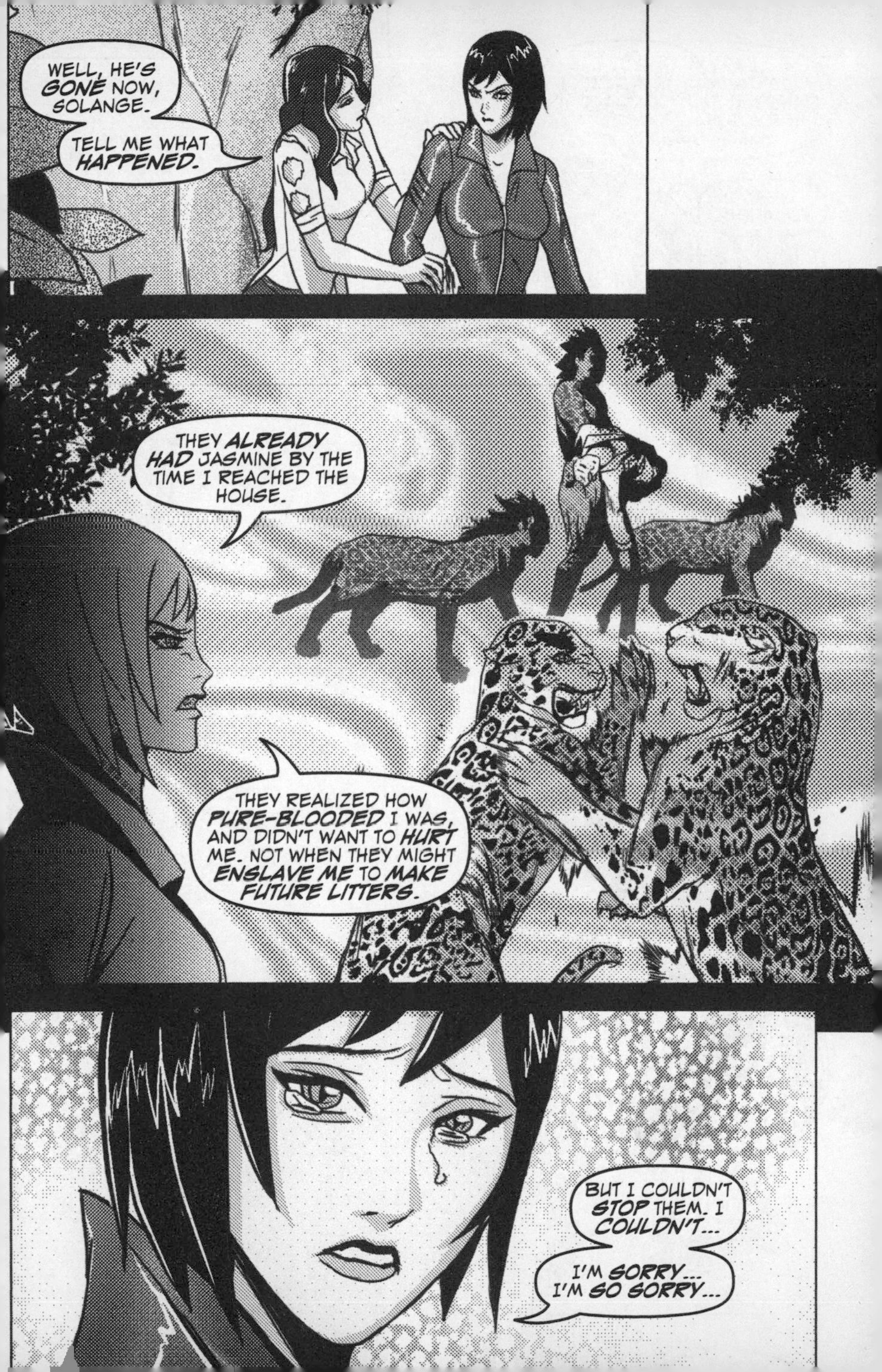
WELL, HE'S GONE NOW, SOLANGE.
TELL ME WHAT HAPPENED.
THEY ALREADY HAD JASMINE BY THE TIME I REACHED THE HOUSE.
THEY REALIZED HOW PURE-BLOODED I WAS, AND DIDN'T WANT TO HURT ME. NOT WHEN THEY MIGHT ENSLAVE ME TO MAKE FUTURE LITTERS.
BUT I COULDN'T STOP THEM. I COULDN'T...
I'M SORRY... I'M SO SORRY...

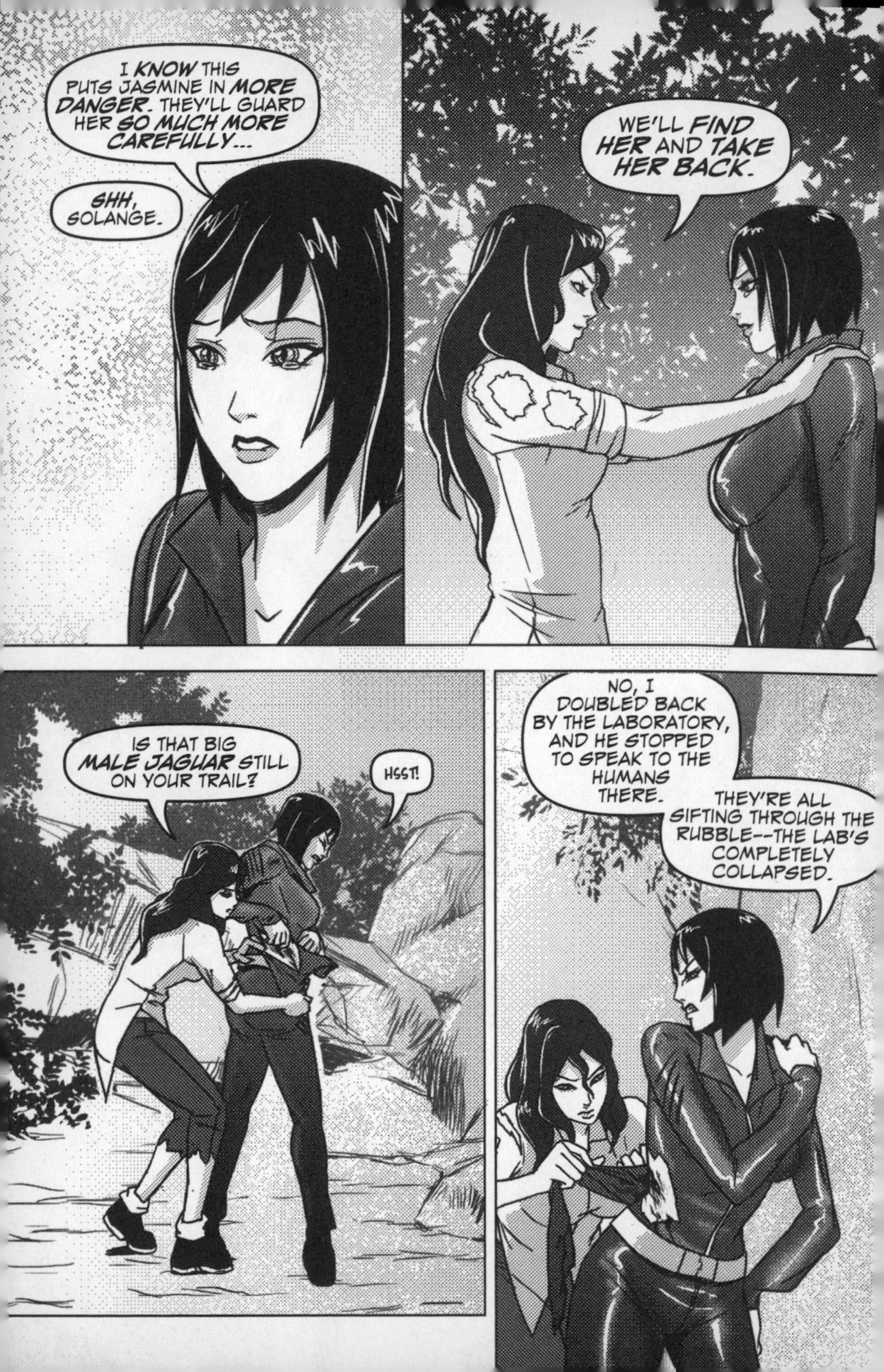
I KNOW THIS PUTS JASMINE IN MORE DANGER. THEY'LL GUARD HER SO MUCH MORE CAREFULLY...
SHH, SOLANGE.
WE'LL FIND HER AND TAKE HER BACK.
IS THAT BIG MALE JAGUAR STILL ON YOUR TRAIL?
HSST!
NO, I DOUBLED BACK BY THE LABORATORY, AND HE STOPPED TO SPEAK TO THE HUMANS THERE.
THEY'RE ALL SIFTING THROUGH THE RUBBLE--THE LAB'S COMPLETELY COLLAPSED.

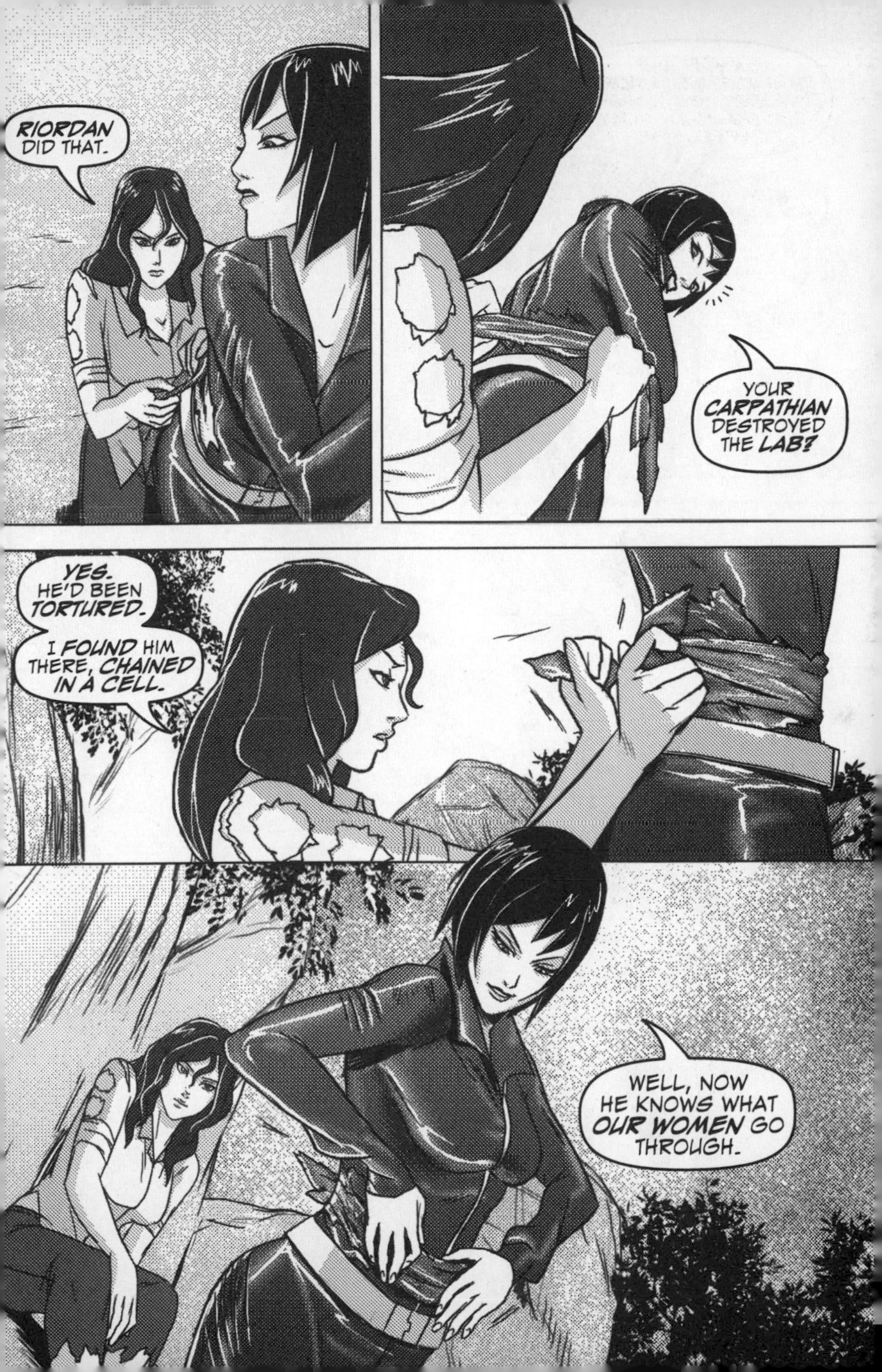
RIORDAN DID THAT.
YOUR CARPATHIAN DESTROYED THE LAB?
YES. HE'D BEEN TORTURED.
I FOUND HIM THERE, CHAINED IN A CELL.
WELL, NOW HE KNOWS WHAT OUR WOMEN GO THROUGH.

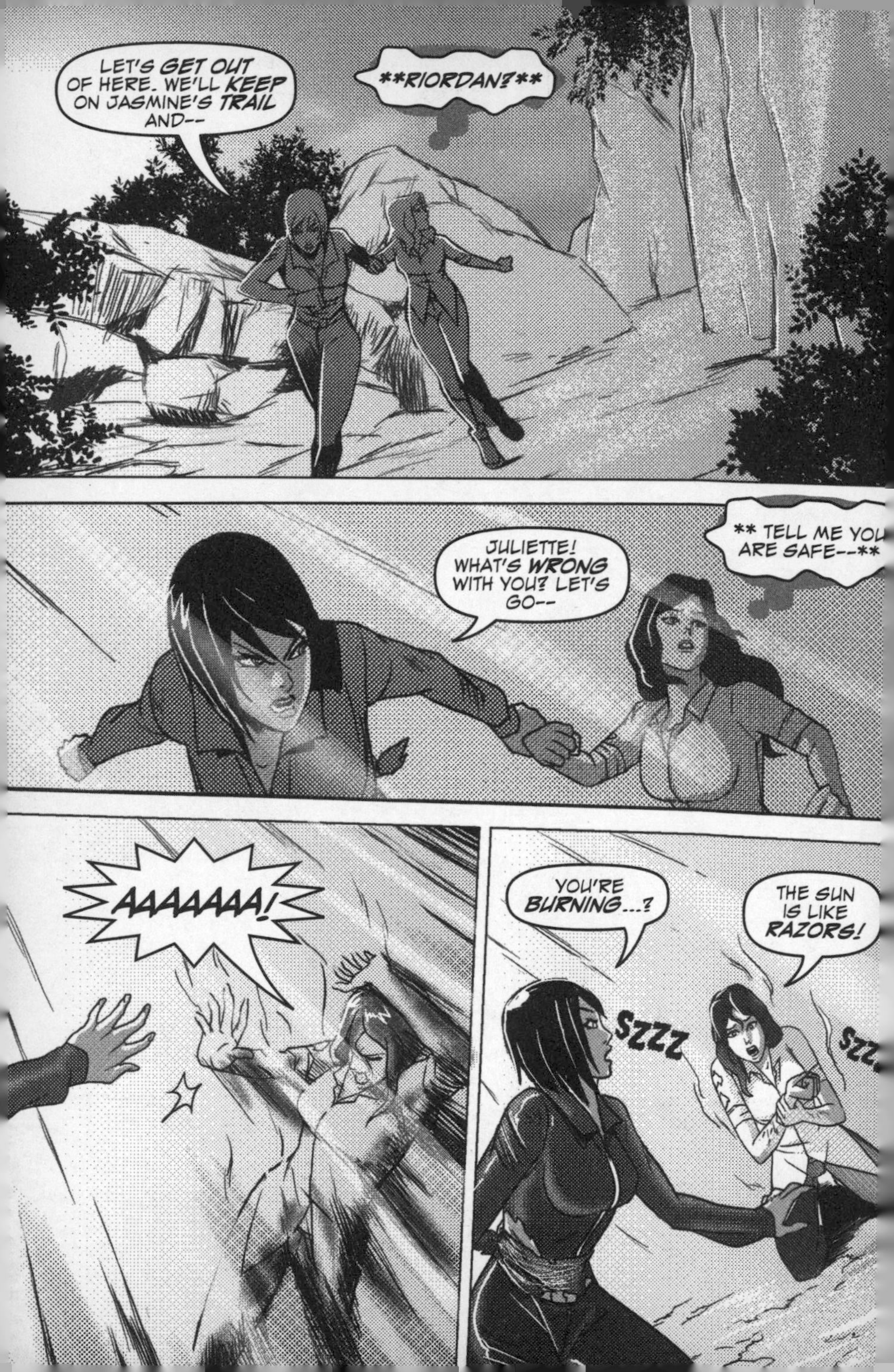
LET'S GET OUT OF HERE. WE'LL KEEP ON JASMINE'S TRAIL AND--
RIORDAN?
JULIETTE! WHAT'S WRONG WITH YOU? LET'S GO--
** TELL ME YOU ARE SAFE--**
AAAAAAA!
YOU'RE BURNING...?
THE SUN IS LIKE RAZORS!
SZZZ

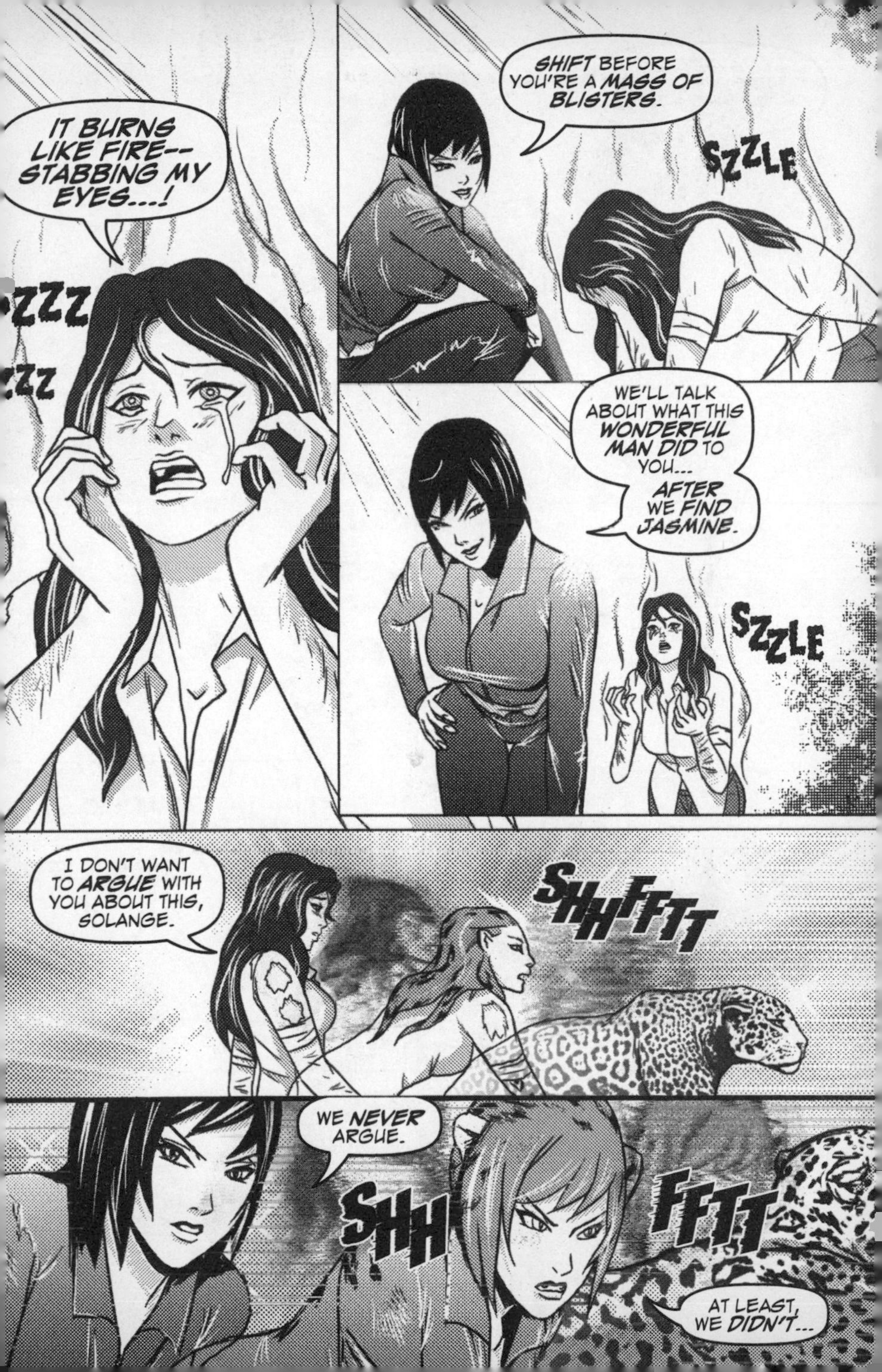
IT BURNS LIKE FIRE-- STABBING MY EYES...!
ZZZZ
ZZZ
SHIFT BEFORE YOU'RE A MASS OF BLISTERS.
SZZLE
WE'LL TALK ABOUT WHAT THIS WONDERFUL MAN DID TO YOU... AFTER WE FIND JASMINE.
SZZLE
I DON'T WANT TO ARGUE WITH YOU ABOUT THIS, SOLANGE.
SHHFFTTT
WE NEVER ARGUE.
SHH
FFTT
AT LEAST, WE DIDN'T...

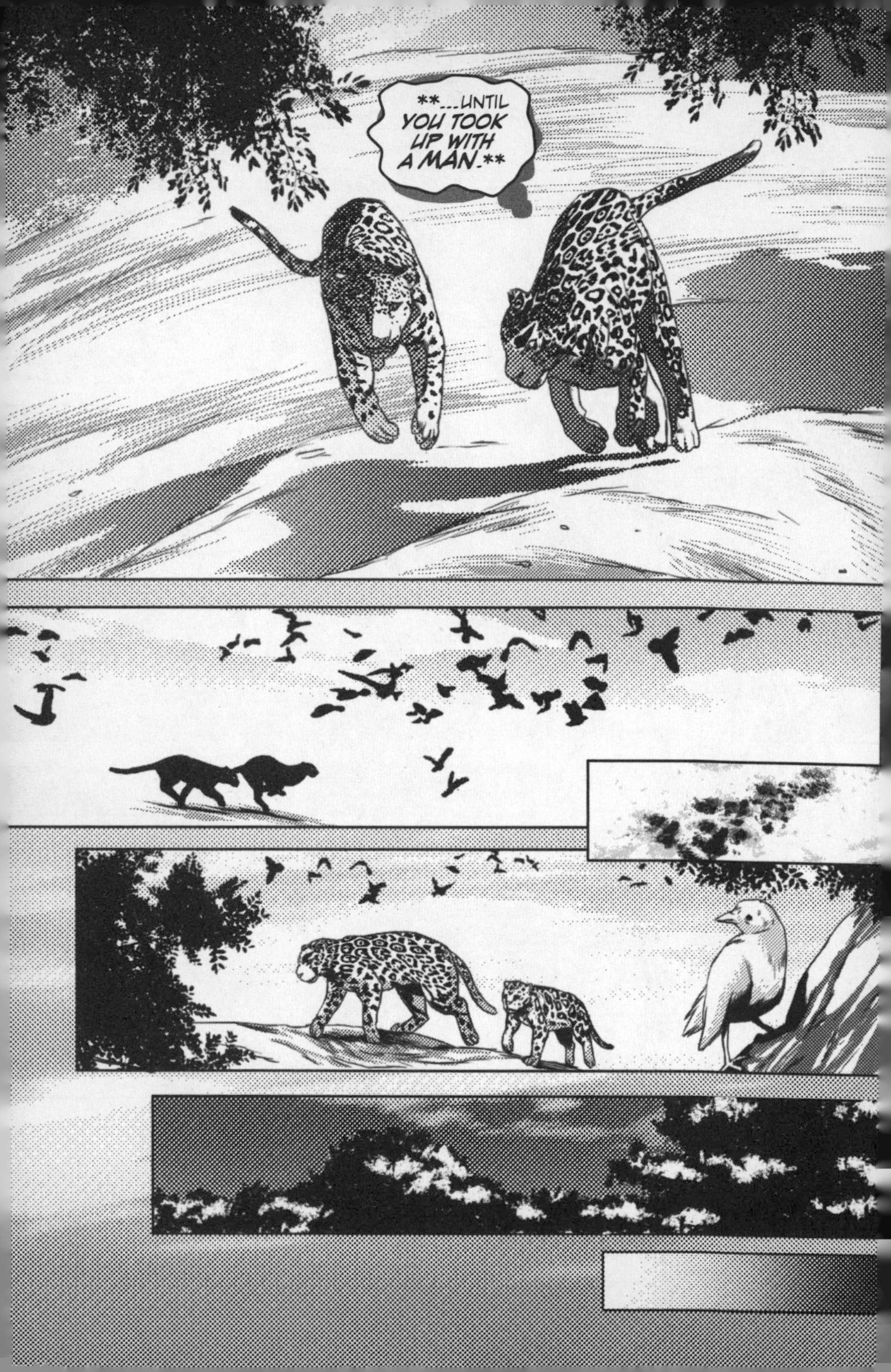
...UNTIL YOU TOOK UP WITH A MAN.

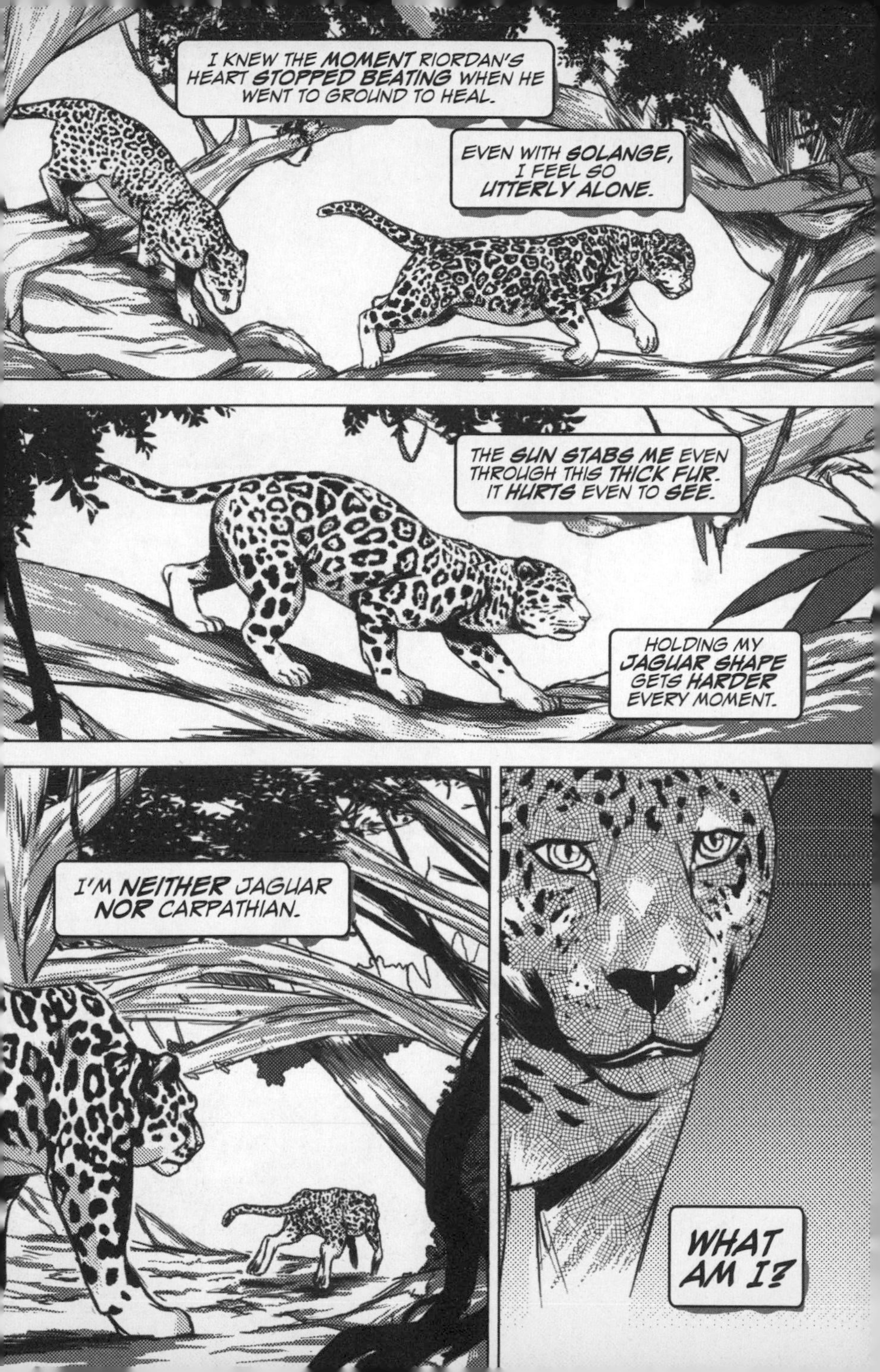
I KNEW THE MOMENT RIORDAN'S HEART STOPPED BEATING WHEN HE WENT TO GROUND TO HEAL.
EVEN WITH SOLANGE, I FEEL SO UTTERLY ALONE.
THE SUN STABS ME EVEN THROUGH THIS THICK FUR. IT HURTS EVEN TO SEE.
HOLDING MY JAGUAR SHAPE GETS HARDER EVERY MOMENT.
I'M NEITHER JAGUAR NOR CARPATHIAN.
WHAT AM I?

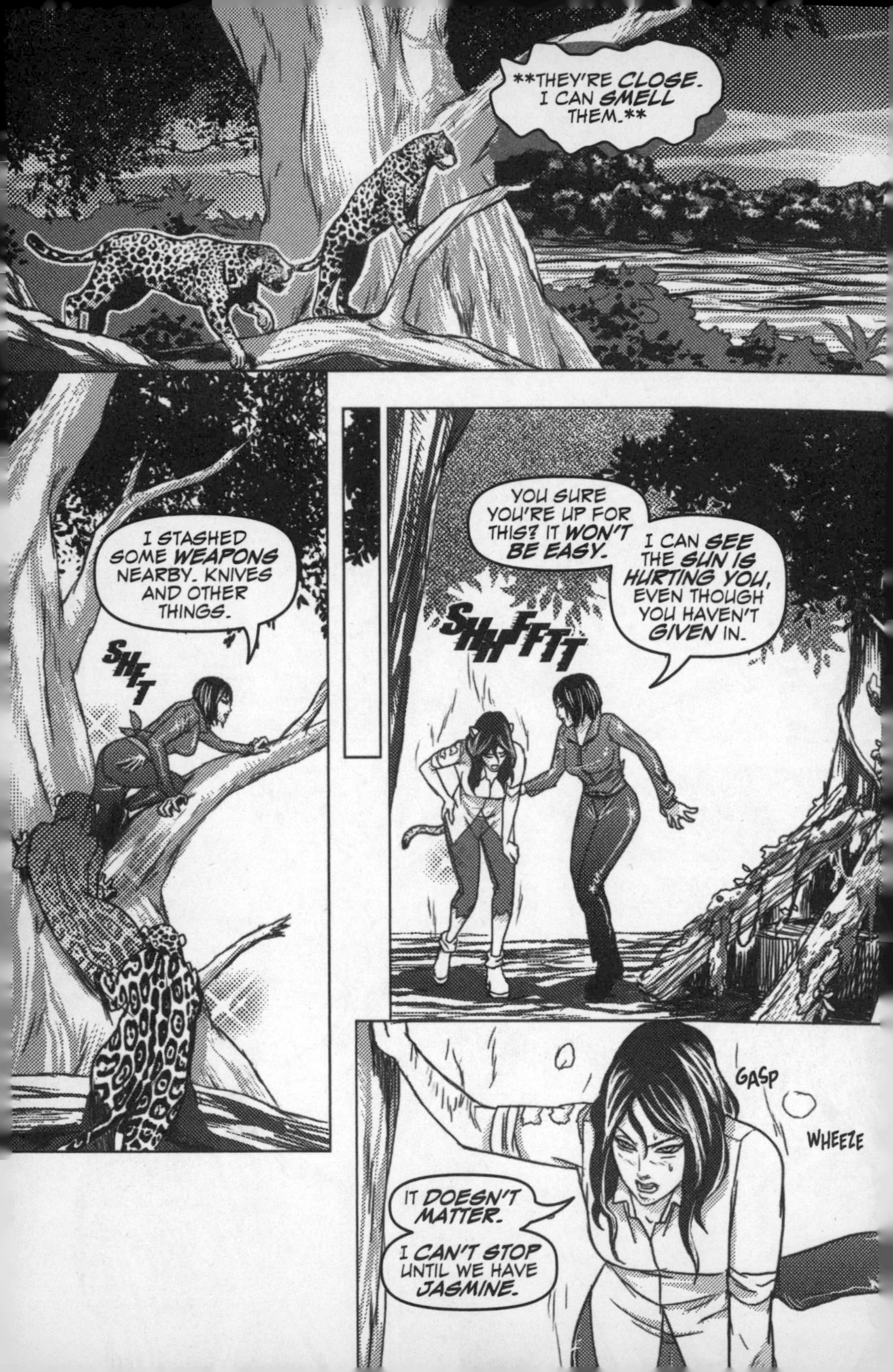
THEY'RE CLOSE. I CAN SMELL THEM.
I STASHED SOME WEAPONS NEARBY. KNIVES AND OTHER THINGS.
SHFT
SHHFFTTT
YOU SURE YOU'RE UP FOR THIS? IT WON'T BE EASY.
I CAN SEE THE SUN IS HURTING YOU, EVEN THOUGH YOU HAVEN'T GIVEN IN.
GASP
WHEEZE
IT DOESN'T MATTER.
I CAN'T STOP UNTIL WE HAVE JASMINE.

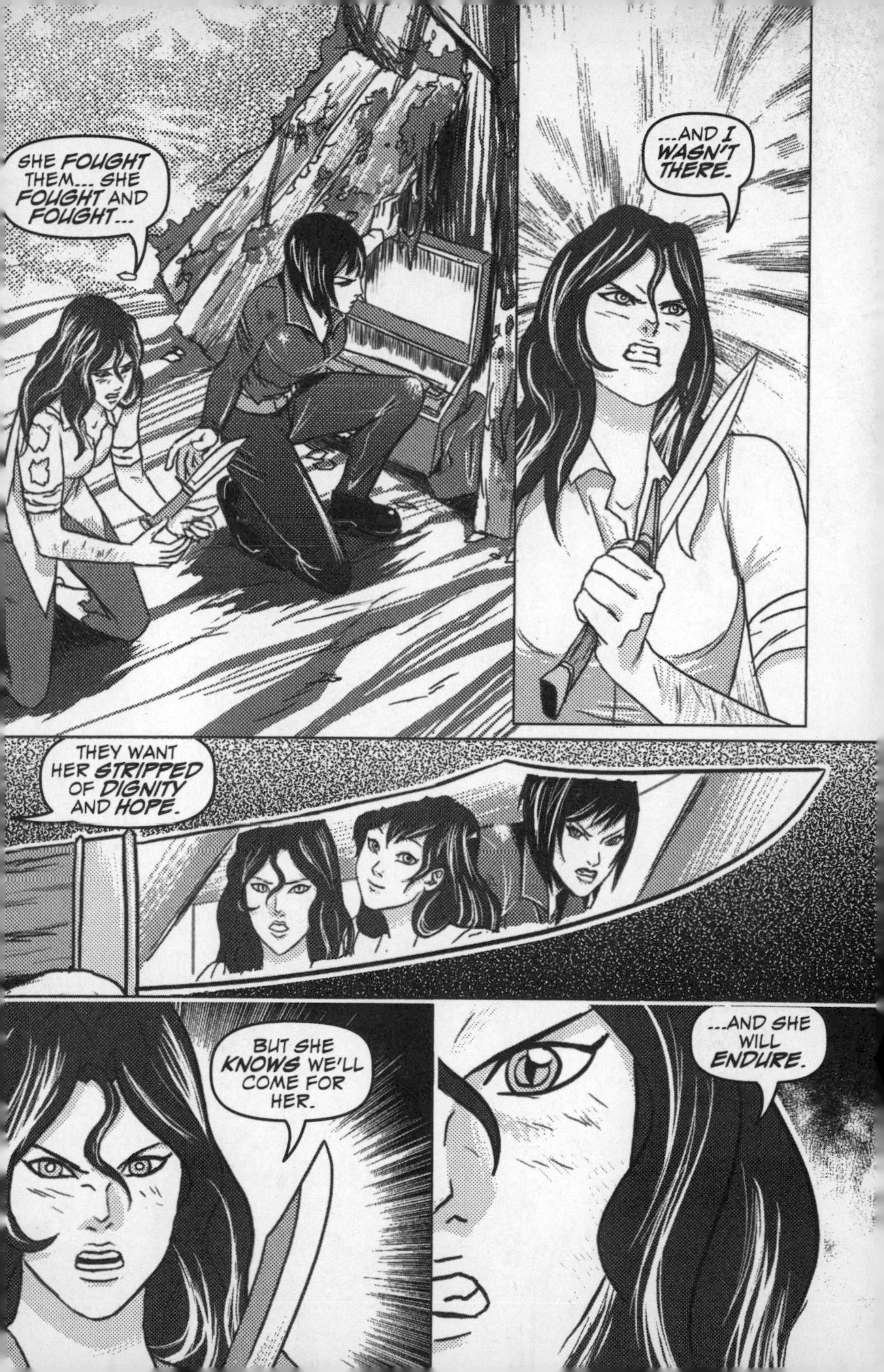
SHE FOUGHT THEM... SHE FOUGHT AND FOUGHT...
...AND I WASN'T THERE.
THEY WANT HER STRIPPED OF DIGNITY AND HOPE.
BUT SHE KNOWS WE'LL COME FOR HER.
...AND SHE WILL ENDURE.

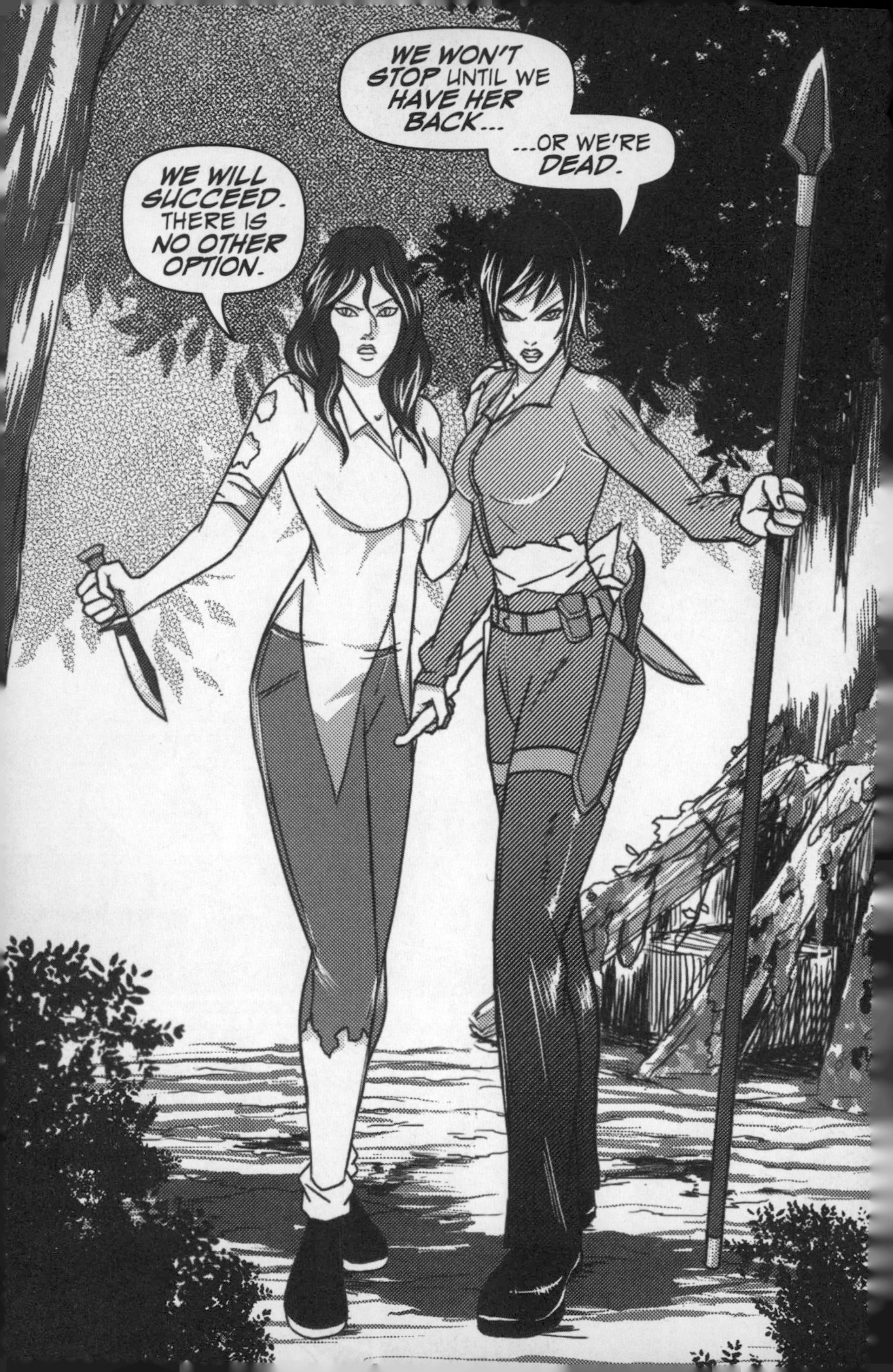
WE WILL SUCCEED. THERE IS NO OTHER OPTION.
WE WON'T STOP UNTIL WE HAVE HER BACK...
...OR WE'RE DEAD.

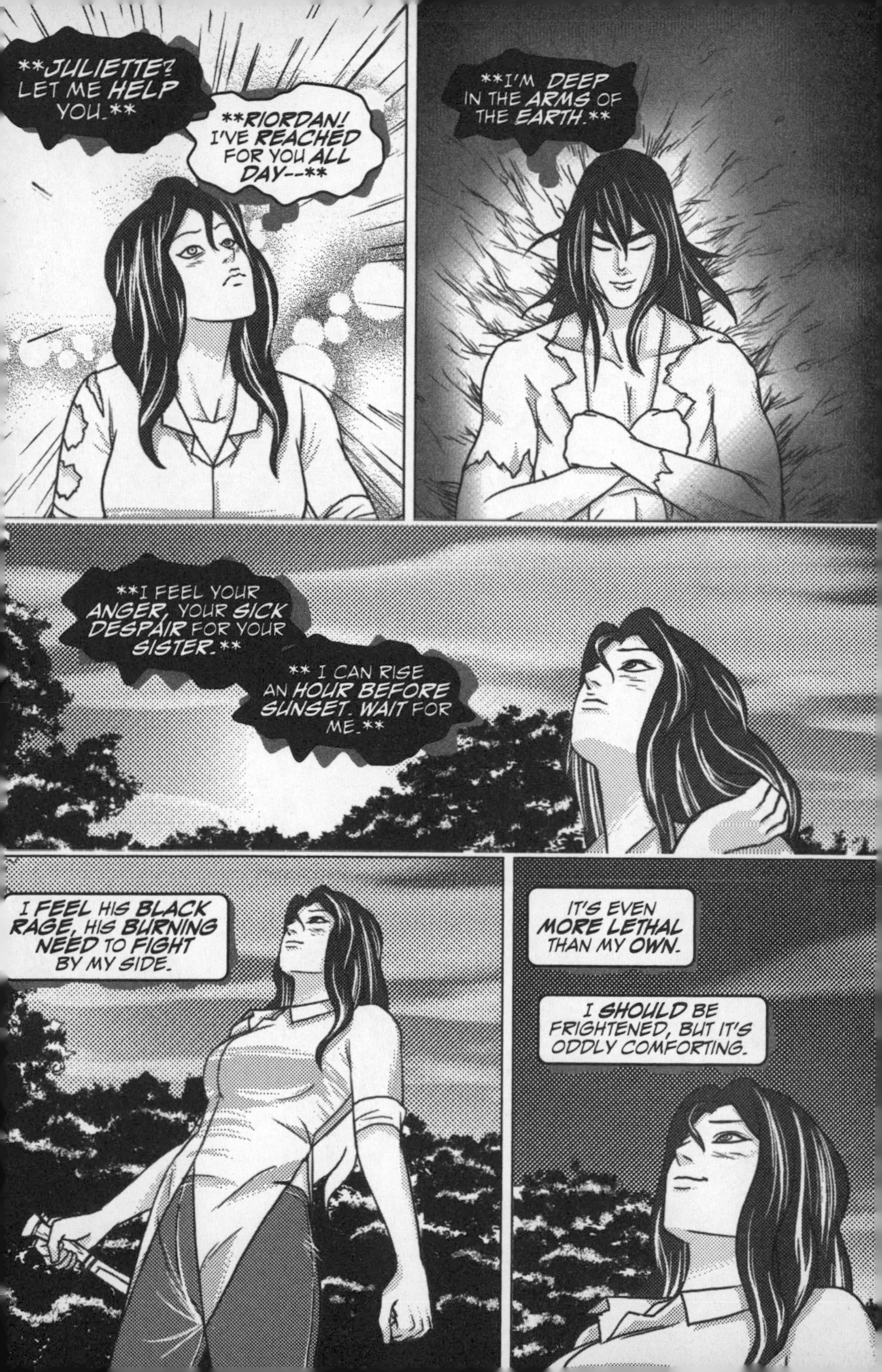
JULIETTE? LET ME HELP YOU.
RIORDAN! I'VE REACHED FOR YOU ALL DAY--
I'M DEEP IN THE ARMS OF THE EARTH.
I FEEL YOUR ANGER, YOUR SICK DESPAIR FOR YOUR SISTER.
** I CAN RISE AN HOUR BEFORE SUNSET. WAIT FOR ME.**
I FEEL HIS BLACK RAGE, HIS BURNING NEED TO FIGHT BY MY SIDE.
IT'S EVEN MORE LETHAL THAN MY OWN.
I SHOULD BE FRIGHTENED, BUT IT'S ODDLY COMFORTING.

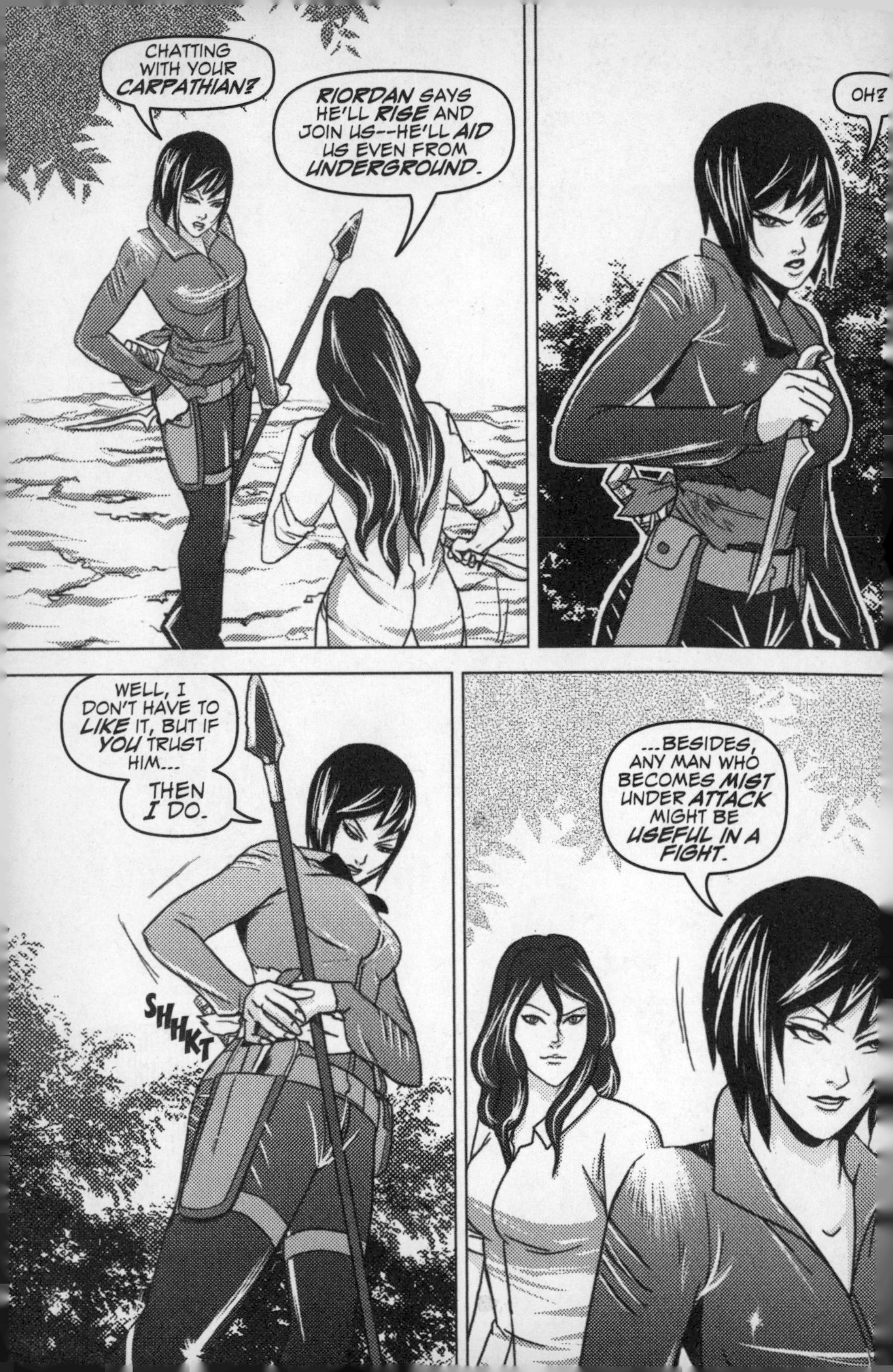
CHATTING WITH YOUR CARPATHIAN?
RIORDAN SAYS HE'LL RISE AND JOIN US--HE'LL AID US EVEN FROM UNDERGROUND.
OH?
WELL, I DON'T HAVE TO LIKE IT, BUT IF YOU TRUST HIM...
THEN I DO.
SHHKT
...BESIDES, ANY MAN WHO BECOMES MIST UNDER ATTACK MIGHT BE USEFUL IN A FIGHT.

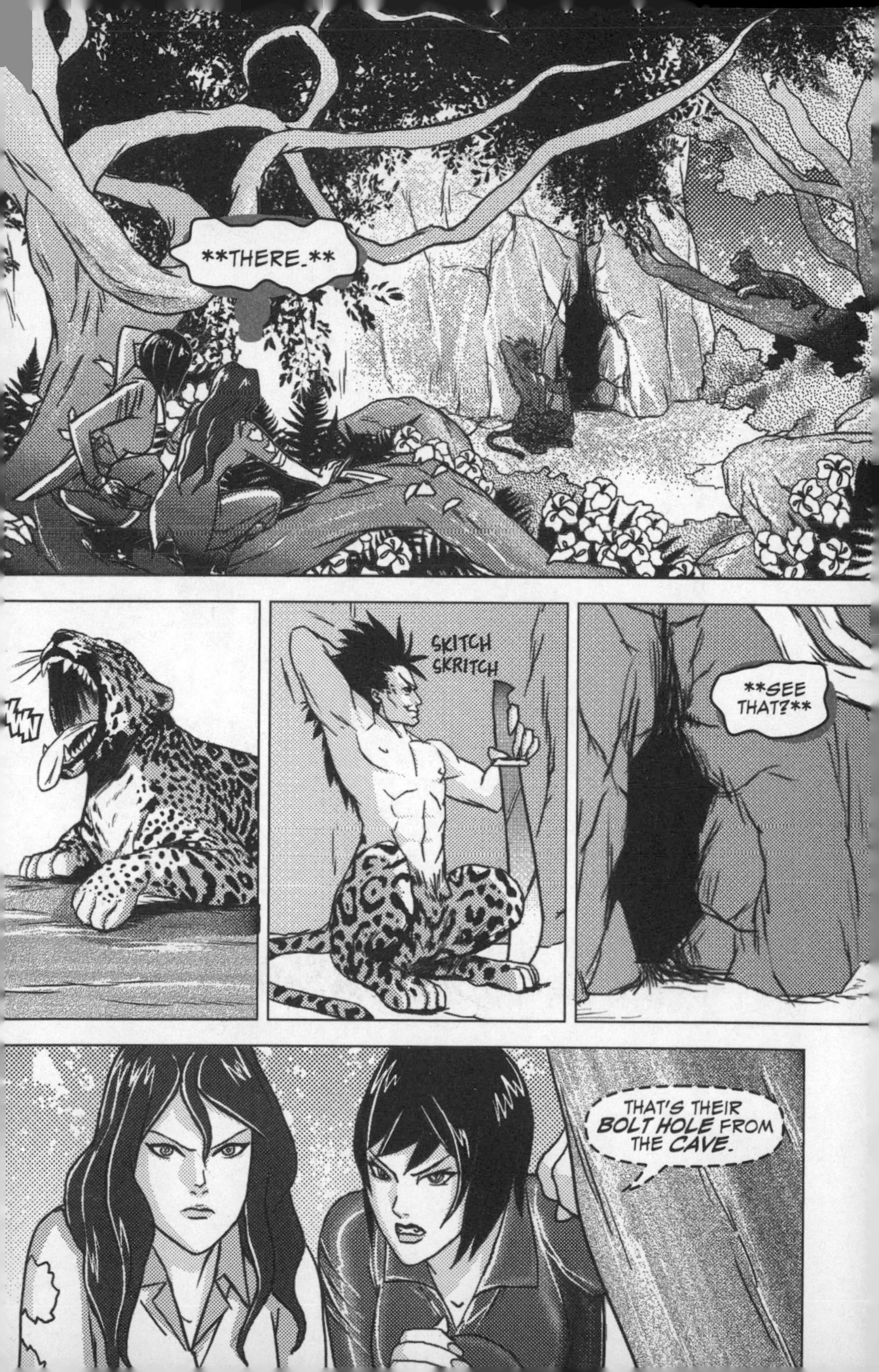
THERE.
SKITCH SKRITCH
SEE THAT?
THAT'S THEIR BOLT HOLE FROM THE CAVE.

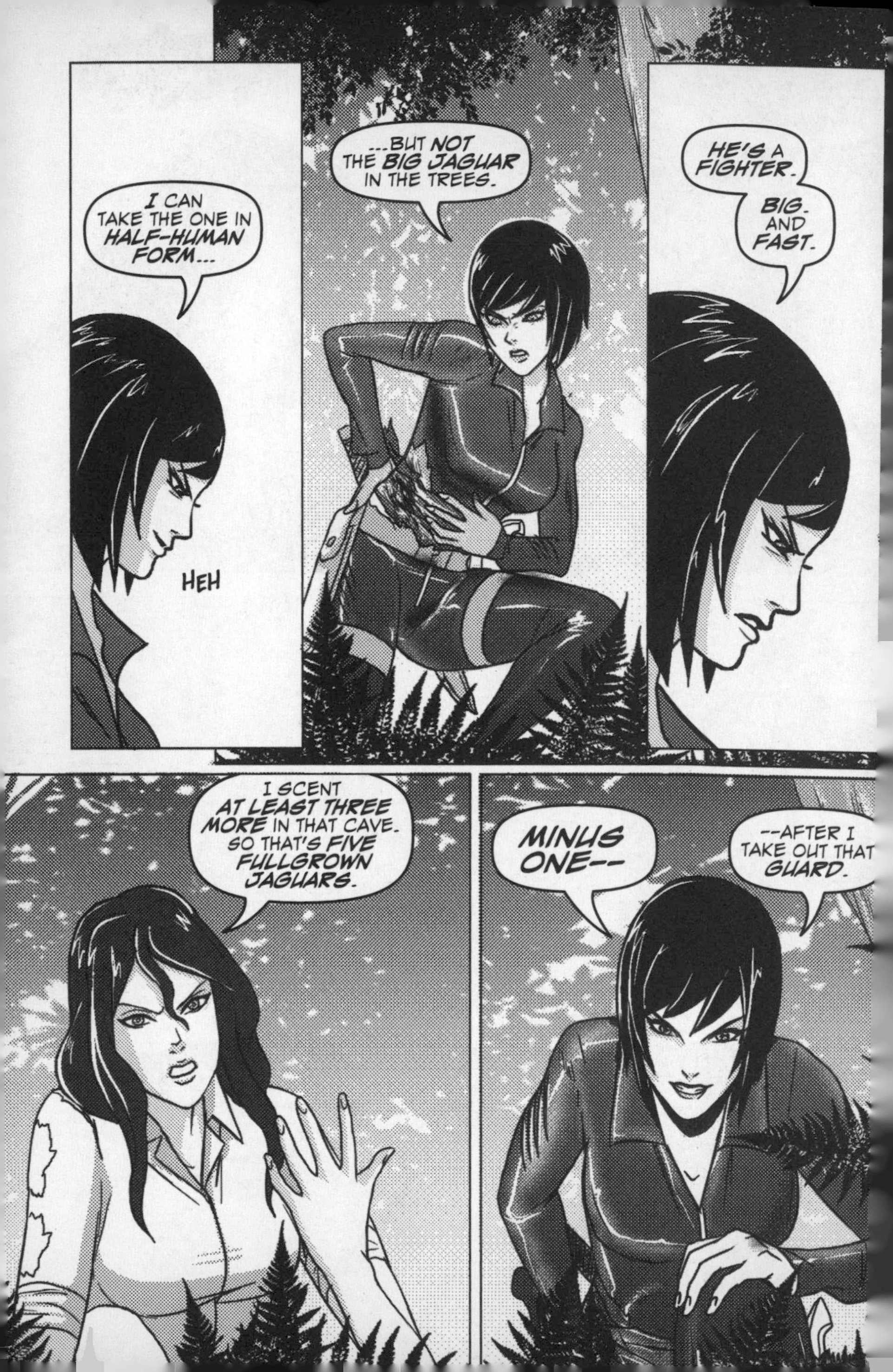
I CAN TAKE THE ONE IN HALF-HUMAN FORM...
HEH
...BUT NOT THE BIG JAGUAR IN THE TREES.
HE'S A FIGHTER.
BIG. AND FAST.
I SCENT AT LEAST THREE MORE IN THAT CAVE. SO THAT'S FIVE FULLGROWN JAGUARS.
MINUS ONE--
--AFTER I TAKE OUT THAT GUARD.

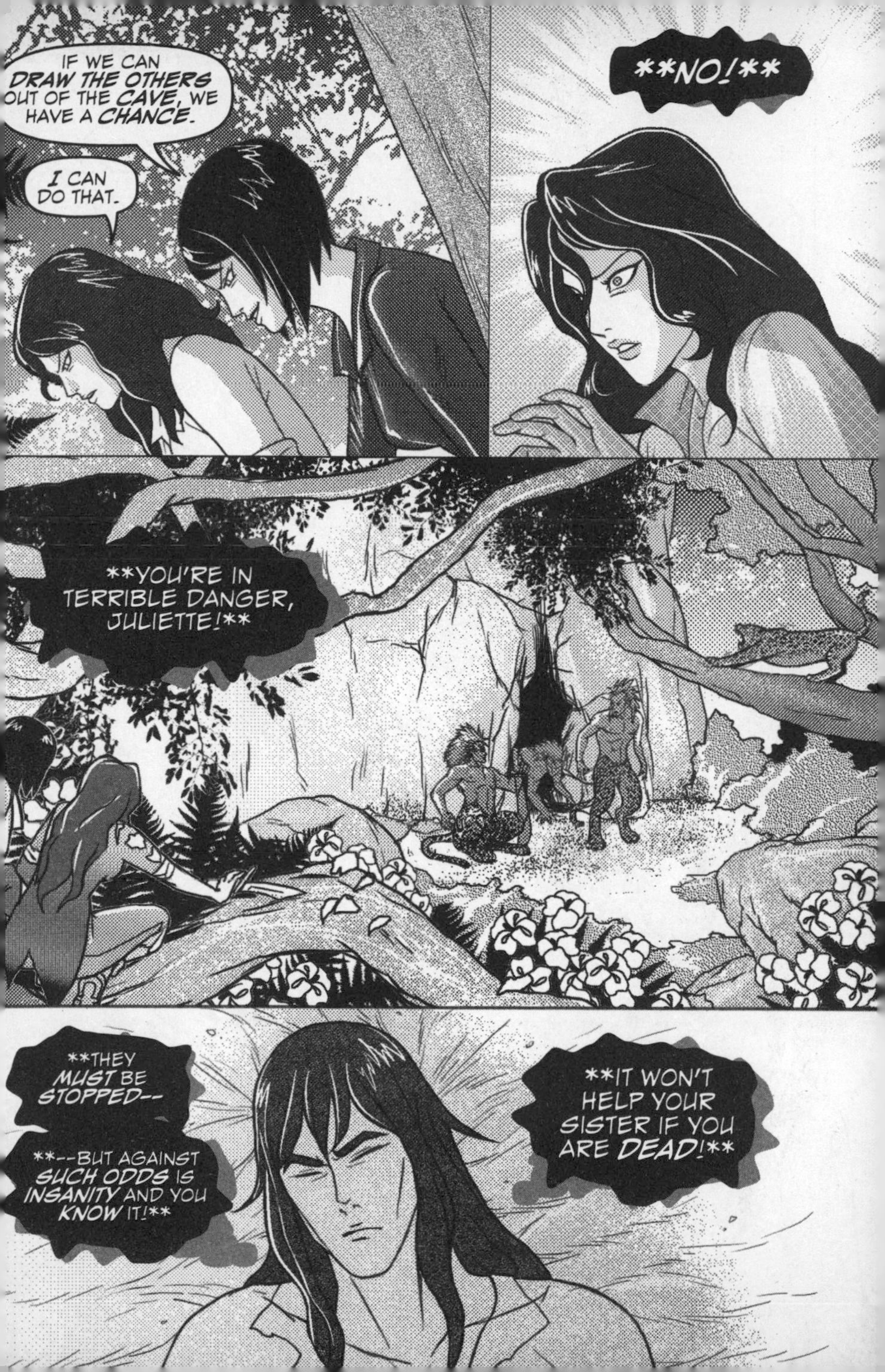
IF WE CAN DRAW THE OTHERS OUT OF THE CAVE, WE HAVE A CHANCE.
I CAN DO THAT.
NO!
YOU'RE IN TERRIBLE DANGER, JULIETTE!
**THEY MUST BE STOPPED--
--BUT AGAINST SUCH ODDS IS INSANITY AND YOU KNOW IT!
IT WON'T HELP YOUR SISTER IF YOU ARE DEAD!

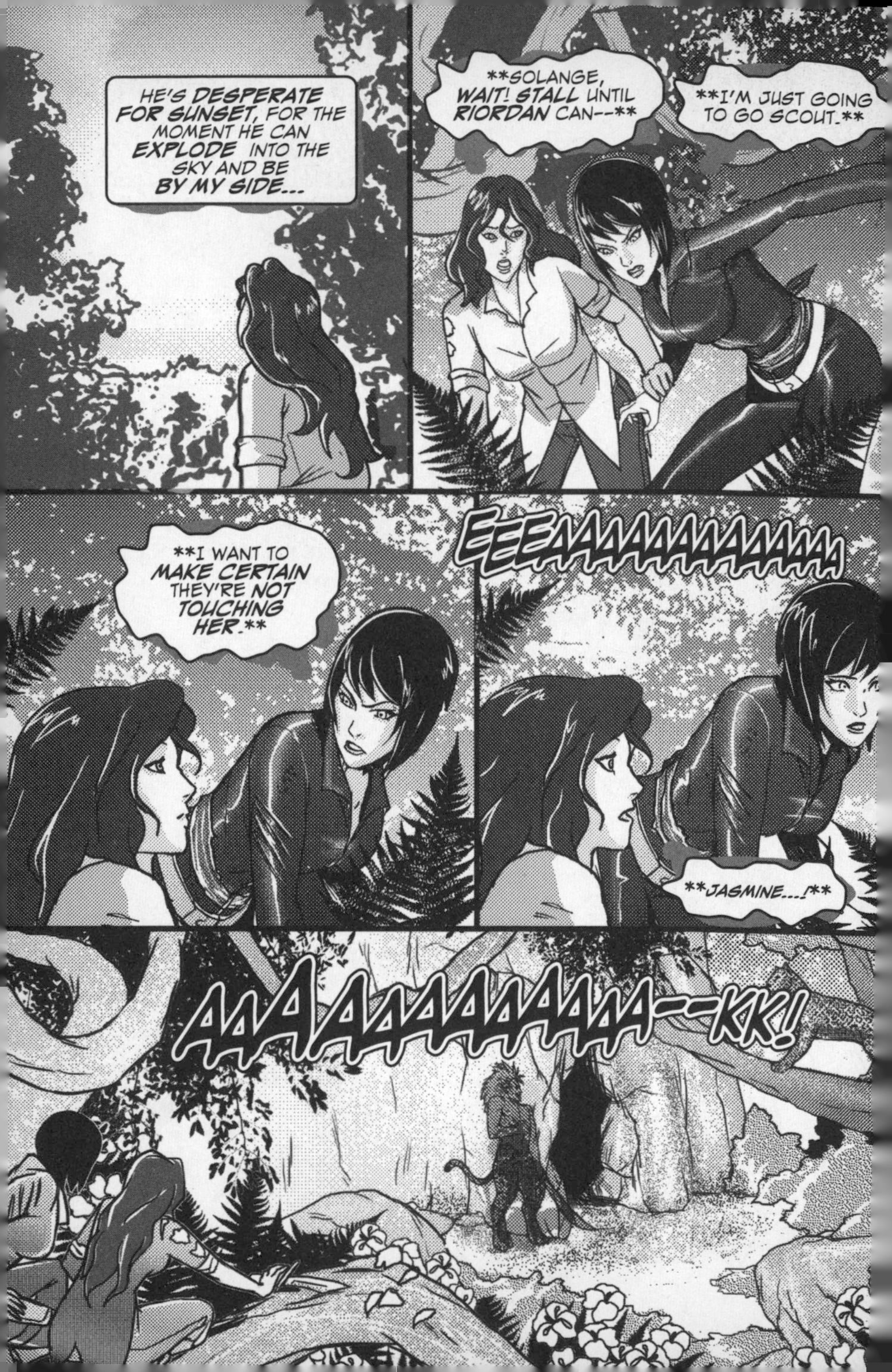
HE'S DESPERATE FOR SUNSET, FOR THE MOMENT HE CAN EXPLODE INTO THE SKY AND BE BY MY SIDE...
SOLANGE, WAIT! STALL UNTIL RIORDAN CAN--
I'M JUST GOING TO GO SCOUT.
I WANT TO MAKE CERTAIN THEY'RE NOT TOUCHING HER.
EEEAAAAAAAAAAAAA
JASMINE...!
AAAAAAAAAAAAA--KK!

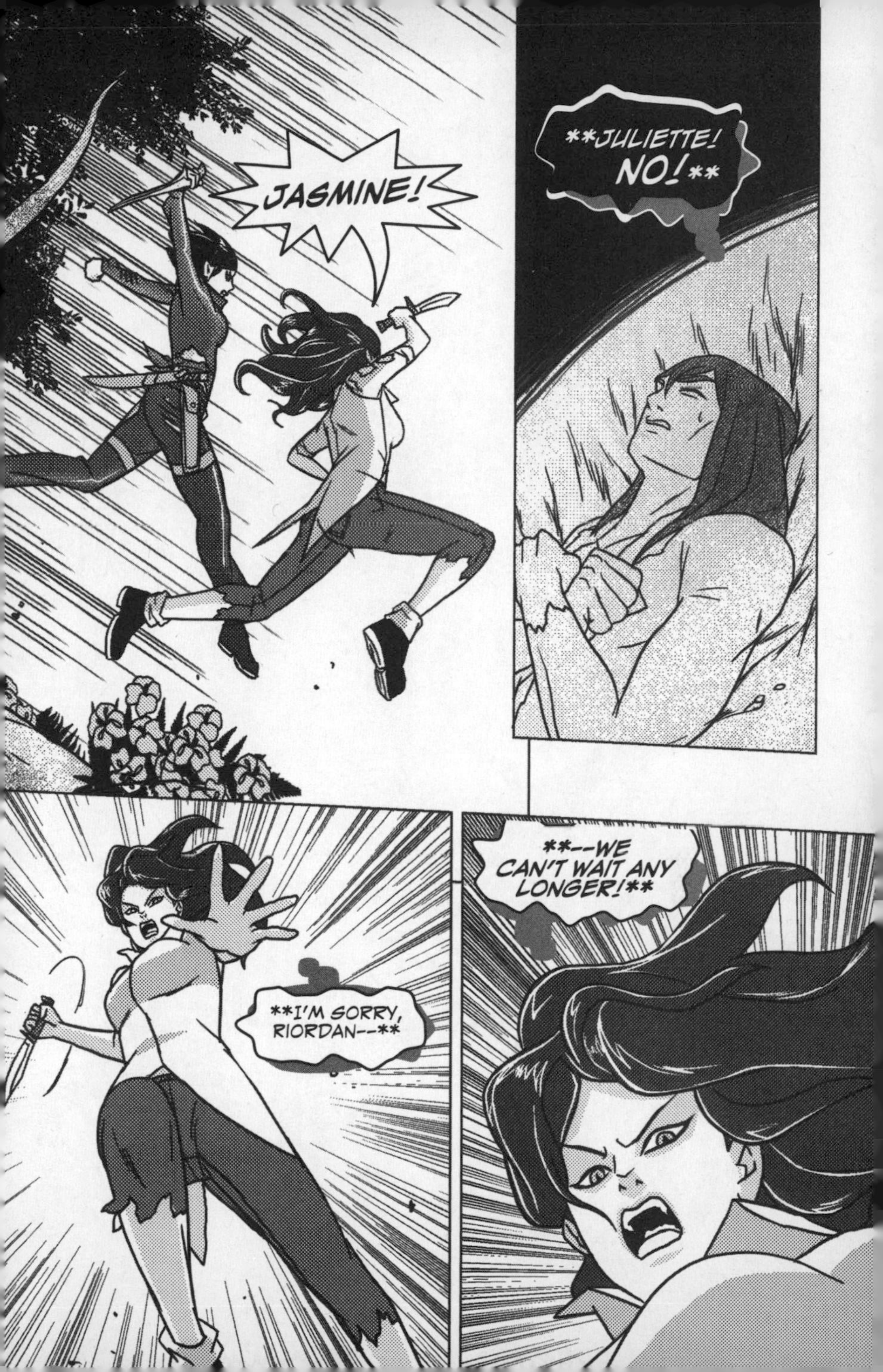
JASMINE!
JULIETTE! NO!
I'M SORRY, RIORDAN--
--WE CAN'T WAIT ANY LONGER!

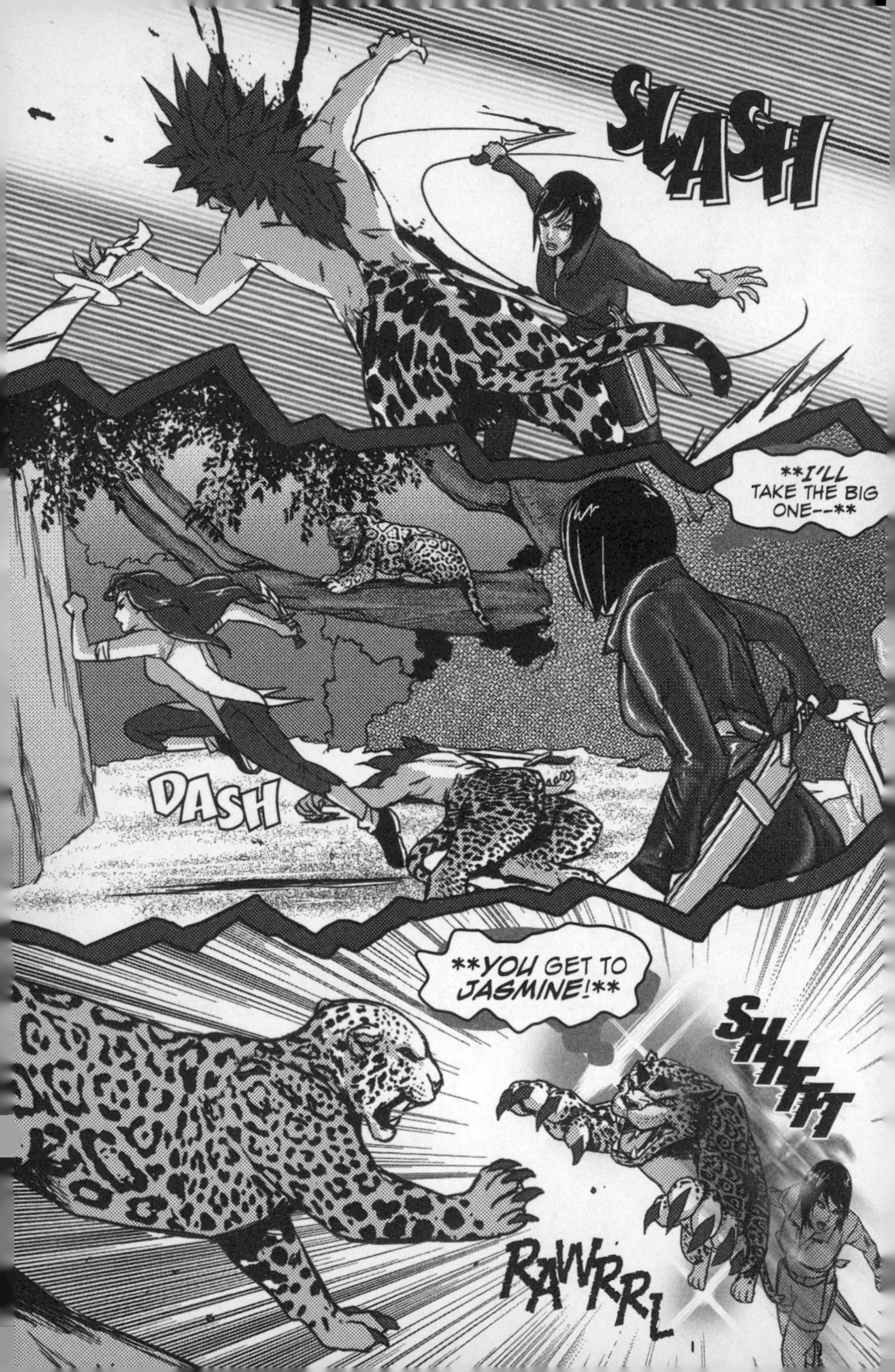
SLASH
I'LL TAKE THE BIG ONE--
DASH
YOU GET TO JASMINE!
SHHHFFT
RAWRRL

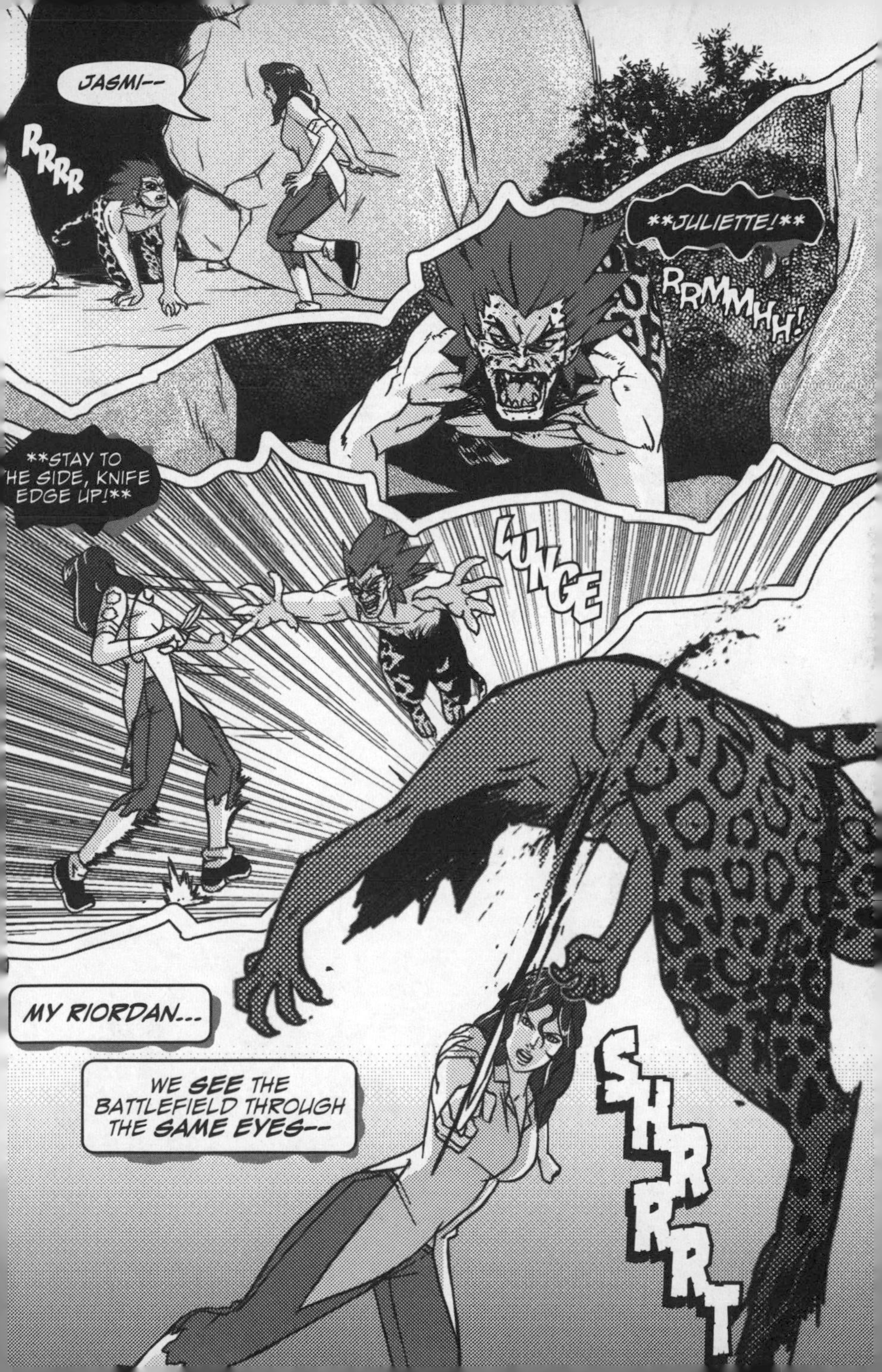
JASMI--
RRRR
JULIETTE!
RRMMHH!
STAY TO THE SIDE, KNIFE EDGE UP!
LUNGE
MY RIORDAN...
WE SEE THE BATTLEFIELD THROUGH THE SAME EYES--
SHRRRT

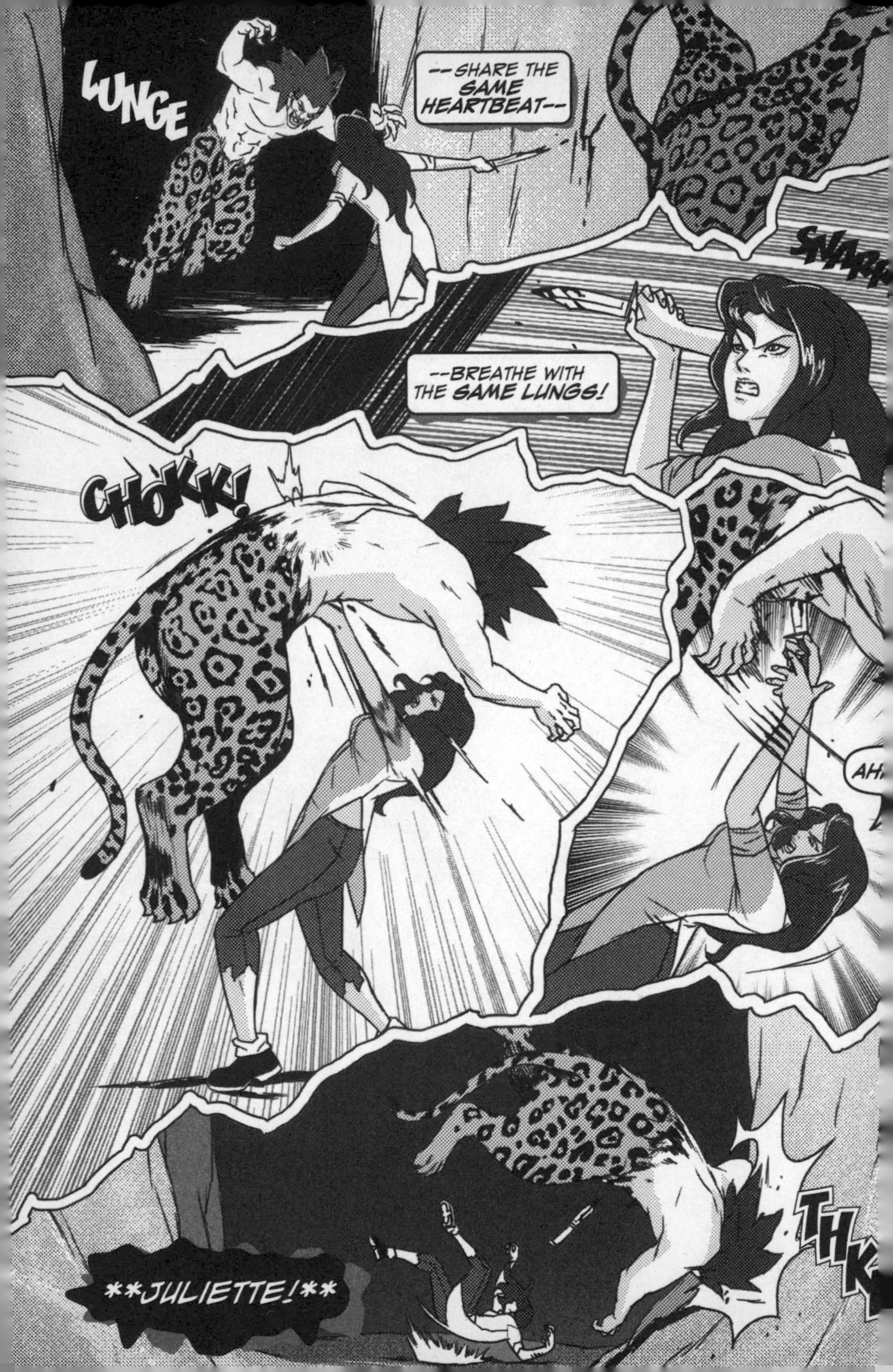
LUNGE
--SHARE THE SAME HEARTBEAT--
SNARR
--BREATHE WITH THE SAME LUNGS!
CHOKK!
AH
THK
JULIETTE!

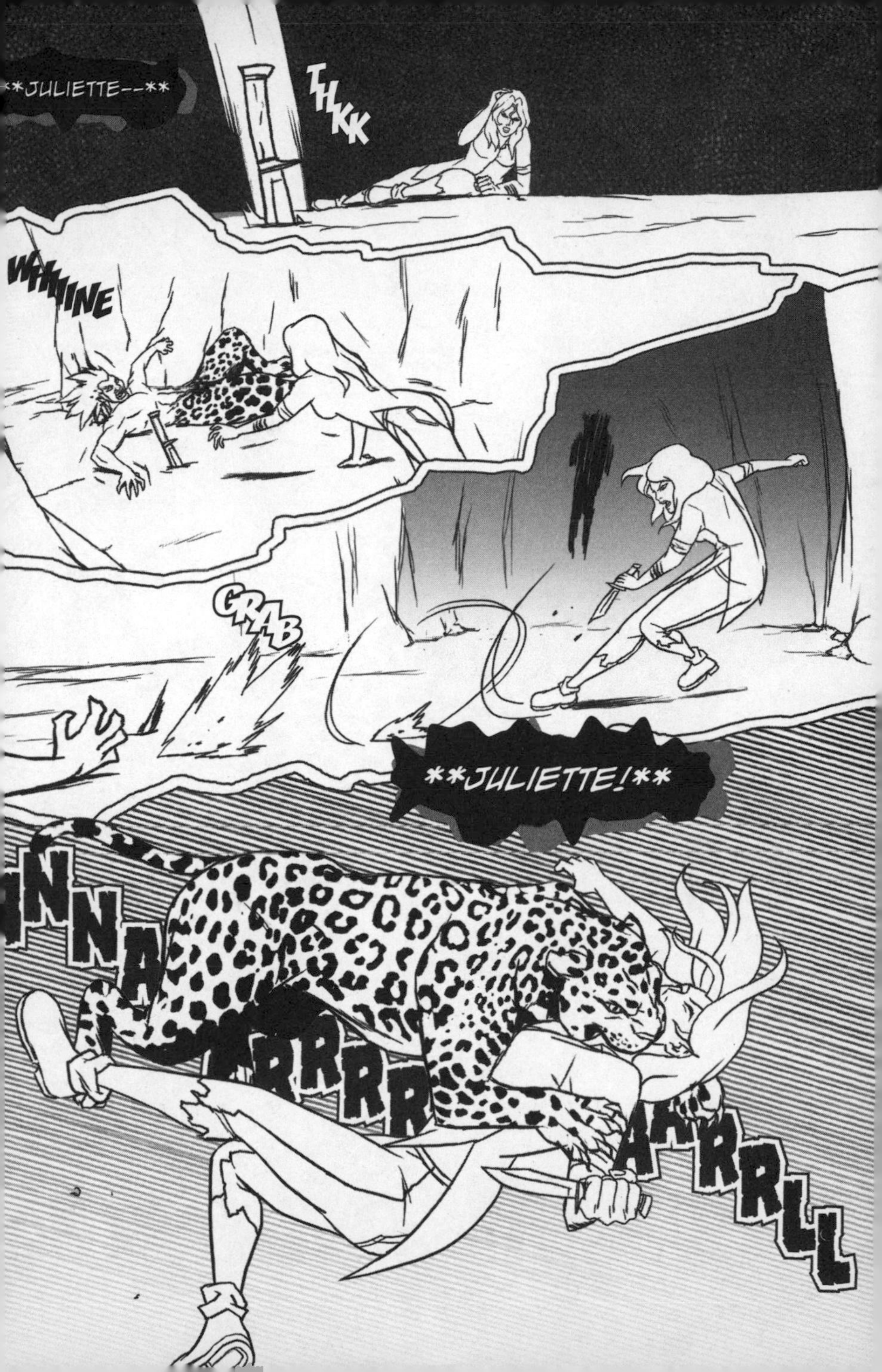
JULIETTE--
THKK
WHHINE
GRAB
JULIETTE!
NNAARRRRR
AHRRLL

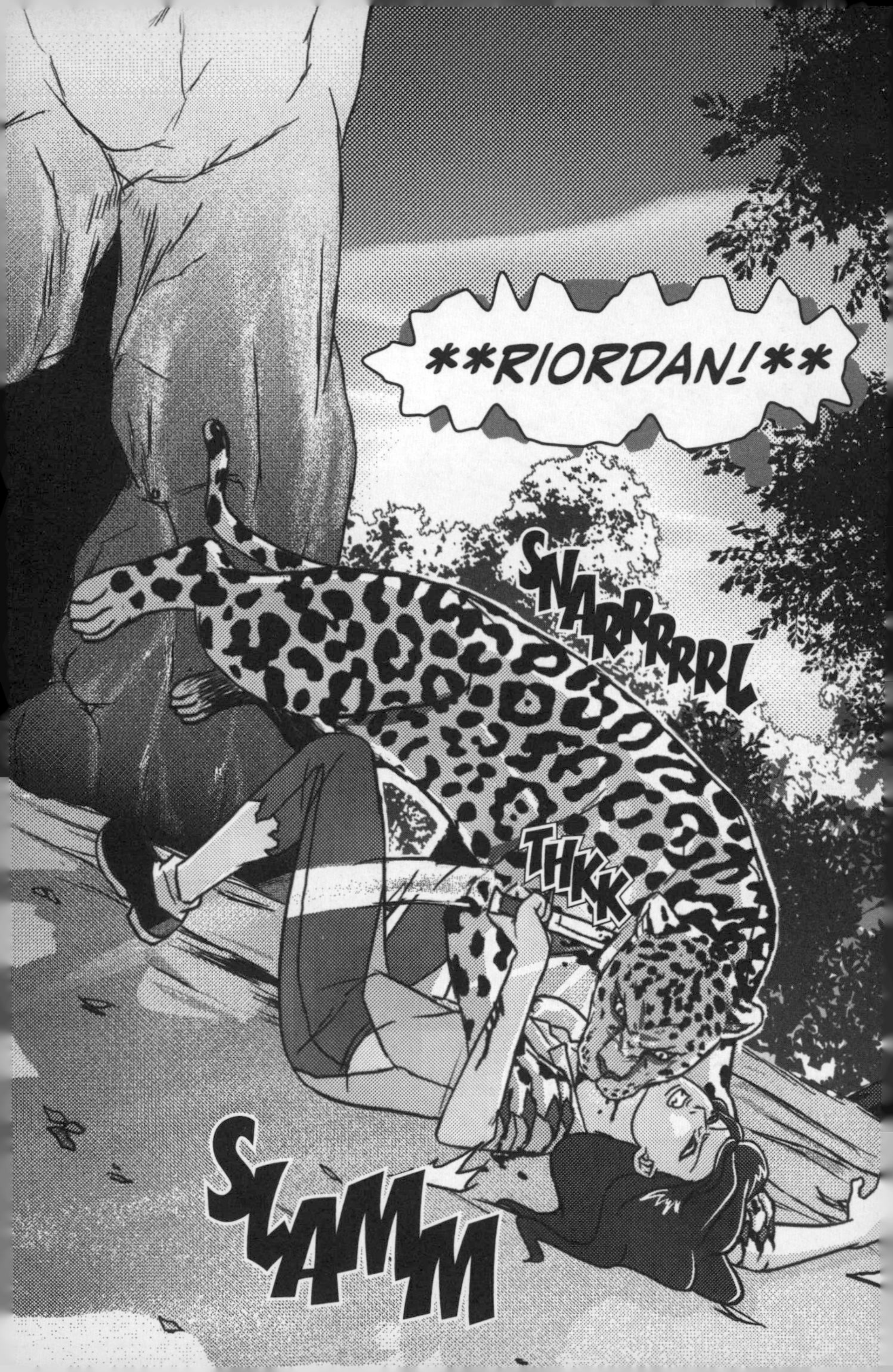
RIORDAN!
SNARRRRRRL
THKK
SLAMMM

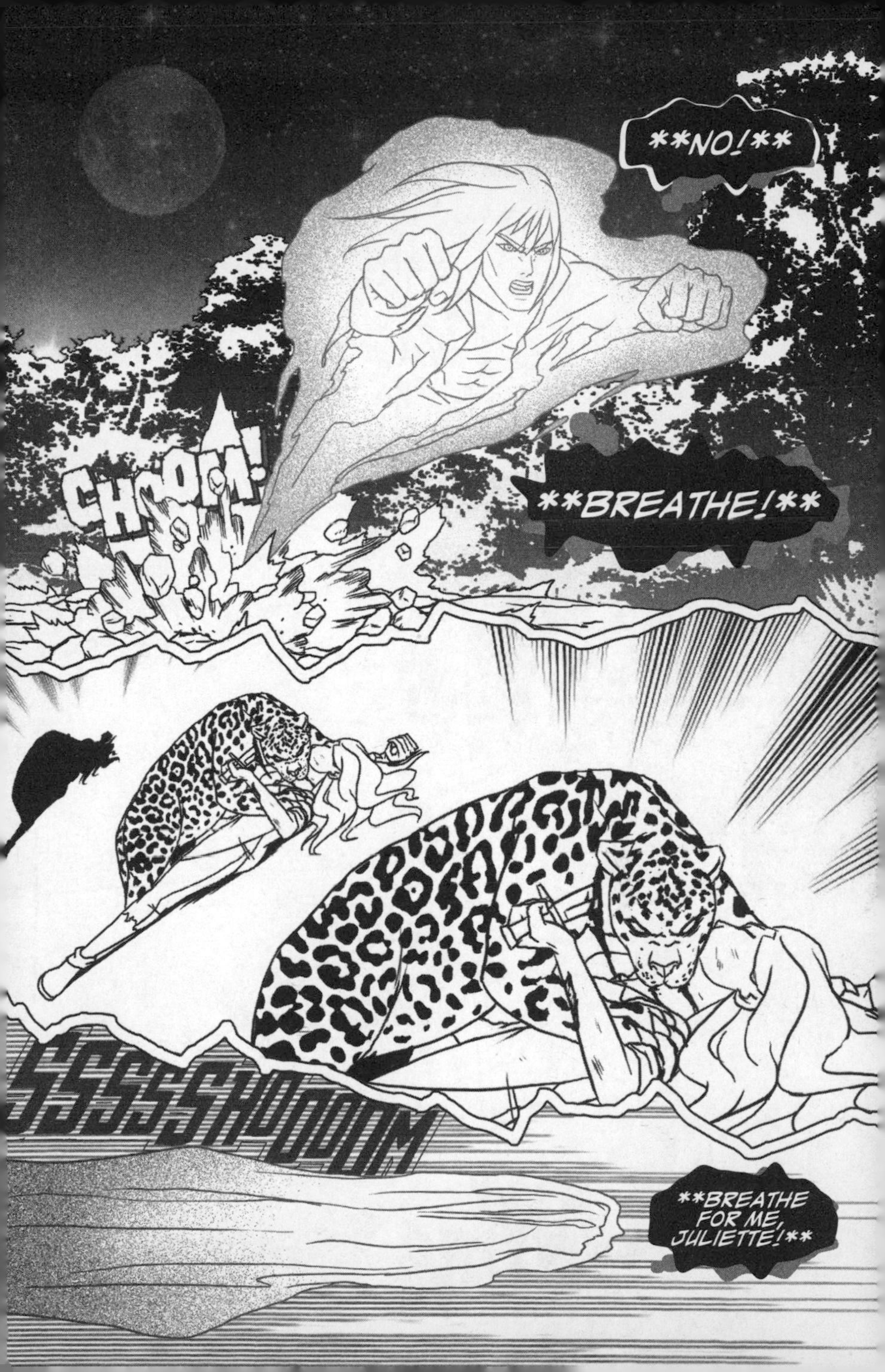
NO!
CHOOM!
BREATHE!
SSSSSSHOOOOM
BREATHE FOR ME, JULIETTE!

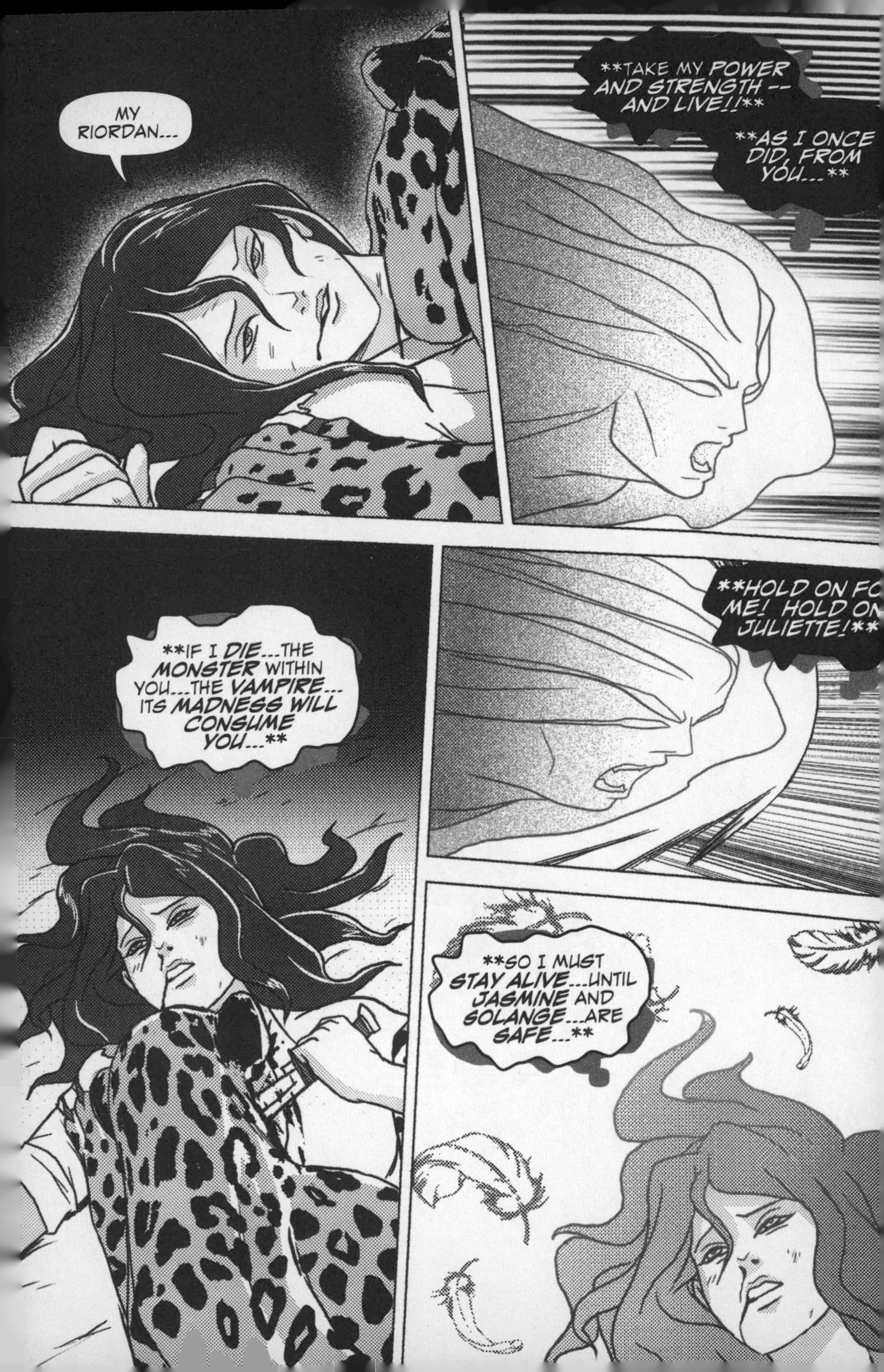
MY RIORDAN...
TAKE MY POWER AND STRENGTH -- AND LIVE!!
AS I ONCE DID, FROM YOU...
IF I DIE...THE MONSTER WITHIN YOU...THE VAMPIRE... ITS MADNESS WILL CONSUME YOU...
HOLD ON FO ME! HOLD ON JULIETTE!
SO I MUST STAY ALIVE...UNTIL JASMINE AND SOLANGE...ARE SAFE...

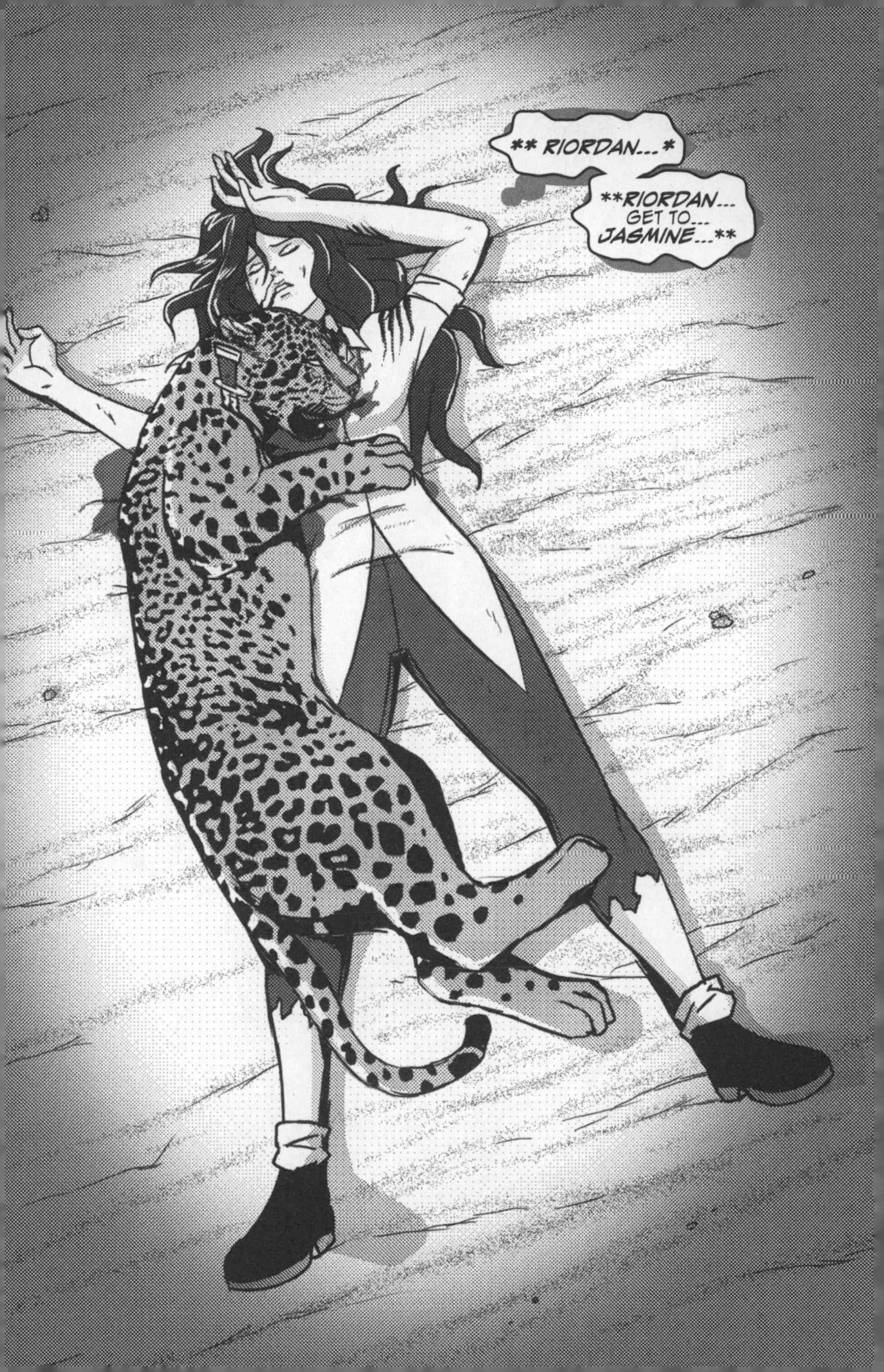
** RIORDAN... *
RIORDAN... GET TO... JASMINE...

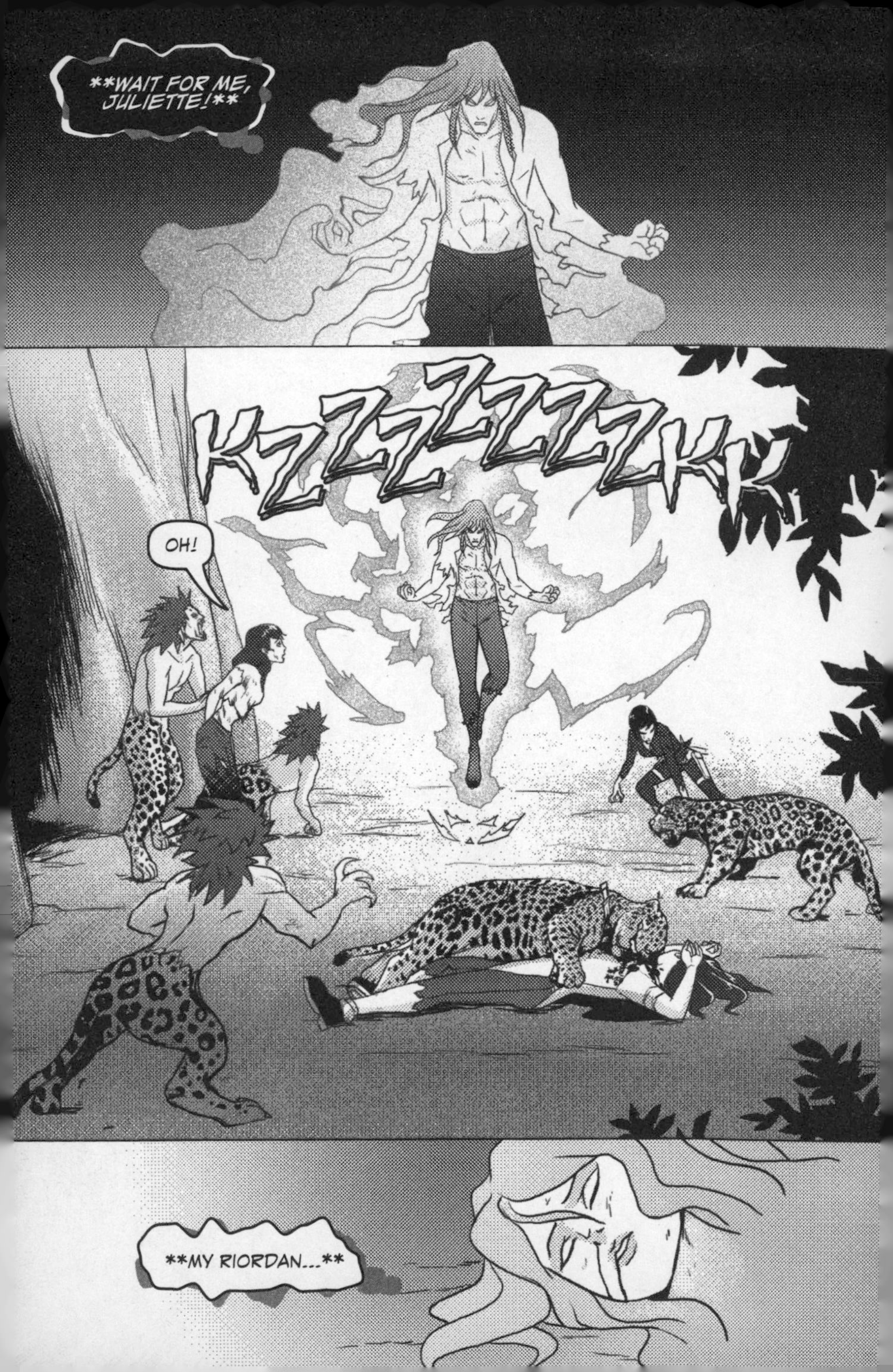
WAIT FOR ME, JULIETTE!
KZZZZZZZZKK
OH!
MY RIORDAN...

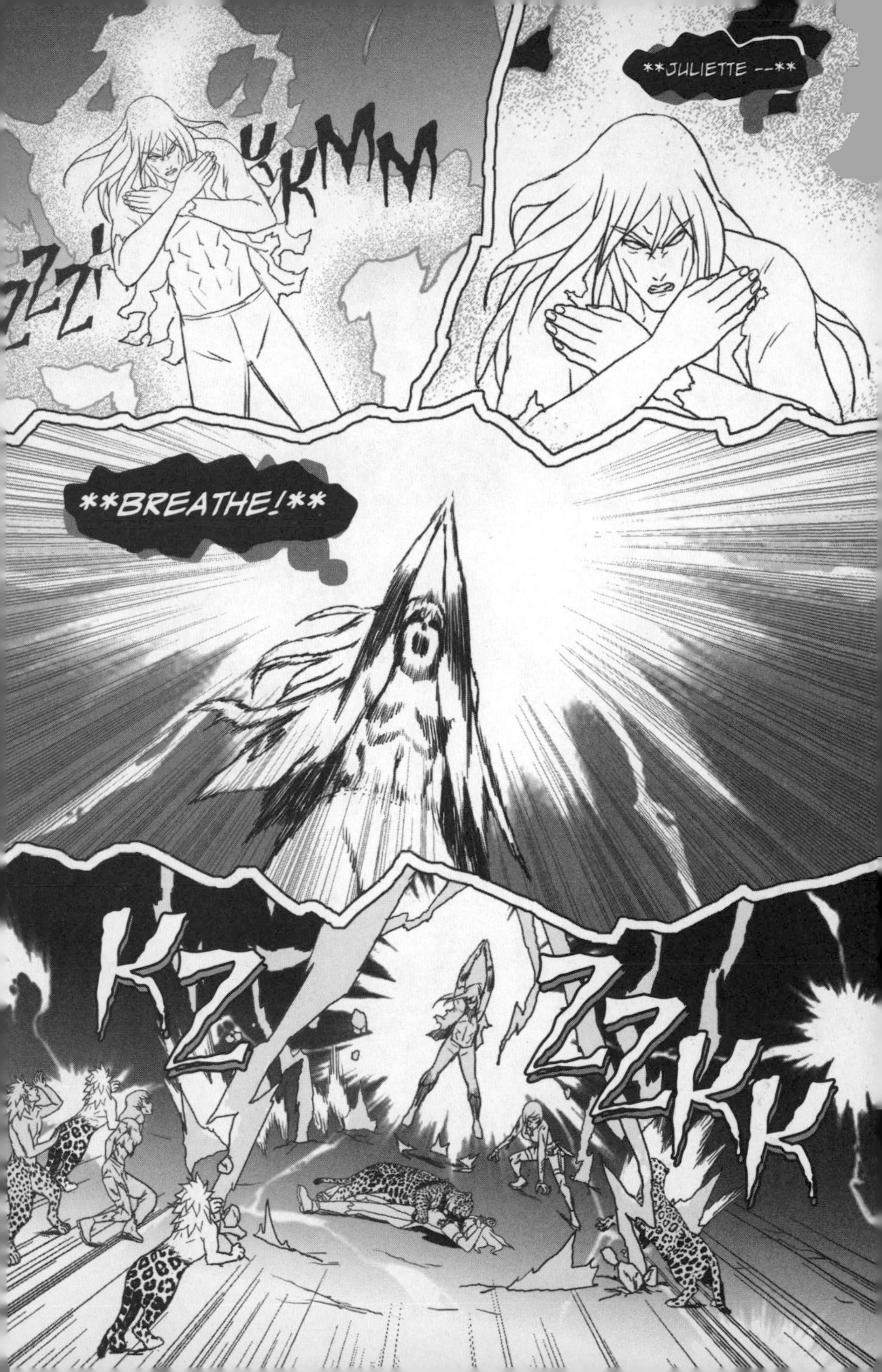
ZZZT!
YKMM
JULIETTE --
BREATHE!
KZZ
ZZKK

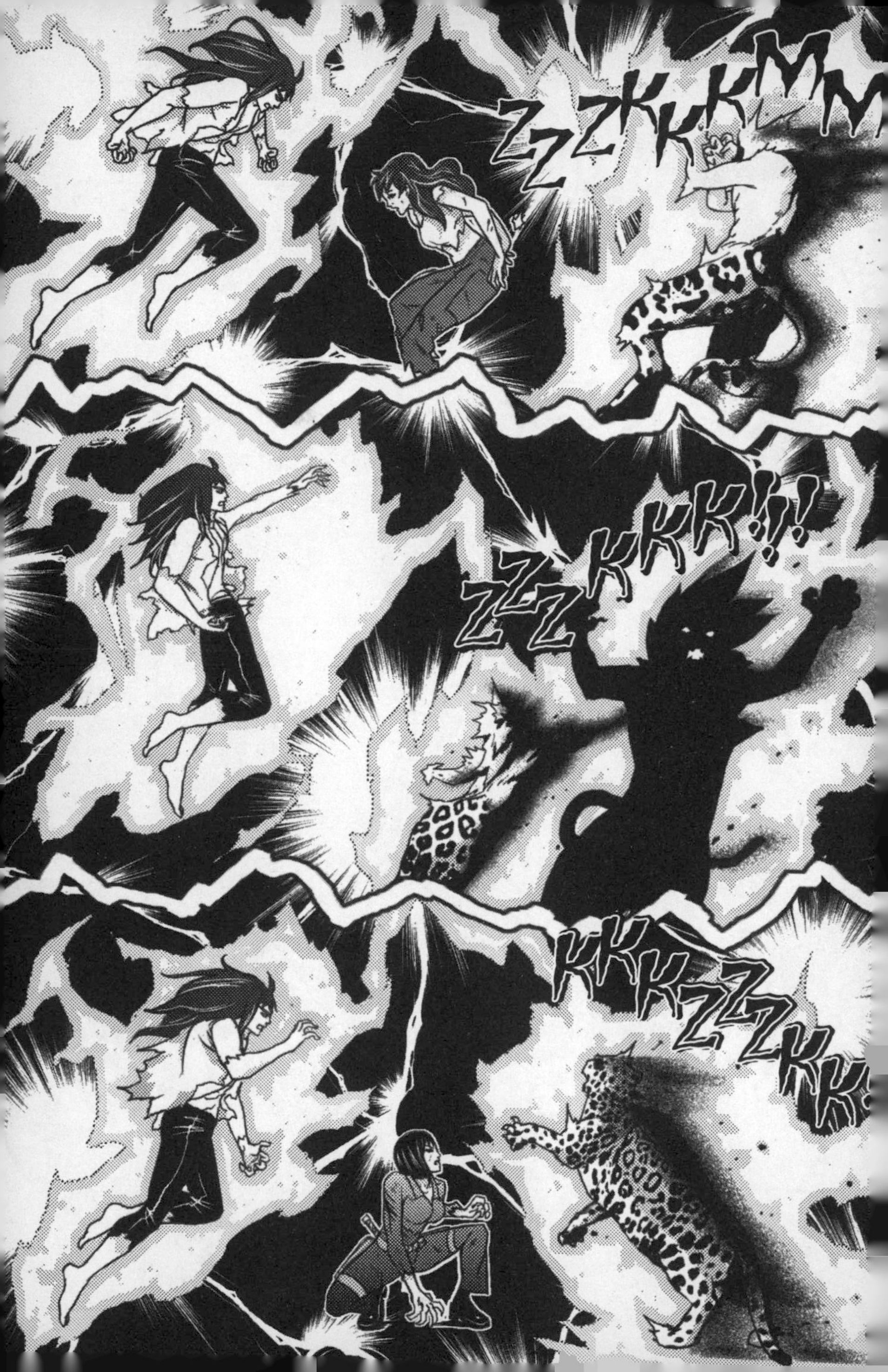

ZZZKKKMM
ZZZKKK!!!
KKKZZZKK

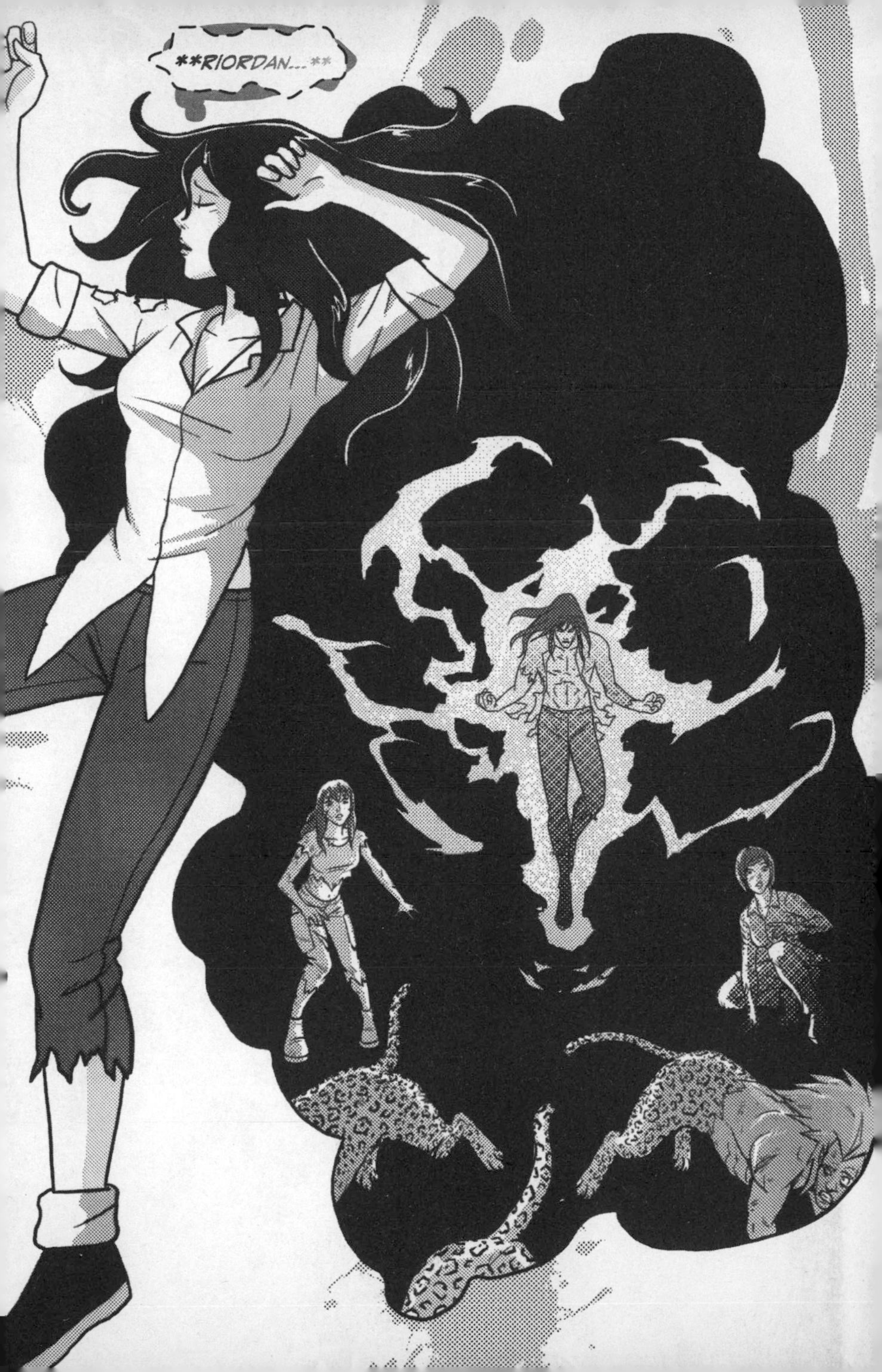
RIORDAN...

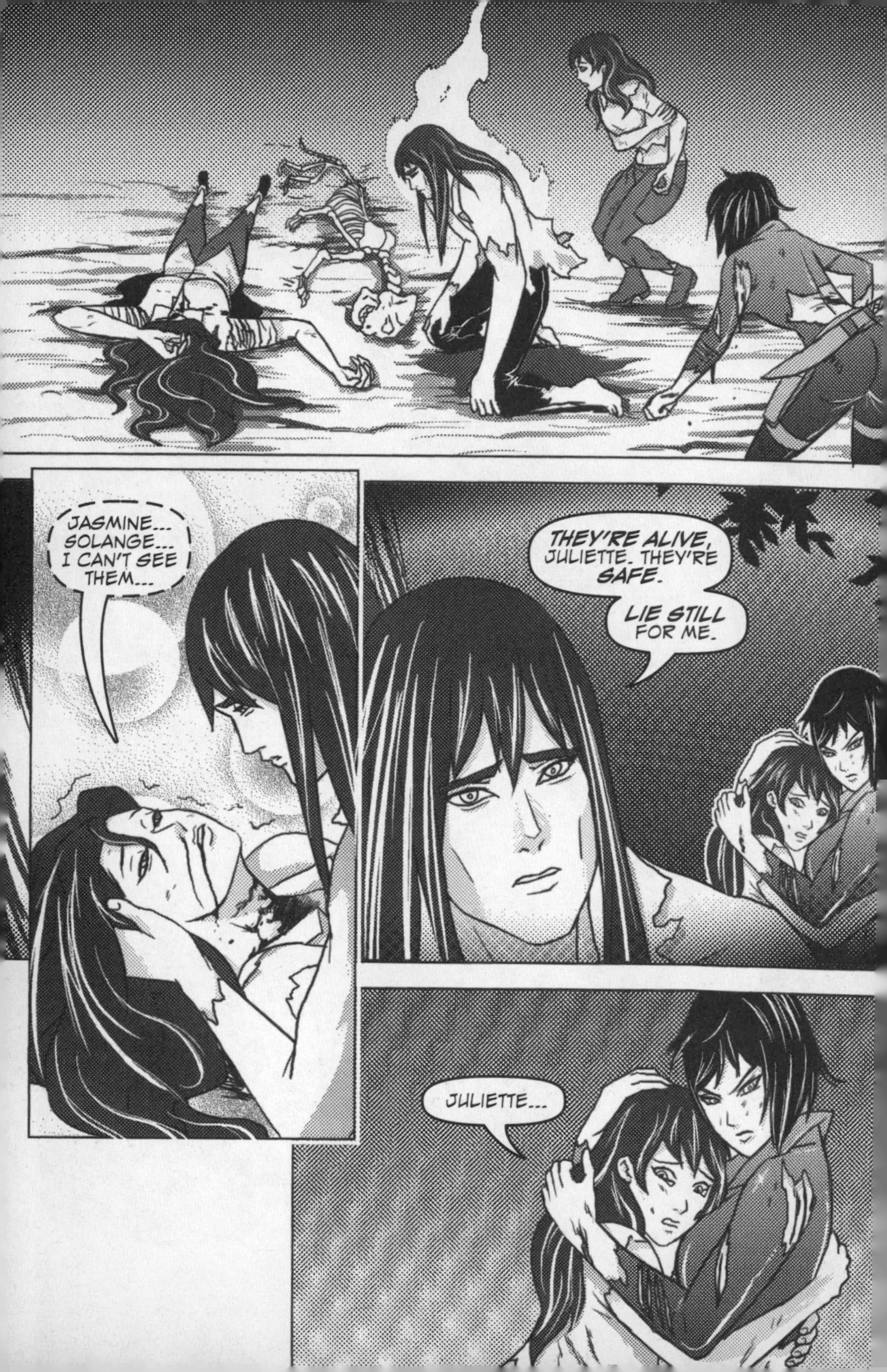
JASMINE... SOLANGE... I CAN'T SEE THEM...
THEY'RE ALIVE, JULIETTE. THEY'RE SAFE.
LIE STILL FOR ME.
JULIETTE...

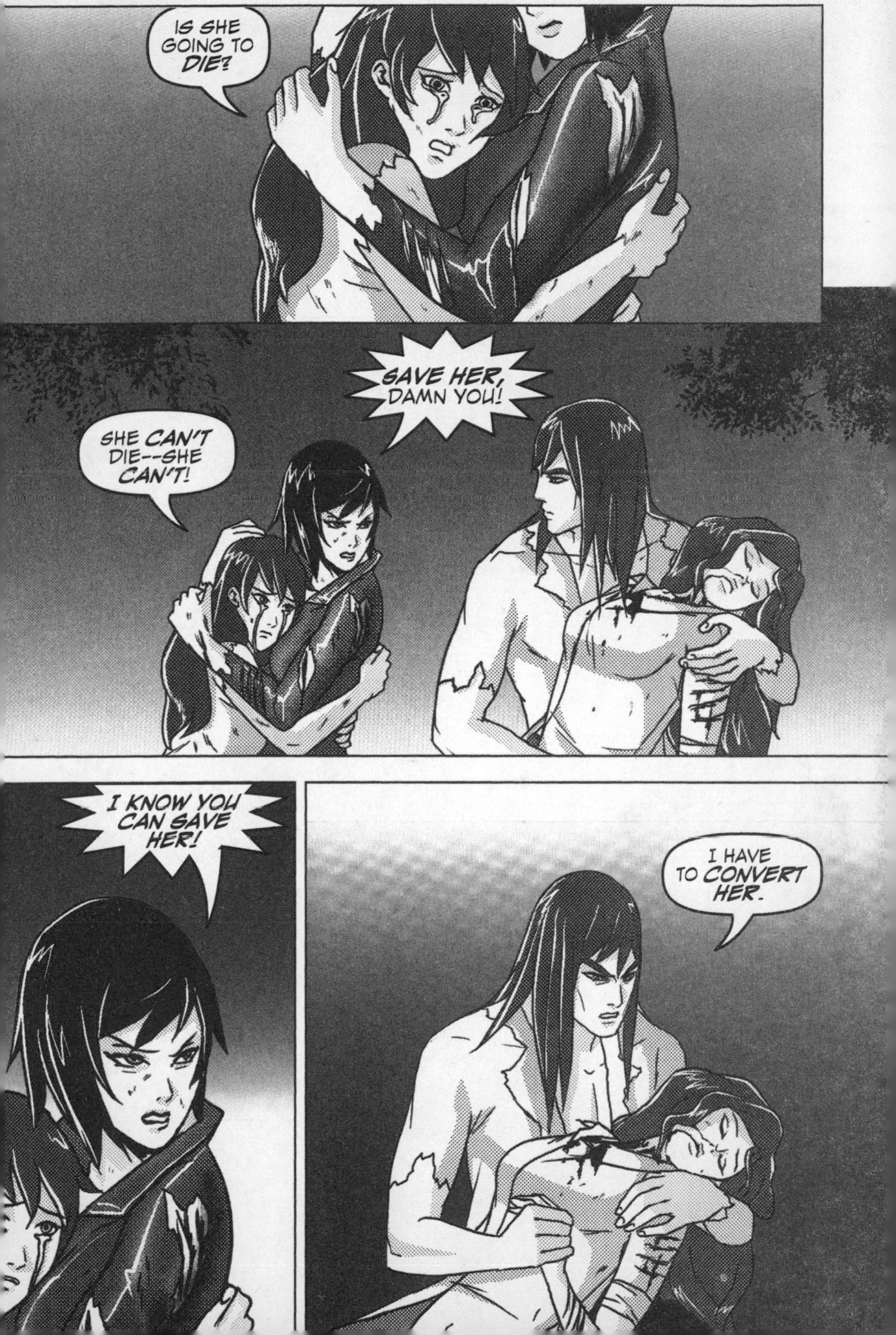
IS SHE GOING TO DIE?
SHE CAN'T DIE--SHE CAN'T!
SAVE HER, DAMN YOU!
I KNOW YOU CAN SAVE HER!
I HAVE TO CONVERT HER.

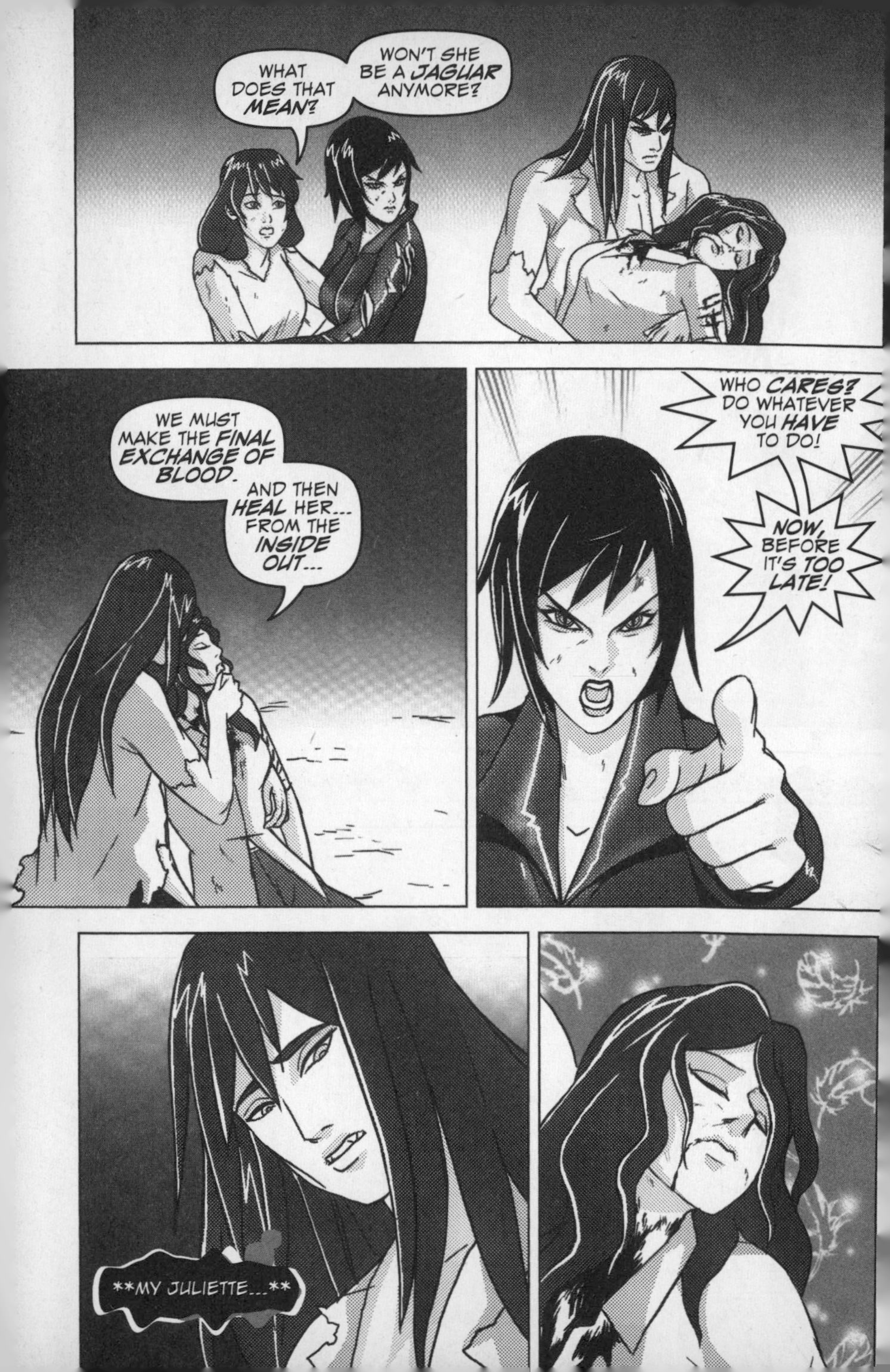
WHAT DOES THAT MEAN?
WON'T SHE BE A JAGUAR ANYMORE?
WE MUST MAKE THE FINAL EXCHANGE OF BLOOD.
AND THEN HEAL HER... FROM THE INSIDE OUT...
WHO CARES? DO WHATEVER YOU HAVE TO DO!
NOW, BEFORE IT'S TOO LATE!
MY JULIETTE...

SHHHHHIINNNGGG

WITH THIS THIRD EXCHANGE, WE BECOME ONE.

I OFFER MY LIFE FOR YOU, JULIETTE.

SHHHHINGGG

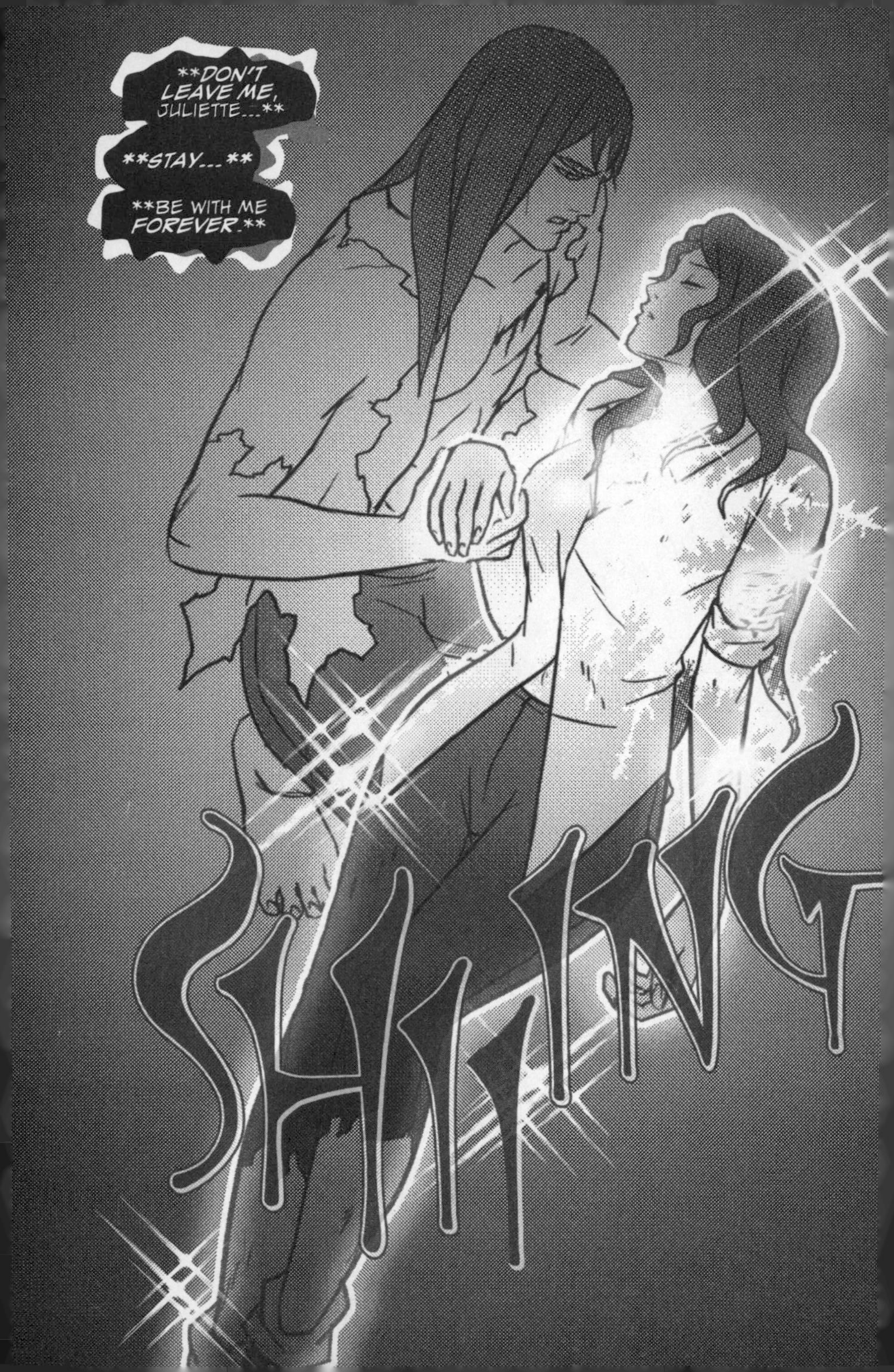
DON'T LEAVE ME, JULIETTE...
STAY...
BE WITH ME FOREVER.
SHING

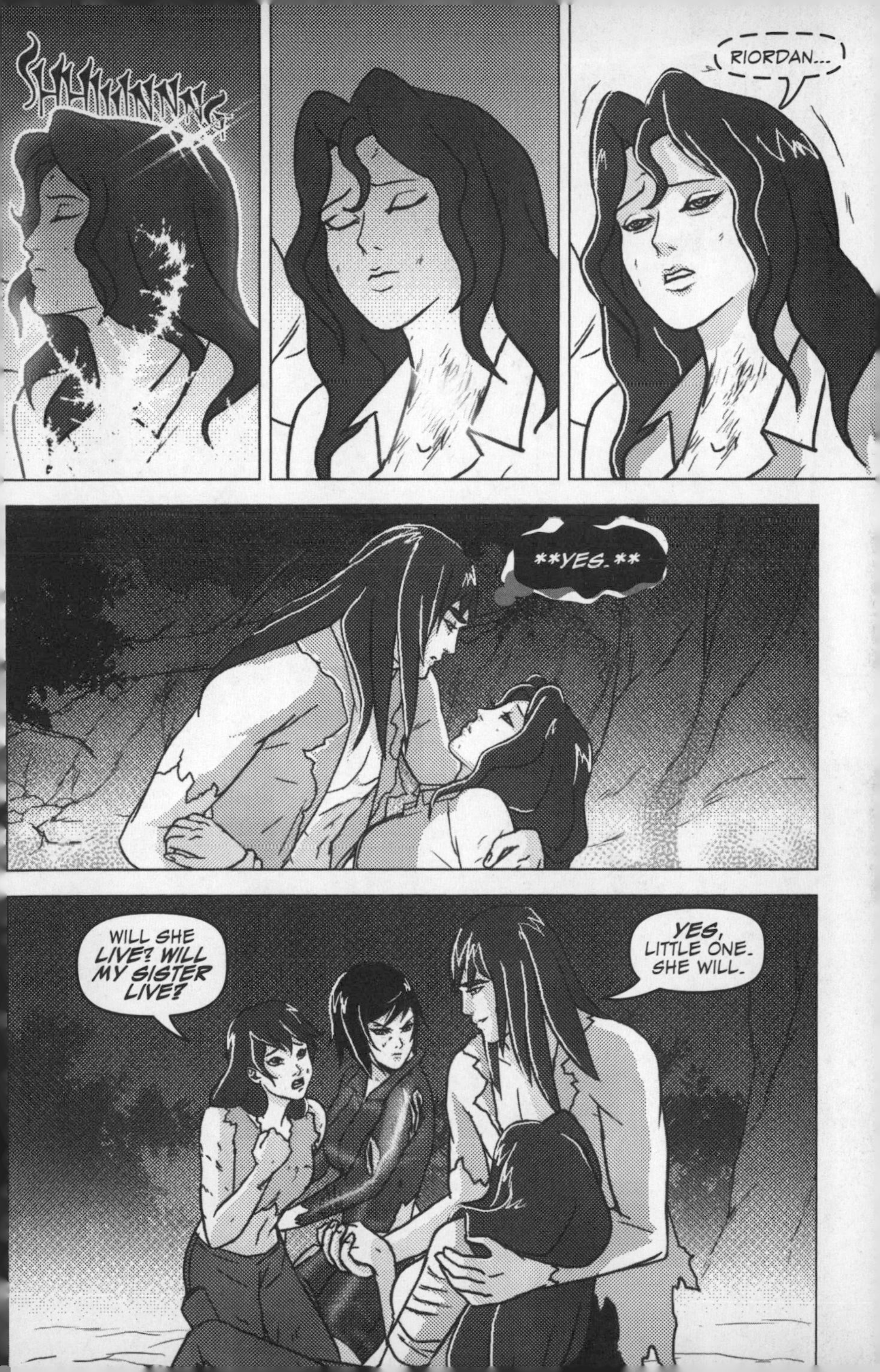
SHHHHINNNNG
RIORDAN...
YES.
WILL SHE LIVE? WILL MY SISTER LIVE?
YES, LITTLE ONE. SHE WILL.

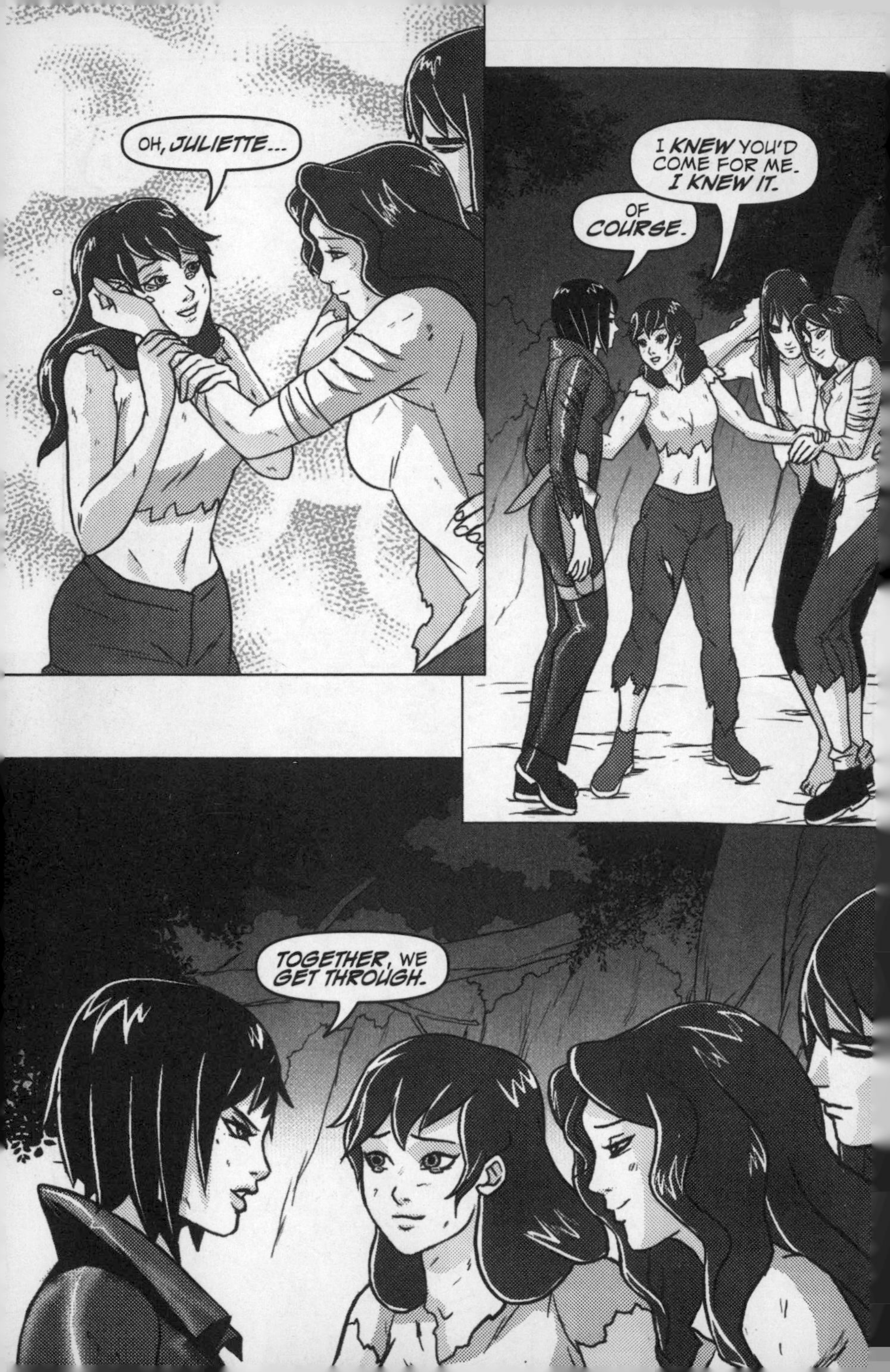
OH, JULIETTE...
OF COURSE.
I KNEW YOU'D COME FOR ME. I KNEW IT.
TOGETHER, WE GET THROUGH.

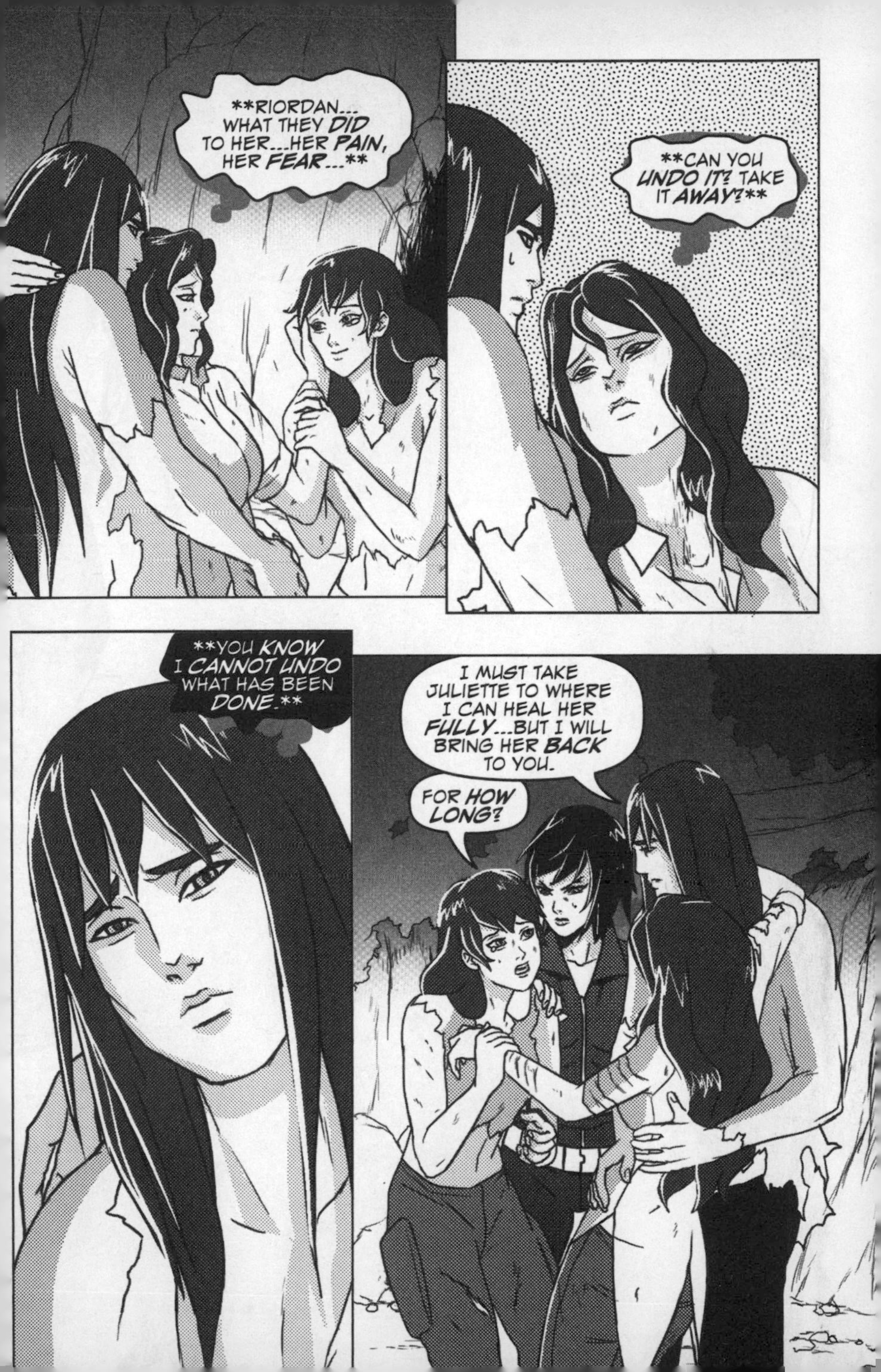
RIORDAN... WHAT THEY *DID* TO HER...HER *PAIN*, HER *FEAR*...
CAN YOU *UNDO IT?* TAKE IT *AWAY?*
YOU *KNOW* I *CANNOT UNDO* WHAT HAS BEEN *DONE*.
I MUST TAKE JULIETTE TO WHERE I CAN HEAL HER *FULLY*...BUT I WILL BRING HER *BACK* TO YOU.
FOR *HOW LONG?*

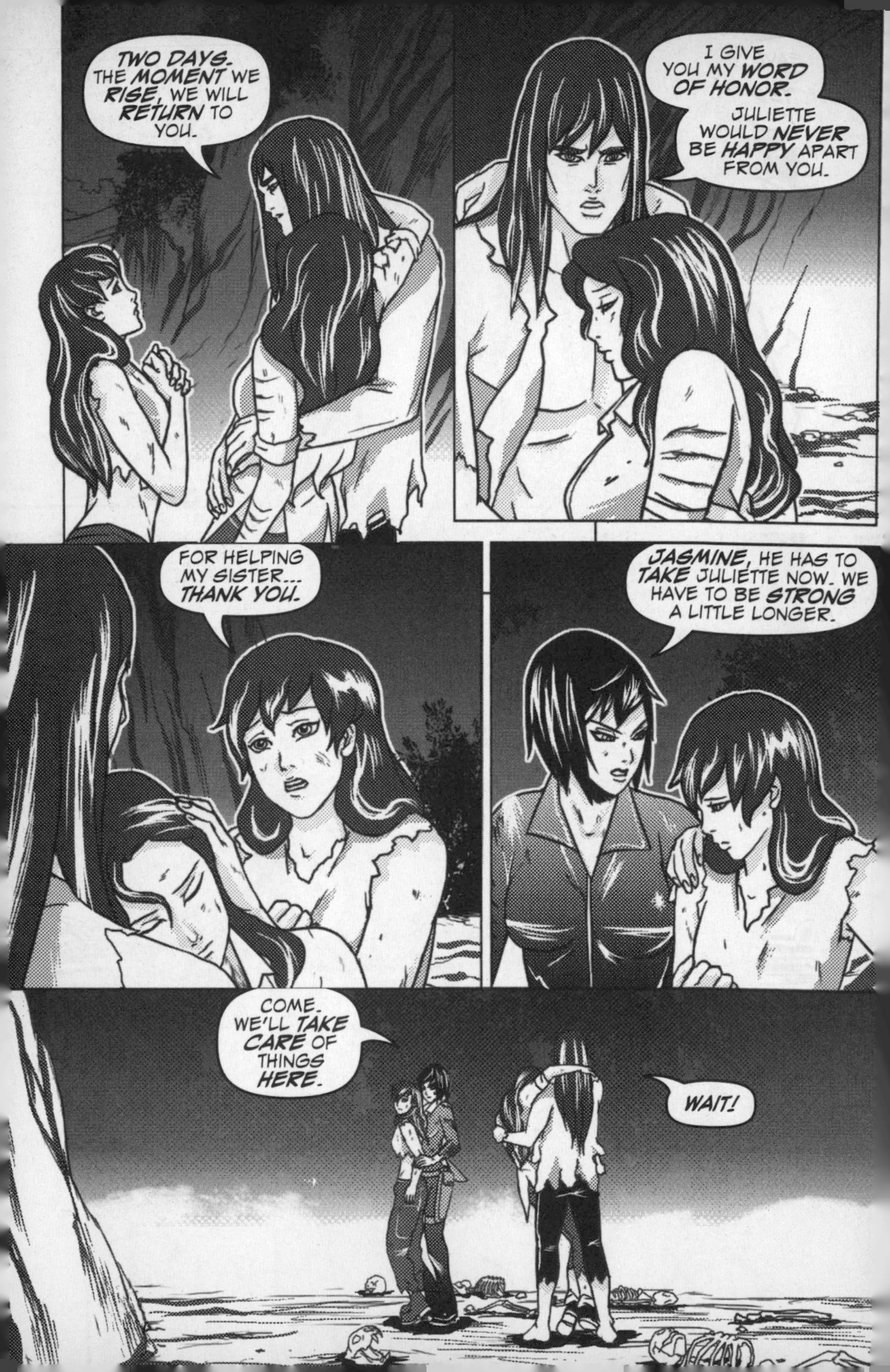
TWO DAYS. THE MOMENT WE RISE, WE WILL RETURN TO YOU.
I GIVE YOU MY WORD OF HONOR.
JULIETTE WOULD NEVER BE HAPPY APART FROM YOU.
FOR HELPING MY SISTER... THANK YOU.
JASMINE, HE HAS TO TAKE JULIETTE NOW. WE HAVE TO BE STRONG A LITTLE LONGER.
COME. WE'LL TAKE CARE OF THINGS HERE.
WAIT!

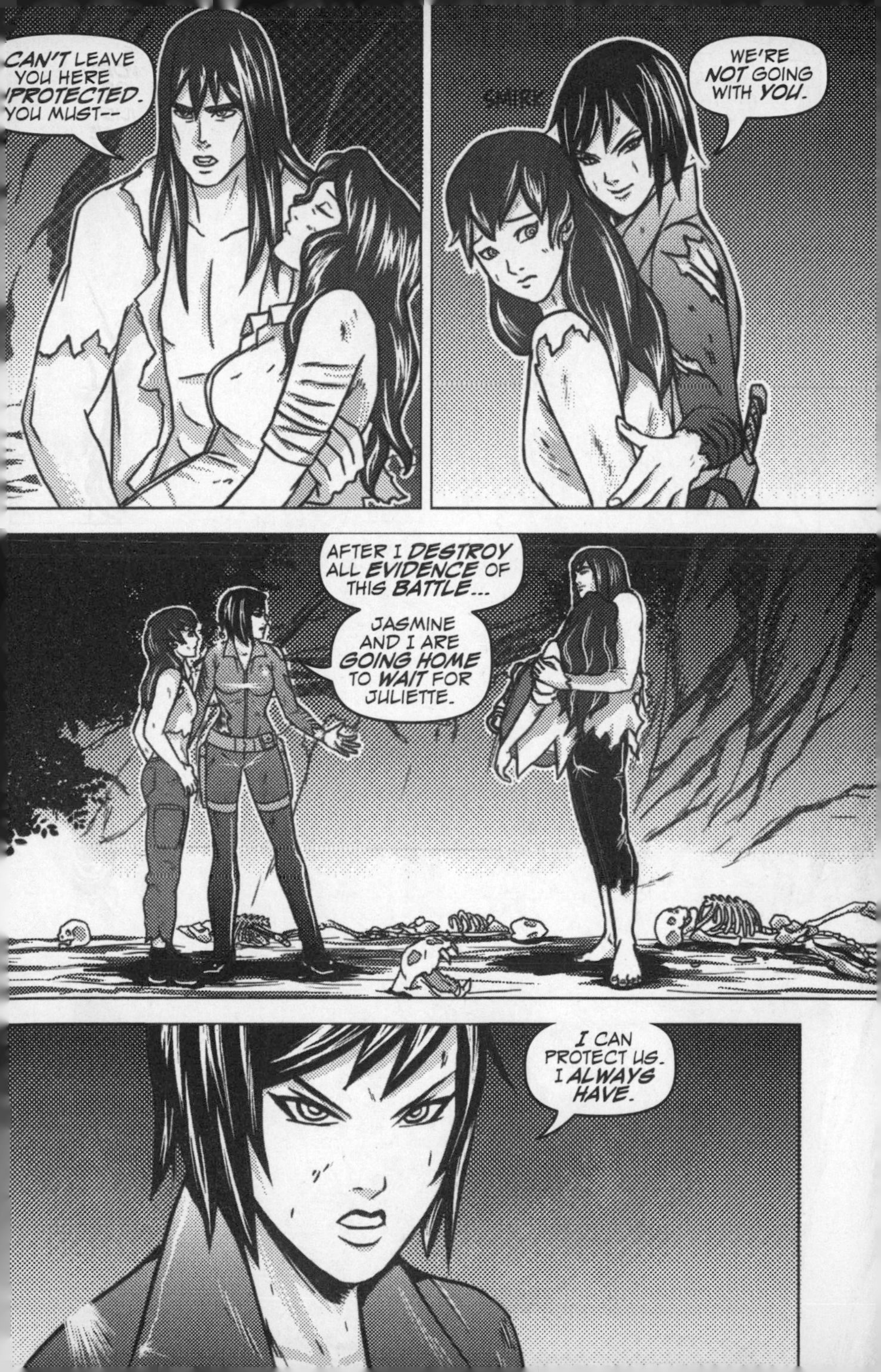
CAN'T LEAVE YOU HERE PROTECTED. YOU MUST--
SMIRK
WE'RE NOT GOING WITH YOU.
AFTER I DESTROY ALL EVIDENCE OF THIS BATTLE...
JASMINE AND I ARE GOING HOME TO WAIT FOR JULIETTE.
I CAN PROTECT US. I ALWAYS HAVE.

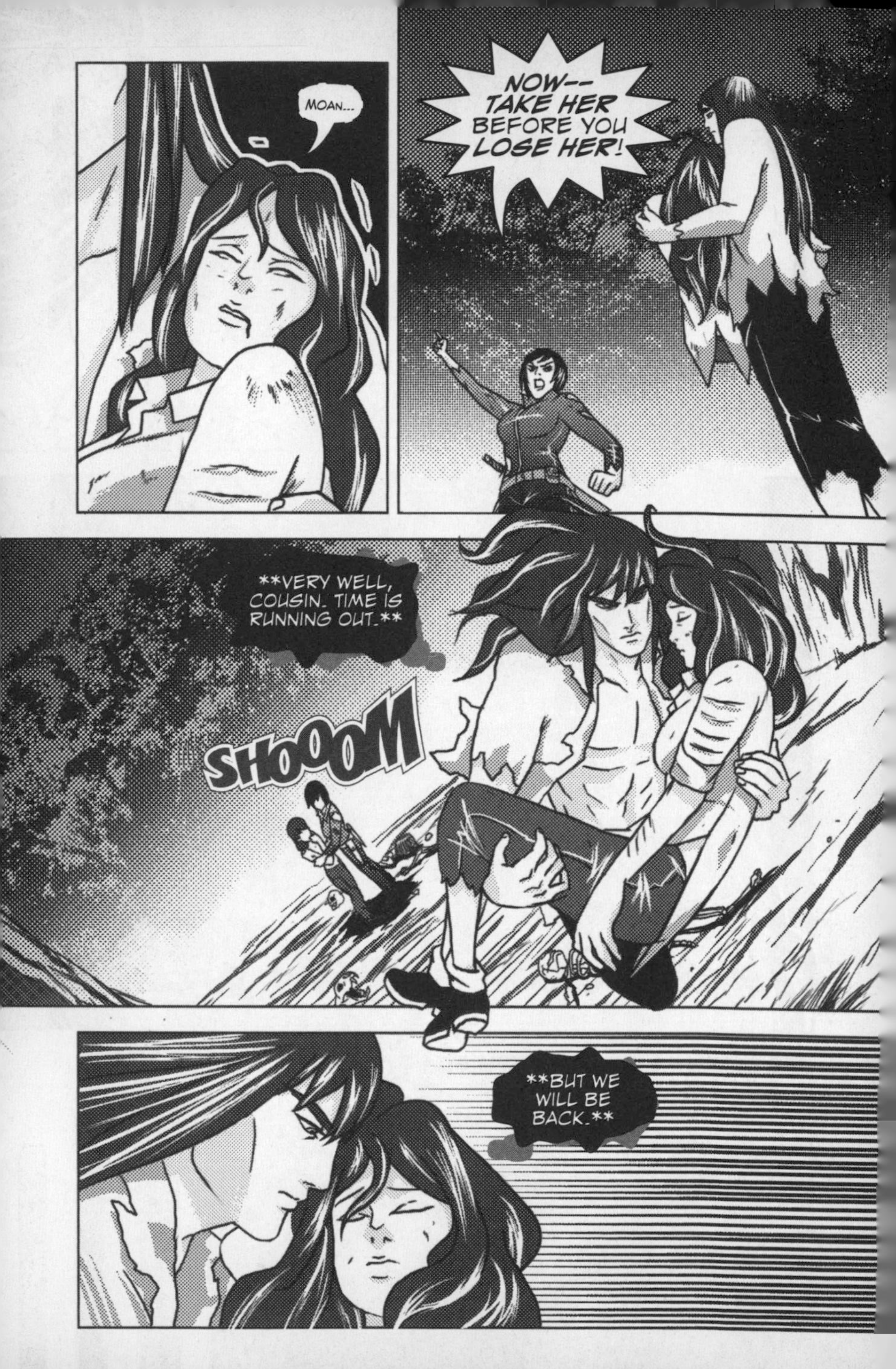
MOAN...
NOW-- TAKE HER BEFORE YOU LOSE HER!
VERY WELL, COUSIN. TIME IS RUNNING OUT.
SHOOOM
BUT WE WILL BE BACK.

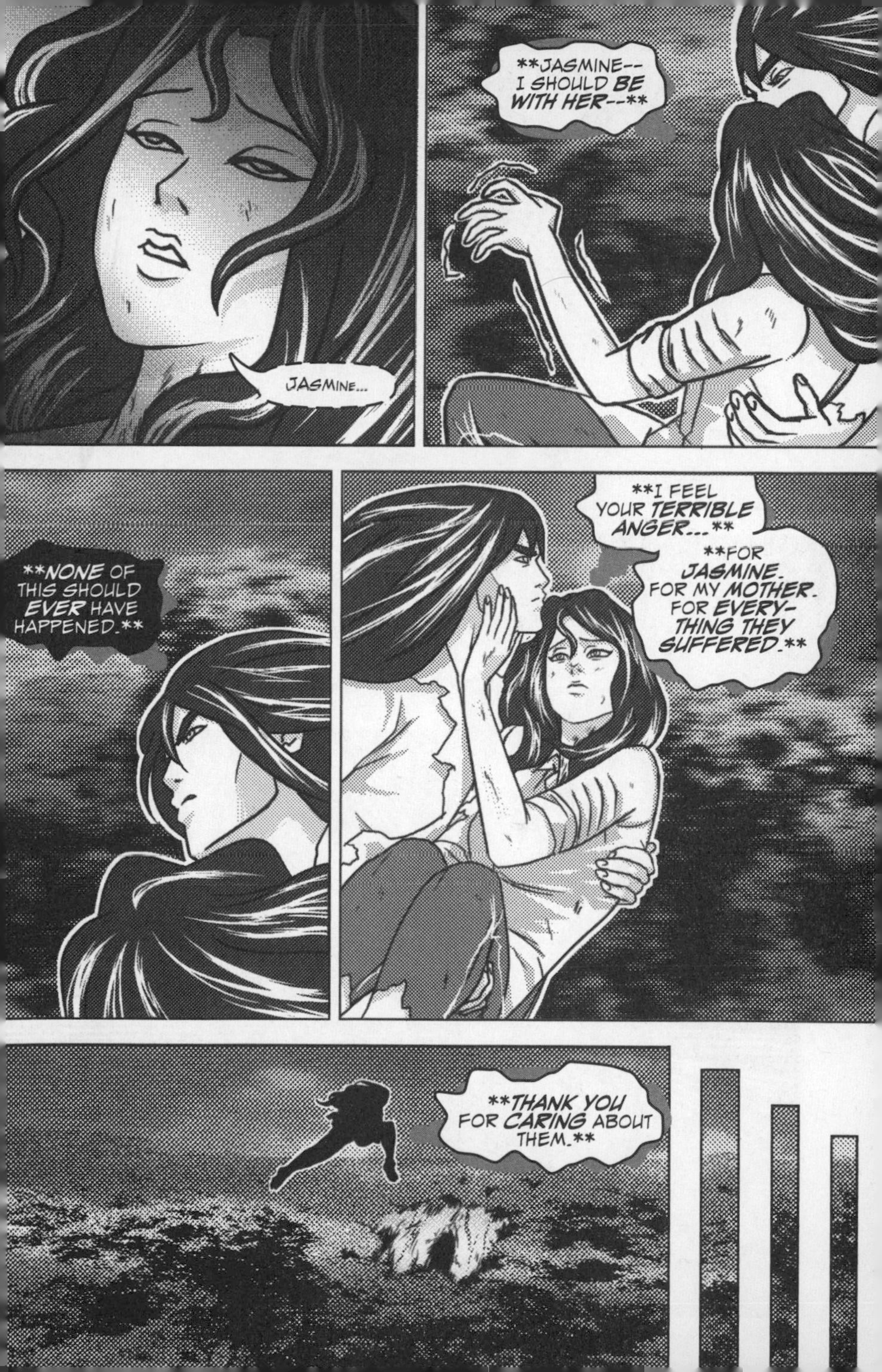
JASMINE...
JASMINE-- I SHOULD BE WITH HER--
NONE OF THIS SHOULD EVER HAVE HAPPENED.
I FEEL YOUR TERRIBLE ANGER...
FOR JASMINE. FOR MY MOTHER. FOR EVERY-THING THEY SUFFERED.
THANK YOU FOR CARING ABOUT THEM.

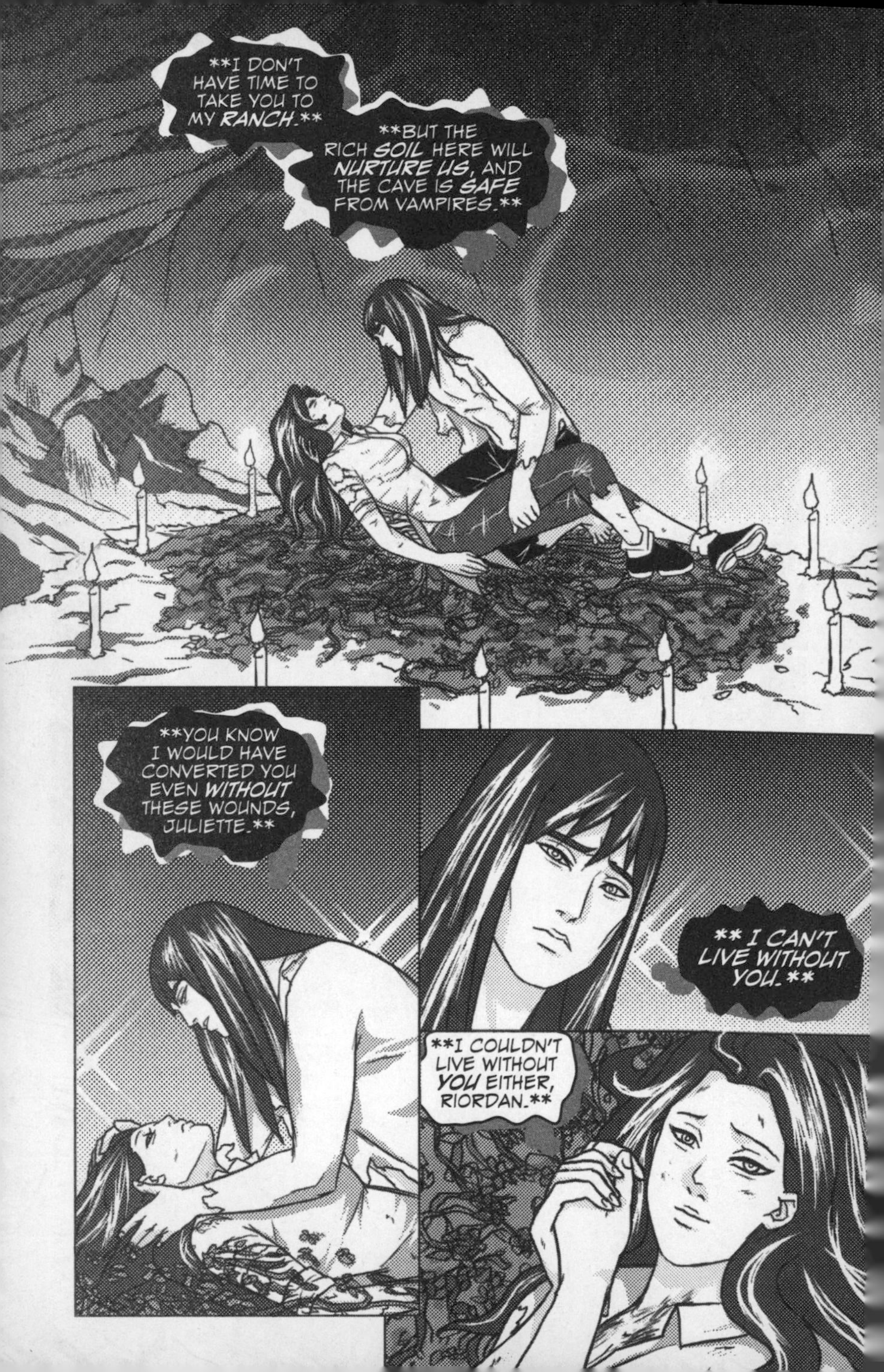
I DON'T HAVE TIME TO TAKE YOU TO MY RANCH.
BUT THE RICH SOIL HERE WILL NURTURE US, AND THE CAVE IS SAFE FROM VAMPIRES.
YOU KNOW I WOULD HAVE CONVERTED YOU EVEN WITHOUT THESE WOUNDS, JULIETTE.
** I CAN'T LIVE WITHOUT YOU.**
I COULDN'T LIVE WITHOUT YOU EITHER, RIORDAN.

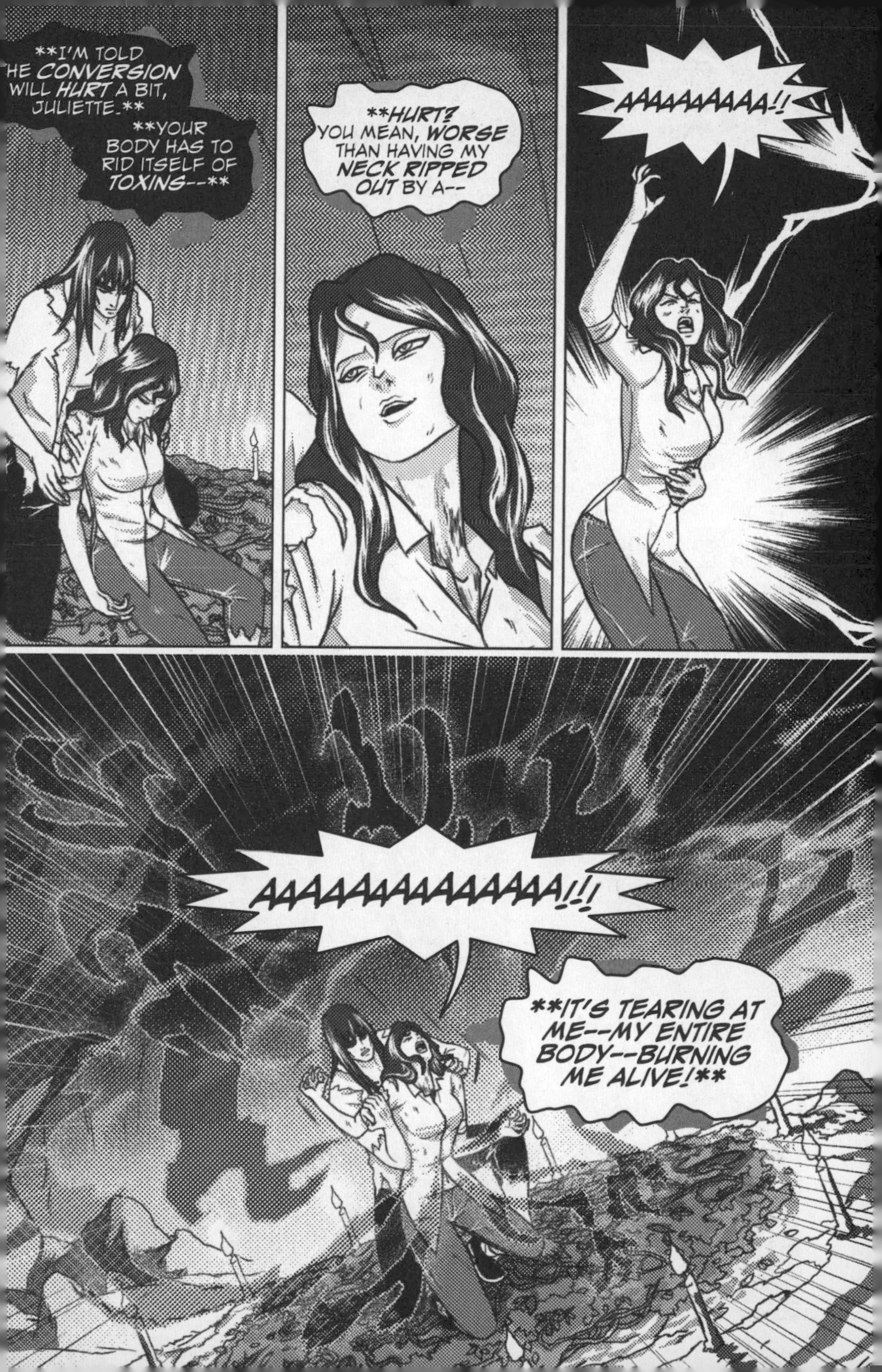
I'M TOLD THE CONVERSION WILL HURT A BIT, JULIETTE.
YOUR BODY HAS TO RID ITSELF OF TOXINS--
**HURT? YOU MEAN, WORSE THAN HAVING MY NECK RIPPED OUT BY A--
AAAAAAAAAA!!
AAAAAAAAAAAAAAA!!!
IT'S TEARING AT ME--MY ENTIRE BODY--BURNING ME ALIVE!

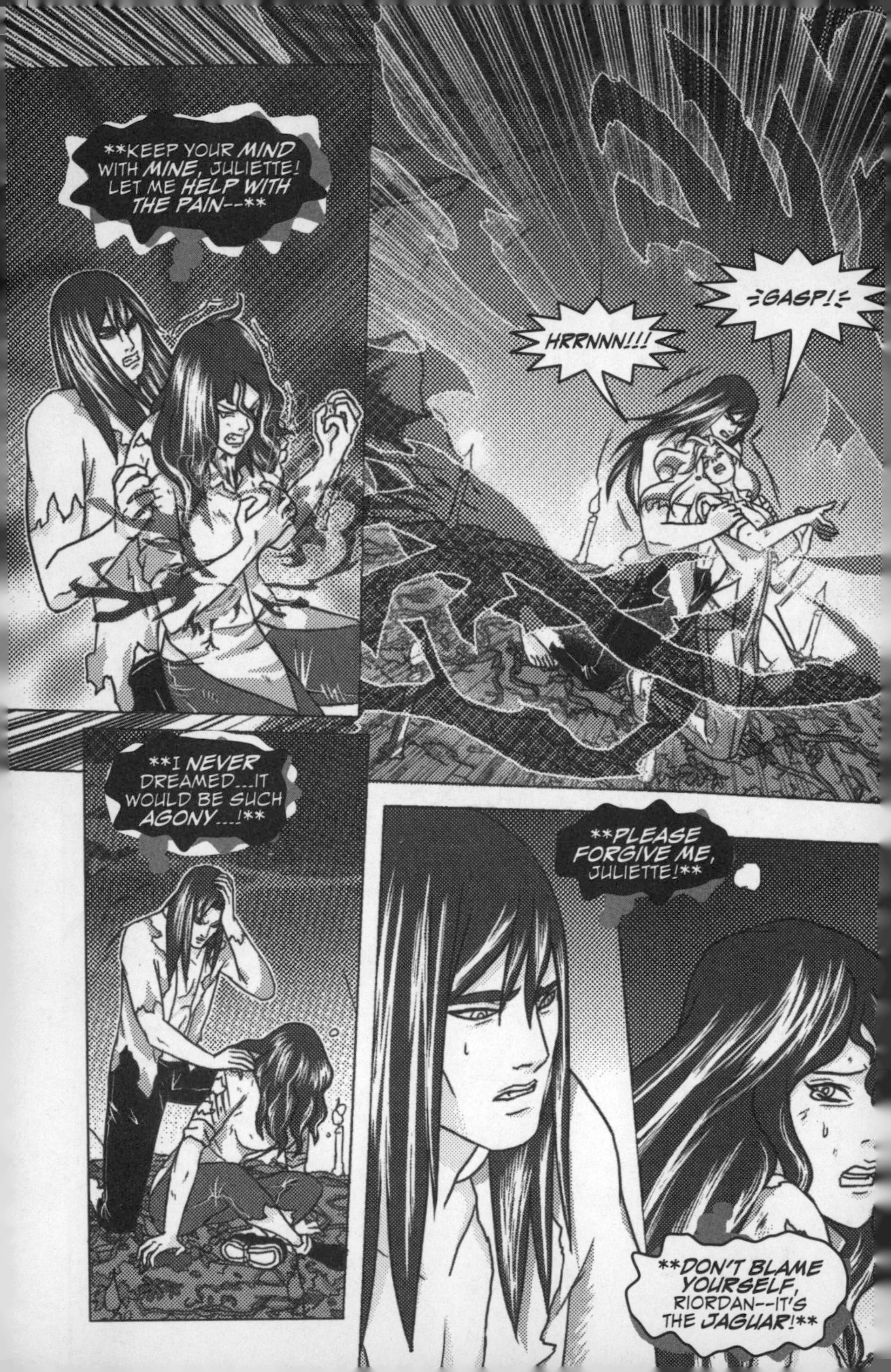

KEEP YOUR MIND WITH MINE, JULIETTE! LET ME HELP WITH THE PAIN--
HRRNNN!!!
=GASP!=
I NEVER DREAMED...IT WOULD BE SUCH AGONY...!
PLEASE FORGIVE ME, JULIETTE!
DON'T BLAME YOURSELF, RIORDAN--IT'S THE JAGUAR!

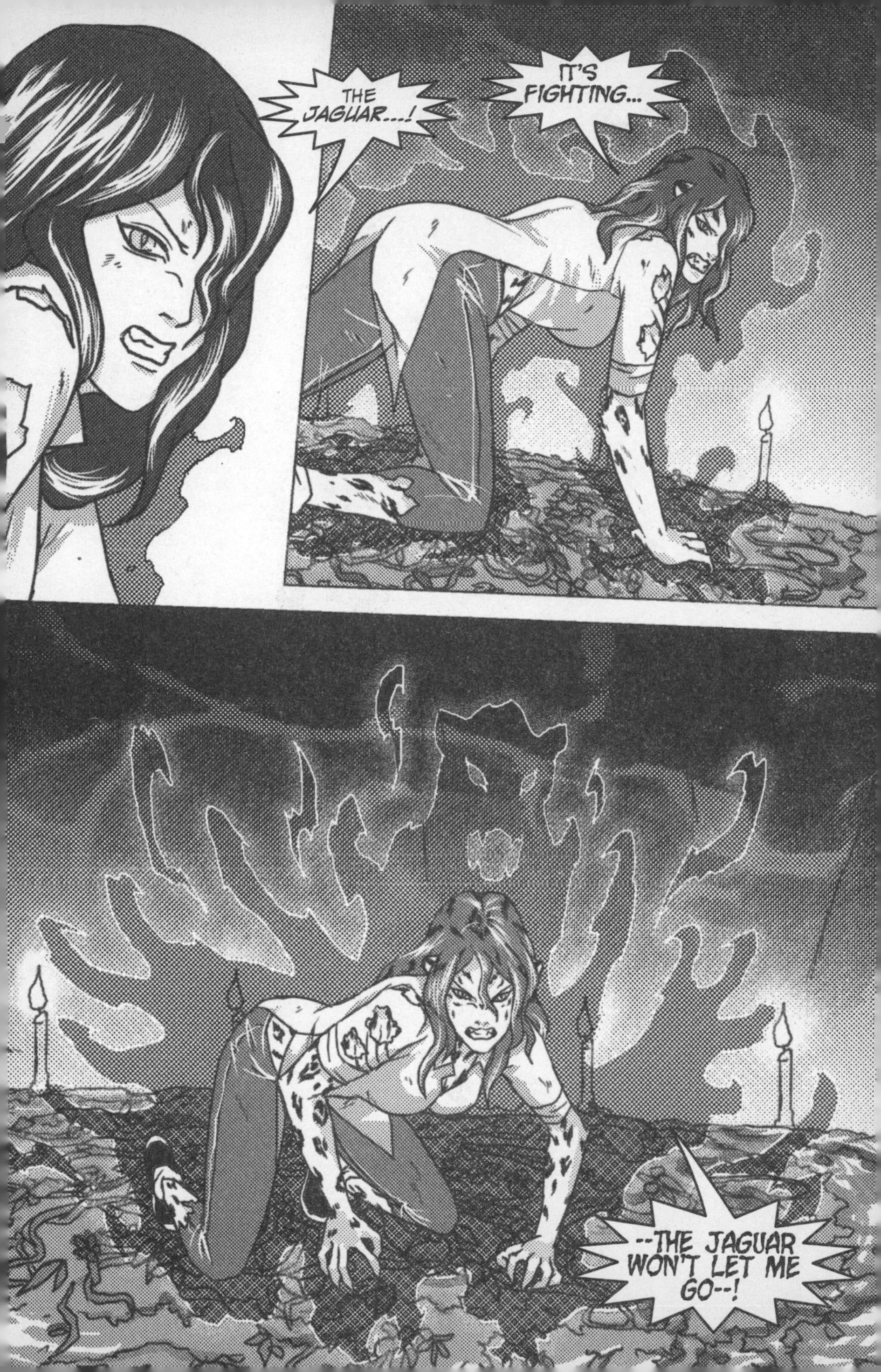
THE JAGUAR...!
IT'S FIGHTING...
--THE JAGUAR WON'T LET ME GO--!

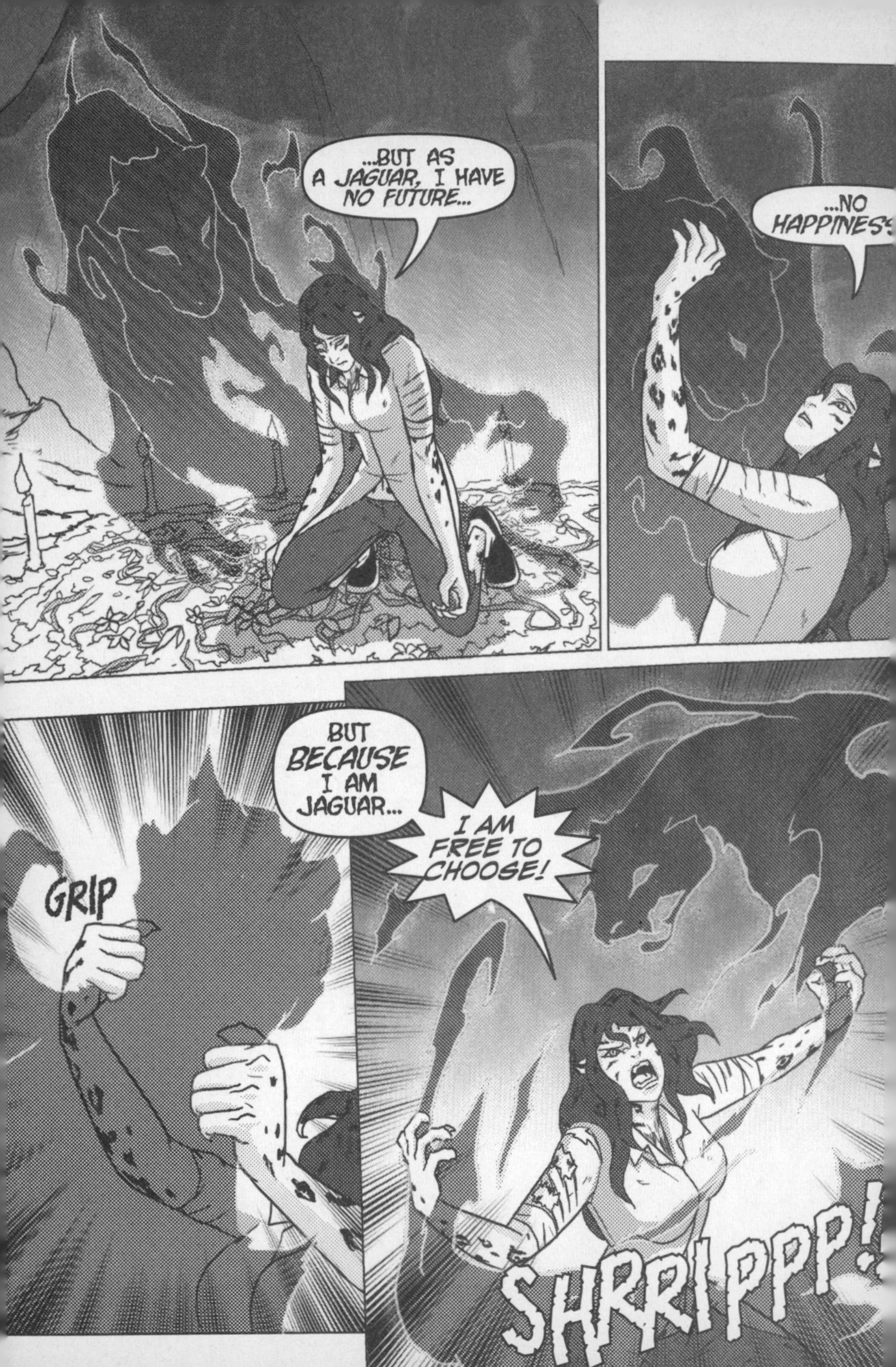
...BUT AS A JAGUAR, I HAVE NO FUTURE...
...NO HAPPINESS
BUT BECAUSE I AM JAGUAR...
I AM FREE TO CHOOSE!
GRIP
SHRRIPPP!

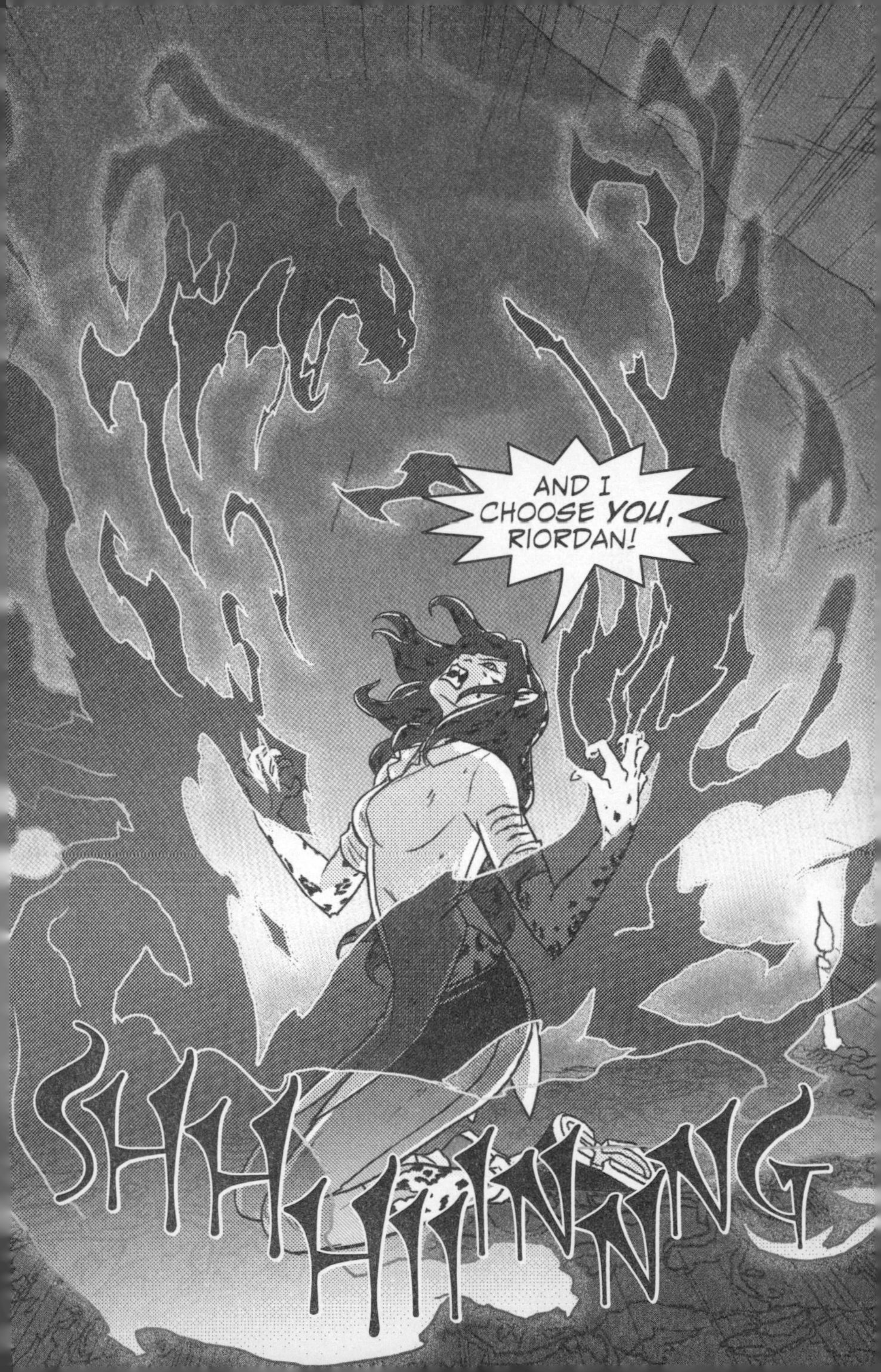
AND I CHOOSE YOU, RIORDAN!
SHHHIIINNNG

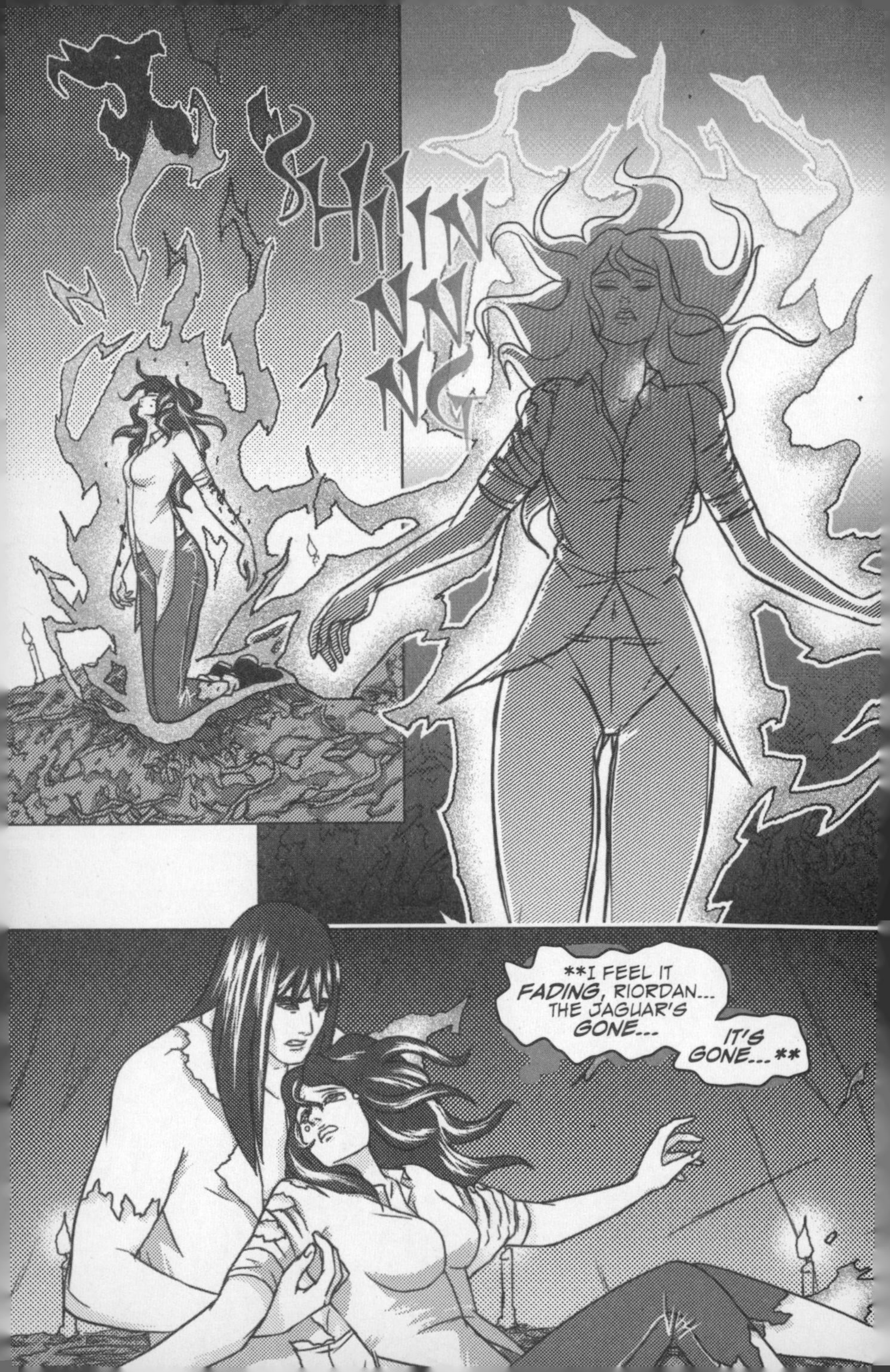
SHIIINNNNNG
**I FEEL IT *FADING*, RIORDAN... THE JAGUAR'S *GONE*...
IT'S GONE...**

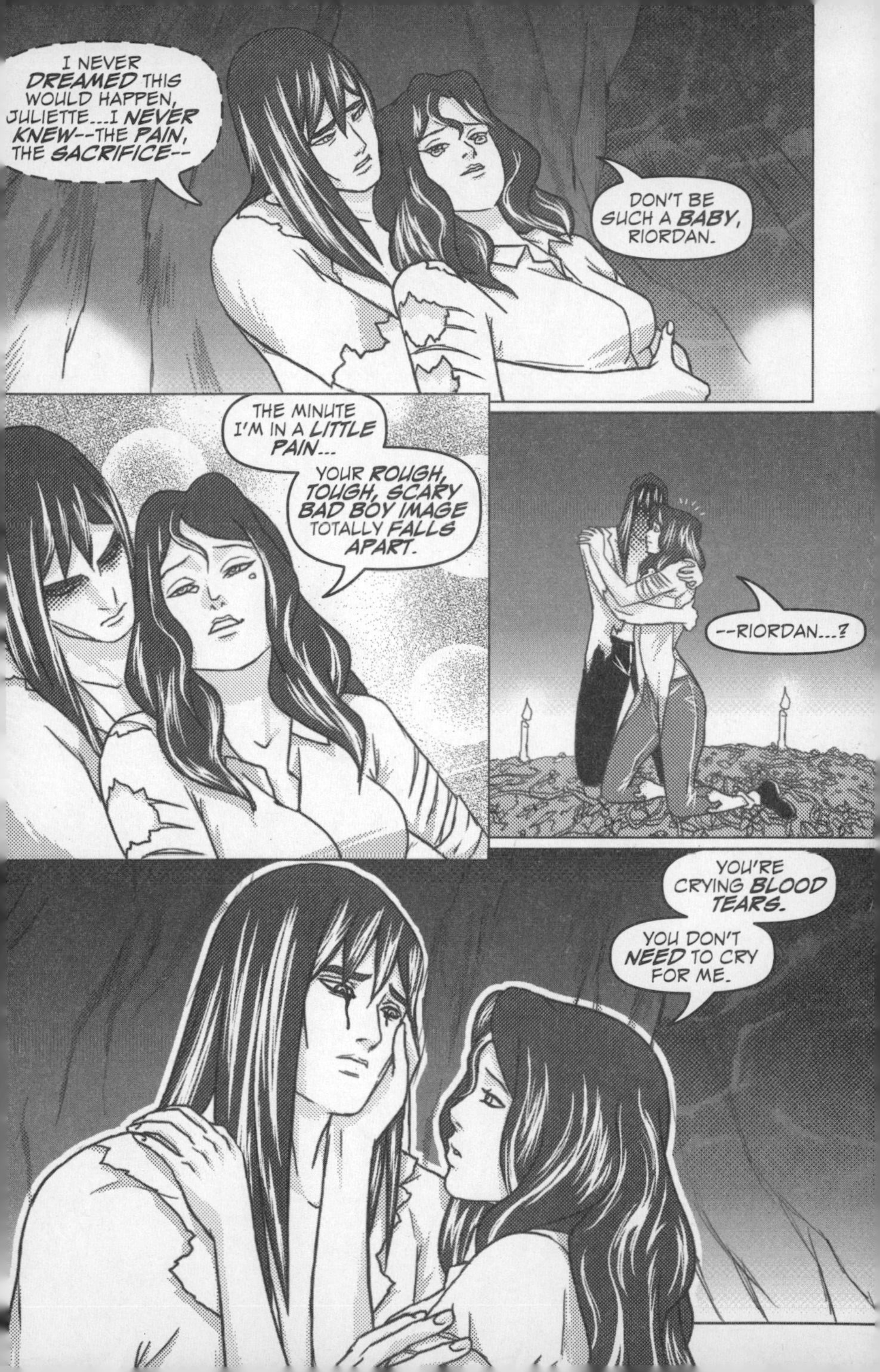
I NEVER DREAMED THIS WOULD HAPPEN, JULIETTE...I NEVER KNEW--THE PAIN, THE SACRIFICE--
DON'T BE SUCH A BABY, RIORDAN.
THE MINUTE I'M IN A LITTLE PAIN...
YOUR ROUGH, TOUGH, SCARY BAD BOY IMAGE TOTALLY FALLS APART.
--RIORDAN...?
YOU'RE CRYING BLOOD TEARS.
YOU DON'T NEED TO CRY FOR ME.

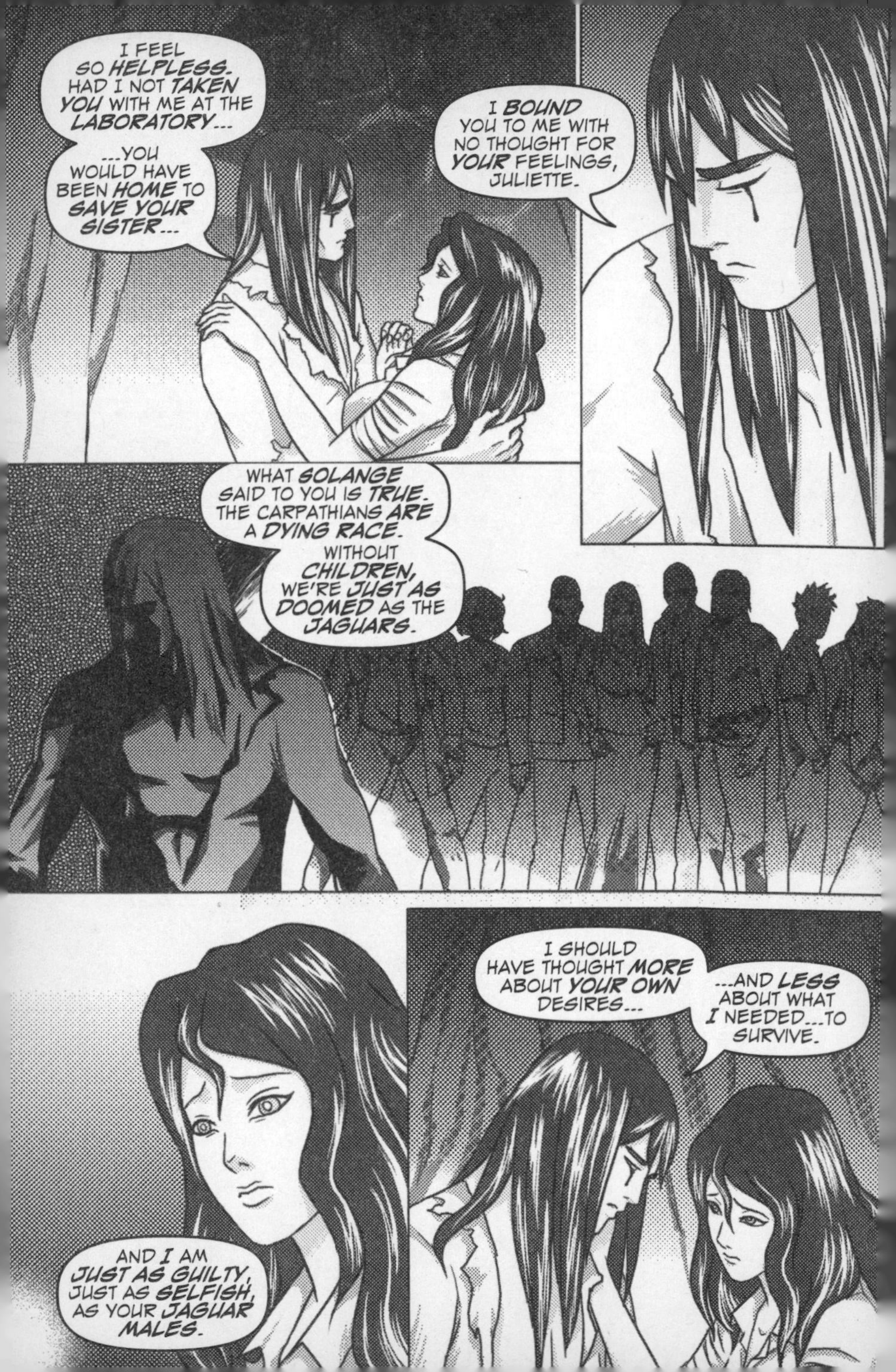

I FEEL SO HELPLESS. HAD I NOT TAKEN YOU WITH ME AT THE LABORATORY...
...YOU WOULD HAVE BEEN HOME TO SAVE YOUR SISTER...
I BOUND YOU TO ME WITH NO THOUGHT FOR YOUR FEELINGS, JULIETTE.
WHAT SOLANGE SAID TO YOU IS TRUE. THE CARPATHIANS ARE A DYING RACE.
WITHOUT CHILDREN, WE'RE JUST AS DOOMED AS THE JAGUARS.
AND I AM JUST AS GUILTY, JUST AS SELFISH, AS YOUR JAGUAR MALES.
I SHOULD HAVE THOUGHT MORE ABOUT YOUR OWN DESIRES...
...AND LESS ABOUT WHAT I NEEDED...TO SURVIVE.

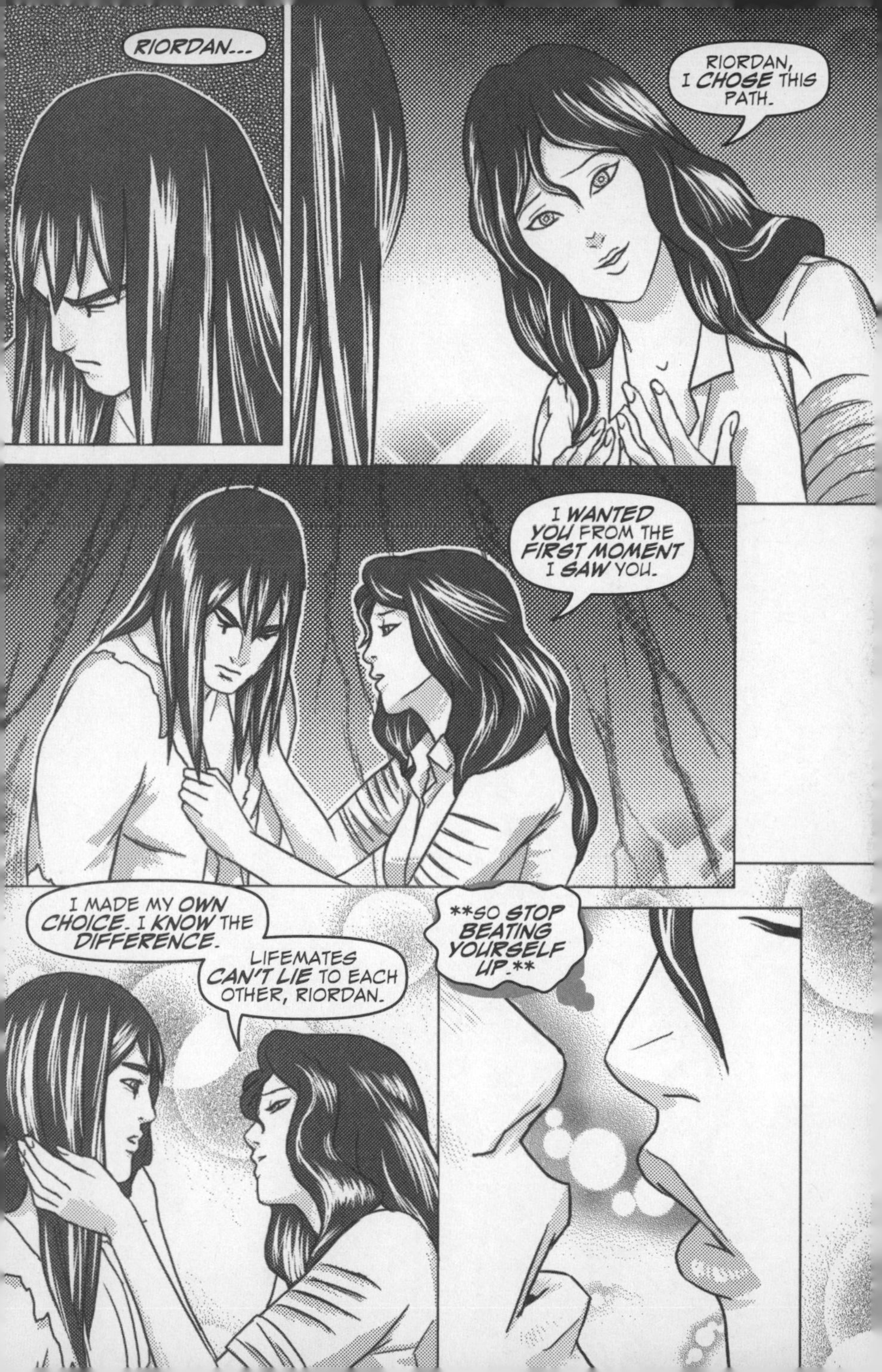
RIORDAN...
RIORDAN, I CHOSE THIS PATH.
I WANTED YOU FROM THE FIRST MOMENT I SAW YOU.
I MADE MY OWN CHOICE. I KNOW THE DIFFERENCE.
LIFEMATES CAN'T LIE TO EACH OTHER, RIORDAN.
SO STOP BEATING YOURSELF UP.

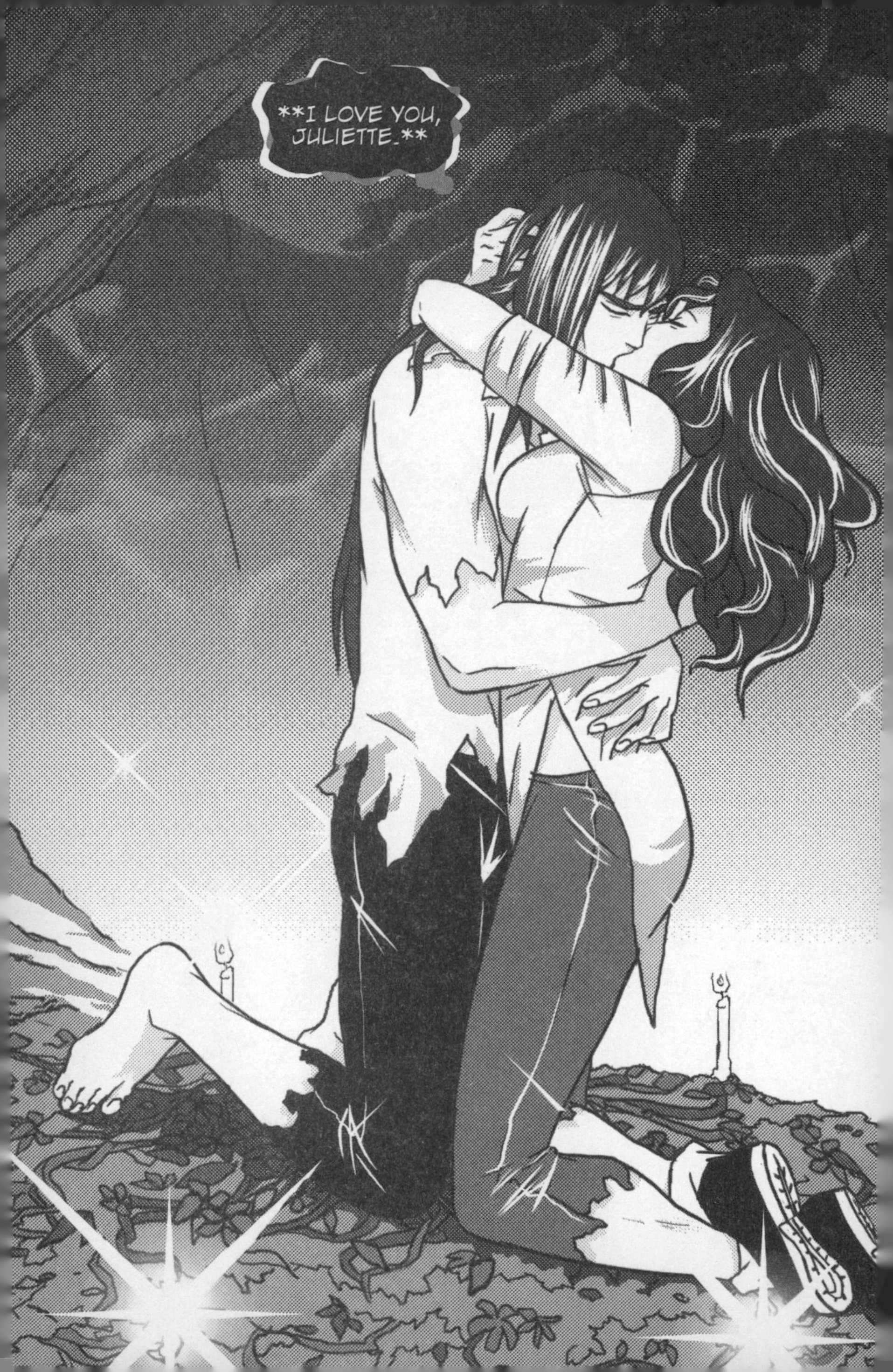
I LOVE YOU, JULIETTE.

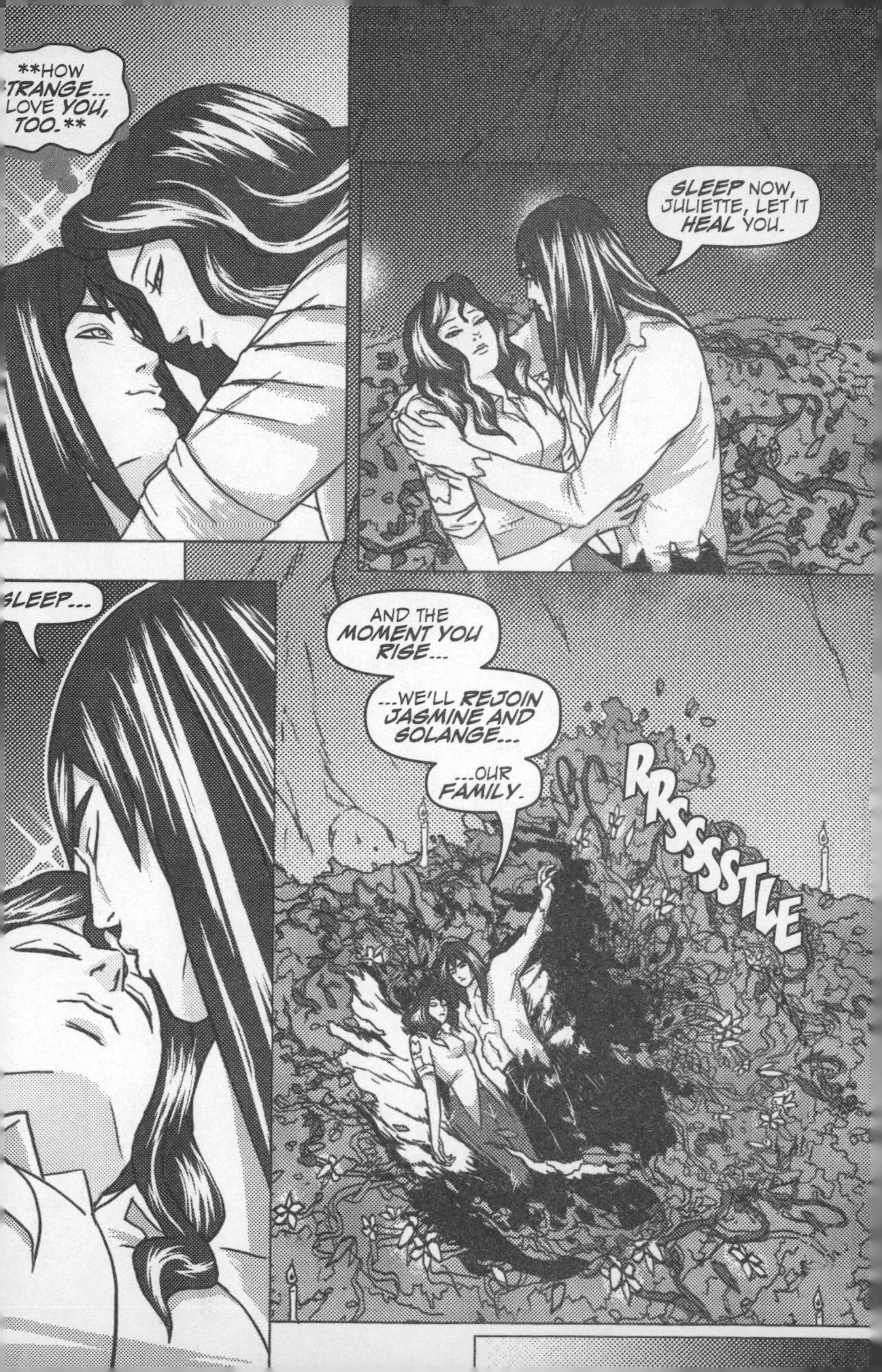
HOW STRANGE... LOVE YOU, TOO.
SLEEP NOW, JULIETTE, LET IT HEAL YOU.
SLEEP...
AND THE MOMENT YOU RISE...
...WE'LL REJOIN JASMINE AND SOLANGE...
...OUR FAMILY.
RRSSSSTLE

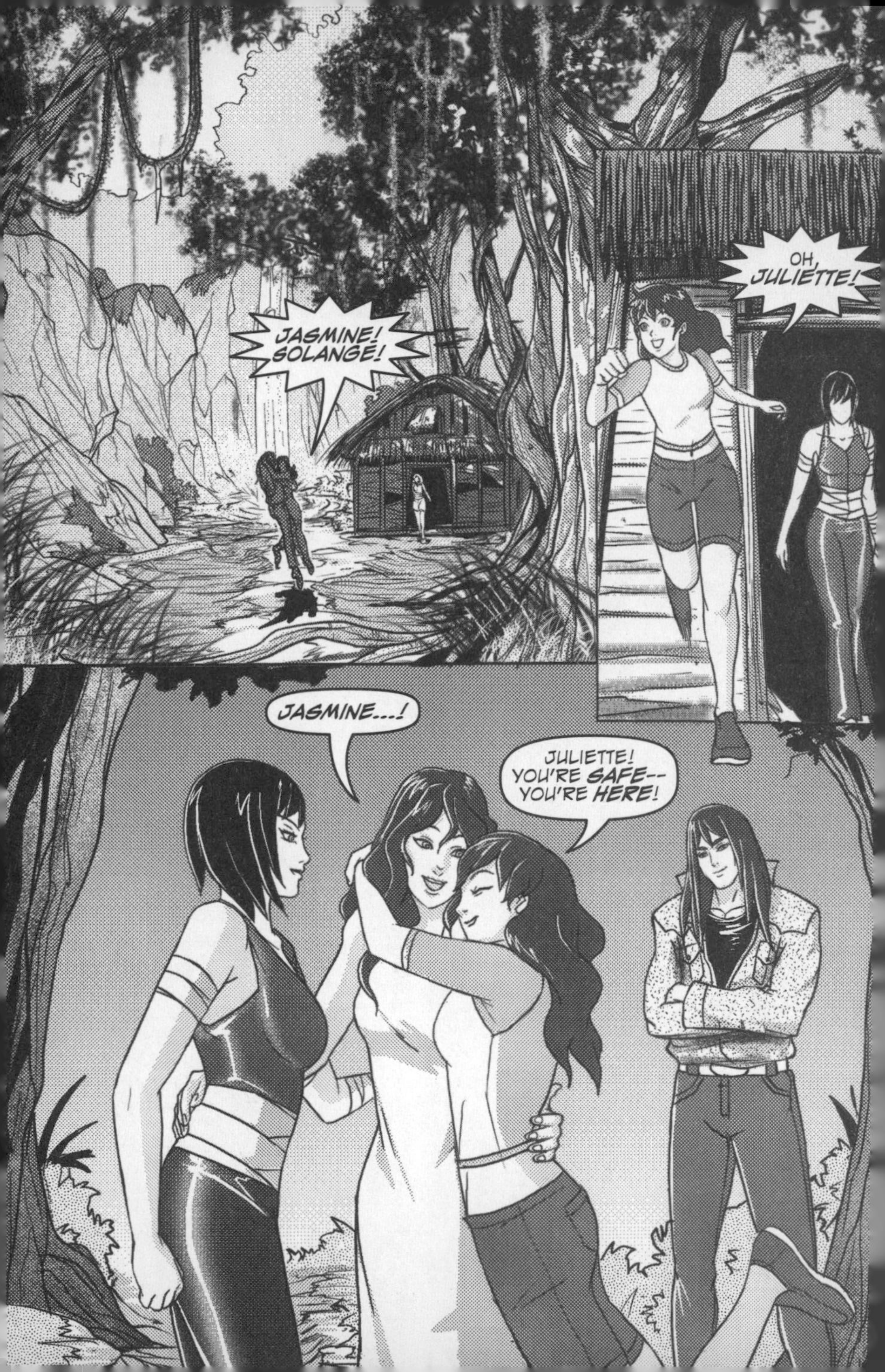
JASMINE! SOLANGE!
OH, JULIETTE!
JASMINE...!
JULIETTE! YOU'RE SAFE-- YOU'RE HERE!

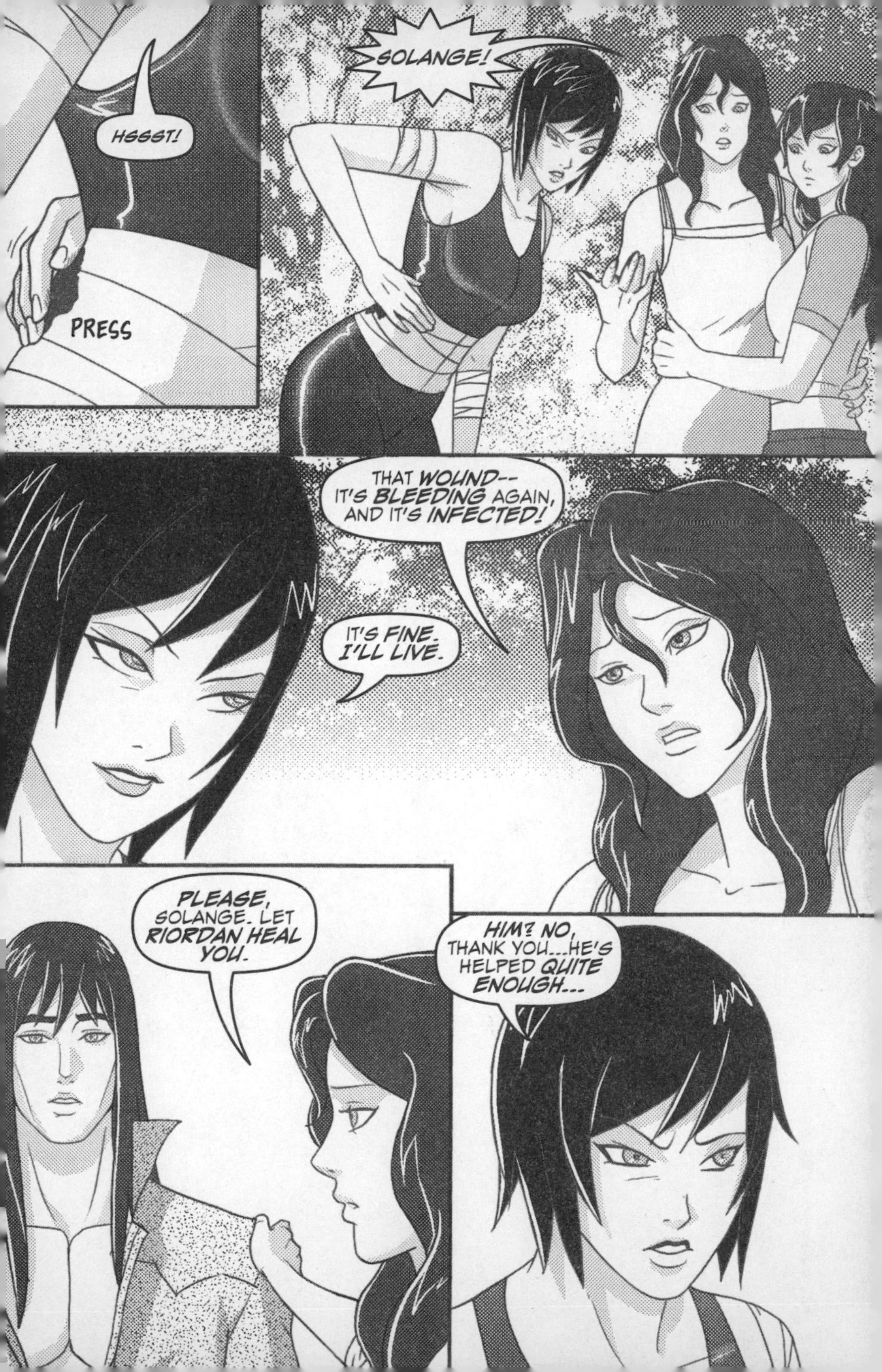
HSSST!
PRESS
SOLANGE!
THAT WOUND-- IT'S BLEEDING AGAIN, AND IT'S INFECTED!
IT'S FINE. I'LL LIVE.
PLEASE, SOLANGE. LET RIORDAN HEAL YOU.
HIM? NO, THANK YOU...HE'S HELPED QUITE ENOUGH...

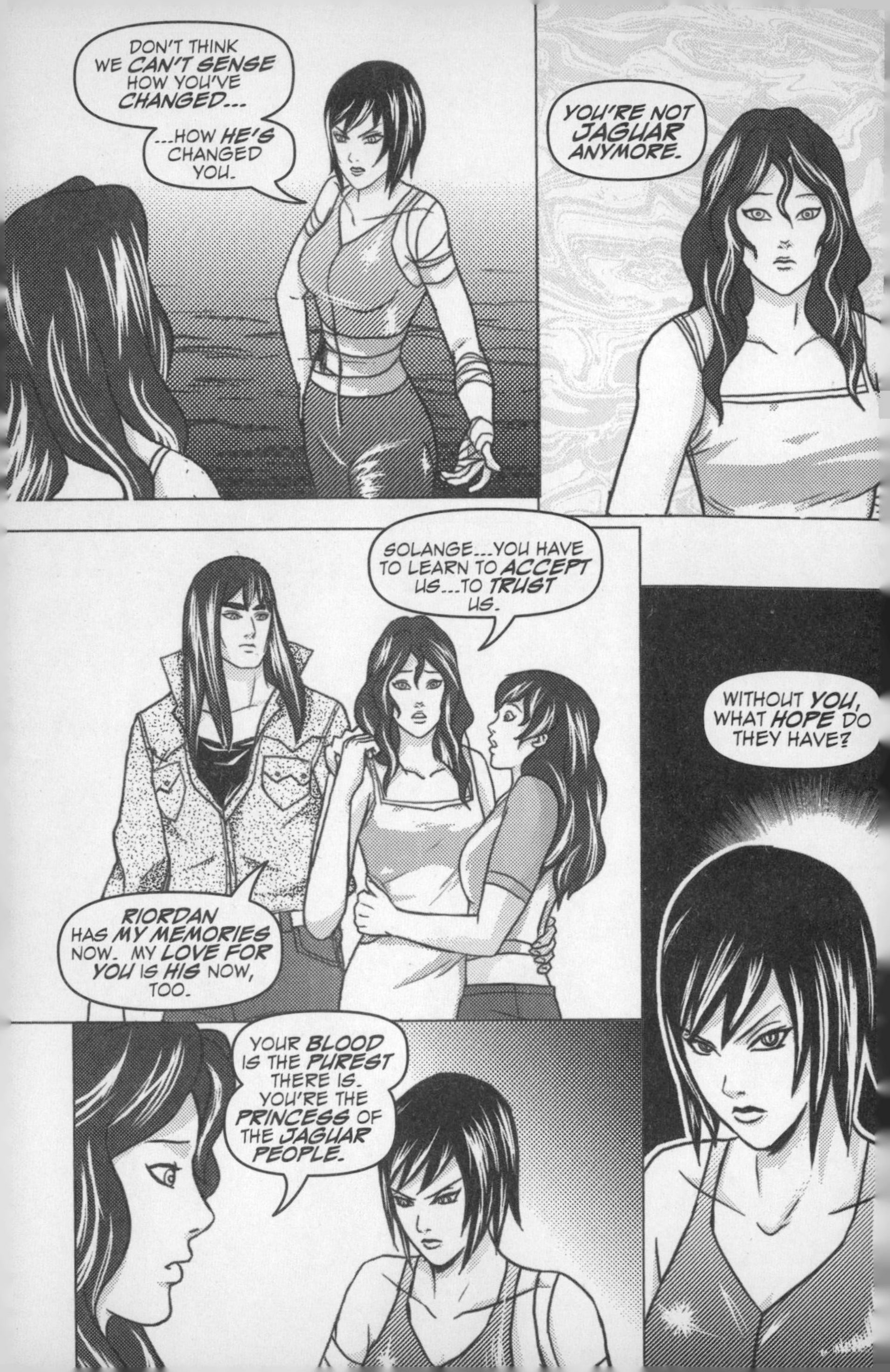
DON'T THINK WE CAN'T SENSE HOW YOU'VE CHANGED...
...HOW HE'S CHANGED YOU.
YOU'RE NOT JAGUAR ANYMORE.
SOLANGE...YOU HAVE TO LEARN TO ACCEPT US...TO TRUST US.
RIORDAN HAS MY MEMORIES NOW. MY LOVE FOR YOU IS HIS NOW, TOO.
WITHOUT YOU, WHAT HOPE DO THEY HAVE?
YOUR BLOOD IS THE PUREST THERE IS. YOU'RE THE PRINCESS OF THE JAGUAR PEOPLE.

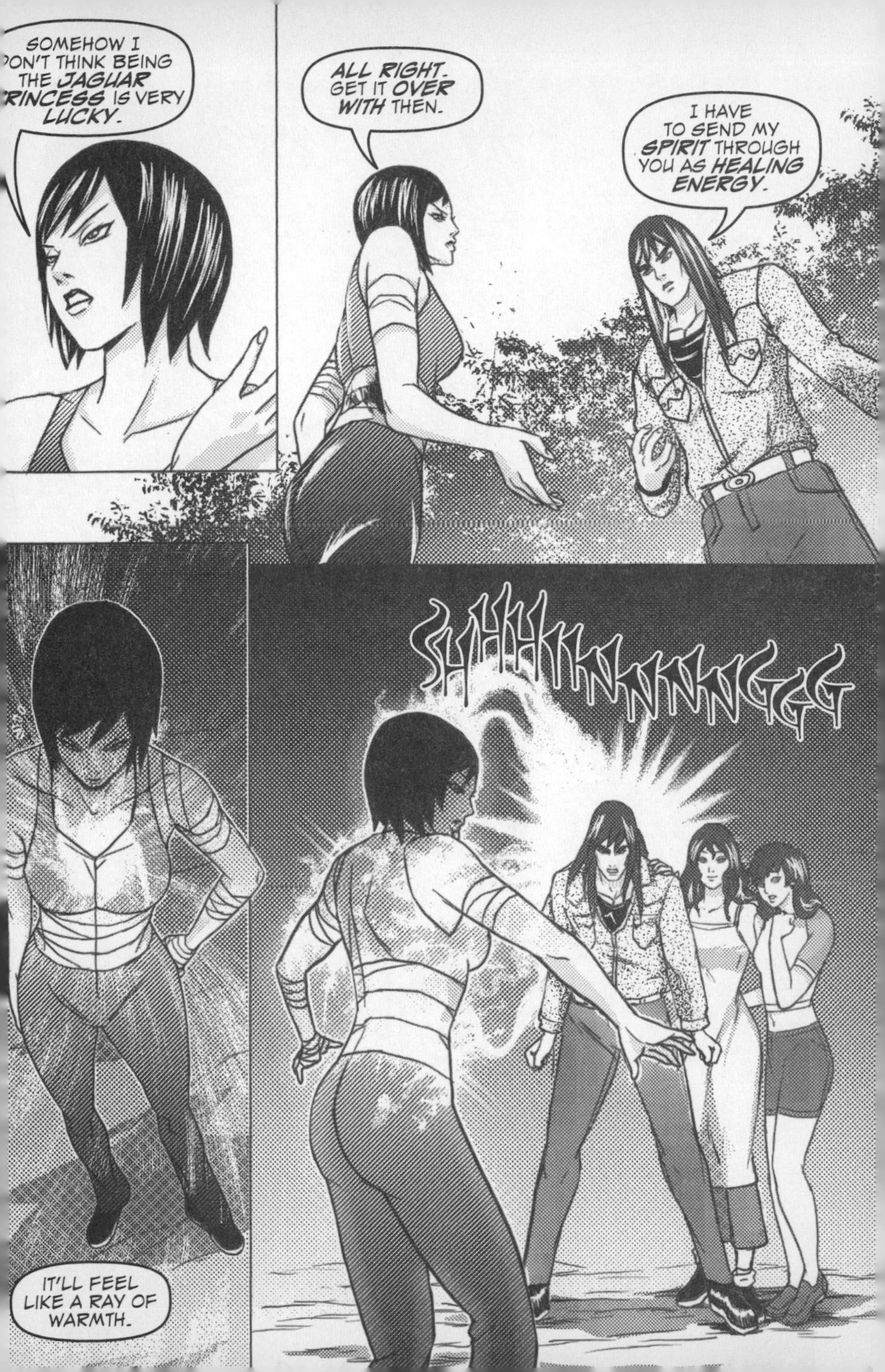
SOMEHOW I DON'T THINK BEING THE JAGUAR PRINCESS IS VERY LUCKY.
ALL RIGHT. GET IT OVER WITH THEN.
I HAVE TO SEND MY SPIRIT THROUGH YOU AS HEALING ENERGY.
IT'LL FEEL LIKE A RAY OF WARMTH.

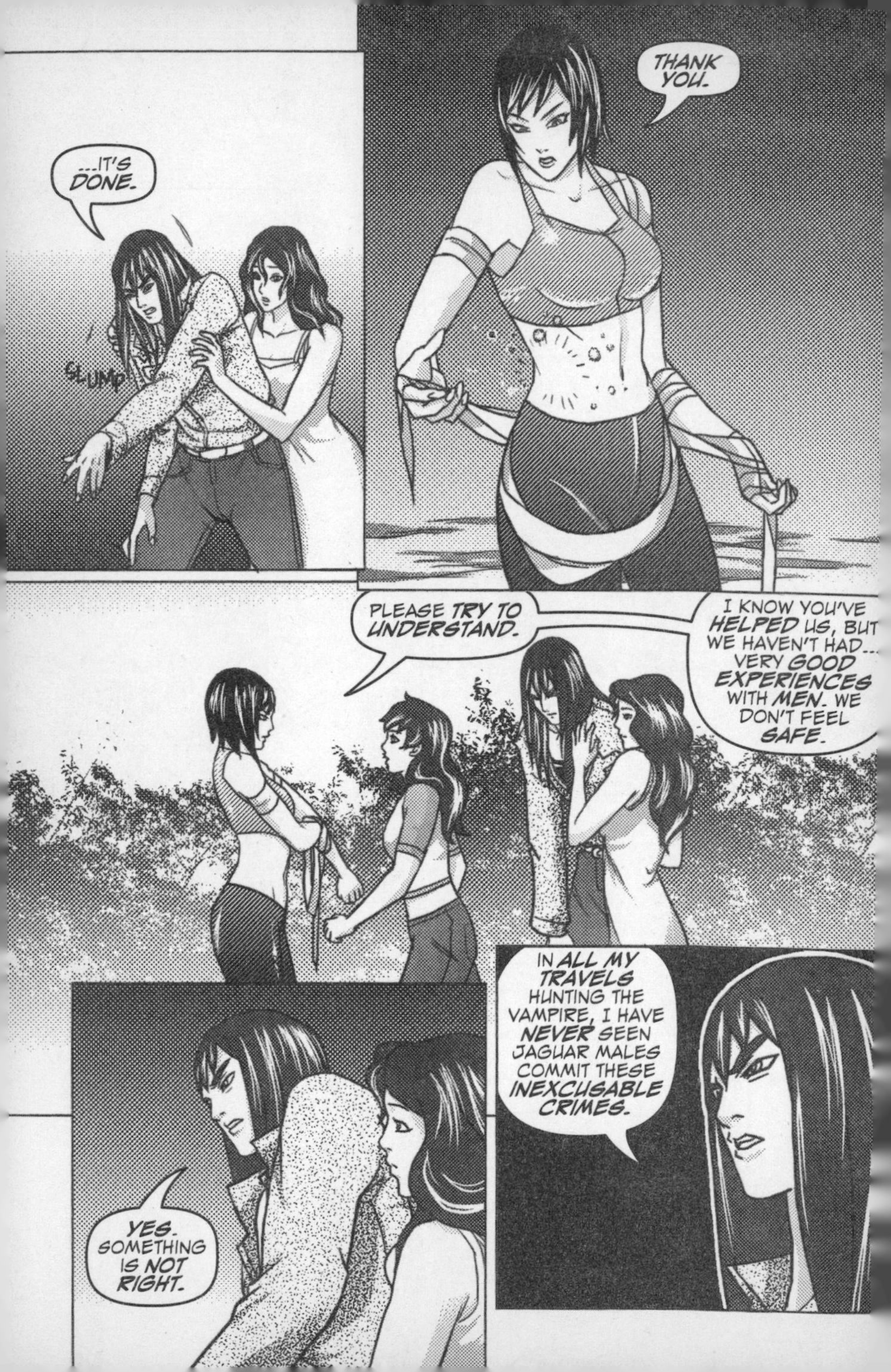
...IT'S DONE.
SLUMP
THANK YOU.
PLEASE TRY TO UNDERSTAND.
I KNOW YOU'VE HELPED US, BUT WE HAVEN'T HAD... VERY GOOD EXPERIENCES WITH MEN. WE DON'T FEEL SAFE.
YES. SOMETHING IS NOT RIGHT.
IN ALL MY TRAVELS HUNTING THE VAMPIRE, I HAVE NEVER SEEN JAGUAR MALES COMMIT THESE INEXCUSABLE CRIMES.

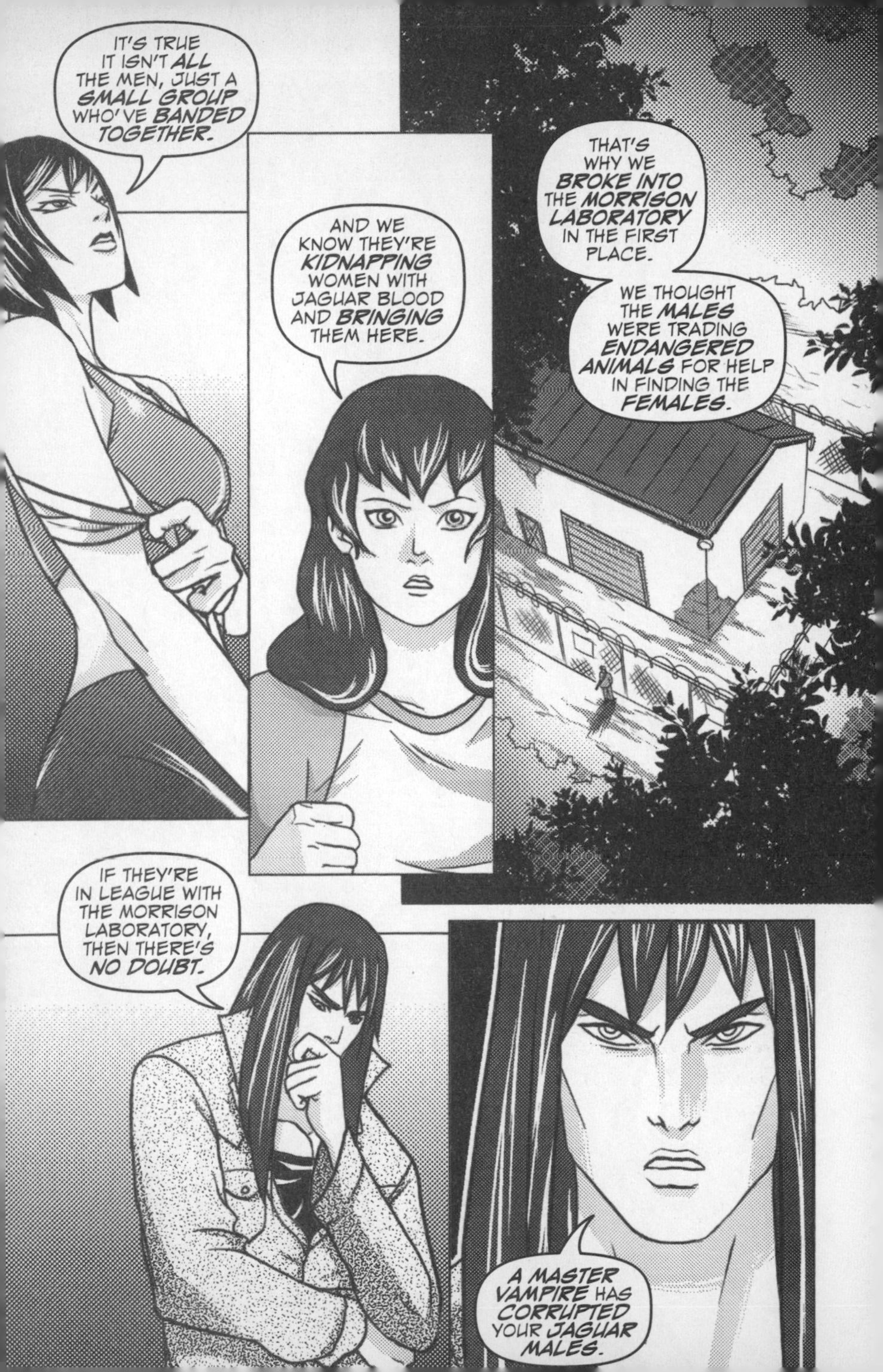
IT'S TRUE IT ISN'T ALL THE MEN, JUST A SMALL GROUP WHO'VE BANDED TOGETHER.
AND WE KNOW THEY'RE KIDNAPPING WOMEN WITH JAGUAR BLOOD AND BRINGING THEM HERE.
THAT'S WHY WE BROKE INTO THE MORRISON LABORATORY IN THE FIRST PLACE.
WE THOUGHT THE MALES WERE TRADING ENDANGERED ANIMALS FOR HELP IN FINDING THE FEMALES.
IF THEY'RE IN LEAGUE WITH THE MORRISON LABORATORY, THEN THERE'S NO DOUBT.
A MASTER VAMPIRE HAS CORRUPTED YOUR JAGUAR MALES.

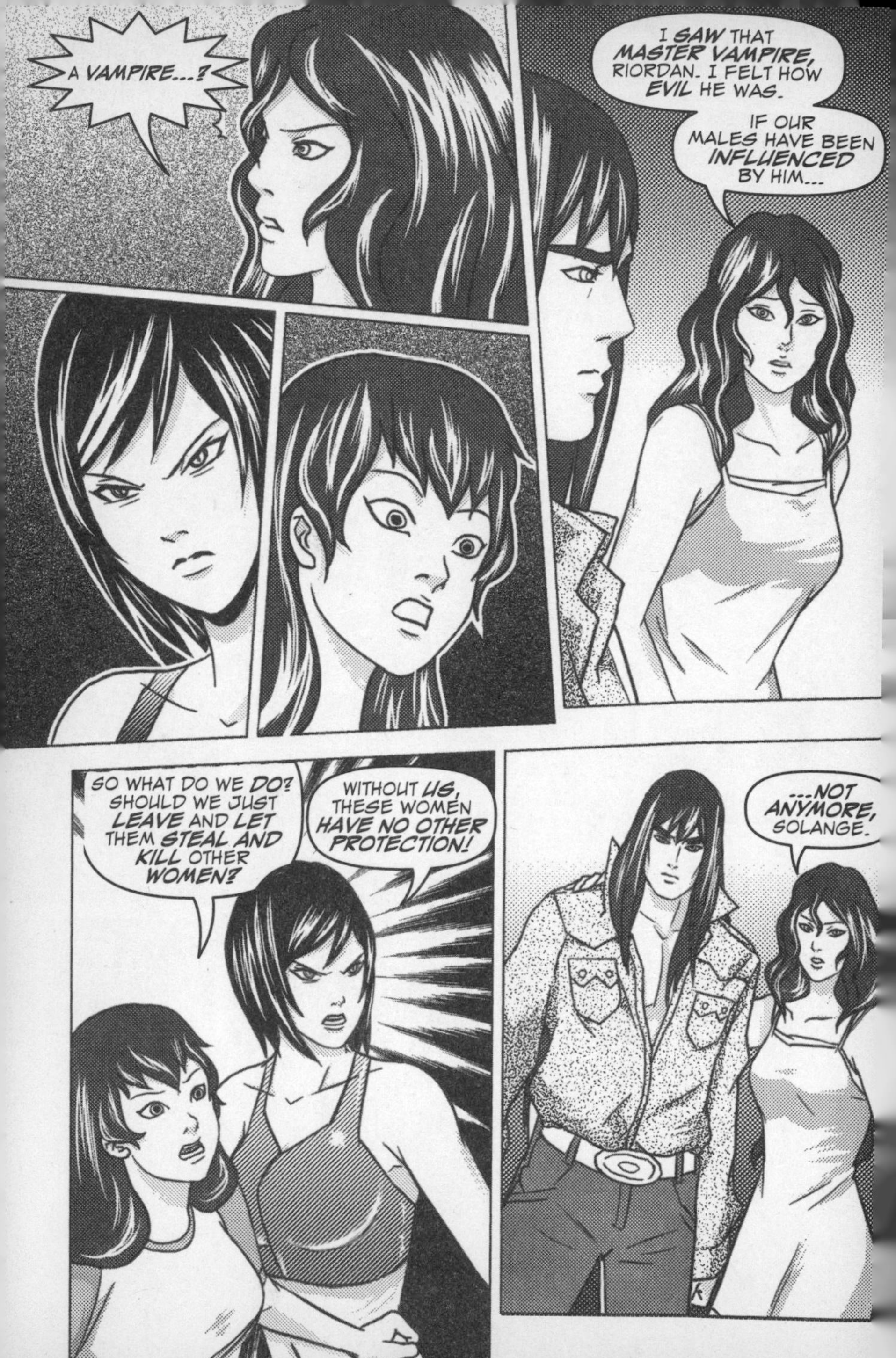
A VAMPIRE...?
I SAW THAT MASTER VAMPIRE, RIORDAN. I FELT HOW EVIL HE WAS.
IF OUR MALES HAVE BEEN INFLUENCED BY HIM...
SO WHAT DO WE DO? SHOULD WE JUST LEAVE AND LET THEM STEAL AND KILL OTHER WOMEN?
WITHOUT US, THESE WOMEN HAVE NO OTHER PROTECTION!
...NOT ANYMORE, SOLANGE.

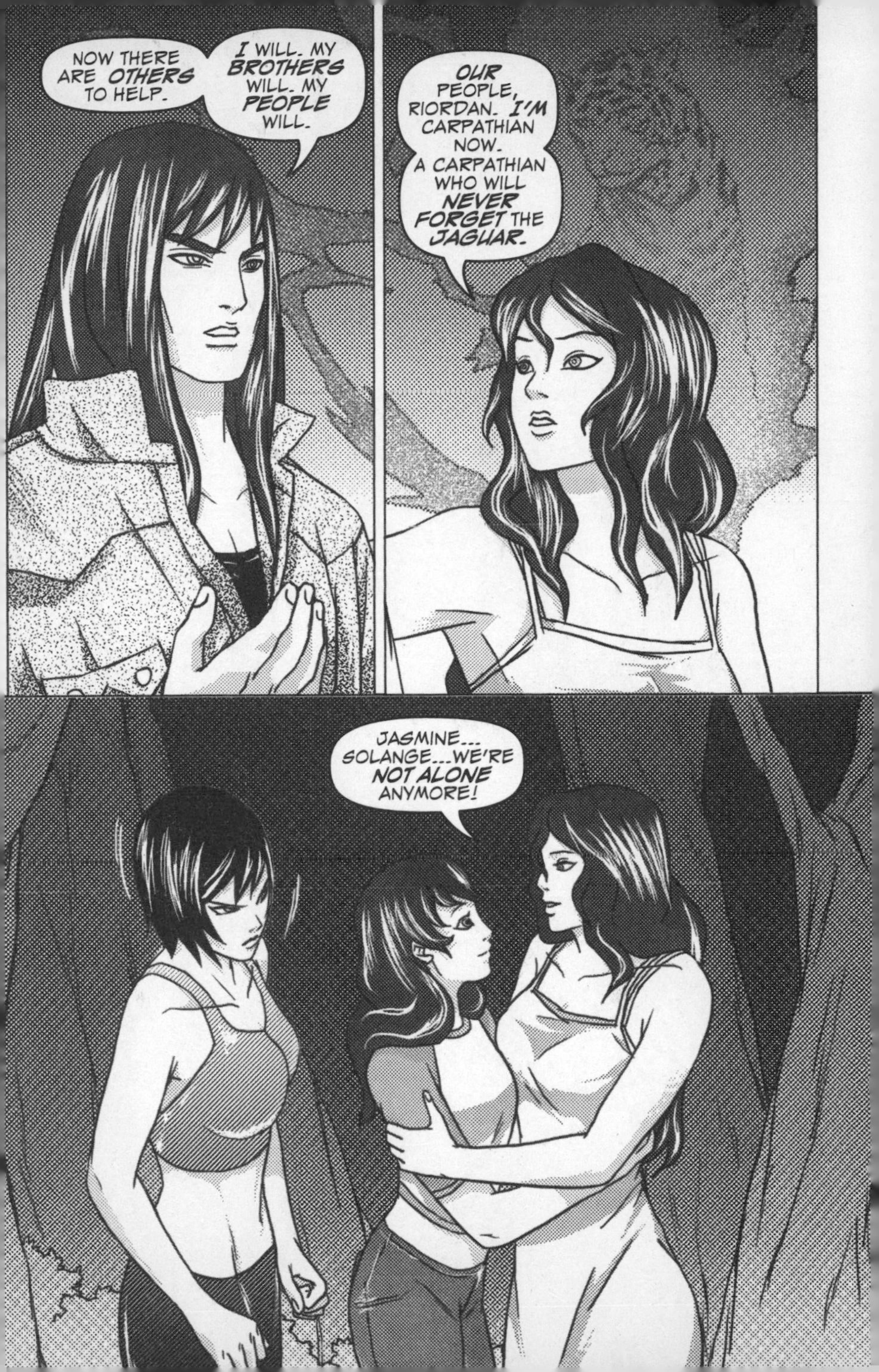
NOW THERE ARE OTHERS TO HELP.
I WILL. MY BROTHERS WILL. MY PEOPLE WILL.
OUR PEOPLE, RIORDAN. I'M CARPATHIAN NOW. A CARPATHIAN WHO WILL NEVER FORGET THE JAGUAR.
JASMINE... SOLANGE...WE'RE NOT ALONE ANYMORE!

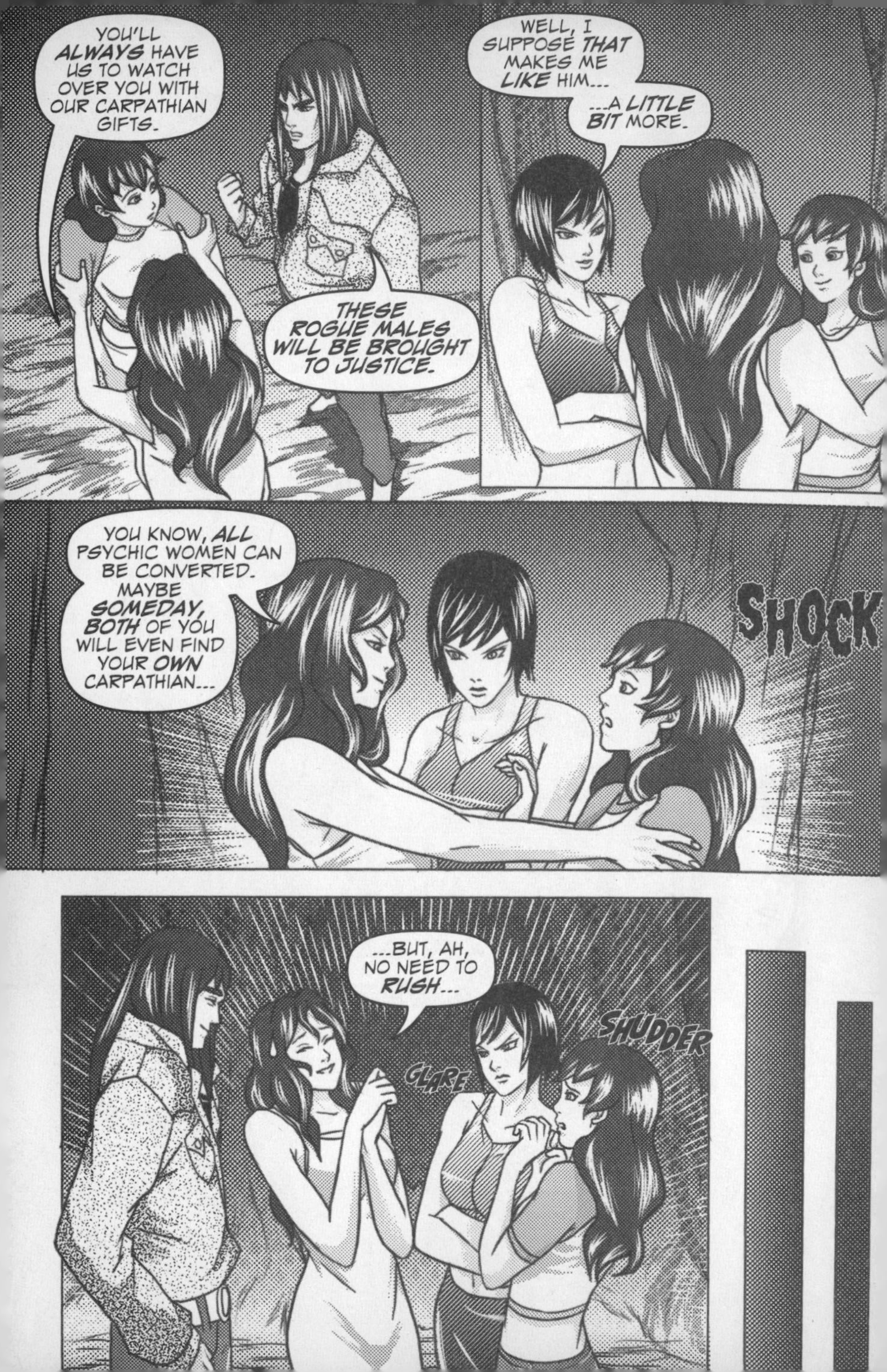
YOU'LL ALWAYS HAVE US TO WATCH OVER YOU WITH OUR CARPATHIAN GIFTS.
THESE ROGUE MALES WILL BE BROUGHT TO JUSTICE.
WELL, I SUPPOSE THAT MAKES ME LIKE HIM...
...A LITTLE BIT MORE.
YOU KNOW, ALL PSYCHIC WOMEN CAN BE CONVERTED. MAYBE SOMEDAY, BOTH OF YOU WILL EVEN FIND YOUR OWN CARPATHIAN...
SHOCK
...BUT, AH, NO NEED TO RUSH...
GLARE
SHUDDER

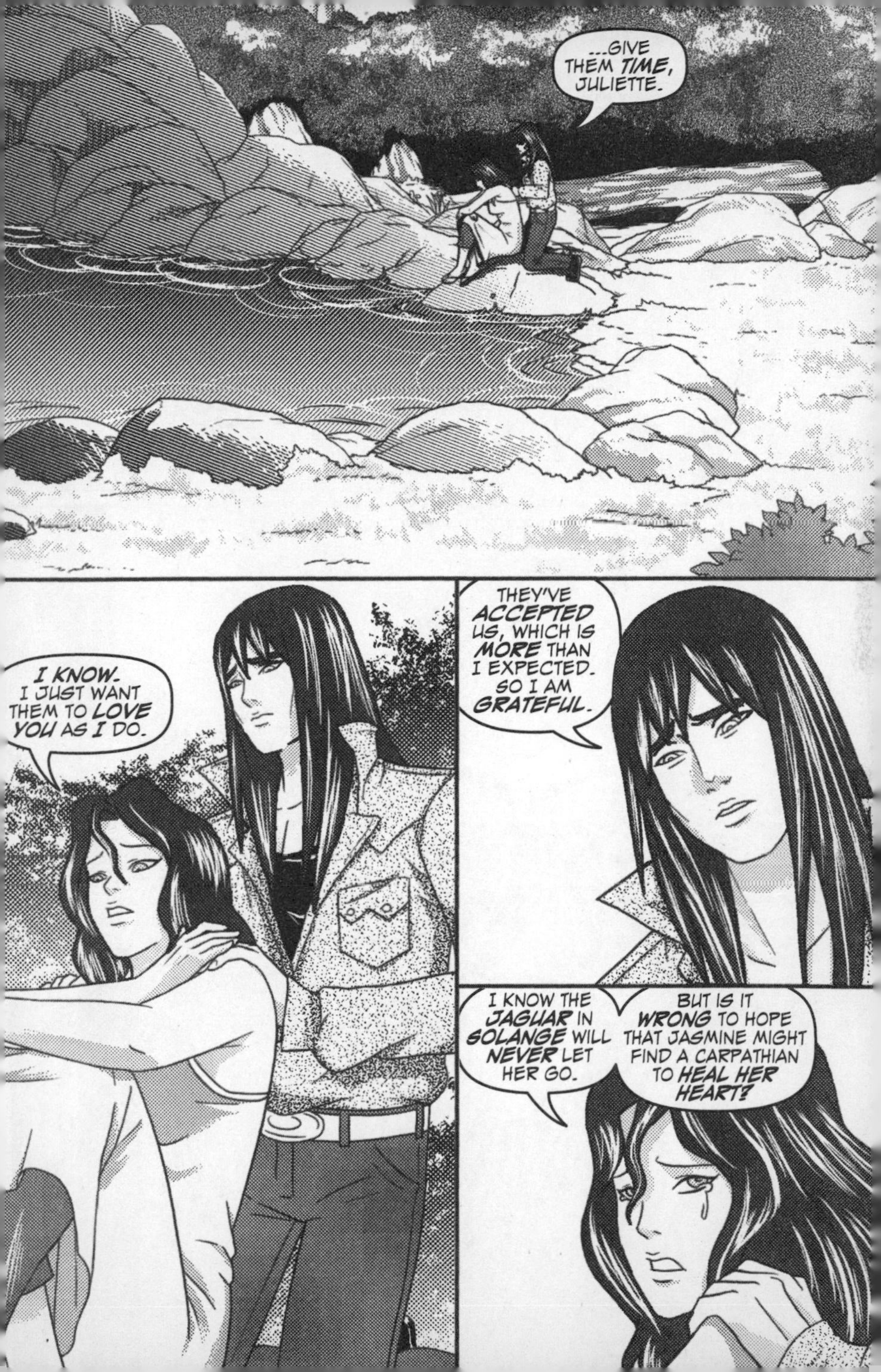
...GIVE THEM *TIME*, JULIETTE.
I KNOW. I JUST WANT THEM TO *LOVE YOU* AS *I* DO.
THEY'VE *ACCEPTED* US, WHICH IS *MORE* THAN I EXPECTED. SO I AM *GRATEFUL*.
I KNOW THE *JAGUAR* IN *SOLANGE* WILL *NEVER* LET HER GO.
BUT IS IT *WRONG* TO HOPE THAT JASMINE MIGHT FIND A CARPATHIAN TO *HEAL HER HEART?*

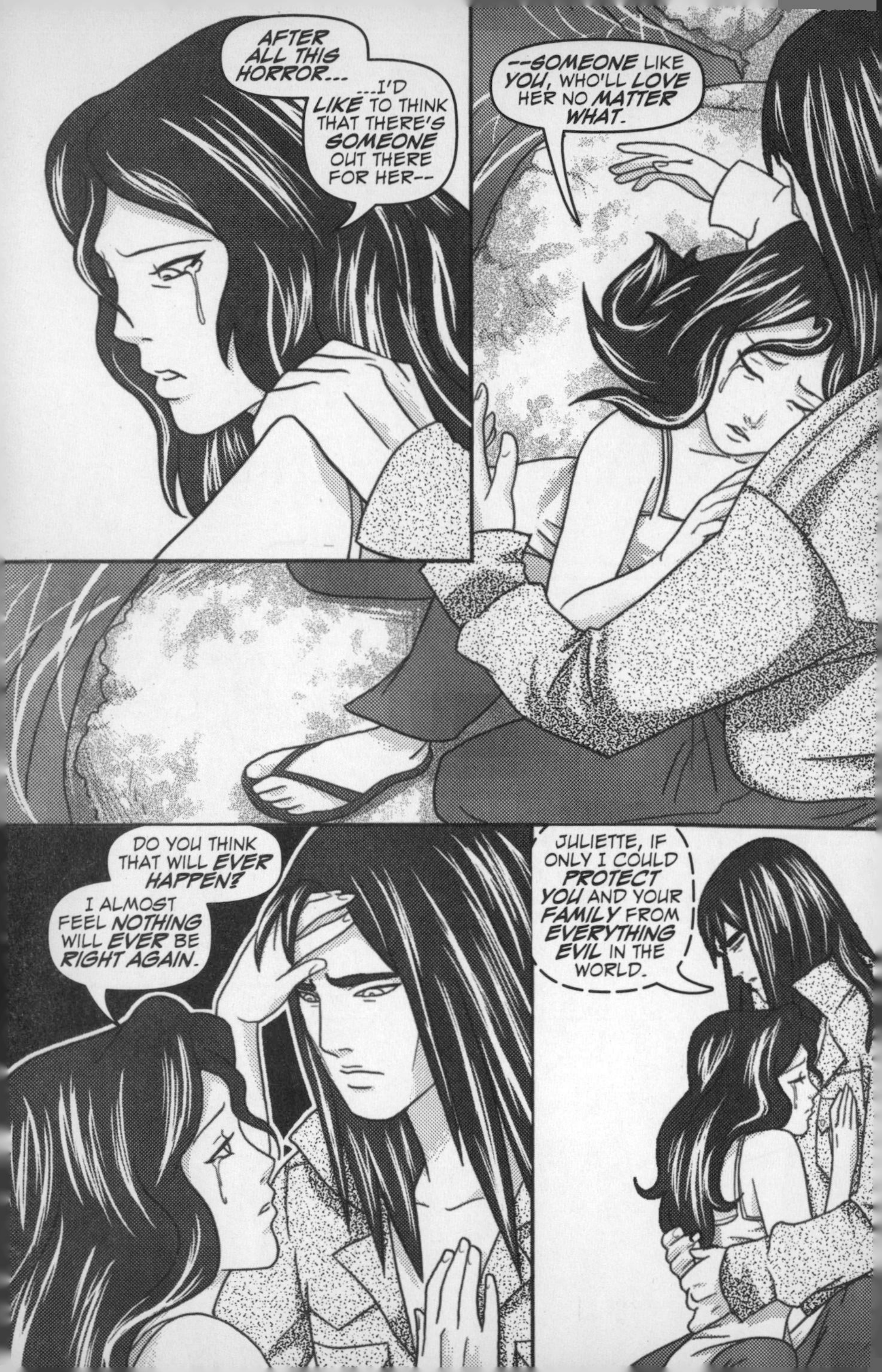
AFTER ALL THIS HORROR...
...I'D LIKE TO THINK THAT THERE'S SOMEONE OUT THERE FOR HER--
--SOMEONE LIKE YOU, WHO'LL LOVE HER NO MATTER WHAT.
DO YOU THINK THAT WILL EVER HAPPEN?
I ALMOST FEEL NOTHING WILL EVER BE RIGHT AGAIN.
JULIETTE, IF ONLY I COULD PROTECT YOU AND YOUR FAMILY FROM EVERYTHING EVIL IN THE WORLD.

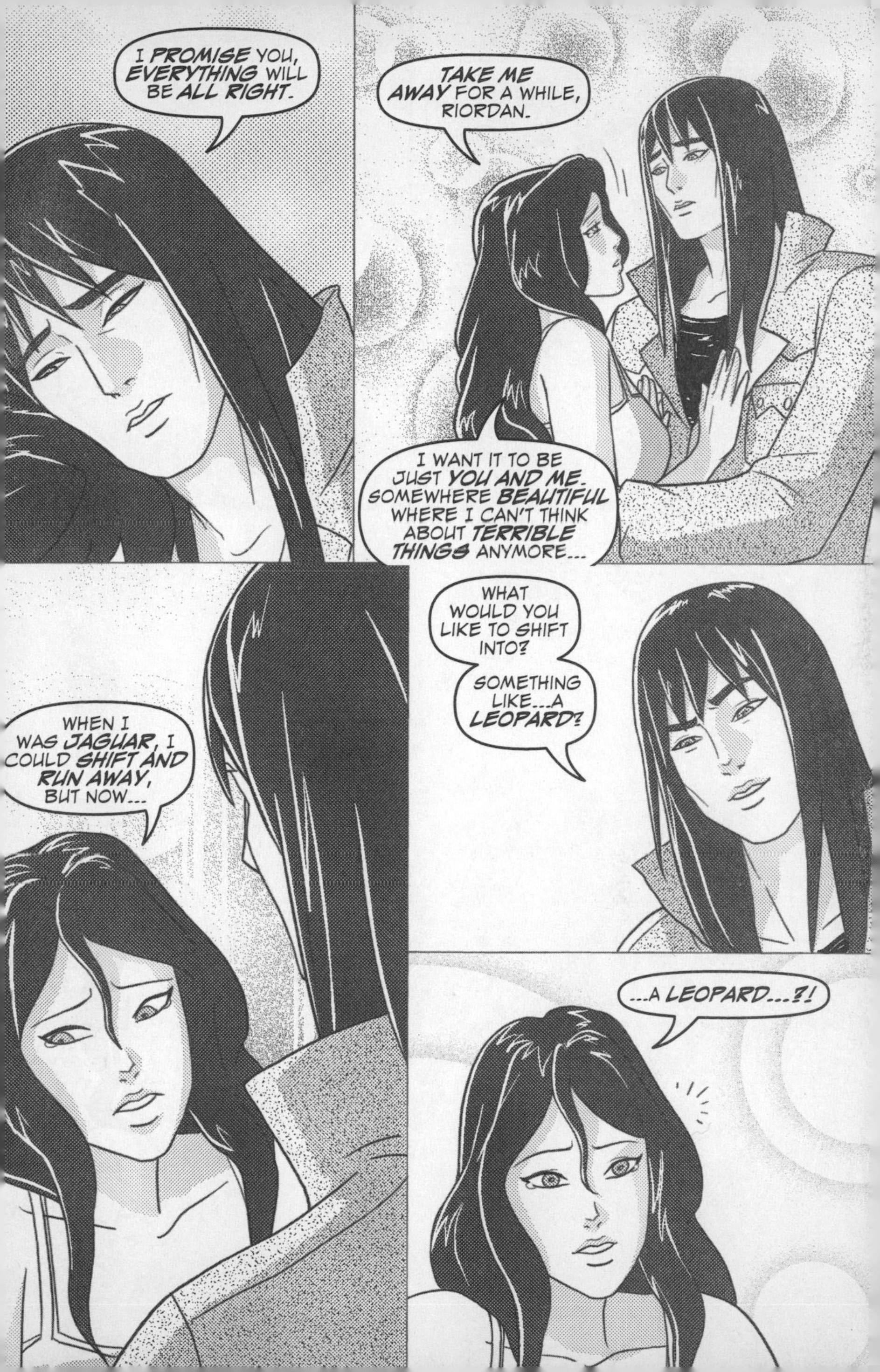
I PROMISE YOU, EVERYTHING WILL BE ALL RIGHT.
TAKE ME AWAY FOR A WHILE, RIORDAN.
I WANT IT TO BE JUST YOU AND ME. SOMEWHERE BEAUTIFUL WHERE I CAN'T THINK ABOUT TERRIBLE THINGS ANYMORE...
WHEN I WAS JAGUAR, I COULD SHIFT AND RUN AWAY, BUT NOW...
WHAT WOULD YOU LIKE TO SHIFT INTO?
SOMETHING LIKE...A LEOPARD?
...A LEOPARD...?!

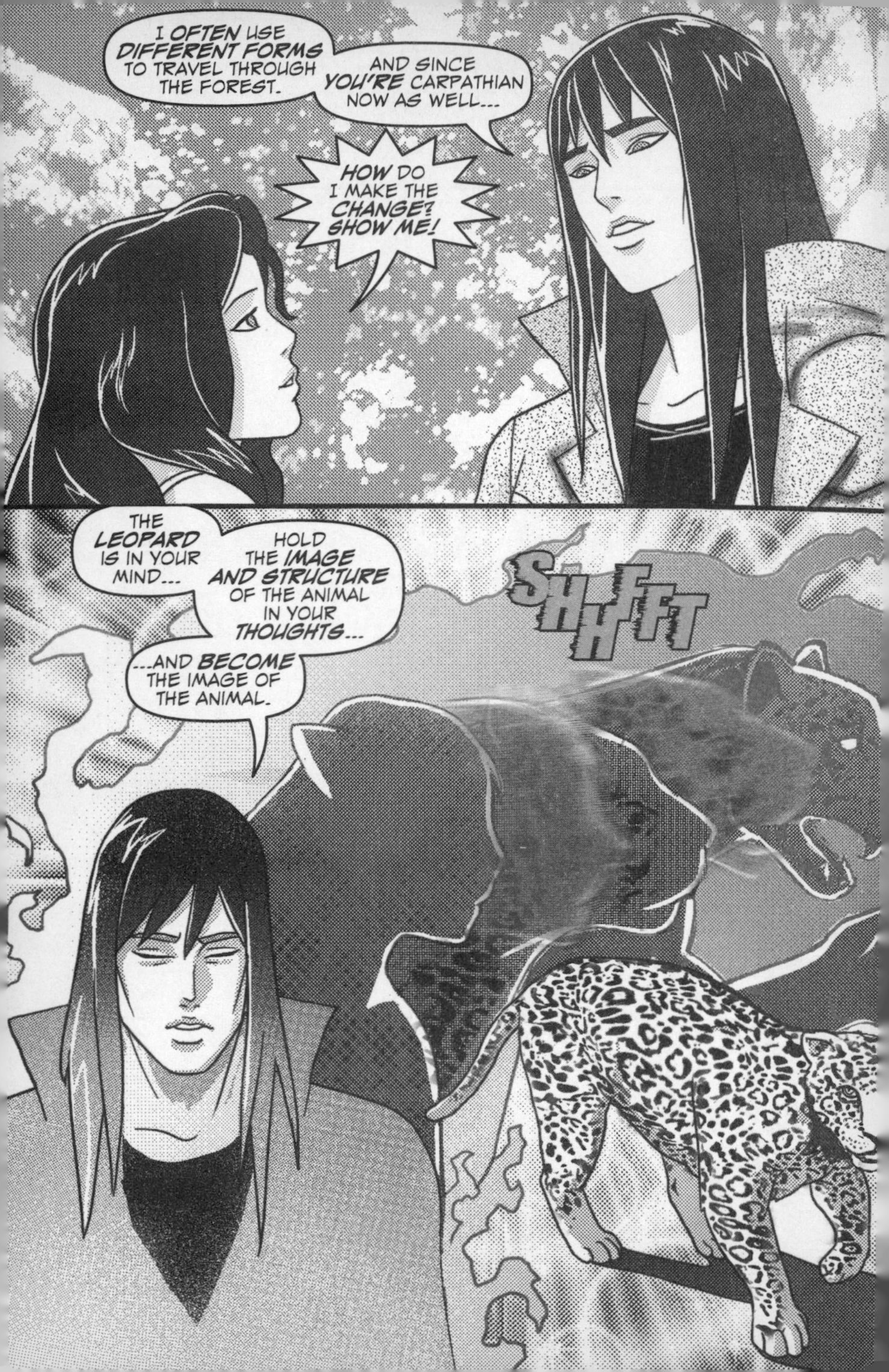

I OFTEN USE DIFFERENT FORMS TO TRAVEL THROUGH THE FOREST.
AND SINCE YOU'RE CARPATHIAN NOW AS WELL...
HOW DO I MAKE THE CHANGE? SHOW ME!
THE LEOPARD IS IN YOUR MIND...
HOLD THE IMAGE AND STRUCTURE OF THE ANIMAL IN YOUR THOUGHTS...
...AND BECOME THE IMAGE OF THE ANIMAL.
SHHFFT

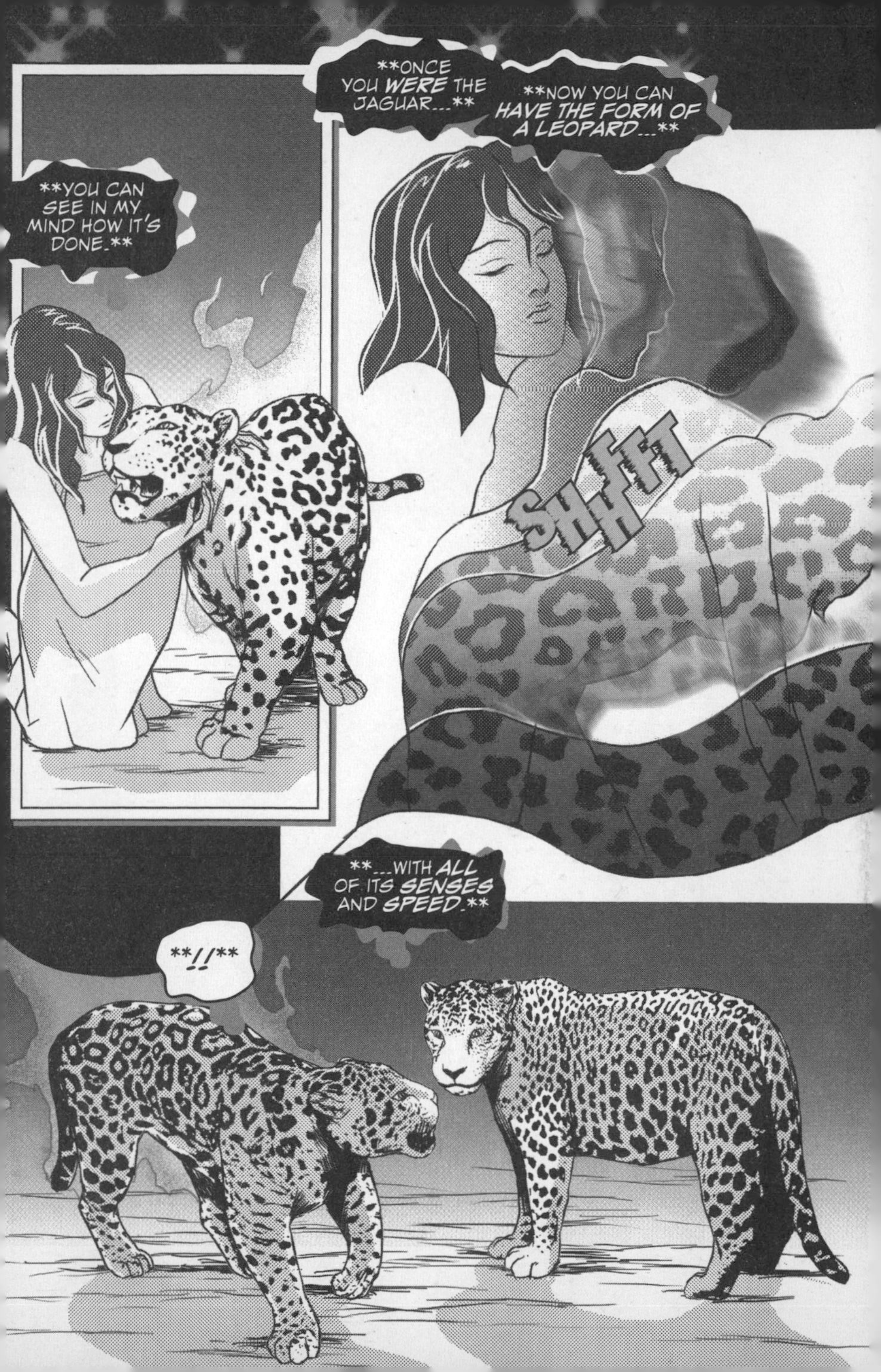
YOU CAN SEE IN MY MIND HOW IT'S DONE.
ONCE YOU WERE THE JAGUAR...
NOW YOU CAN HAVE THE FORM OF A LEOPARD...
SHHHFFT
...WITH ALL OF ITS SENSES AND SPEED.
!!

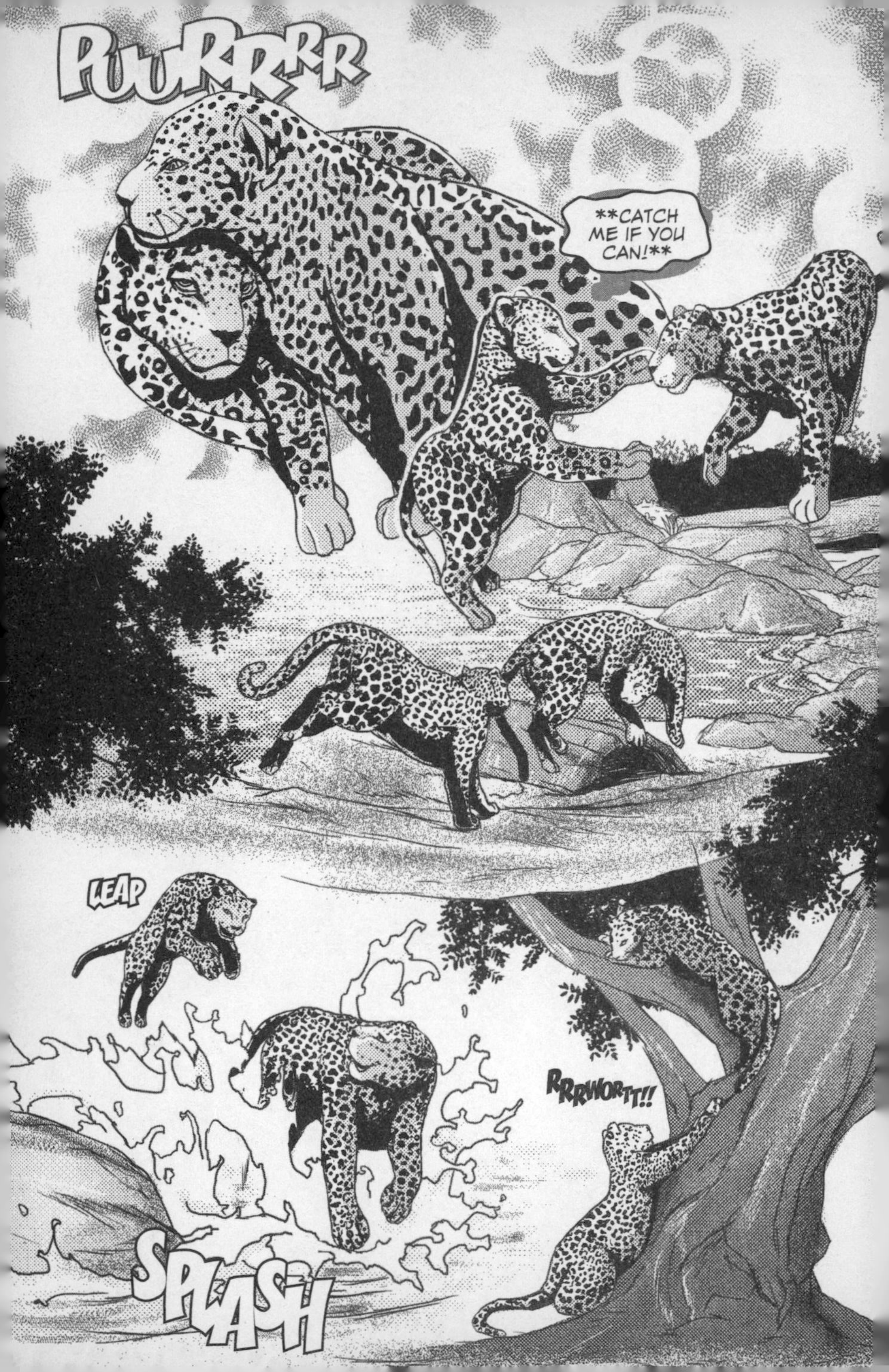
PUURRRR
CATCH ME IF YOU CAN!
LEAP
RRRWORTT!!
SPLASH

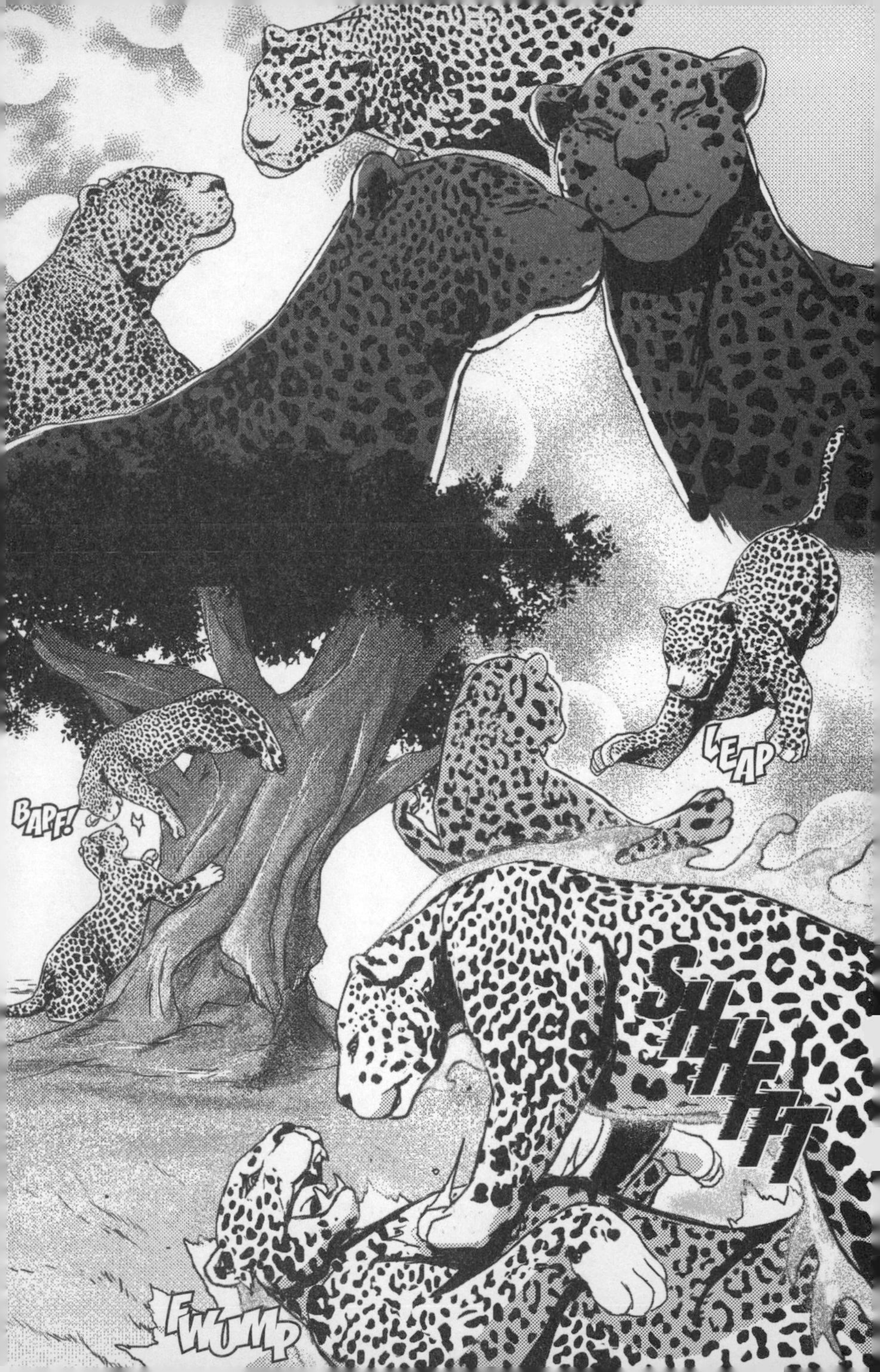
BAPF!
LEAP
SHHFFT
FWUMP

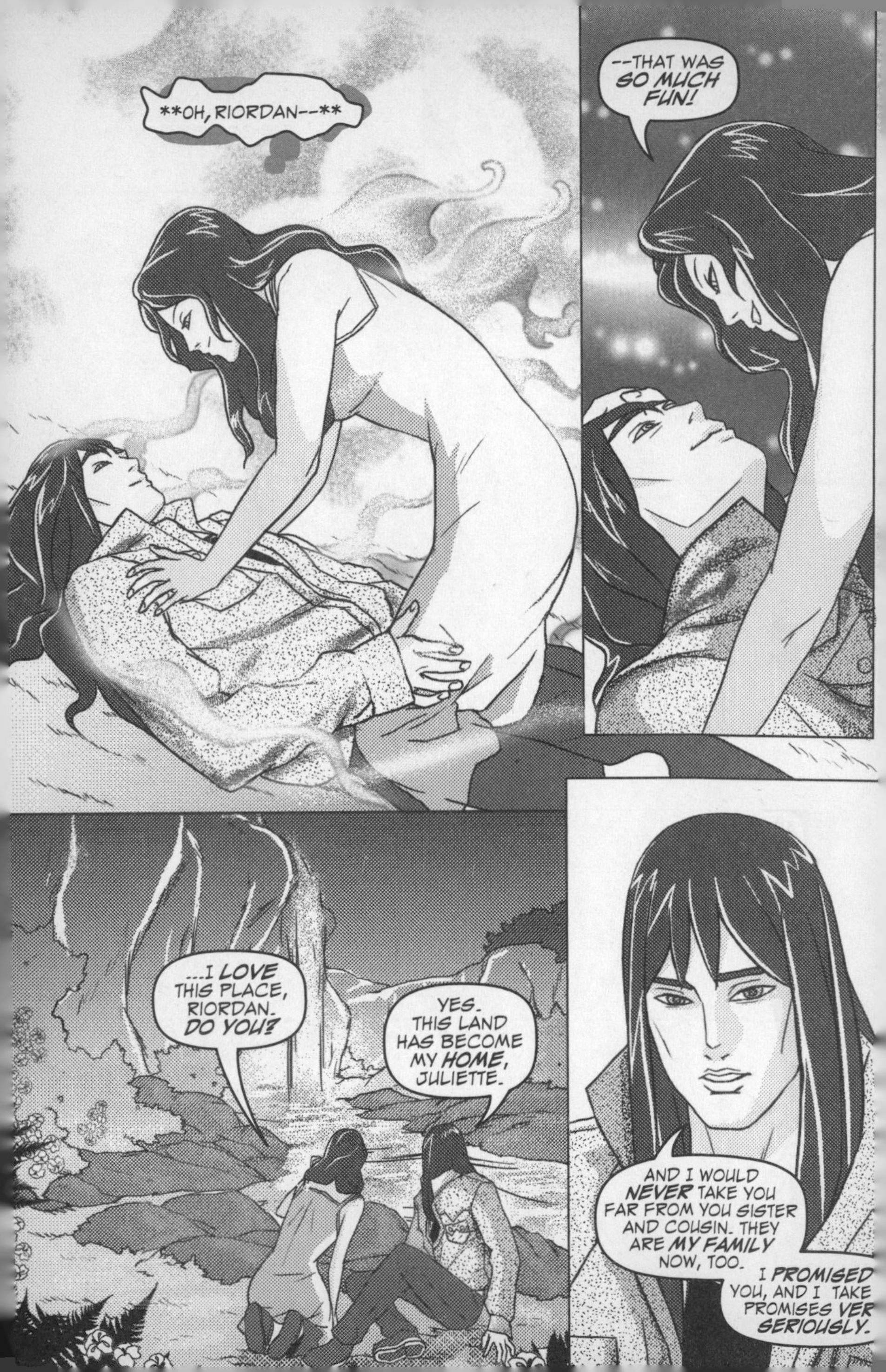
OH, RIORDAN--
--THAT WAS SO MUCH FUN!
...I LOVE THIS PLACE, RIORDAN. DO YOU?
YES. THIS LAND HAS BECOME MY HOME, JULIETTE.
AND I WOULD NEVER TAKE YOU FAR FROM YOU SISTER AND COUSIN. THEY ARE MY FAMILY NOW, TOO.
I PROMISED YOU, AND I TAKE PROMISES VER SERIOUSLY.

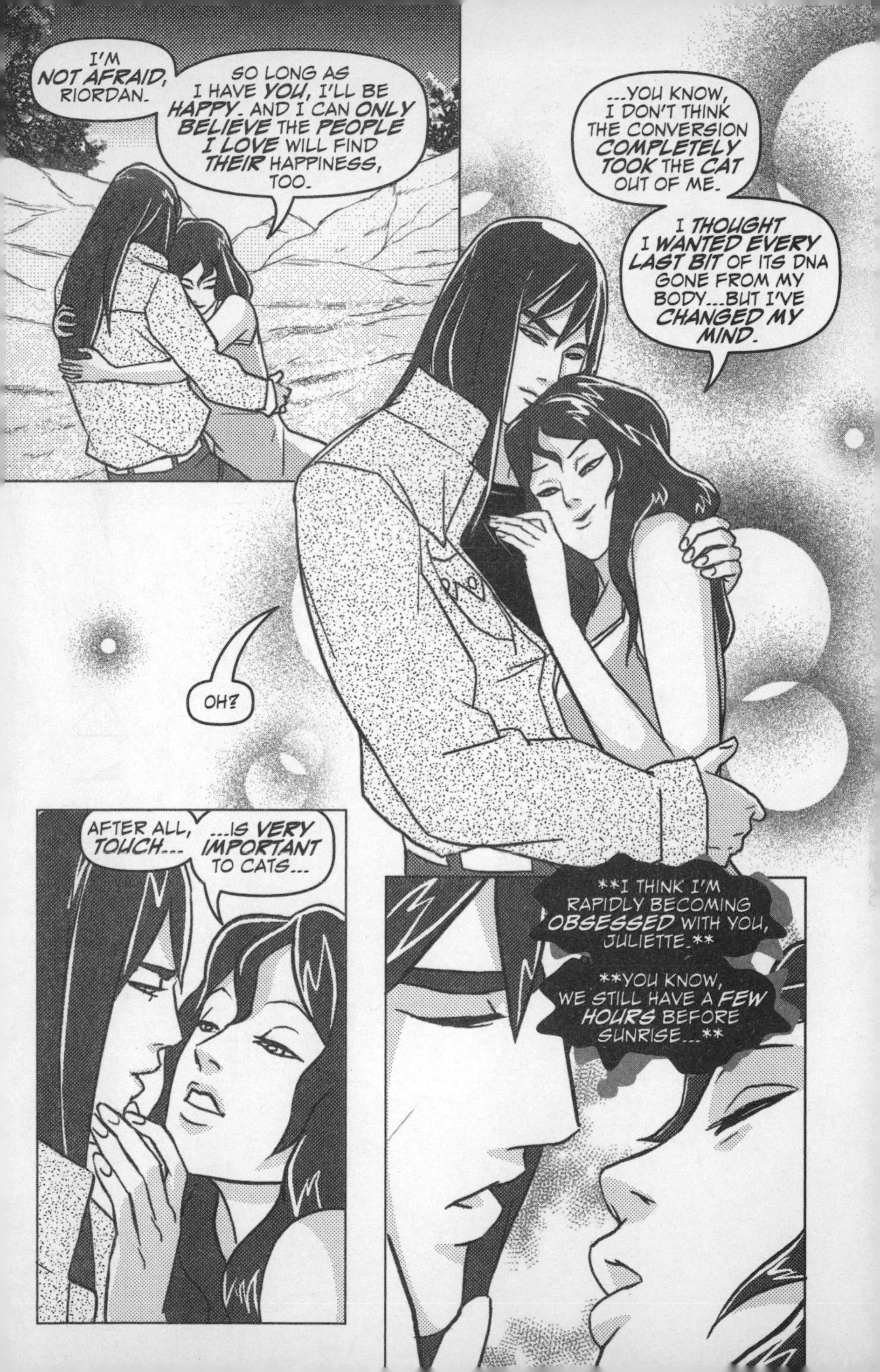
I'M NOT AFRAID, RIORDAN.
SO LONG AS I HAVE YOU, I'LL BE HAPPY. AND I CAN ONLY BELIEVE THE PEOPLE I LOVE WILL FIND THEIR HAPPINESS, TOO.
...YOU KNOW, I DON'T THINK THE CONVERSION COMPLETELY TOOK THE CAT OUT OF ME.
I THOUGHT I WANTED EVERY LAST BIT OF ITS DNA GONE FROM MY BODY...BUT I'VE CHANGED MY MIND.
OH?
AFTER ALL, TOUCH...
...IS VERY IMPORTANT TO CATS...
I THINK I'M RAPIDLY BECOMING OBSESSED WITH YOU, JULIETTE.
YOU KNOW, WE STILL HAVE A FEW HOURS BEFORE SUNRISE...

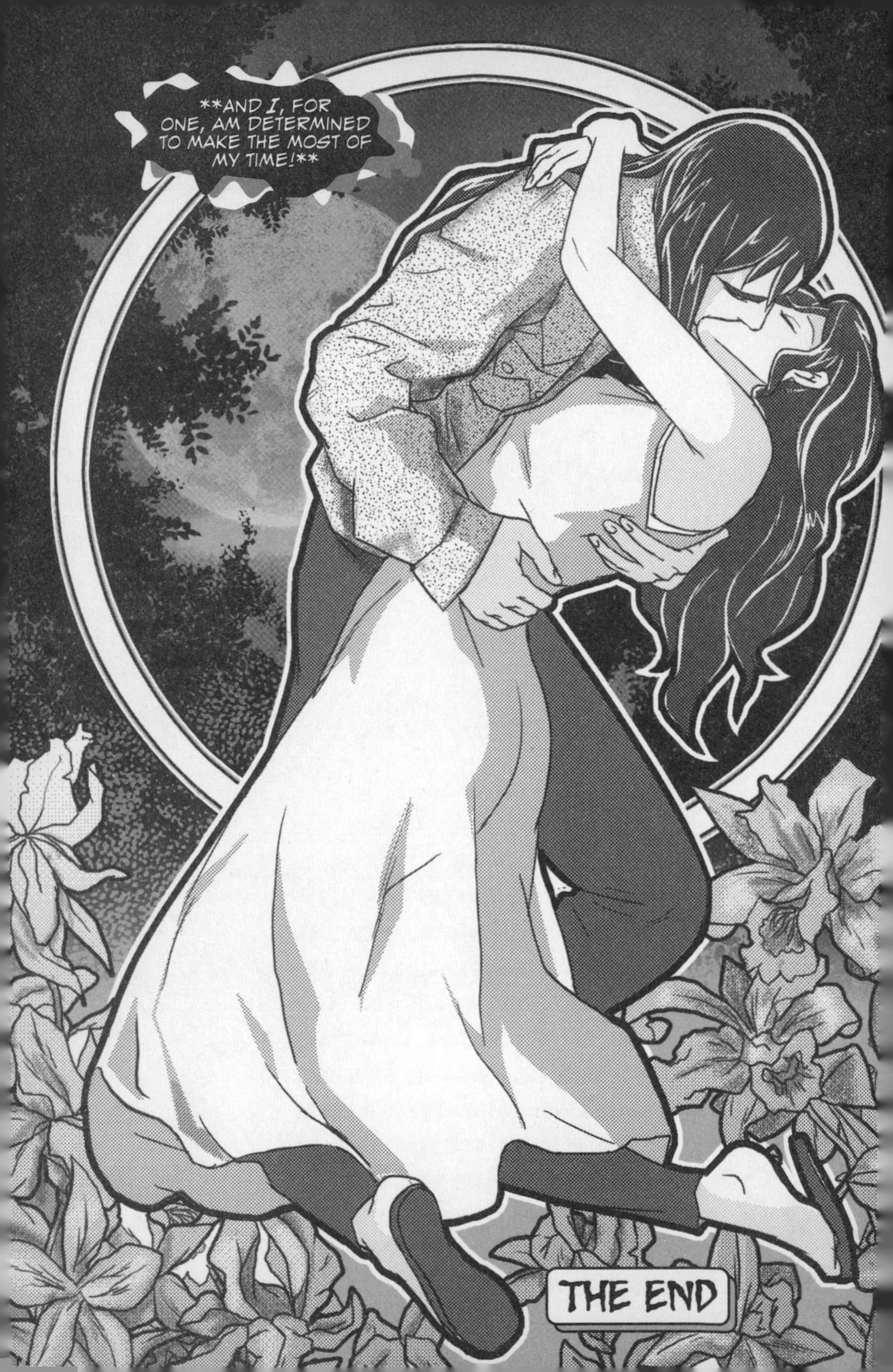
AND I, FOR ONE, AM DETERMINED TO MAKE THE MOST OF MY TIME!
THE END

I live in the beautiful mountains of Lake County California. I have always loved hiking, camping, rafting and being outdoors. I've also been involved in the martial arts for years—I hold a third degree black belt, instruct in a Korean karate system, and have taught self-defense. I am happily married to a romantic man who often inspires me with his thoughtfulness. We have a yours, mine, and ours family, claiming eleven children as our own. I have always written books, forcing my ten sisters to read every word, and now my daughters read and help me edit my manuscripts. It is fun to take all the research I have done on wild animals, raptors, vampires, weather, and volcanoes and put it together with romance. Please visit my website at www.christinefeehan.com.

THE NEXT BOOK IN
CHRISTINE FEEHAN'S
NEW YORK TIMES BESTSELLING
GAME SERIES

PREDATORY GAME

Saber Winter is running from her past when she meets Jess Calhoun, an ex–Navy SEAL who is physically and emotionally compromised by his own mysterious and violent history as a Ghost walker.

Now the riddles of both their pasts are about to collide, shattering the promise of their future with the ultimate betrayal.

COMING MARCH 2008

penguin.com
AD-014803